PENGUIN BOOKS

A NEW GRAND TOUR

'What looks at first like a leisurely guide book rapidly acquires the pace of a detective story ... In Central Europe Hodgson is at his best ... and a major pleasure of the book is to have the great Russian and Czech cities brought back into the European fold. It is a heartening reminder of the way changed politics can open up new vistas ... a highly readable and wide-ranging narrative' – Annette Kobak in *The Times Literary Supplement*

'Written with such a breadth of knowledge that his journey is not just a travelogue but a voyage in the history of ideas and an exploration of precisely what made culture flourish at particular times' – David Robinson in the *Scotsman*

'A pleasure to read ... Hodgson knows exactly where the right connections are to be made. Take the case of Alma Mahler, the ultimate groupie: "Wife of Mahler, mistress of Kokoschka ... pursued by Klimt, her life is a scarlet thread interwoven into the fabric of Vienna 1900." In every city Hodgson alights on these seminal figures, who encapsulated within their individual lives the growing culture around them' – Stephen Brook in the *New Statesman & Society*

D1369045

000147586

Godfrey Hodgson is a Yorkshireman and was born in 1934. He graduated from Oxford with a First in history and went on to do postgraduate work at the University of Pennsylvania. He has worked as a journalist for newspapers and television in Britain, Europe and the United States and as a foreign editor for the *Independent*. His television credits include *The Great Depression* for LWT and *Reagan on Reagan*, a television biography of President Reagan for Channel 4. Among his many books are *An American Melodrama* (1969), written jointly with Lewis Chester and Bruce Page, a bestselling account of the American election of 1968; *In Our Time* (1976), a history of the United States in the 1960s; *All Things to All Men* (1980), a study of the American presidency; and *The Colonel* (1989), a biography of the US statesman Henry L. Stimson. He taught at Harvard and Berkeley and is now the Director of the Reuter Foundation Programme at Green College, Oxford University.

Godfrey Hodgson has two sons and two daughters and lives in north Oxford.

A NEW GRAND TOUR

*How Europe's Great Cities
Made Our World*

Godfrey Hodgson

PENGUIN BOOKS

PENGUIN BOOKS

Published by the Penguin Group
Penguin Books Ltd, 27 Wrights Lane, London W8 5TZ, England
Penguin Books USA Inc., 375 Hudson Street, New York, New York 10014, USA
Penguin Books Australia Ltd, Ringwood, Victoria, Australia
Penguin Books Canada Ltd, 10 Alcorn Avenue, Toronto, Ontario, Canada M4V 3B2
Penguin Books (NZ) Ltd, 182–190 Wairau Road, Auckland 10, New Zealand

Penguin Books Ltd, Registered Offices: Harmondsworth, Middlesex, England

First published by Viking 1995
Published in Penguin Books 1995
1 3 5 7 9 10 8 6 4 2

Printed in England by Clays Ltd, St Ives plc

For Hilary: my fellow traveller

CONTENTS

PREFACE

MOST BOOKS HAVE A PREHISTORY AS WELL as a history. The prehistory of this one lies in more than forty years of exploring European cities, since my father first took me to Paris as a boy of thirteen in 1947. In my teens, in company with friends from school, especially the late Alasdair Clayre, I got to know Paris better, and I was subsequently lucky to be given many postgraduate courses in the city's history and topography by my son Pierre and by his grandfather, the late Jacques Vidal.

As a reporter I visited most of the great cities of western Europe on many occasions. I worked in Brussels for some months in 1961 for the *Observer* and in Rome off and on for a couple of years in the middle 1970s. I made a film in Berlin for the TV current-affairs programme 'This Week' in 1967. In 1968 I first got to know Prague when I covered the 'Prague Spring' for the London *Sunday Times*. My knowledge of western Europe as a whole was refreshed when I spent some months working for the German weekly *Stern* in 1976. I worked in Vienna for ITN in 1983. As for London, I have spent countless hours exploring it on foot from Whitechapel to Notting Dale: my interest in the history of London was greatly stimulated by reading Simon Jenkins's *Landlords to London*, and I have been a member of the London Topographical Society for many years.

It was in 1989 that I proposed to my friend Geraldine Cooke, then an editor at Penguin Books, a book about the history of Europe through a tour of European cities. For some months my family and I engaged in the party game of deciding which cities should be included and which left out. (Dublin? Cambridge? Cracow? Barcelona? Trieste? . . .) Then I took a full-time job, and Geraldine generously agreed not to press me for a manuscript until I was free to concentrate on it. In the meantime Alexander Chancellor sent me to Brussels to write an article for the *Independent* Magazine, which he never published, and which has become the core of Chapter 8.

When, as a result of what can tactfully be referred to as 'unforeseen circumstances', I found myself free again in 1992, Peter Carson, the editor in chief at Penguin Books, kindly agreed to edit the book personally, a great compliment and a great help. I am indebted to him, probably more than he realizes, for giving me confidence that the book would finally appear, as well as for his wise judgement and good advice.

At that point crucial and timely help came from Ann Spackman, an editor at the *Independent* in London, who asked me to do a series of travel articles about Europe's great cities. This enabled me to revisit Paris, Rome, Prague, Berlin and Vienna and to visit St Petersburg for the first time. She also devised for the series the title we have chosen for the book: 'A New Grand Tour'. That title in turn gave me the theme around which the book is organized: the idea that, instead of visiting the vestiges of classical antiquity and Renaissance and baroque Europe, as so many tourists do, it might be interesting to look for the traces and settings of the beginnings of modern and modernist Europe: *our* Europe, with all its splendours and miseries.

Once armed with that idea, which I felt justified in interpreting in a very freehand way, I set off on my tour: or rather on two different, interwoven journeys. The first was a physical tour of half a dozen European cities. Anyone who has realized how much more enjoyable travel becomes when it has a purpose will be able to imagine what fun that was, even though the journeys were made in the dead of winter, with drenching rain at Tivoli and deep snow in St Petersburg.

The second was, so to speak, a voyage of internal exploration. I returned to books I had read years before and read other, less-well-known books by writers whose masterpieces I already knew. I read Kafka's *Diaries*, poems I did not know by Baudelaire, Mallarmé and Apollinaire and – in translation – the verse of Akhmatova, Mandelstam and Blok. With dictionary at my side and with growing pleasure I explored Hofmannsthal and Rilke. I retraced the history of the Commune and the October Revolution and visited the ruins of the Gestapo headquarters in the Prinz-Albrecht-strasse. I discovered biographies of Dostoyevsky and essays by Walter Benjamin, reread Gissing and Musil, *Svejk* and T.S. Eliot. Armed with Donald Olsen's *The City as a Work of Art*, I looked carefully at buildings in Vienna's Ringstrasse which I had passed a dozen times without seeing. Hillairet's *Évocation du vieux Paris* in hand, I picked like an archaeologist at the layers of history on the Left Bank laid down from Roman times to the German occupation. I saw paintings from the Musée d'Orsay to the Sezession with a new eye, visited Alma Mahler's Hohe Warte and Wittgenstein's house, and listened with a newly adventurous ear to Stravinsky and Schoenberg. I have rarely had such a good time. My only hope is that my tour will inspire a few others to embark on similar explorations of their own, and that they will find their own journeys half as enjoyable as I did mine.

ACKNOWLEDGEMENTS

AS I HAVE EXPLAINED ELSEWHERE, THIS
project owes everything to the trust and patience of two editors at
Penguin, Geraldine Cooke and Peter Carson, and to the imaginative enthusiasm of Ann Spackman at the *Independent*. What little I
know of Paris I owe to my French family, especially to my former
father-in-law, the late Jacques Vidal, to Noële Vidal and to my son
Pierre. In St Petersburg, I do not know how I would have
managed without my guide and interpreter, Masha Avrabach. In
Prague, I am indebted to Jana Frankova, my researcher in 1968,
who has since become a friend of the family, and who is known to
be the best interpreter in Prague. I am also indebted to Sir Stephen
and Lady Barrett and in particular for Alison Barrett's kindness in
letting me see her notes on the intellectuals under the Husak
regime, analysed with wit and sympathy in her contemporary
letters to her sons. My interest in Prague and its literature was
sustained by that of my son Francis. In Vienna, Sabine Egger was
my patient and cheerful guide and Hedda Egerer not only gave
me an insight into the *genius loci* but took me into the Vienna
Woods and introduced us to her favourite *Heuriger* (an inn selling
new wine). I am also grateful for my polyglot son Pierre for
travelling to Vienna with me and insisting that I go to the opera
every night. If we were punished by a bizarre production of
Nabucco, we were rewarded by extraordinary productions of *Fidelio*

and *Rosenkavalier*. In Berlin, I must thank Hanne Gamnes, who accompanied me on my explorations, and Dr Eckart Stratenschulte, press secretary to the mayor of Berlin, who explained contemporary developments with such enthusiasm. In Rome, I was entertained with great kindness by Patricia Clough, and in Brussels I was fortunate enough to be taught by Dr René Schoonbrodt, founder of ARAU, one of the most remarkable of the practical visionaries who are trying to save the great cities of Europe from the combined assaults of ignorance and greed.

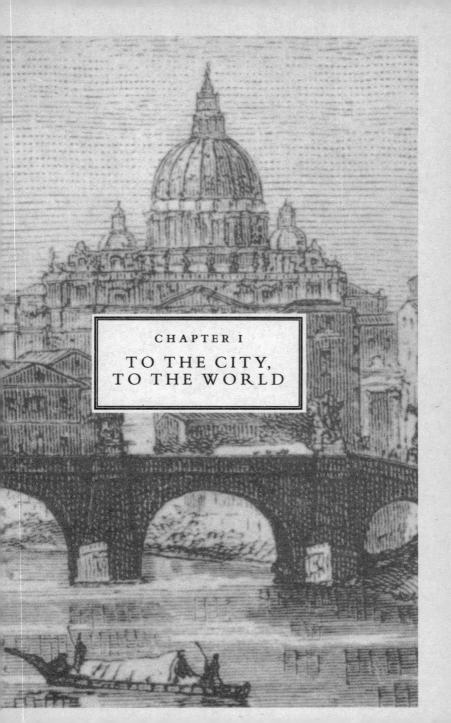

CHAPTER I

TO THE CITY,
TO THE WORLD

'I HAVE HARDLY HAD ONE HOUR TO MYSELF
this week,' wrote the British minister to Florence, Francis Colman,
in 1775, 'by reason of the great concourse of English gentlemen
that are here at present, of whom there have been above twenty.'[1]
Seven years later the ambassador in Paris, James, Earl Waldegrave,
echoed Colman. 'The town swarms with English,' he complained.
'I had near a dozen newcomers dined with me yesterday, and shall
have near as many more today.' One year in the 1730s there were
twelve English visitors at Turin, thirty-four at Bologna, forty in
Rome. From time to time between 1740 and 1786 Sir Horace Mann,
the British minister in Florence, noted the number of British
tourists there in his letters to his friend Horace Walpole: the
number was never less than twelve, or more than sixty.[2]

These were, of course, only the grander sort of travellers, those
who would expect that their own or their family's position and
celebrity would entitle them to be invited to dinner by the British
ambassador or minister if they signed his visitors' book. But in the

eighteenth century, aside from a handful of students, painters, musicians, soldiers and priests who travelled in order to acquire skill or promotion in their various specialities, most English travellers were of just that sort.

Compare those numbers to the herds of tourists from Britain, the United States and many other countries who graze the 'sights' of Europe as the numberless millions of buffalo devoured the grasslands of the Great Plains, and they are almost invisible. But in their day they already reflected a significant increase in the num of English people who travelled abroad. cultural event of great importance: the reintroduction of at least the élite of British society to the mainstream culture of Europe after the interruption caused by the Reformation and the religious wars.

Two centuries earlier, in Queen Elizabeth's time, British travellers abroad were so infrequent, and so suspect, that you can track their individual movements in the state papers as nervous English diplomats report their arrival and departure.[3] In the Middle Ages, after all, England was an integral part of a European civilization which stretched from the Lithuanian marshes to the kingdom of Granada. Dangerous as the Channel crossing was in the tubby boats of the time, there was a constant two-way traffic. Just as Norman men-at-arms, Burgundian monks and Lombard bankers sought fortune or salvation in England, so English archers made themselves a reputation for ferocity and courage in the wars, from Italy to Aquitaine, and English wool merchants were well known in the markets of Champagne and the Low Countries. British monks prayed in the cloisters of the Rhineland, and British scholars studied in Paris and Padua, while a French-speaking English aristocracy moved between estates on both sides of the narrow seas.

That age ended symbolically in 1558, when England lost Calais, its last possession on the continent of Europe. For three generations, contacts between England and Europe dwindled to a trickle. Some English Protestants went to fight for the Dutch in their wars against Spain after 1575, and a handful of English fought in the armies of France and Spain. But in those formative generations in the second half of the sixteenth century, the English lost contact with Europe; Shakespeare's contemporaries grew up believing in the black legend which made of their neighbours either the devils of the Inquisition or the dupes of superstition.

In the seventeenth century, this began to change.[4] A great nobleman, Thomas Howard, Earl of Arundel, visited France and Italy in 1612, and then again in 1613–14, the second time taking with him Inigo Jones, who taught England the classical purity of the Palladian Renaissance. Lord Arundel brought back with him paintings, gems, Latin and Greek manuscripts and, above all, his great collection of 'marbles', the classical sculptures which adorn the Ashmolean Museum in Oxford.

Even so, travel across the Channel did not really pick up until peace with France was signed in 1630. During the English Civil War, a growing number of wealthy or intrepid Englishmen were to be found in the Low Countries, Paris and elsewhere in France, some because England was too hot for them, more because they wanted to absorb the ideas and techniques of baroque Europe. Among the Englishmen you might have bumped into in Paris in the middle of the century were Sir Christopher Wren, Thomas Hobbes and John Milton, and the work of all three owed much to what they learned on their travels. John Evelyn,[5] a wealthy gentleman from Kent, brought back with him ideas that were to transform the English garden and English woodland.

After the Restoration, with a king who had lived in France and the Low Countries on the throne, the custom of sending rich young Englishmen abroad to put a high polish on their education became firmly established. The statesman and historian Lord Clarendon, looking back after the Restoration, recalled that 'We can all remember when very few Men travelled beyond the Seas, except it was to be a Soldier, which is now a Profession we have learned too much of without Travel. Now very few stay at Home, or think they are fit for good company if they have not been beyond the Seas.'[6]

By the early eighteenth century, this habit was sufficiently ingrained for it to have acquired a name: the Grand Tour. There was no set pattern to it. Young noblemen and gentlemen were sent off, often with tutors who were known as 'bear-leaders', appropriately in view of the uncouth pranks some of the young gentlemen got up to.

Within the bounds of the assumption that travel broadened the mind and polished a gentleman's knowledge of the world, there were many different motives for going on, or sending one's son (and occasionally a well-chaperoned daughter) on the Grand Tour. The opportunities the great European cities offered for gambling, drinking and sexual adventures were not neglected. Paris and Venice, in particular, were prized for their sexual freedom, and the young Britons managed to get involved with princesses, countesses, opera singers, innkeepers' daughters and serving-maids, and of course with countless prostitutes of every degree, from the courtesans of Venice, reputed for their style and skill, to the 'votaries of Venus, for the most part of the lowest class' who thronged the Tuileries, the Palais-Royal and the Pont-Neuf in Paris at nightfall. Venereal disease was a constant danger and preoccupation. One young gentleman announced that he preferred women who admitted they had the clap, since their frankness meant it was less likely that they had the pox.[7]

James Boswell, the ambitious son of the Laird of Auchinleck, was the classic example of the young man whose tour was a ceaseless agony of hesitation between self-indulgence and self-improvement. When he went to Holland in 1763 he fell in love in the most respectful manner with the famous bluestocking Belle de Zuylen, 'so much above me in wit, learning and good sense'. Getting no change out of her, he spent six months visiting the minor German courts, and then Switzerland, before moving on to Italy. In spite of endless Calvinist plans of self-amendment, he amused himself with numerous women, from the wife of one of Frederick the Great's guardsmen to the warm-hearted lady of the mayor of Siena. But Boswell also met the literary lions of the day.

He was received by Rousseau and Voltaire, and had audiences with the Cardinal of York, the brother of the young Pretender, and with the Pope; and made friends with General Paoli, the liberator of Corsica, whom he hero-worshipped.[8]

High-blooded young British noblemen certainly took advantage of the opportunities for debauchery abroad, but they did not need to go beyond Covent Garden or Shepherd Market to find sexual adventures. Their letters home suggest that even if they did sow bushels of wild oats, they were also thrilled by the architecture, painting, music and statuary, and by the freshly excavated archaeological sites they discovered in their travels. The Grand Tour, in fact, was one of the chief conduits by which French and Italian taste, and through them the influence of classical antiquity, reached Britain.

If the wealth of antiquities was one motive for travelling, another was the fact that, with the industrial revolution and imperial trade roaring towards their zenith, Britons found that their golden sovereigns went a lot further abroad than they did at home. When the young Benjamin Disraeli visited Italy in 1826, he wrote home to his father that Florence was a city where

real cheapness is to be found. On five hundred a year [you can almost hear the wonder in his voice] you may live in a palace built by Michael Angelo [*sic*], keep a villa two miles from the city with vineyards, fruit and pleasure gardens, keep *two* carriages, have your opera box and live in every way as the first Florentine nobility.[9]

There was no fixed route for these eighteenth-century travellers. Many visited the Low Countries and the German Empire. Some intrepid spirits ventured to Russia, where one traveller was shocked by 'a monstrous scene of beastly women and indecent men mixed together naked' in a bathhouse. More daring still, some visited the Ottoman Empire, where the Revd Robert Stockdale was surprised to find that he was not as horrified as he had feared he would be by 'the first impalement we had seen': it was very old 'and did not strike one with those feelings of horror which a more recent execution produces ... [more like] an old gibbet in England.'[10]

The isles, and the mainland of Greece, sacred earth to generations brought up to revere classical antiquity, were occupied by a dangerously hostile and, to contemporary European eyes, barbarous government.

So the great majority of eighteenth-century British travellers, after visiting Paris, headed for Italy. Usually they went by way of Switzerland, whose mountains and lakes were just beginning to form the romantic sensibility of generations of Englishmen and Englishwomen. With mounting excitement they descended on the lakes and plains, the flowers and vines and the golden cities of Italy.

Often they headed first for Venice. Byron captured what the 'most serene' city meant to his generation in the Fourth Canto of *Childe Harold*:

> I loved her from my boyhood; – she to me
> Was as a fairy city of the heart,
> Rising like water-columns from the sea,
> Of joy the sojourn, and of wealth the mart;
> And Otway, Radcliffe, Schiller, Shakespeare's art,
> Had stamp'd her image in me, and even so,
> Although I found her thus, we did not part;
> Perchance even dearer in her day of woe,
> Than when she was a boast, a marvel, and a show.[11]

Later Ruskin was to take the stones of Venice and use them as a sort of pattern book for the characteristic architecture of Victorian Britain, the Gothic. But before Ruskin, and only a few months after Byron left, an Englishman more gifted than either of them arrived in Venice: Joseph Mallord William Turner. Astonishingly, on this first visit – he was to be back in the 1830s and 1840s – he spent no more than five and perhaps as few as three days there. It was long enough to produce not only seventy-four detailed sketches up and down the Grand Canal, but also four watercolour sketches, or impressions.[12] They are among his most brilliant achievements and a turning-point in the history of painting. Yet, after this brief visit he, like Byron, was on the move again.

Byron and Turner visited other Italian cities: Milan and Bologna, and the towns and cities of the Marches, Umbria and Tuscany. But for them, as for Keats and Shelley, Browning in 1844 and Thackeray in 1846, and for numberless other English visitors in the late eighteenth century and even more in the nineteenth, the chief goal of the Grand Tour, the visit which crowned the experience of modern Europe because it sent back the richest echoes of the ancient civilization of which they felt themselves the heirs, was Rome.

Which is the best view of Rome? The *cognoscenti* differ. From the Janiculum hill, which lies to the west of the city, says one school of thought, and, for preference, first thing in the morning. From that point of vantage, and at that hour, said G.M. Trevelyan, the historian of Garibaldi's campaigns to free Italy, you can look down on 'the city spread beneath our feet in all its mellow tints of white and dark and red and brown, broken here and there by masses of dark green pine and cypress and by shining cupolas raised to the sun'.[13] Behind it, on a fine day, you can see the 'grander dome' of the Alban Hills, the *mons Albanus*, from which, some time before 753 BC, the first Romans came down to the Tiber valley to found the city.

Nonsense, says E.V. Lucas, who wrote a travel book about Rome in the 1920s.[14] From the Janiculum, he points out, you can't even see the dome of St Peter's. He prefers the view Corot painted, from the great marble basin under the umbrella pines on the Pincio, the hill at the top of the Spanish Steps. There, in the evening, you can look out over the stuccoed walls and tiled roofs of the city, broken by the silhouetted façades and humped domes of its great baroque churches, into the Roman sunset, 'stained' – someone said – 'with the blood of the martyrs'. There across the Tiber is the brick drum of the Castel Sant'Angelo, where Hadrian is buried, and where the great goldsmith Benvenuto Cellini laid and fired the cannon at the imperial soldiers before the sack of the city in 1527;[15] and beyond it the dome of St Peter's, floating over the Vatican like the flagship of an armada of churches.

Climb the Janiculum in the morning, by all means, and climb the Pincio at sunset as well. But don't forget what the classic guidebooks will not warn you about, that in the foreground of every view of Rome there will be . . . Romans. On the Janiculum, where Garibaldi's legion of red-shirted heroes mounted its heroic defence against the French infantry in 1849, the foreground will consist of vendors selling balloons shaped like cartoon animals, and puppets, and sweets and soda. The accompaniment will be the steady beat of Roman rock. You can see the Alban mount, but only through a frieze of young men snapping pictures of their girlfriends. At nightfall, at the top of the Spanish Steps, where Keats lived and Goethe bought a fragment of old Roman terracotta which gave him 'extraordinary pleasure', as the city darkens against an opal sky, snogging couples, keen to be seen, perch precariously on the balustrade. The soundtrack to this incomparable panorama is the steady snarl of small, fast-revving motors, the rowdy shouts of young people skateboarding up the hill to the Villa Medici towed by Japanese four-wheel-drives, and raucous bursts of strictly non-traditional song.

What is true of the views of Rome, of course, is true of the city itself. We want it to be *our* Rome, the Rome we have brought with us, pieces of which have been buried in our minds since childhood, and to which we have been adding ever since. In this imagined city, Mark Antony came to bury Caesar, not to praise him; St Peter was crucified and St Paul beheaded; and the noble army of martyrs were thrown to the lions. Here St Gregory saw blue-eyed children in the slave market and said they were not Angles, but angels. Here Borgias feasted and poisoned, Michelangelo sculpted and Raphael painted. This is the city where Keats died and Shelley, drowned at sea, was buried; where on 15 October 1764, as he sat 'musing amid the ruins of the Capitol, while the bare-footed friars were singing vespers in the Temple of Jupiter',[16] the idea of writing its decline and fall first occurred to Edward Gibbon; and where, in Macaulay's hardly less lapidary phrase, the Church 'may still exist in undiminished vigour when some traveller from New Zealand shall, in the middle of a vast solitude, take his stand on a broken arch of London Bridge to sketch the ruins of St Paul's'.[17]

That is *our* Rome, one of the most potent symbols and richest seedbeds of the civilization dominating Europe from the time of Augustus until that of Michelangelo, and inspiring the age of the baroque and the second Augustan age which succeeded it. But the Rome of the pilgrim, the traveller and the tourist has always been an intrusion on the Romans' Rome.

Few of them, for a start, live in what we think of as Rome, and they call the *centro storico*, the historic centre. It is too inconvenient, too expensive, too impossible to park. They live in modern suburbs out on the Via Flaminia, Via Cassia or Piazza Bologna, or in EUR, the modern business city Mussolini built. Theirs is a world of modern plumbing, designer furniture, terrazzo floors, giant supermarkets and intimate bars, decorated with the triangular pennants of football teams, where the TV is always on in the corner. Their Greater Rome sprawls thirty miles from the Tivoli to the sea, a motor city of some four million people, like Paris or Los Angeles, only with fewer freeways than Los Angeles and a far less ambitious metro than Paris.

It remains as memorable to visit as it was for Poussin and Goethe, Gibbon and Macaulay. You can still trudge the five kilometres of the Vatican galleries and see masterpieces every yard of the way, to the extent that you can see them at all over the heads of the thousands of others who have come, like you, to see them, or to say that they have seen them. You can muse like Gibbon on the ruins of the imperial forum, much excavated since his day – though I was accosted there by a motorized prostitute who mistook my musing for more purposeful loitering. Besides the universal favourites – the forums and the Colosseum, the Baths of Caracalla and Diocletian, the ochre temples and the crumbling walls of rose brick, and the four great basilicas of the Roman see – you will find smaller favourites for yourself. There is the quiet cloister of Santa Maria della Pace, just off the noisy

Piazza Navona; the elephant Bernini sculpted to hold up the Egyptian obelisk in the tiny Piazza Minerva, because, as he quaintly said, 'the elephant is the most robust of beasts'; the wonderful gallery of Renaissance maps in the Vatican; and the exquisitely earthy, though headless, Venus of Cyrene in the Baths of Diocletian.

The Rome you visit as a tourist, Rome inside the Aurelian walls, built by Marcus Aurelius in the second century AD, divides into four unequal parts. The biggest, lying south of the Piazza Venezia, consists of the ruins of the heart of ancient Rome. First comes the Capitol, once the fortress citadel which the geese saved from attack by the Gauls, now an elegant piazza designed by Michelangelo at the top of a long flight of steps, like a stage setting for a baroque masque. Tiny as it is there is room for two museums. The one on the left houses such masterpieces of ancient sculpture as the *Dying Gaul* and the *Capitoline Venus*, which is a Hellenistic copy of the Aphrodite by the greatest of Greek sculptors, Praxiteles.[18] In the other, besides paintings and sculptures by the greatest masters of the Renaissance, you can see the famous bronze, attributed to the Greek master Myron, of a boy pulling a thorn from his foot. At the top of the hill is the Franciscan church of Santa Maria d'Aracoeli, St Mary's of the Altar of Heaven, and near by, crowded together in a space so famous that it is hard to believe how tiny it is, are the remains of the first Roman temple of Jupiter, which dates from the sixth century before Christ; the Tarpean rock, from which criminals were thrown to their death under the Republic; the Mamertine prison of the same period; and the even more sinister lower dungeon, the *carcer Tullianum*, where enemies of the Roman state such as Vercingetorix were held before their execution and where, according to legend, St Peter struck a spring from the rock before his own crucifixion. To the south stretch rough hummocks, covered with grass and dotted with umbrella pines, which are the ruins of the old city. Here are the imperial forums, of Caesar, Augustus and Trajan, the palaces of Augustus and his wife Livia and of

Tiberius, the arches of Titus and Constantine, and the oblong site of the chariot races in the Circus Maximus. And that is not the end. In one direction the ruins stretch to the terrifying oval of the Colosseum and the remnants of the Domus Aurea, Nero's Golden House. Beyond the Circus there are the massive brick ruins of the Baths of Caracalla, now the cyclopean sounding-board for grandiose open-air productions of opera on summer nights. Verdi's *Aida* with live camels is quite in the antique Roman tradition.

Repeatedly sacked by the barbarian invaders, and again by the Spanish and German mercenaries of the Constable of Bourbon in 1527,[19] ravaged by plagues and epidemics, Rome shrank to a shadow of its ancient glory. In the late fourteenth century the population of Rome, which has been estimated at two million at the height of the Roman Empire, is thought to have fallen to as little as 17,000.[20] The forum itself, covered by rich grass, was seen as valuable pasture and came to be known as *il campo vaccino*, the 'cow field', and cattle roamed where Cicero once orated and Caesar rode in triumph. It was not until the late eighteenth century, after the ruins of Pompeii, Herculaneum and other Roman sites had already been excavated, that the ruins of Rome began to be uncovered, and it was only after Rome had joined the rest of the newly unified Italy, in 1870, that archaeological investigation began in a systematic way.

Between the Capitol and the Tiber lies the ghetto, next to the early medieval church of Santa Maria in Cosmedin and the simple but supremely elegant Temple of Vesta.[21] And from the ghetto northwards to the Piazza del Popolo, between the Tiber and the Corso, is Renaissance Rome – though here, too, in that promontory like a dog's nose drawn by the curves of the river, there are traces of ancient Rome. Here is the site of the Ara Pacis, the great Altar of Peace given to Augustus by the Senate in commemoration of his pacification of Gaul and Spain; its bas-reliefs are mostly elsewhere, in the Vatican and in Florence. Here is the Pantheon, a Christian church in the almost intact building of a Roman temple. Here, too, is one of the loveliest spaces in Rome, the Piazza

Navona, with Bernini's fountain of four rivers in the centre, shaped as it is because it was once the hippodrome, the *circo agonale*, built by Domitian. And here, in the charming flower market of the Campo dei Fiori, where Giordano Bruno was burned at the stake in 1600, was the *porticus Pompeiana*, Pompey's theatre. That is where the conspirators plunged their daggers into Julius Caesar.

Nevertheless it is in the dark streets and gloomy palaces of this quarter that you feel the opulence and the new classical taste of Renaissance Rome. Here are the great houses built by the finest architects of the day for the papal families: the Farnese, now the French embassy, started by Sangallo the Younger and finished by Michelangelo; the Montecitorio, Bernini's creation for the Ludovisi, and now the home of the Chamber of Deputies; the Madama, which belonged to the Medici; and many, many more, presenting for the most part sombre, dignified façades to the street, and hiding their sumptuous interiors and their opulent collections of masterpieces, especially the Doria gallery. Here, in this same Renaissance neighbourhood, are the two imposing churches built by the Jesuits in the baroque style which took the passionate missionary message of their order all over Catholic Europe and the Americas: the Gesù itself and its neighbour, Sant'Andrea della Valle. For it was in this same corner that the Jesuit Order began. In three little rooms, just behind the Gesù, St Ignatius Loyola and his friends, among them St Francis Xavier, directed the missionary enterprises of the Society of Jesus from China to Paraguay. It takes an effort, as the green taxis dice with the scooters in the Corso Vittorio Emanuele, to imagine the Rome of the sixteenth and seventeenth century: crowded, dirty, dangerous, the home to cynics, courtiers and sensualists like Benvenuto Cellini and the Borgia, but also the cradle of the Counter-Reformation.

If you return to the farthest limits of the Rome of the ruins, on the south side of the Circus Maximus, and climb the slope, you are on another of the Seven Hills, the Aventine. With permission from the head office of the order, you can visit the priory of the

Knights of St John of Malta, and there, through the keyhole, perfectly framed, you can see the dome of St Peter's. It was not until 1377, after the Avignon schism, that the popes made the Vatican their home. Before that, they lived in St John Lateran, at the extreme opposite corner of Rome, where Constantine the Great built his first basilica in the fourth century, on land brought to him by his wife Fausta in her dowry. In Roman times, the right bank of the Tiber was suburban. Rich people, including emperors, had parks and pleasure grounds there, and it was in Trastevere that Nero burned Christians as human torches in his gardens. In early times it was a poor neighbourhood, the home of Rome's Jews, where Christianity made its first converts; Santa Maria in Trastevere, built in the third century, is said to be the first church to be dedicated to the Virgin Mary. (There are churches as old in Cairo.) It is in the Borgo, between the Vatican and the Castel Sant'Angelo, and Trastevere, between the steep ridge of the Janiculum and the river, that the traditional Roman working-class life survives today. Trastevere has remained a popular quarter, full of ancient streets and restaurants serving traditional Roman dishes. But the withdrawal of the popes into their Vatican enclave since 1870 has cut the right bank of the river off from the life of the city far more effectively than the river itself ever did.

As the self-indulgent luxury of the High Renaissance and the fierce missionary faith of the Counter-Reformation mellowed, comparatively speaking, into the eighteenth century, fashionable Rome moved into the regular street pattern of the third section of the city. At its northern end is the Piazza del Popolo, just inside the gate in the northern wall, the tip of the arrowhead drawn by three long straight streets. The middle one of these is the Corso, the main street of Rome. Between it and the cliff of the Pincio lie the eighteenth-century streets: Via Frattina, Via Condotti, Via della Croce and the rest. As recently as the late nineteenth century they were quiet places, favoured by foreign tourists. Now they are the home of high-fashion shops selling shoes, handbags and clothes, and thronged with window shoppers. In the Corso, which cuts through the district, the Caffè Nazionale used to be the gathering place for politicians and journalists, and this is still the district where Romans gather on Sundays or on a summer evening to walk and admire one another's shoes and more personal attributes. This, too, is where foreigners used to stay, until the palace-hotels of the turn of the century were built along the Via Veneto, at the top of the Spanish Steps.

If we climb the steps and turn right, we are moving, through the once-smart Ludovisi quarter, into the fourth segment of the inner city: nineteenth-century Rome. Street after street consists of modern houses, mostly split up into flats, with few traces of the ancient city and even fewer monuments from the Middle Ages or the Renaissance. Here Rome's first railway station was finished in 1873, but closed a year later. Mussolini built a new terminus, but the present building, in the modern style, was not finished until the 1950s.

Until 1870, when the city became once again the capital of the Italian state, it slumbered in deeply lethargic tradition. It was of course the capital of the pope's temporal domain. Until 1848 this included Emilia, the Marches, Umbria and the whole of central Italy down to the frontier of the even more reactionary Kingdom of Naples. If the papal regime was not quite as brutal as that of King Ferdinand of Naples – King 'Bomba', as he was called, after he turned his artillery on the population of Messina and massacred most of them – the Papal States were nevertheless a byword for reaction and oppression.[22] In the city, only one tenth of the population could read or write. That was a great improvement on the rural parts of His Holiness's domains, where it was estimated that only 2 per cent were literate. The slightest suspicion of liberalism, freemasonry or modern thought of any kind was proscribed. Under the notorious Pope Gregory XVI, who reigned from 1831 to 1846, it was even forbidden to study the immortal Dante, father of Italian literature, and both the railway and the telegraph were kept out of the papal territory as dangerous agents of modernism and change. One cardinal sent orders that a man should be kept under strict watch because, although he was not subversive in the slightest, there was reason to fear he might be a 'thinker'.[23] Torture was freely used to turn such suspicions into proof, and the Papal States crawled, every bit as much as Russia under Stalin, with police spies, the hated *sbirri*, who handed freethinkers and other suspected enemies of religion over to the mercies of ecclesiastical justice, and with the centurions of the Holy Faith, who all too often carried out their own idea of justice for themselves. Twice, in 1821 and again in 1844, commissions of inquiry sent hundreds to rot in filthy jails or in the 'galleys' at Civita Vecchia, when they were gibbeted, guillotined or shot. Jews were persecuted – a hundred years after their emancipation in Austria – with special savagery. A decree of 1843 made it a crime, punishable by the Inquisition, for a Jew to have any social contact with a Christian. Even in the last ten days of papal rule, two young men were sent to the galleys for at least twenty years, for being in possession of 'Writings that are subversive, anti-political, calculated to overthrow the present order of things, containing irreverent words on the persona of a most eminent Cardinal of the Holy Roman Church'. The writings in question were one copy, between the two of them, of a liberal newspaper from Florence.[24]

After 1870, the city was the capital of the Italian state, and it has remained essentially a political and administrative capital, where business takes second place. It took a long time before the swelling army of bureaucrats and the invading hordes of tourists transformed the atmosphere of the town. Photographs of Rome in the 1870s and 1880s, and indeed as late as the second decade of the twentieth century, show a sleepy, backward, southern town such as you might have found in Sicily or Greece in the 1950s. In the 1870s goats grazed and their owners hung out their washing in the forum. There was almost no traffic. In the early twentieth century, the Via Veneto, now throbbing with tourists and Romans in search of *la dolce vita* in cafés and nightclubs, was all but deserted. Even in the Via Nazionale, one of the proud new thoroughfares built after the Risorgimento, the new trams shared the roadway with clip-clopping hackney carriages, and traffic was so scarce that pedestrians walked in the middle of the road.

Only a third, or at most a half, of the area within the Aurelian walls, built by Marcus Aurelius at the height of Rome's ancient splendour, was occupied at the end of the nineteenth century. That is less surprising if you remember the deep trough of the city's historic population figures. As we have seen, from two million in the second century, it fell to a few thousand in the tenth century and perhaps 17,000 in the fourteenth, and had recovered to only a little over 200,000 by 1870, when the popes gave up the last major portion of the Papal States and retreated into the tiny enclave of the Vatican City.

This modern Rome is not the industrial capital of Italy; that is Turin, the home of Fiat. Nor is it the business capital; that is Milan, the home of the stock exchange and of 'made in Italy' fashion and design. Rome is the political capital: the capital, that is, of the discredited system that lurched along, conveniently concealing monstrous overmanning, waste, incompetence and corruption, so long as the Christian Democrats could persuade the voters to keep them in power whatever they got up to, just so as to keep the Communists out. The official monuments of this modern, political Rome are to be seen: the Quirinale, the president's palace up the hill above the forums, the Palazzo Chigi, the prime minister's office, just off the Corso, the long, narrow street that was the main street of nineteenth-century Rome. The Senate sits in the Palazzo Madama, close to the Pantheon (close, that is, in the topographical sense); and the Chamber of Deputies is in the Piazza Montecitorio, next to the Piazza Colonna, called after a column on which are commemorated, in bas-relief, the campaigns of the philosopher-emperor Marcus Aurelius against the Germans in the second century AD. There have been all too few philosopher-kings in modern Italian politics. It is worth seeing the *transatlantico*, the elegant, elongated lobby (supposedly reminiscent of the deck of a liner) where the parliamentarians wheel and deal with legendary convolution. But such official buildings do not tell the true story of Italian political life in the twentieth century.

That story is better told by the hideous monument to Vittorio Emanuele, disfiguring the very oldest part of the city, the Capitoline Hill; by the Palazzo Venezia, across the swirling traffic of the square, from whose balcony Mussolini used to harangue the crowd; and by the headquarters of the two parties which have run the country since Mussolini's fall. The Christian Democrats, appropriately, are in the Piazza del Gesù and, scarcely a hundred yards away, in the Via delle Botteghe Oscure, the Street of the Dark Shops, the old Communist Party has been rechristened the Party of Democratic Socialism, and the hammer and sickle replaced as its badge by the green oak tree. The most sinister monument of all to the Italian system that has now been made obsolete by the collapse of Communism, however, is not a building or a column that you can visit or photograph. It is simply a place; an undistinguished spot in Via Caetani, the short, gloomy street without a pavement which joins the Botteghe Oscure and the Piazza del Gesù, command posts of the Red Italy and the White. That is where, with cruelly deliberate political symbolism, the body of Aldo Moro, the politician who wished to achieve a historic compromise between the two forces, was dumped by the Red Brigades, stuffed into the boot of an old red Renault 4.

Since the Risorgimento, in the middle of the last century, Italian political life has been a story of disappointment and tragedy, of hard-headed, often impressively clever protection and advancement of cynical private interest, broken only by occasional periods of hope and idealism. Rome has been the forum of that stylish but dour and ruthless political warfare. It has the Food and Agriculture Office of the United Nations and two separate sets of diplomatic missions, to the Republic and to the Vatican. It has Cinecittà, one of the biggest film industries in Europe. It is also the home to a journalism that seems to reflect the political culture: subtle, accomplished, brilliant even, but rather tenuously related to the real world except in so far as it is highly profitable to its owners. It is still, in a quiet way, a place where you can live a sweet life, though calling it *la dolce vita* would be to betray that you are hopelessly out of date. But most Romans work in a bureaucracy which is relatively well-paid and – except at the top – not particularly demanding. It is not the impartial civil service of the Victorian ideal, where you lean over backwards not to seem to be doing any favours; far from it. Nor is it the intellectually pretentious but genuinely expert bureaucracy of Paris. If anything, it more closely resembles the Washington bureaucracy, locked in a *pas de trois* with Congress and the organized special interests. But the Roman bureaucracy is less careful to maintain the proprieties. It is a vast, hardly concealed system of what the Italians call *clientelismo*, in which the wary bureaucrat takes good care to know whose interests it is to his advantage to serve.

The point is that the city, in modern times, to paraphrase Oscar Wilde's wisecrack about the United States, has passed from political barbarism to political decadence without passing through modernism. There are brilliant, pioneering architects in Italy; but not in Rome. There have been great modern Italian artists and schools, in painting and sculpture; in Milan, not in Rome. There have been philosophers, novelists, and critics who have played an important part in creating the European consciousness of the twentieth century: Benedetto Croce, D'Annunzio, Gramsci, Carlo Levi, Calvino, Primo Levi, Fellini, to take half a dozen names almost at random. None of them were Romans.

Rome, in fact, in spite of its experience of fascism and war, for all its sophistication in the uses of power, has remained strangely insulated from the realities of modern Europe. The Church now, compared to the stifling constriction of Italian politics, seems to breathe a wider air. I have felt it when I wandered by chance into St Peter's during a pontifical High Mass, and walked up past row upon row of priests and nuns, Indian, Chinese, Mexican, African, to the scarlet company of the cardinals under the ornate baroque *baldacchino* over the high altar. You sense it, too, when the Holy Father, in Rome between his ceaseless voyaging to encourage the faithful in every corner of the world, appears for the Angelus on the stroke of noon at his window high above the crowd crammed between the horned arms of the colonnade, and speaks, as the ancient formula has it, *urbi et orbi*: to the city and to the world.

The truth is that Rome has meant too much to too many for too long to be the exclusive property of either the city or the world. Seedy and august, solemn and cynical, eternal and frivolous, Rome has always been a place of pilgrimage, and in the eighteenth and nineteenth centuries it became the favourite goal of a new, secular form of pilgrimage: the Grand Tour.

There is a delightful drawing in the royal collection at Windsor Castle which depicts a young English milord arriving at last in Rome at the climax of his Grand Tour.[25] The Scots artist, David Allan, shows him as he has just stepped from his carriage in front of the Spanish Steps at the height of the Roman Carnival. As a handsome young woman dances with a masked man to the music of violin, mandolin and tambourine, the tourist is surrounded by importunate vendors selling food, drink, religious paintings and every other conceivable service.

But if Roman life had its temptations and its comforts, that was not what drew the visitors who made Rome the climax of the Grand Tour. It was the massive, mysterious relics of the ancient Romans and the brilliant achievements in marble and paint of the Renaissance that fascinated them. From the beginning of the eighteenth century, right through Georgian and Victorian times, even as late as the days of the artistic tourists gently mocked in the novels of Henry James and E.M. Forster, Britons travelled to Rome, not for luxury, still less to understand the culture of the present. Almost to a man, they were repelled by what they saw as the religious superstition and political repression of contemporary Italy. They travelled to learn about, and to learn from, the classical past.

It is sad, perhaps, but it is no longer our past. In the twentieth century, and especially in the last fifty years, the classical origins of

European civilization have come to seem, if not irrelevant, at least inaccessible to most of us. It is not so long since almost every educated man and woman in Britain or France or Germany knew Latin and Greek. Now, to study the classical languages is unusual, and even carries with it a faint hint of pretension. To study the art of the Renaissance and the Baroque, while less suspect, is also out of fashion. Few would see either classical antiquity or the Renaissance as promising fields in which to look for new ideas.

In the heyday of the Grand Tour architects were thrilled by studying Diocletian's palace at Split, on the far shore of the Adriatic, like the brothers Adam, or the villas of Palladio, like Colen Campbell, or the palaces of Venice, like Ruskin, but modern architecture has other sources and wrestles with different problems. Writers as influential as Goethe, Byron, Keats and Shelley, painters like Claude Lorrain and Nicolas Poussin, Jacques-Louis David and Turner were thrilled by the legacy of classical antiquity and found it natural to turn to Italy for the most powerful, the most challenging ideas. But the painters who shaped the way we see the world were rebels against the classical vision. The writers who formed the modern consciousness found their inspiration elsewhere, often – like the painters – in the teeming streets and shabby rented rooms of the modern city.

C.S. Lewis once said that the greatest division in the history of the West was not that between the ancient world and the Dark Ages, or between the Dark Ages and the medieval world, but between the modern world and the world of Jane Austen.[26] The French critic Roland Barthes put the Great Divide around 1850. Since then, he wrote, new forms of organization in society, new classes, new methods of communication have destroyed 'classical' writing. We could go further and say that they have created a new civilization in Europe, descended from, but quite different from, the civilization which acknowledged the ancient world as its model and master.

Some of that change has been brought about by science and technology. The technical base of modern cities has influenced them in more ways than the obvious ones. For example, the coming of the railways made possible the modern megalopolis, the city with one million or even almost ten million inhabitants. Railways and steam navigation created trade on a scale which demanded the great markets and counting-houses of nineteenth-century Paris, Chicago, Moscow and Berlin, the commercial empires of London and New York. But railways created a new city culture in other ways, too. Railways, and light railways, made suburbs possible. That meant that a very important class of people in the cities, businessmen, went into the centre of the city to work, but left their wives and children in the healthier air of the suburbs. It happened first in London in the 1850s, then in some American cities, and eventually in every city that was big enough. That had non-economic effects. It created a split in values and consciousness between the unforgiving Darwinian contest of business in the city and the more softer, more 'feminine' values of home, now that home was no longer over the shop or the counting-house. Again, railways and light railways, from the 1870s on, implied a journey to work. That in turn created a new reading public, for the clerk and the typist wanted new, bright reading matter for the train or the tram. The first newspapers with circulations of a million copies a day appeared in the cities – London, Paris, New York, Berlin – where the commuting habit was first established. Mass readership meant mass advertising, and advertising created a new cultural tone, bustling, brash, impatient and irreverent, because it addressed a wider and more impressionable audience than the solemn newspapers and three-volume novels of the mid-century. The new industrial and commercial world of the Victorian age, the age of driving pistons and clacking looms, lifts and light-bulbs and typewriters, corresponded with changes in the minds and spirits of men and women.

Among other things, the new age created a new tourism. It was an Englishman called Thomas Cook, in mid-century, who put an end to all that. Or rather he and his many imitators and competitors were responsible for the beginning of the end of that happy world where, for a few British sovereigns, a man could live like a prince for months on end as he toured the sights and the watering-places of the Continent. A writer called Charles Lever, in *Blackwood's Magazine*, sardonically observed, as through his monocle, that 'some enterprising and unscrupulous man', by which he meant none other than the much-derided, much-followed Cook, was proposing to carry forty or fifty people to Naples and back for a fixed sum. Why Lever should have been so horrified by this plan is not plain. It is hard to believe that he already foresaw, in the 1850s, like some prophet whose eyes penetrated the generations, the tour buses parked in their ranks around the Louvre, the Colosseum, the Houses of Parliament, the airports full of bare-legged tourists, the gift shops and Shoppes, the hotel pools and cheap nightclubs, the wholesale debauching of monuments, landscapes, even cultures. Already then, 'the cities of Italy are deluged with droves of these creatures'.

Steadily, the columns converged on the famous cities and idyllic landscapes. Victorian clergymen and schoolteachers' daughters sought to immortalize the pagan beauties of Italy and Greece in sepia photographs to hang on the walls of Hampstead villas and Lincolnshire rectories. Soon Russian grand-dukes, then German burghers, the French, insatiable for artistic information, and inexhaustible armies of Americans thronged round the culture circuit.

Each generation changed the emphasis of its explorations. For British and American travellers between the wars, it was first and foremost France. Many, when war came, looked back, like Cyril Connolly, with bitter nostalgia on those pre-war summers: 'peeling off the kilometres to the tune of "Blue Skies", sizzling down the long black liquid reaches of Nationale Sept, the plane trees going sha-sha-sha through the open window, the windscreen yellowing with crushed midges, she with the Michelin beside me, a handkerchief binding her hair'.[27]

During the Second World War there were many in Britain who shared Connolly's fear that foreign travel would be no more than the memory of a vanished world. Instead, there was more than ever

– and more meant less. By the 1960s, the great travel boom was under way. First the Scandinavians, then the Germans, and with rising prosperity all Europe joined the lemming migration to the sun and the southern sea.

We all kill the thing we love, and inexorably the sheer numbers of people wanting to see the sights and scenes of Europe began to transform the scenes and sights themselves. Tourist hotels, great multistorey slabs, began to disfigure bays whose landscapes had been a symphony of sea, sand and hills covered with olives and scented herbs since Odysseus sailed into them. The aisles of cathedrals where quiet believers had worshipped for centuries filled up with loud disbelievers in shorts, cameras slung at the ready. No doubt the tourist industry has not been wholly destructive. Norman Lewis has graphically described the bitterly impoverished Catalan village where he lived in the very year before the first hotels appeared.[28] Most of its inhabitants worked all their lives at back-breaking labour in the fields or the fishing boats, tyrannized by an ignorant priest and a handful of mean-spirited notables. To the inhabitants of hundreds of villages like that, from Portugal to Turkey, work as a waiter or a maid in a new hotel, however ugly, was an improvement on millennial want. Still, the golden tide from the north did drown the places it chose. The effluent from hotels pollutes the beach where the naked Odysseus hid from the king's daughter as she played ball with her maidens. Trampling feet have worn away inches from the paving-stones of the Temple of Zeus at Olympia and the Athenian acropolis has had to be closed because visitors' feet have made it too slippery for safety.

It became fashionable to draw a rather snobbish distinction between explorers, who were heroic, travellers, who were respectable, and tourists, who were beneath contempt.[29] But we are all, in differing proportions, travellers and tourists, even – if we get the chance – in some modest degree explorers. Which of us has not, when tired or convalescent or plain bored, hankered for a cheap, uncomplicated trip to a warm place with no greater ambition than to lie in the sun and to go to bed at night hot, full of wine and far from the office?

Still, a law of diminishing returns does apply to tourism. When a Byron or a Richard Burton visited Greece or Arabia, he took his life in his hands. He spent several years of that life getting there. By the time he returned, having coped with uncertain facilities for transmitting and changing money, with arbitrary and potentially ferocious beys, pashas and governors, with rascally innkeepers, shipwrecks, bandits and fevers, and with the effort spent in acquiring fluency in half a dozen languages, the traveller was profoundly transformed by his experience. The tourist whose visit lasts a week or a fortnight, who needs to learn no more words of a foreign language than the words for 'please' and 'thank you', 'beer' and 'wine', 'Ladies' and 'Gents', is hardly affected at all. A kind of 'factorization' has taken place: as travel has given way to tourism, more and more people spend less and less money in seeing less and less of more and more places. Many of us who cannot afford the time or the money to become 'travellers' in the manner of the Grand Tour nevertheless hanker for a new tourism that is a little less of a production line.

We can put that another way. Something called modernism is now well over a hundred years old. Old enough, in fact, to deserve a kind of tourism of its own. So now is the time to think in terms of a new Grand Tour. Those who sign on for it will not necessarily refuse to look at the Leonardos in the Louvre or the Hermitage, the treasures of the Vatican galleries or the British Museum. But they will be more interested in tracing the roots of our own culture, which is largely the culture of modernism. It did not, for the reasons I have suggested, grow in Rome, nor in the other capitals of humanism, Venice, Florence, Bologna. It was the new civilization of great cities, swollen by empire, and industry, and the great migration from the countryside.

This book has grown out of journeys I made to seven cities: Rome, Paris, Brussels, Berlin, Prague, Vienna and St Petersburg. I tried to understand the contribution that each of them, and London, has made to the world we live in. That sent me back to books I had heard of but not read, to lesser-known books by writers I had read, and to read more about the writers whose books I had read. I have tried to think myself back into the past of the cities, to understand what they were like roughly a hundred years ago, and how they got that way. It became a journey in time as well as in space, an exploration of ideas as well as of buildings. Its simple project is to propose a new kind of tourism for the modern traveller, to map a new Grand Tour of some of the cities which were the cradle and the imaginative backdrop to the books and the buildings, the ideas and the movements, which made the world we live in.

CHAPTER II

LEFT BANK, RIGHT BANK

THE AVERAGE FRENCHMAN, THE OLD
saying goes, keeps his heart on the left and his wallet on the right.
For the whole of this century, at least, the same has been true of
Paris. The Right Bank of the Seine, the Rive Droite, where the
Bourbons had their palaces, is the realm of power and money.
That's where you'll find the President of the Republic, the Bourse,
the bourgeois quarters of the 16th and 17th *arrondissements*, big
business, *haute couture* and serious shopping.

The Left Bank, the Rive Gauche, has been since the Middle
Ages the kingdom of the heart and the mind. Before the Revolution it was the realm of the Church: of great abbeys – Cluny,
Ste-Geneviève, St-Germain, the Bernardins and the Jacobins – and
of the University. It is still the home of the university and of the

grandes écoles: the Polytechnique, until it moved out a few years ago; 'Sciences Po'; the École Normale Supérieure, which turns out university teachers; and the École Nationale d'Administration, which cranks out formidable bureaucrats; not to mention others less well known outside France.

There are focuses of power on the Left Bank, among them the prime minister's office at Matignon, in a quiet corner halfway up to Montparnasse; the Assemblée Nationale; and the foreign ministry on the quai d'Orsay. The old aristocratic quarter, too, the spiritual home of Proust's duchesses, was the Faubourg St-Germain, on the left bank of the Seine. But the Left Bank is *par excellence* the home of that endangered but tenacious species, the French intellectual. In the old days he came up from the provinces on a scholarship to one of the crack Paris *lycées*, he did his higher education in Paris, and in Paris he stayed for the rest of his life, in and out of the cafés, the bookshops and the publishing houses, teaching, writing and inextinguishably arguing, in print and face to face. Between the wars,[1] most literary publishers were clustered round St-Germain-des-Prés: Gallimard in the rue Sébastien-Bottin, Grasset in the rue des Saints-Pères, Flammarion in the rue Racine; and when les Éditions du Seuil came along, they were near by in the rue Jacob. In tiny cubbyholes in these warrens, literary fashions and reputations were launched and destroyed, and incidentally a lot of notable books were written, too. Many French writers doubled as editors. André Malraux, for example, was an editor at Gallimard. Once, at a cocktail party in the garden at Gallimard – publishers of Proust,[2] Gide, Sartre and Simone de Beauvoir, among so many others – an old gentleman said to me, 'If someone threw a bomb into this garden, *Monsieur, la France serait décervelée* [France would have her brains blown out]!'

Fifteen years ago, he was right. The publishers are still clustered round St-Germain-des-Prés, the students still throng the Latin Quarter, where Loyola taught in the sixteenth century, Aquinas in the thirteenth and Abelard in the twelfth; where Villon boozed and wenched in the fifteenth century, Rabelais in the sixteenth and Rodolfo and Mimi, the hero and heroine of *La Bohème*, in the nineteenth. For three quarters of a millennium, these streets between the Montagne Ste-Geneviève and the Seine have been a myth. Still, the fact remains that a great and probably irreversible transformation is taking place in the social geography of Paris. The balance is slow but unmistakably shifting back towards the Right Bank; the empire of the Left is in inexorable decline.

In part, this is the capricious movement of fashion. When I first visited Paris as a schoolboy in the 1950s, St-Germain-des-Prés was the centre of the Existentialist universe. Sartre and Simone de Beauvoir drank their coffee at the Montana, next to the Café de Flore. Sidney Bechet gave concerts at the Mutualité, in the hall where the giant student demos against the Algerian war took place, and someone in the rue du Vieux Colombier had invented a new word: *discothèque*, which then meant a bar where you could ask for records – *disques* – as you asked for books at the *bibliothèque*.

A quarter of a century before that, in the 1920s, it was Montparnasse,[3] and in particular the four big cafés at the intersection of the boulevard de Montparnasse and the boulevard Raspail – the Dôme and the Select, the Rotonde and the Coupole – that were the intellectual centre and the nightlife capital of the world. There you might see Ernest Hemingway and Gertrude Stein, Alfred Jarry, the creator of *Ubu Roi*, or Kiki, the model whose back appears as a violin in Man Ray's famous photograph. Montparnasse inaugurated intellectual tourism. In 1921, the whole world poured out of the Métro at the Vavin station, 'Americans in checked shirts, Scandinavians in sweaters and heavy boots, playboys in tuxedos, women in men's clothes, dipsomaniacs, dope fiends, schizophrenics and Hindu mystics',[4] all hoping to catch a sight of Matisse and Picasso, Modigliani and Chagall. Down the road was the bookshop, Shakespeare & Company, where the English and the Americans went in the hope of becoming famous, and where the owner, Sylvia Beach, called her customer and friend James Joyce, 'melancholy Jesus' behind his back.[5]

Twenty years before that, and indeed for the whole of the forty-odd years between the Commune of 1870 and the 1914 war, the magnet both for Parisian pleasure-seekers and intellectuals was on the Right Bank, and specifically Montmartre. From Baudelaire and Zola, Manet and Renoir to Matisse and Picasso, all the great writers and painters lived in Montmartre, or if they didn't, they spent their evenings there, rubbing shoulders with grand-dukes and *grands bourgeois* slumming for the evening, and working-class girls from Belleville and Ménilmontant on the Butte de Montmartre, with its windmills and dancehalls, its bearded painters and its cancan girls, and on the *boulevards extérieurs*, with their wandering males and loitering females. In 1890, when the great picture-dealer, Ambroise Vollard,[6] went to live in Montmartre, he just missed Vincent van Gogh at a little restaurant, Au Tambourin, run by Madame Segatori, in the boulevard de Clichy. But Cézanne and Renoir, Manet and Degas were all painting in the *quartier*. All four of them had just transferred their custom from the Nouvelle Athènes to the Rat Mort, and you could buy their paintings for a song, which the shrewd Vollard proceeded to do. Another acquaintance, Henri de Toulouse-Lautrec, could not be dragged away from the dancing at the Moulin-Rouge.

Twenty years later the action had moved to the Lapin Agile.[7] Picasso used to eat there; an 'extraordinary radiance' hovered over him; but his fellow Cubist Max Jacob had both his thumbs broken by a black pimp who thought he was taking the micky when Jacob talked about religion to his girl. After a while, the artists moved to the Billard-en-Bois, a scruffy dive, but with, on its walls, two Renoirs and a Marie Laurencin – the beautiful woman who was the lover of Apollinaire, incomparable poet of the streets and bridges of Paris.

So the pendulum of fashion has swung, Left Bank, Right Bank, since the Revolution and even longer. The one constant is that in Paris, quite unlike London or Berlin or Vienna, the rich and the poor, the intellectuals and the bourgeois, the working classes and the dangerous classes, have always spent their evenings and taken their pleasures, if not together, at least in the same neighbourhoods.

In the beginning, there were not two Parises – Rive Droite and Rive Gauche – but three.[8] There was also the Cité, on the islands. There are now only two islands, the Île de la Cité and the Île St-Louis, but in the Middle Ages there were more. That was royal Paris, though before long the kings of France began to build great fortresses – the Châtelet, the Louvre – on the mainland as well. There was the *Université*, on the Left Bank: Church Paris, which was not just the home of students and their teachers, but also of great religious houses. And there was the *Ville*: Town Paris, the home of the merchants.

Roman Paris, Lutetia, lay on the Left Bank, where you can still see its traces: the *Arènes de Lutèce* (the ancient arena) in the rue Monge; the Roman Baths, complete with *tepidarium, frigidarium* and *caldarium*, on the site of the monastery of Cluny, in the heart of the modern university district; remains of an aqueduct, of a theatre (in the grounds of the famous Lycée Louis-le-Grand); and, preserved in the Cluny Museum, inscriptions which prove that at the time of Christ there was a community of boatmen on the Seine who raised an altar to the Emperor Tiberius. They decorated it with a bas-relief of bearded warriors, the remote ancestors of many generations of moustachioed warriors from the banks of the Seine.

The Petit Pont joining the island to the Left Bank, the Roman *parvus pons*, rebuilt at least eleven times, was guarded by the Petit Châtelet, the little castle, and led into a quarter so crowded that it reminded the chronicler Joinville, who had visited Egypt on crusade, of the streets of Damietta. From there began the rue St-Jacques, the street of St James, the beginning of the pilgrimage road which led all the way to the great shrine of St James at Compostela in north-western Spain. As it left Paris, the road passed the great convent of the Dominicans, the Jacobins: *Jacobus* is the Latin for 'James'. It was founded by the Preaching Brothers of St Dominic only three years after his first house in Toulouse, set up to combat the Albigensian heresy in 1215. St Louis loaded it with gifts of lands and money. The bodies or the hearts of twenty-three princes of the royal houses of France were buried there, as well as poets and priests. St Albert the Great and St Thomas Aquinas were both members of the Jacobins, and from it, indirectly, the Jacobins of the French Revolution take their name, because they rented another Dominican building as their first meeting place. Rich as it was, the convent of the Jacobins was by no means the only great monastery on the Left Bank. There was Cluny, the Paris house of the great reforming Benedictine order based in Burgundy. There were the Bernardins, the Paris house of the Cistercians, who reformed Cluny in its turn. Oldest of all was the monastery of Ste Geneviève, founded by King Clovis as long ago as 510; and, outside the walls, the great abbey of St-Germain-des-Prés, 'in the fields' when it was founded, but now surrounded by swirling modernism.

In fact, Paris, since the Dark Ages, has been a great capital of Christianity, comparable almost to Rome. And, since the twelfth century it has also been a great university centre, indeed, *the* great university centre. Before the Revolution it was a federal university, made up of colleges, much like Oxford or Cambridge, and on the Left Bank you can still see traces of a couple of dozen. In 1762, after the Jesuits were expelled from France, their great college, which was never subject to the authority of the university, was merged with thirty little colleges, and there were still a round dozen left to be closed at the Revolution, among them the Irish and Scots colleges.

The whole earth, said Thucydides, is the grave of famous men. The Latin Quarter, as the university came to be called – because Latin was the language of the Church and of the schools – has been holy ground for the Grand Tour for centuries. Here, for example, was the Collège Ste-Barbe, where Ignatius Loyola and St Francis Xavier studied – the one founded the Society of Jesus and the other became an apostle to India, China and Japan – and were fellow students of Jean Calvin, the future arch-Protestant of Geneva. Ignatius was insulted by a medical student called François Rabelais, who scribbled something offensive about the 'stink' of the 'Hespaniards' in general and 'Fray Inigo' in particular.

In the rue du Chat Qui Pèche, near the bridgehead, Elliott Paul wrote his tender and touching book of reminiscences of Paris before the Second World War, *The Last Time I Saw Paris*. Not far away is the site of a medieval fortress, the Tour de Nesle, the scene of the grim love story of the two squires who became the lovers of the princesses of Burgundy, wives of the king's brothers. The king's daughter saw the squires wearing rich purses she had given to the princesses. The young men were flayed alive, and the princesses, their hair shaven, were locked up for life in the grim tower of Château Gaillard, built by Richard the Lionheart. Their sister, Jeanne, only escaped because her husband succeeded as king. She is said to have been the lover of the theologian Buridan, then a schoolboy; he later fought a duel over another mistress with a rival who became Pope Clement VI.

A few streets further on, past the beautiful dome of the Institut, gift of Cardinal Mazarin, where the Immortals of the Académie Française meet in their green robes, and you are in the rue de l'Ancienne Comédie and back in the late seventeenth century. Here was the theatre which opened, on the night of 18 April 1689, with a notable double bill: Racine's *Phèdre* and *Le Médecin malgré lui*, by Molière, who had died a dozen years earlier.

Next door, in 1670, a noble Sicilian, Francesco Procopio dei Coltelli, set up in a new business he had been taught by two Armenian refugees from the Ottoman Empire: for two and a half *sous* a cup, he sold the 'new aroma', coffee. The Café Procope is still there. In it Voltaire scribbled a venomous quatrain about an enemy and the *Encyclopédie* was born, from a conversation between Diderot and d'Alembert. It was here that Beaumarchais waited to hear what kind of reception the *Marriage of Figaro* was getting up the road at the Odéon. Marat, who was murdered in his bath by Charlotte Corday round the corner, was a regular, and so in later years were Balzac, Anatole France and Verlaine. This is the oldest café in Paris: ancestor of all those thousands of establishments, from tiny rooms, their windows curtained with gingham, in the outer suburbs, to the brass-fitted, mirror-lined palaces of the *grands boulevards*.

The Cité is as ancient as the Left Bank, and as rich in memories. Here is Notre-Dame de Paris, the home of Hugo's hunchback, where Charles de Gaulle stood upright when everyone else threw themselves on the floor as a sniper's shots ricocheted round the nave during the *Te Deum* sung for the Liberation in 1944. Here is the Sainte-Chapelle, supreme masterpiece of the High Gothic, built by St Louis to house what he believed to be the Crown of Thorns, brought back from the Crusades by Baldwin, Count of Flanders. Here is the quai des Orfèvres, where Chief Inspector Maigret used to look out of the window, savour the smell of Paris, compounded of grey tobacco, petrol and chestnut trees after the rain, and send out to the café for a bock and a sandwich to encourage his suspects to talk. Fourteenth-century detectives used harsher methods: when the Tour Bonbec – the 'canary tower' we might call it – was demolished in the nineteenth century fragments of instruments of torture were found in the ruins. Here were the *tapis francs*, the lowest dives of early-nineteenth-century Paris; and here was the royal palace of the Capetians. From its windows, Philippe le Bel watched Jacques de Molay, Grand Master of the Templars, being burned alive on the sandbank called *l'Îlot des Juifs*.

The Right Bank was the slowest of the three parts of the city to develop. In Roman times it was deserted marshland, flooded by the stream of Ménilmontant. Philip Augustus, who went on crusade with Richard the Lionheart, built a castle on the site of the Cour Carrée of the Louvre. Its foundations, and the king's gilded helmet, were found when I.M. Pei's additions to the museum were built in the 1980s. Gradually the Right Bank was drained and built upon. By the time of the Hundred Years' War it had become one of the richest trading communities in northern Europe. Near the end of the fourteenth century, Charles VI's chancellor built himself a palace, the House of Turrets, in the district called the Marais, 'the marsh', long drained to provide gardens for the convents and private palaces in the neighbourhood. After Agincourt, the brother of Henry V of England, John, Duke of Bedford, lived there for a while. In 1559 Henri II was killed there by accident in a joust with the Duke of Montgomery. His widow, Catherine de Médicis, could not bear to stay on in the palace, and had it demolished. The area then became the great horse market of Paris, where two thousand horses were bought and sold every Saturday. Finally, in 1605, Henry of Navarre built the first great square in Europe there, the place Royale (renamed, after the Revolution, the place des Vosges), and around it there were built, until the court moved to Versailles in the time of Louis XIV, palaces and town houses in the rich Renaissance style.

By the early part of this century, the Marais was a shabby neighbourhood. When Simenon moved there in the 1930s it was 'a jumble of shops, craftsman's studios, tumbledown palaces and dubious alleys', and the nearby rue des Rosiers had become the ghetto and reception area for poor Jewish immigrants from eastern Europe. It has now been restored, speculated over and gentrified; it remains one of the most handsome quarters of any city in Europe.

As the city grew, the walls shaped its growth: you can read the city's history in them, as you can read the rings of a tree. The first ring of fortifications to be built round the whole city since Roman times was started by Philip Augustus. Although Paris already had some 200,000 inhabitants, making it almost as big as Constantinople at the time, the walls enclosed much open ground, and it was some 150 years before the city had filled them. After the battle of Poitiers when the English captured the King of France, the merchants' great leader, Étienne Marcel, began a new and more extensive ring of walls to keep out the marauding English. By the time they were finished, in 1383, there were 300,000 Parisians. There were seven gates on the Right Bank and four on the Left. In the Middle Ages, there were eight quarters, then sixteen, and under Louis XIV there were twenty; shortly after his death the first street names appeared, carved on stone.

In Louis XIV's time, after the end of the religious wars, Paris remained a dark and dangerous place. In the Middle Ages chains were pulled across the streets at night to keep out wagons and carriages. Even in the sixteenth century there were no more than a handful of coaches in the whole town. But by the middle of the seventeenth century the first horse-cabs, the *fiacres*, had appeared. The first oil lamps were put up in 1763, and the world's first gas lighting appeared there in 1829. There was a chronic shortage of water (only a litre a day for each Parisian) until the first Napoleon built the Canal de l'Ourq; the streets were full of robbers and footpads.

From the middle of the seventeenth century on, with Louis XIV's armies probing deep into Holland and Germany, the city was at last safe from foreign invasion. The fourteenth-century walls were razed and on them were laid out the *grands boulevards*, the inner ring of boulevards that runs from the Madeleine up the boulevard des Capucines and the boulevard des Italiens to the place de la Bastille and, on the Left Bank, as the boulevard St-Germain, curves from the eastern tip of the Île St-Louis to the Assemblée Nationale.

A little over a hundred years later, in the last years of the *ancien régime*, a new wall was built, this time not to keep enemies out, but to raise excise taxes. This was the *mur des fermiers-généraux*. The Fermiers-Généraux was a syndicate of rich bankers who 'farmed' the monarchy's revenue, paying the king the money he needed, and raising it from the increasingly restive commoners in taxes, including the hated *octroi*, a sort of internal customs tariff. Two roads ran round the oval course of the stout stone wall, one on the inside and one on the outside, so that, when the wall itself was pulled down, the broad double roadway of the *boulevards extérieurs* was formed. They run from the quai de Bercy, near the Gare de Lyon, round the boulevards of La Villette, Clichy and Batignolles, past where the Étoile now is and, on the Left Bank, out along the rue de Grenelles and the rue de Vaugirard to the neighbourhood of Montparnasse. As we shall see, the trace of that wall has shaped the intellectual as well as the social geography of Paris.

No fewer than sixty gates were planned in the wall, and in 1785, only four years before the French Revolution, the greatest of French eighteenth-century architects, Claude-Nicolas Ledoux, was commissioned to design them. He called them rather grandly 'Propylaeas', after the Greek for a gatehouse. You can see eight of his designs in his book on architecture, handsome structures in the neo-classical style, with rotundas, wings, colonnades. Only forty were actually built, and of those traces of only four remain: the best-preserved is the rotunda of La Villette, behind the Gare du Nord. The rest were pulled down in the Revolution.

That was not the last wall around Paris, however. In 1840, a new ring of fortifications was built still further out, earthworks faced with brick, to resist the artillery of the day. The *fortifs* enclosed a ring of new development. There were trim, regularly built streets, tiny cottages put up individually by *rentiers* like the *petits-bourgeois* savers and scroungers of Balzac's 'Comédie Humaine', the great series of novels in which he painted the whole social gamut of Paris in the 1820s and 1830s, and crowded tenements in slums like Belleville in the east or the Goutte d'Or in the far north-east. Beyond these varied, sprawling developments, in the muddy wildernesses towards the *fortifs*, were the shanties of the poorest of the poor: the *chiffonniers* – rag pickers – and what came to be called, not without justification, 'the dangerous classes': thieves, pimps and the roughest prostitutes. The *fortifs* were eventually razed and the Boulevard Périphérique, six lanes of howling traffic, was built where they stood. Their line is still the boundary of Paris proper, though another eight million or so inhabitants of the *région Parisienne* now live beyond it.

There is a geography of pleasure in Paris, as well as a geography of work, and it follows that slow process whereby the city grew to fill in one ring of walls after another. This is not just a matter of boozing and wenching. Paris has always had its red-light districts, like London's Soho and New York's Tenderloin. What is peculiarly Parisian, however, is the way different classes have come together in particular places, not only to drink and to pick up, or be picked up by, members of the opposite sex, but also to dance, to talk and to enjoy themselves at every level, from the grossly fleshly, even the perverse, to the cerebral, the aesthetic and sometimes the spiritual. Pleasure, too, fell subject in the nineteenth century to the process of specialization that affected the city's working and residential geography.

Under the *ancien régime*, rich people and poor people in Paris lived jumbled up together in a way which shocked English visitors. Noblemen built private houses, H-shaped, *entre cour et jardin*, lived in the middle wing and rented off space to pensioners, tradesmen and widows. Even in the late nineteenth century, the middle-class narrator in Proust's great sequence of novels gets to know the aristocratic Guermantes because his parents live in a flat carved out of the Guermantes' town house. Or a rich man might live in the first floor of a five-storey house, with craftsmen or shopkeepers on the ground floor and tenants of diminishing means on the upper floors. Balzac tells a cynical story of a publisher who meets a poet at a party and wants to see his poems so as to decide whether he wants to bring them out. They go back to the poet's attic, and, says Balzac, the advance went down by 100 francs for every floor they climbed. Gradually, after the Revolution, Paris acquired a class geography. (Not for nothing did Marx write a book on 'the class struggle in France' in those years.) The bourgeois lived in the *beaux quartiers*, in the west; the workers, were pushed into *les quartiers populaires* in the east, north-east and north.

It was the same with the geography of pleasure and with the geography of the intellect. Under the *ancien régime*, people crowded into the narrow streets around the Pont-Neuf where there was a continual fair. Then, in the last years before the Revolution, the duc d'Orléans carried out one of the great real-estate speculations in the history of Paris when he transformed the Palais-Royal, long abandoned by the kings, who had moved to Versailles a hundred years before, into a place for elegant dissipation: fashionable restaurants, expensive prostitutes, gambling for high stakes. Today the Palais-Royal is a quiet corner of central Paris. Its dusty stamp and coin dealers' shops and the stuffy elegance of a great restaurant, Le Grand Vefour, give no hint of the smart dissipation and revolutionary frenzy that filled its oblong, colonnaded space in the years immediately before the Revolution.[9] Philippe d'Orléans was the prototype of the limousine liberals and Bollinger bolsheviks of the next two hundred years. Immensely rich and devoted to freemasonry at a time when it was the dangerous religion of revolutionaries, he was suspected by the court party of wishing to overthrow his cousin and become king himself. He affected every kind of liberalism and libertinism, and in 1792 he formally requested of the communal government of Paris that his name should be changed to Philippe Égalité. His real-estate speculation in the Palais-Royal became from the middle 1780s the place where the 'action', social, intellectual, sexual and political was to be found. What was more, the Duc d'Orléans forbade the intrusion of any of the half dozen police forces of the *ancien régime*.

Choderlos de Laclos, the author of *Les Liaisons dangereuses*, worked for Orléans in the Palais-Royal and the Marquis de Sade opened a pornographic bookshop there. The colonnades were the beat of the boldest and most expensive prostitutes in Paris. The promenade of shops in the centre of the Palais, known as the Galerie de Bois or the 'Tartar Camp', was the place where assignations were made, and at its centre was a wax statue of a naked woman, *'la belle Zulima'*. In the centre of the garden the duke had laid out an oval space, a hundred metres long, for parades and sports. The surrounding colonnade was lined with wax-model and magic-lantern shows and cafés, and underground there were more sinister dives like the Café des Aveugles (Café of the Blind) and blatantly pornographic displays. The cafés above ground were the focus of furious politicking; the verb *'politiquer'* was probably invented as part of the private language of the Palais, along with the names of multicoloured drinks like the *non-lo-sapraye*, dog-Italian for 'you'd never know'.

The very centre of this dizzy world of pleasure and politics was the Café Foy, and it was there precisely, at 3.30 p.m. on Sunday, 12 July 1789, that the French Revolution began. That was where a firebrand journalist from Picardy, Camille Desmoulins, jumped up on to what he called his magic table, pulled a bunch of leaves from the chestnut tree overhead and stuck them in his hat as a cockade of liberty, and began to harangue the crowd about the news, which had just arrived from Versailles, of the fall of the reforming minister, Jacques Necker. *Aux armes!* he cried, and the crowd poured out of the Palais into the streets, carrying waxwork busts of Orléans and Necker, to look for weapons. Two days later the same mob stormed the Bastille. Arguably that was the moment when, for better and for worse, the modern world began.

The gates Ledoux built in the eighteenth-century wall were known as *les barrières*. Most of them were pulled down within a few years. But in their brief life they made sure that the focus of pleasure and intellectual life in future would not be in the centre, like the Palais-Royal, but on the city's periphery. One of the main commodities brought into Paris was wine, which cost substantially less outside the *barrière* than inside it. It became the custom to flock to drink *le vin des barrières*,[10] particularly at a row of *barrières* to the north of Paris: the barrière Blanche, the barrière Pigalle, the barrière de Clichy. North of the gates, there had always been a cluster of windmills on the Butte, or hill, of Montmartre.

So it is an eighteenth-century wine tax which explains why, in the late nineteenth and early twentieth century, bohemians and intellectuals, thieves and prostitutes looking for a killing, and tourists and wealthy Parisians looking for fun, congregated where the exterior boulevards had replaced the *octroi* wall in the south and in the north of the city.

It was the journalist Henri Murger who found a name for the poets, painters, sculptors and their long-suffering women folk: he called them *les gens de Bohème*.[11] To be sure, Murger wrote in his preface that 'Bohemia, which this book is about, is not a tribe that first saw the light of day in our time.' He traced a pedigree for his bohemians, back to François Villon, student and poet, killer and thief, who was twice tortured and once sentenced to death, and wrote some of the most haunting poetry in the French language. But Murger had a point when he said that there was nowhere like Paris in his day, the Restoration and the July Monarchy, for leading the bohemian life.

As early as the 1820s a group of young artists had installed themselves in the old houses on the slopes of the hill: among them George Sand and her lover, Chopin, the painter Delacroix, the engraver Gavarni (great rival of Daumier), opera singers like La Malibran.[12] The most famous of the old dancehalls, the Élysée-Montmartre, was founded in 1806, the year after Trafalgar (or after Austerlitz, if you are French). By the Restoration, after Waterloo, plenty of entrepreneurs were beginning to cater for the custom of going to the *barrières* to drink and dance. The Boule Noire was founded, by a retired prostitute, in 1822; the Moulin de la Galette at about the same time. Balzac and Victor Hugo spoke of prostitutes euphemistically as *lorettes*, after the church of Notre-Dame de Lorette, not far north of the *grands boulevards*.[13] But by the palmy days of the Second Empire the game had moved further out, to the exterior boulevards – Clichy, Rochechouart – on the line of the *barrières*. In 1857 the writer Alphonse Daudet met in the Brasserie des Martyrs a girl called Marie, who lived in the passage of the Élysée, just off the place Pigalle. Thirty years later, an old man, limping on the arm of a young admirer, he stopped suddenly and said, 'I'm seeing ghosts tonight. There is the house where I knew the bugger [*bougresse*] I made into Sapho', the heroine of his Montmartre novel of the same name.[14] Zola's good-time girl, Nana, ranged from the sleazy dancehalls of the Goutte d'Or to the boulevards and the Butte in her search for love and luxury.[15]

By the heyday of Napoleon III, while Baron Haussmann was rebuilding the city centre and driving his broad new boulevards through the centuries-old, tumbledown rookeries, Montmartre was rocking. The Élysée-Montmartre dancehall was so big – 1,000 square metres, or say 100 × 90 feet – that it took a two-hundred-piece orchestra, belting out Verdi, Rossini and Gounod, to be heard over the noise of the dancers stamping to and fro in the waltz, the polka and the newly fashionable lancers quadrille.[16] In summer, they danced in the garden, in the winter in the vast ballroom with its cascades and its plantations of exotic trees and flowers. Inside or out, they stamped and swirled when Olivier Métra played his signature tune, the cherry-time waltz, 'Le Temps des Cerises'. There society ladies, great courtesans like Liane de Pougy, with her seven strings of pearls, or Caroline Otéro, with crowned heads among her scalps, waltzed together with grisettes – shopgirls – and maids on their day off. Russian grand-dukes and tough young butchers from the abattoirs of La Villette waltzed with some of the most brilliant men in Europe. Freud's teacher, Dr Charcot, from the hospital of the Salpêtrière, was a friend of Daudet and used to spend evenings with him in Montmartre;[17] Murger and Baudelaire, and the painters Courbet and Monet, all drank in the Brasserie des Martyrs and the Nouvelle Athènes, place Pigalle. In 1880 a little, bearded man, crippled by a childhood fall from a horse, but lineal descendant of the almost royal Count of Toulouse who helped to lead the First Crusade, arrived in Montmartre and started to paint.[18] In 1889 Henri de Toulouse-Lautrec discovered the Moulin-Rouge and its dancers, Boneless Valentin, La Goulue and the girl whom they called Sewer-grill. He made their fame and his own, and the glory of Montmartre, and in the end he destroyed it too. For in the 1900s, it was the influx of outsiders, drawn by the myth of Montmartre, which drove the people who had made Montmartre famous across the city to Montparnasse. But in the meantime, Paris had passed through an epic transformation, and a heroic catastrophe. Both would contribute to the city's legend. Both help to explain why Paris is where the world of modernism began. It was in 1857 that Baudelaire's collection of poems, Les Fleurs du Mal, 'The Flowers of Evil', was first published; some of the poems date from before the revolution of 1848.[19] And it was in 1863, a full generation before the *fin de siècle* made itself felt in London or Vienna, that Impressionist painting first appeared at the Salon des Refusés.

Marxist critics, including Marx himself, interpret the history of France in the first half of the nineteenth century in terms of the bourgeoisie taking over the Revolution. Certainly the bourgeois used and controlled the multifarious instruments of the state, strengthened by Napoleon's reforms, but in many ways recognizable as the same powerful entity it had been under the kings and their intendants. Thus the Collège de Navarre on the Montagne Ste-Geneviève, from which Villon was suspected of stealing 500 gold coins in the fifteenth century,[20] and where princes, nobles and prelates were educated under Louis XIV, Louis XV and Louis XVI, became the Polytechnique under Napoleon and throughout the nineteenth and twentieth centuries turned out engineers for the service of the French state and of private industry.

Another consequence of the years of restored monarchy from 1815 to 1870, under Louis XVIII, Louis-Philippe and Napoleon III, was that many of the most intelligent and the most idealistic of the intellectuals, especially in Paris, were driven into emotional sympathy and sometimes activist fraternizing with the working class, as it was beginning to be called, or with the *petit peuple* of Paris. This was the origin of that phenomenon of the twentieth century, which so many in Britain and in the United States find so inexplicable and so irritating: the comfortable, state-salaried intellectual of the socialist and even the Communist Left.

'*Le vieux Paris n'est plus*,' wrote Baudelaire under the Second Empire,

> (*la forme d'une ville*
> *Change plus vite, hélas! que le cœur d'un mortel*); . . .
>
> *Paris change! Mais rien dans ma mélancolie*
> *N'a bougé! palais neufs, échafaudages, blocs,*
> *Vieux faubourgs, tout pour moi devient allégorie,*
> *Et mes chers souvenirs sont plus lourds que des rocs.*

> (The old Paris is no more; (the shape of a city,
> Alas! changes more quickly than a mortal's heart); . . .
>
> Paris changes! But nothing in my melancholy
> Has budged! New palaces, scaffolding, blocks,
> Old suburbs, all for me becomes allegory,
> And my dear memories are heavier than the rocks.)[21]

During the Second Empire of Louis Napoleon, that pompous, ruthless but, until the final disaster, curiously effective figure, the economy of France was transformed, and so was the face of Paris. Industrialization, long delayed, hit France like a breaking wave and acquired a new impetus after the free-trade treaty with England in 1860. Coal and iron mining began in the north and the east, textile manufacture in the north and the Rhône valley. Railway mileage expanded from 3,000 km in 1850 to 16,000 km in 1869, and railways needed more coal, more steel. By the end of the Second Empire Charles de Wendel was employing 5,000 in Lorraine and Eugène Schneider 10,000 at Le Creusot in the centre of France. There were close links between politics and business. Schneider was president both of the Comité des Forges, the guiding cartel of French heavy industry, and of the Corps Législatif, the closest France came to a parliament under the empire. Wendel sat in the legislature. Achille Fould was a director of the Crédit Mobilier and a minister; the Foulds were connected by marriage to the powerful banking clan of the Péreire, rivals to the Rothschilds, and the Rothschilds, besides investing heavily in railways, were also connected with the Schneiders.

Cities grew furiously. Between 1853 and 1869, Lille grew from 70,000 to 160,000, Paris from 1,287,000 to 1,850,000.[22] And the growth went on: in 1891 the population was 2,447,000; in 1911, at its peak, it was 2,888,000. To meet this growth, and to establish his claims to match his great-uncle's glory as Emperor of the French, Napoleon ordered the prefect of the Seine to rebuild Paris.[23] The *coup d'état* which brought Napoleon to power, one historian has written, 'had two great victims: the Republic and Old Paris. We know today that the Republic was only wounded, but the old Paris, struck in the heart by Baron Haussmann, never rose again.'[24] That is true: Paris today owes its surface personality, the images that everyone recognizes, to the *grandes percées* through the ancient alleyways, the broad, straight streets and ornate seven- or eight-storey façades of Haussmann's Paris. Still, you have only to poke around on foot[25] behind Haussmann's grand boulevards and splendid avenues, especially but not only in working-class neighbourhoods like the Goutte d'Or, Belleville or behind the Gare de Montparnasse, and you will find alleys and courtyards, houses and tenements that date from Balzac's Paris, if not indeed from before the Revolution.

It was widely believed at the time,[26] and has often been said since, that Haussmann's activities were politico-military in motivation: that he punched wide streets through crowded working-class neighbourhoods to make a *journée révolutionnaire* less likely, because it would be harder to build barricades, and easier to rush troops to trouble spots, and would provide, if necessary, an open field of fire for the artillery. Haussmann himself admitted that his plans did serve military purposes, but that was not their original motive, and since kings and visionaries, from Major Pierre L'Enfant in Washington to the builders of the Vienna Ringstrasse in the same era shared Haussmann's love of the sweeping gesture and the grand vista, there is no reason to disbelieve him.

One of Haussmann's achievements was the *grands boulevards*, and he also built what was called the *grande croisée*. This was the great cross formed by extending the boulevard de Sébastopol southwards across the Île de la Cité and south along a new boulevard St-Michel, and at the same time knocking through the rue de Rivoli to join the rue St-Antoine and form a grand east–west axis.

The German critic Walter Benjamin wrote an essay about Paris at this period which he called 'Paris – the Capital of the Nineteenth Century'.[27] In it, he stressed the modernism of Paris under Napoleon III and even before, not only in the intellectual sense, but also in the enthusiasm with which Parisians, like the New Yorkers of the twentieth century, embraced new ideas, new materials, new processes and new fashions. He cited the Paris arcades, glass-roofed iron structures, gaslit, and mostly built in the 1820s and 1830s, which became the home of the luxury-goods trades; the dioramas, which led directly to the development of photography, since Daguerre was apprenticed to a diorama painter, and it was in Paris that the theory of photography was first studied, especially in its impact on painting; the exhibitions, in 1855, 1867, 1889, blazoning the new creed of consumerism; Haussmann's rebuilding, and the speculative building fever it promoted. The Second Empire was a bubble of speculation, both in real estate, as the new smart neighbourhoods between the Champs-Élysées and the Seine and around the place de l'Étoile were built, and on the Bourse. Money was being made and spent with all the abandon of a boom time. Newspapers flourished, in spite of the censorship. Huge advances had already been paid in the 1840s to Eugène Sue, to Alexandre Dumas for his romances, even to the poet Lamartine for *Feuilletons*, the 'review section' of the day. Now there was money for fashions, furnishings, painting, the theatre, the opera. Even under Louis-Philippe, before 1848, cafés flourished. Men went there to read the papers, and the habit of the *apéritif*, taken among men in the café, spread. Respectable ladies still went to the *patissier* rather than to the café or to the *bal*; but not all ladies were invariably respectable, and not all women were ladies. *Bals*, dancehalls of varying degrees of respectability, dated back to the *ancien régime*. But in the free-spending, pleasure-loving atmosphere of the Second Empire, they were all the rage. It was at the Mabille, on the Champs-Élysées, which opened in 1843, that professional dancers were first hired to encourage the others. They were soon dancing the *chahut*, later known as the cancan, to such good effect that it was not unusual for them to be arrested, on the request of the civil and religious authorities, for indecency. The result was disappointing for the guardians of morality: high-kicking dances moved indoors, to the racier establishments growing up around the *barrières*, where Baron Haussmann finally knocked down the wall of the Fermiers-Généraux in 1859.

The rebuilding of Paris did not end with Haussmann. It reached a climax in the 1870s: Garnier's magnificent opera-house was inaugurated in 1875, the bridge joining the *grands boulevards* of the Left Bank to those of the Right was finished in 1876, and the avenue de l'Opéra, the most elegant shopping street Paris had yet seen, was opened in 1877. By 1880, the rebuilding of Paris was at its climax, and a few years later no less an authority than Karl Baedeker, in his guidebook, gave it as his opinion that Paris was 'more uniform than ... most other towns of its size ... on account of the vast schemes of improvement carried out in our day'.[28]

The Second Empire was a fiesta for the bourgeoisie, but life was increasingly tough for the growing armies of industrial and service workers. The middle of the nineteenth century was the period of dramatic change in Paris's economy and in the pattern of employment. Industry was expanding and spreading even beyond the fortifications to the outer suburbs. But jobs in service trades — department stores, trams, insurance, the fashion industry, restaurants, bars and entertainment, amongst others — doubled in the twenty years after 1866.[29] Paris, by the end of the sixties, was acquiring something of the profile of the modern commercial and administrative metropolis.

Then, suddenly, the city's development was interrupted. It was exposed to brutal traumas which have affected the Parisian subconscious to this day.[30] In 1870, responding foolishly to a campaign of provocation from Bismarck, Napoleon III made the fatal mistake of rushing to war. The Franco-Prussian war was declared on 19 July. There has never been such a disaster. Exactly a month later Marshal Achille Bazaine surrendered the fortress of Metz, in which he had been cooped up with 155,000 men by the Germans' brilliant manoeuvring. On 1 September, six weeks after Napoleon had threatened to march on Berlin, his army was annihilated by Moltke at Sedan and he himself was captured. Within three weeks Paris was surrounded by a German army and suffered the hardships of siege. At the end of October there was an abortive insurrection led by the Garde Nationale, many of whose officers were also officials of the French section of the Workers' International, as the French socialist party was called. By Christmas, Parisians were counting themselves lucky to buy rat meat at 2 or 3 francs a piece and dog at 5 francs a pound, and in January the Left Bank came under fire from German siege guns.

On 19 January the Garde Nationale made a mass sortie, the sortie of Buzenval, not against the Germans, who were investing the city to the north and east, but against the republican army with its headquarters in Versailles. The Gardes took their objectives, only to be ordered to retreat. They believed that they had been deliberately exposed in order to weaken them. On 22 January there was a riot at the town hall, at which the Gardes shouted 'Vive la Commune!' On 28 January, an armistice was signed with the Germans by the high command in Versailles, and the next day the German flag flew over the city.

The politicized part of the working class all over the city, but especially in the Red quarters in the north and east, and more especially their leaders in the National Guard, many of them as we have seen committed socialist revolutionaries, believed that they were being deliberately sacrificed by a government which feared and disliked them more than the enemy. It is true that the war had revealed the mutual hostility between the peasant conscripts in the army of Versailles and the radical citizen soldiers from the Paris streets. The peasants thought the Parisians were immoral, irreligious and unreliable; the Parisians thought the conscripts were swede-bashers, meat-heads – all the city boy's liturgy of contempt for his country cousins down the centuries.

On 18 March the government withdrew from the turbulent city to Versailles, and Paris celebrated its 'liberation' from the government of France. Ten days later the members of the Commune were elected, and the next day the Commune was proclaimed. In the last week in May, for ever remembered in Paris as the 'bloody week', the government determined to retake the city. On 23 May, without too much difficulty, its troops entered the city at the western tip, and the next day they occupied the centre of the city.

The Fédérés, as the Communards were called, expected the whole population of the city to rise against the government troops. But that didn't happen. Perhaps as many as 20,000 fought. But even of those, only a few held on to the last. There were individual heroes – and heroines. Louise Michel and a group of women defended the barricades in the place Pigalle and the place Blanche, at the foot of the Butte de Montmartre. Some of the Polish volunteers, survivors of Russian repression after the rising of 1863 in their homeland, fought with conspicuous courage, as did Eugène Varlin, one of the last of the leaders to fall.

By the third day, summary executions of those caught in arms became general. Atrocities were committed by both sides. The Fédérés shot the archbishop of Paris. They also executed two generals, Clément Thomas and Leconte, who had ordered brutal reprisals after the uprising of 1848. Several dozen hostages were shot by the Communards too, including eleven priests, most of them Jesuits, thirty-five policemen and four alleged police spies.

The government's retribution was on quite another scale. Interestingly, it seems that those who had fought in the *contre-guérilla* in Mexico – including Commandant Durieu and General Gallifet – started the killings. They were not the result of indiscipline. The worst atrocities were carried out under the orders of generals, though the commander-in-chief, the future President MacMahon, and the president of the Republic, Adolphe Thiers, took some trouble to distance themselves from what was done. In any case, the army was brought into politics for the first time since the fall of the first Napoleon, with fateful consequences in the Dreyfus affair and in 1940. Anyone who was found fighting, or suspected of fighting, for the Commune, was summarily shot. The officers would ask suspects what they had done the previous day. If they said 'Nothing', the officer would say, 'Aha! You admit you were not at work!' and tell his men to march the man away to be shot. Batches of prisoners were executed in prisons, barracks and, most famously, in the cemetery of Père Lachaise. The *mur des Fédérés*, where they died, has become one of the most sacred shrines of the French Left. Some were shot in cold blood. Some were shot after courts martial. Others again were executed on the orders of councils of war. Altogether, according to the best estimates, something between 17,000 and 30,000 people, most of them ordinary working people of Paris who had taken up arms to defend their city, some of them revolutionaries who thought their lives well lost in the class war, lost their lives. Although some were killed in the fighting, the great majority of them were executed without trial or with little more than a travesty of justice.

That was not all, however. Somehow, in the course of the fighting, fires were started. Some of them, at least, were started on purpose by the army firing red-hot bullets into crowded neighbourhoods. In any case, the damage was far worse than anything the German bombardment had done. The medieval Hôtel de Ville was burned to the ground. So was the rue de Rivoli. To observers looking out over the city from the hill of Montmartre, it looked as if the whole of Paris was on fire.

During the bloody week of the Commune, Montmartre threw itself without hesitation into the fight on the side of the people, its people. Even before the army broke into Paris, it was a group from Montmartre who went down to the place Wagram and dragged the cannon which had been left there up to the top of the Butte so that they would not fall into the hands of the Prussians. It was on the boulevard Rochechouart that a little boy recognized General Thomas and General Leconte. They were tried in the Élysée-Montmartre dancehall (during the siege, it had been a factory for the postal balloons which were Paris's only link with the outside world) and they were shot on a piece of waste ground near the top of the hill. Montmartre fought for the Commune, workers, toughs, bohemians and intellectuals together, and Montmartre died for the Commune: Varlin was shot at the same spot as the two generals.

The trauma of the siege, the Commune, the fires and the

massacres explains a good deal of the sharpening of the class lines in French politics in the last quarter of the century. It provides the emotional background to the angry division of the country over the Dreyfus case in 1894 and even the split between socialists and communists at the Congress of Tours two generations later. On the other hand, just as France recovered with a speed which astonished the world from the economic consequences of the war and paid off, with unexpected ease, the reparations with which the Prussians had intended to cripple the French economy, so too, at least on the surface, Paris, and within Paris Montmartre in particular, recovered with amazing speed from the blood and rage of the Commune. The years after the killings, in fact, were the Golden Age of Montmartre.

The revolution in French painting took place in successive waves, 'each generation trying to sweep away yet more of the convention in which the official art of the academies had got stuck'.[31] The first wave is associated with Eugène Delacroix. He was in every sense a Romantic. He rebelled against the cool classicism of the schools of Poussin and David. He reverted to the opulent manner of Rubens and the Venetian masters, rejoicing in the texture and colour of paint. Above all, he reacted against the classical canon of subject-matter. He visited north Africa and did intensely exciting paintings there, replete with feeling.

The second wave was associated with a group of painters in the middle of the century, some of whom chose to paint from nature around the village of Barbizon on the Marne above Paris. Their rebellion concerned the subject-matter of painting above all. Jean-François Millet painted ordinary people, especially peasants, and celebrated their work and the hardness of their life. Gustave Courbet, technically and visually the most gifted painter of the group, coined a name for what all of them were trying to do. He called it 'realism'.

Courbet was at the height of his powers in the 1850s, and Delacroix died in 1863. By that time the third wave of the painting revolution was ready to break. In 1862 Claude Monet bought himself out of the army and started to paint. In 1863 Édouard Manet had his own first show at the Galerie Martinet. One of the fourteen paintings in it was his crowded and original canvas, *Musique aux Tuileries*. As a reminder of the close relationship between the revolution in painting and the modern style in literature, Manet fitted into it his close friend, Charles Baudelaire, who had called for a painter of modern life who could 'show how great and poetic we are in our frock-coats and patent-leather boots'.

The jury at the Salon that year was exceptionally stiff and unfriendly to the new painting. It was Napoleon III himself, of all people, who suggested that the rejected paintings should have an exhibition of their own: the Salon des Refusés. Among the painters shown there were Boudin, the American James McNeill Whistler, Pissarro and the young Paul Cézanne. But the show's sensation, in two senses, was Manet's *Déjeuner sur l'herbe*. The moralists were shocked by the libertinism suggested by two naked young women settling down to a picnic with two gentlemen in top hats; the painters were overwhelmed by the freshness and originality with which Manet had painted the scene. There was to be an even greater uproar among the bourgeois when, two years later, Manet exhibited his *Olympia*. The subject was based on Titian's Urbino *Venus*. But where Titian had painted a goddess, Manet made no bones about the fact that he was painting an expensive prostitute, and painting her in a spirit of realism, without implied criticism or comment.

Even before the Commune, a whole cluster of young painters had gathered around the banner raised by Manet and his young Norman friend, Claude Monet. Such generalizations are always dangerous, but it can safely be said that nowhere, not in fifth-century Athens, nor the Florence of the fifteenth, the Rome of the sixteenth or the Venice of the seventeenth century has there been such a talented group of artists. Édouard Manet, Claude Monet, Camille Pissarro, Alfred Sisley, Vincent van Gogh, Edgar Degas, Berthe Morisot, Henri de Toulouse-Lautrec, Auguste Renoir, Paul

Gauguin, Paul Cézanne: these were only the most august of the painters, most of whom knew one another, all of whom shared a commitment to the new realism in painting and to the exploration of how the technique of painting could be used to capture the visible world in colour and in light.

After the Commune, it looked as if the new painters were going to get an exhibition of their own arranged by the dealer Durand-Ruel; in the end, they had to organize it themselves. It was held in April 1874. By a significant coincidence, it was in what had previously been the studio of the photographer Nadar; for the new painting was, among many other things, a response to the perception that, since the invention of photography, painting could never be the same again. It was one of the canvases in that exhibition which gave the new painting a name. It was a hazy riverscape, a red moon reflected in the water. Monet had been teased for giving his pictures dull titles. So he called this one *Impression, Sunrise, 1872.* A critic jeered at it. Once again, the name stuck. The new painters became, for ever, the Impressionists.

They were as different as you could imagine in their class origins and political loyalties: Manet and Degas, for example, were conservative in politics, and Degas a violent anti-Semite, while Pissarro, of Spanish-Jewish descent, was a convinced socialist. They responded to a welter of different influences, from Japanese woodcuts to English watercolour painting. Monet, Sisley, Pissarro all worked in England; Van Gogh and Cézanne (who belonged to the first wave of Post-Impressionism rather than to Impressionism in the strict sense) worked in the bright light of Provence; others explored the watery light of Normandy and others again loved to work along the banks of the Seine. But it was in Paris, and specifically in Montmartre, that most of them gathered, argued, quarrelled, lived and painted. Their favourite subject was none other than the city itself. Always their subjects were those which would have seemed low, banal, popular to the academicians: Monet's railway station, Degas's dancers and racehorses, and always the night-time pleasure-seekers, the good-time girls and punters of Renoir's *Moulin de la Galette*, Toulouse-Lautrec's prostitutes from the brothel in the rue des Moulins and his artistes at the Moulin Rouge.

It was in 1881 that two bohemian entrepreneurs, Émile Goudeau and Rodolphe Salins, met for a drink in the Grande Pinte in the avenue Trudaine[32] and decided to start what has been called the world's first cabaret,[33] the Chat Noir in the boulevard Roche-chouart. It was an instant success. The artists all turned up, but so did the fashionable world and the pimps with their girls, so much so that Salins moved across the road to a quieter street. There, the story goes, he welcomed the Prince of Wales, later Edward VII, with bows and scrapes. 'What an honour for my house!' he said. 'I don't know how to thank your Royal Highness.' Then he leaned forward and murmured, '*Comment va la maman?* – 'How's mum?'

Le Chat Noir was not just a cabaret. It was also one of the two reviews which acted as the midwives of the movement in poetry which corresponded in importance, and in its essential modernism, with Impressionism in painting. Poetry, like painting, in nineteenth-century France was transformed by three successive waves of change. First, in the early part of the century, came the great Romantics: Alfred de Musset and, above all, Victor Hugo. Then, under the Second Empire, there came the sway of the group who were called, from the name of the review which published them, the Parnassians: Théophile Gautier, Théodore de Banville, Leconte de Lisle. Baudelaire was published in the *Parnasse contempo-rain*.[34] But even at the time, it was clear that he was not quite at home with the Parnassians, that he looked forward to something new. Baudelaire died in 1867. By the time of his death, a whole generation of new poets were growing up as his disciples. One of them was Paul Verlaine. Another was Arthur Rimbaud. In 1872 Verlaine and Rimbaud ran away together and lived together in a homosexual relationship, in northern France, England and Brussels. It ended disastrously. Verlaine served a prison term in Brussels for shooting Rimbaud in the wrist. Rimbaud departed, having written some poetry of the highest quality, to become, among many other things, a gunrunner in Africa; he never wrote another line in his life. In 1882, after various other adventures, Verlaine returned to Paris, or rather to Boulogne-sur-Seine, where the giant Renault plant now is, with a boy he had fallen in love with when the latter was still at the *lycée*, Lucien Létinois.[35] For a year or so Verlaine would take the horse-tram in to the Left Bank and do the rounds of the literary cafés there. In 1883, hearing that Lucien was dying, he left Paris again. With his mother he bought Lucien's parents' farm, and eventually lost all his money and served another brief prison sentence for threatening his mother when drunk. But by then he had plunged back into the very centre of the literary world in Paris; and Symbolism, as a school of poetry, was established for ever.

Salins and Goudeau, the founders of the Chat Noir, had met some years before when Goudeau founded a club called the Hydropaths, which met in a room over a café in the boulevard St-Michel on the Left Bank. ('Hydropaths' was an obscure pun on Goudeau's name: Goudeau equals *goût d'eau*, a taste for water – which neither Goudeau nor Salins were conspicuous for.) Goudeau wrote a collection of poems called *Les Fleurs du bitume* ('Flowers of the Tarmac'), one of which fashionably explored the decadence of the late Roman Empire, comparing the courtesans of the Champs-Élysées to the lascivious freedwomen of Rome.[36] Goudeau and his friend Salins migrated to the Right Bank and, as we have seen, set up the Chat Noir as both café and publishing venture. Their main rival was the periodical, the *Nouvelle Rive Gauche*, which significantly changed its name in 1883 to the *Lutèce*. Its offices were open to poets and anyone else on Thursday and Friday afternoons, after which the poets would adjourn to the Café de l'École de Médecine to talk over the two great fashions which were sweeping the world of the younger poets.

One was 'decadence': poetry was obsessed with the idea that the nineteenth century was a time of decadence like that of the last days of Rome. Poets sought a language that might express, as they imagined the 'silver' Latin of the late empire could, subtle nuances of aesthetic appreciation, sensuality and emotion. That was what Baudelaire had done. Now a new generation of poets, decadent and symbolist, would be added to the canon. Through the help of friends, including a man called Léon Vanier, who sold poetry and fishing tackle, if you please, in a shop on the quai St-Michel, and the Greek writer, Giannis Papadiamantinipoulo, who called himself, very sensibly, Jean Moréas, Verlaine was beginning to be published. In December 1882 the critic Charles Morice published an attack on Verlaine in the *Nouvelle Rive Gauche*, to which Verlaine replied by defending himself, uncharacteristically tactfully. Morice and he became friends, and Morice published in his review a series by Verlaine on 'Les Poètes Maudits' – 'the accursed poets' – which rehabilitated not only his own reputation, but also those of Rimbaud and Stéphane Mallarmé, who admittedly needed it less, as well. In 1884 the Belgian novelist Joris-Karl Huysmans brought the names of Verlaine and Mallarmé before a much wider public when he praised them in his best-selling novel, *À Rebours*.[37] And the second label for their poetry, Symbolism, came into currency as a result of an article about them in 1886 in the *Figaro littéraire*, the paper *par excellence* of the bourgeois who wanted to keep up with what was going on among the artists and the avant-garde.

Mallarmé was a very much tamer sort of person than Verlaine or Rimbaud. An English teacher, he had married a German girl when he was studying in England as a young man. When he was nearly forty, in the emotional tumult after the death of a son, he fell in love with one of the great courtesans of the age, Méry Laurent.[38] Her claims to fame included having appeared naked, in a giant seashell, on the stage of the Théâtre du Châtelet. She was safely kept by an improbable character, the Philadelphia dentist, Thomas Evans, who parlayed his professional relationship with the Empress Eugénie's teeth into a real-estate fortune by proposing to Haussmann an avenue linking the Étoile to the Bois de Boulogne. Evans left Méry free, when not in his company, to be the muse of a whole Parnassus of poets, not to mention the painter Manet, and Marcel Proust's future lover, the musician Reynaldo Hahn. Tall,

red-haired, with breasts which, as someone unkindly said, spoke
more eloquently than her lips,[39] Méry was compared by no less a
connoisseur of women and flowers than George Moore to a tea
rose. She inspired a passion in the gentle Mallarmé which was
none the less intense for being almost certainly almost wholly
Platonic.[40] She also inspired his great poem, *L'Après-midi d'un
faune*, the prelude of which inspired Debussy in his turn to write
one of his greatest pieces of music.

A rival establishment to Salins's and Goudeau's Chat Noir in the
1880s and 1890s was the Mirliton of Aristide Bruant. He was a
chansonnier whose speciality was insulting the upmarket clients. As
soon as they came in the door, they were greeted with a withering
blast of put-downs,[42] delivered in his rich vocabulary of *argot*.
(Bruant later published a magnificent two-volume dictionary of
argot, the slang of the Paris *faubourgs*.[42]) Toulouse-Lautrec illustrated
several of his songs, many of them named after working-class
districts: for example, '*A Batignolles*'.

In 1886 the artists, who had previously done their drinking and
arguing in the Nouvelle Athènes – they included Degas, Cézanne,
Renoir, Manet and the critic Duranty – migrated to the Rat Mort.
In those days, you could have masterpieces by all those painters for
a song. Manet's *Woman on a Sofa*, which had belonged to
Baudelaire, was sold at auction for 1,500 francs, and as a young
dealer Vollard sold a Renoir for 400 francs in his shop in the rue
Laffitte.

It was characteristic of this extraordinary period, the time when
modernism in literature and the arts was incubating in Paris, that
the writers and painters knew one another, were interested in what
each were doing and felt a sense of solidarity. Baudelaire, we have
seen, was painted by Manet and bought one of his paintings. There
are two pictures, one by Bazille and one by Fantin-Latour, showing
Zola in artists' studios. Zola was brilliantly painted by Manet, but
repaid his Impressionist friends' affection badly with his novel
L'Oeuvre, in which they, and especially his particular friend Cézanne, were unkindly portrayed, not to say caricatured. But if the

central character in *L'Oeuvre*, Claude Lantier,[43] seems to be based on Cézanne, the view from his studio window on the Seine is of a coal wharf just like the one in Argenteuil which Claude Monet painted in his wonderful *Déchargeurs de charbon* ('Unloading Coal').[44]

The contact of writers and painters continued in the next generation. Around 1900 the place to be of an evening in Montmartre was no longer the dead rat but the nimble rabbit, Le Lapin Agile, run by a character called Frédé, whose son was eventually murdered in the joint as a result of some obscure quarrel in the *milieu*, the criminal underworld which was no longer far away from the happy bohemian romps of Montmartre. One of the happiest of the pranks dreamed up in the Lapin was the adventure of Frédé's donkey, Lolo. Some bohemian, desperate for money, attached a brush loaded with paint from tubes of many colours to the donkey's tail. The result, named by a happy inspiration *And the Sun Goes Down over the Adriatic*, was shown at the Salon des Indépendants, to enormous acclaim.[45] Picasso, Max Jacob, the inventors of Cubism, the pitifully alcoholic Maurice Utrillo and his mother, Suzanne Valadon, Derain and Georges Braque were all regulars for a time at the Lapin; but so, too, was the writer Pierre MacOrlan, a robust seafarer with a gift for composing ballads, and author of the story on which the classic film *Quai des brumes* was based. So was Francis Carco, who made a corner in writing novels about tough pimps and golden-hearted tarts in Montmartre. But the greatest writer of that company was the poet Guillaume Apollinaire, lover of the painter Marie Laurencin. Apollinaire kept himself alive by writing pornographic novels such as *Onze mille verges*. He also wrote unforgettable lines that will stand with Villon's ballads or the sonnets of the Pléiade in the private treasury of all who love the French language:

> *Passent les jours et passent les semaines*
>
> *Ni temps passé*
>
> *Ni les amours reviennent*

Sous le pont Mirabeau coule la Seine

Vienne la nuit sonne l'heure
Les jours s'en vont je demeure.[46]

(The days pass and the weeks pass
Neither time past nor loves come back
Under the Mirabeau bridge flows the Seine

Come the night sound the hour
The days go and I remain.)

By 1913, the toffs and the tourists were invading Montmartre. Long before that the anarchists and the pimps had moved in. On Bastille Day 1902, a tough boy from Belleville met a girl called Amélie in a dancehall between the place de la République and Belleville. She left him for a Corsican. Each of her lovers recruited a gang and they fought, thirty apaches a side, over the girl. Her nickname was Casque d'Or, and in 1952 Jacques Becker immortalized her story in a film with Simone Signoret.[47] In 1907 the first adventure of Arsène Lupin, the French Sherlock Holmes, was set in the *quartier*. Soon there was a big change. Bourgeois men had always come to play in Montmartre. Now they brought their women with them to slum. In 1913 all-night pharmacies opened, some of them a front for a new vice that was replacing absinthe: cocaine. Just before the war, the fashion changed and rich people went slumming, not in Montmartre, but in the rue de Lappe. While working-class girls in tight skirts and their *jules* in baggy caps danced the *java*, the tango was all the rage, and upper-class women must have gigolos, Italian, Spanish or best of all Argentine. Montmartre was becoming a place of legend, then a theme park, for tourists. The pendulum was swinging back to the Left Bank, to the Latin Quarter and to Montparnasse.

If French literature, as they say, is about Man, with a capital M, it is also about *les filles*, girls, and, from the Commune to the Nazi occupation, that did not mean any girls, it meant girls who were available. Of course in London or Vienna, Berlin or St Petersburg, writers and bohemians lived in close proximity, as close as they could manage, with young women who were not too iron-clad in their virtue. But nowhere was the link between sheer pleasure-seeking and the serious search for innovation in all the arts quite so intricately many-knotted as in Paris.

So much so that foreigners, especially the British and the Americans, tended to see Paris almost exclusively as a city of luxury, a vast emporium of fashion and frivolity, a city of restaurants, cafés, bars, *bals*, and outright brothels, which were, after all, legal until after 1945; in fact, as *Sodome et Gomorre*, as Proust, the greatest novelist to write about the city in this century, called it. This is, of course, a travesty. Paris in the Belle Époque, between the 1880s and 1914, was a great commercial city, a Chicago with its wholesalers and its debt collectors, its railway terminals and its stockyards, its commodity markets and hotels, its salesmen and its markets for every kind of merchandise. It was also a Washington, a city of civil servants, carefully trained by the *grandes écoles*, carefully disciplined by the *grands corps d'état*, stuffy, meticulous, cultivated and unimaginative; a city of politicians, imaginative and unstuffy, getting what they could for *la France profonde* and for themselves out of the verbose exchanges and frequently lethal manoeuvres of the Chambre; a city of journalists, literate and frequently venal. It was a city of craftsmen, in ancient luxury trades and the new metal industries, where the new engineers built the Eiffel Tower and the new Métro, the first line of which opened in 1900, and where the torch of the Statue of Liberty, which was being made in a yard in Passy, could be seen rising over the roofs; an industrial city which would eventually manufacture more cars than any single city outside Detroit, where sprawling factories would each employ tens of thousands of workers: Renault, at Boulogne-Billancourt; Simca, at Poissy; Citroën, at the quai de Javel.

Successive waves of modernism would burst on the Left Bank in the 1910s and 1920s and on until the 1950s and 1960s: Cubism, Futurism, Dada, Surrealism, Communism, fascism, anti-fascism, Existentialism, Structuralism, New Left, New Right. But by 1890 the mould was set. *Lycées*, *grandes écoles*, publishers, galleries, newspapers, artists, critics, writers, *cafés*, *salons* and their hostesses, all were fixed in the intricate mechanism, the game of love and money, rivalry and reputation that was Paris. Whatever the ostensible beliefs, commitments, shibboleths of each school, however bitter their reciprocal and internal quarrelling, there was a strange consistency about their style. Even the typography of the posters announcing their manifestations was strangely conventional, given their desperate determination to be different. Modernism, in fact, is now a centenarian.

Why was it that Paris, having been 'the capital of the nineteenth century', became and has to a remarkable extent remained the capital of modernism? Paris, first of all, was the home of the great Revolution itself, the shrine, for all the sins that were committed in their name, of liberty, equality, fraternity. The Revolution set out to destroy Crown, Church, nobility, privilege. If in their place it erected the sovereign bourgeoisie, and if the bourgeois took over from the Bourbons the machinery of the French state, glorious and generous as well as ruthless, and gifted with an infinitely patient attention to bureaucratic detail in each of its successive avatars, still Paris remained until the end of the nineteenth century and into the twentieth the capital of change. There were sociological reasons as well. Paris in the nineteenth century was young, growing, bursting with energy. It attracted the young and the ambitious, first from every province of France, then from every corner of Europe: Huysmans and Simenon from Belgium, Van Gogh from Holland, Modigliani from Italy, Whistler and Cassatt, Gertrude Stein and Man Ray from America, Picasso and Miró from Barcelona, Spaniards, Romanians, Russians, Greeks, Poles, even Englishmen. Paris was a city open to the talents: all talents.

It was also a city where restraints which still lay heavily on writers and artists in St Petersburg, Vienna, Berlin, not to mention Rome or London, had to all intents and purposes disappeared. It is true that a Baudelaire or a Verlaine could still be prosecuted for *outrage aux moeurs*, but in practice, intellectuals in France, at least from the Commune on, could afford to laugh at censorship. It was also a society which, while far from equal, either in terms of wealth or of opportunity, was free from the tyranny of an aristocratic culture, such as still counted in London or Vienna. More to the point, if the churches were still full, if the Catholic Church was still strong enough to try conclusions with the Third Republic on the issue of education as late as the 1890s and, less overtly, over Dreyfus in the 1900s, Paris, the Paris of painters and writers, was a lay society. Partly as a consequence, it was also, in the American sense, a wide-open city, as we have seen: tolerant of the search for pleasure in all its forms: music and theatre, gambling, dancing, absinthe and *haute cuisine*, and exceptional tolerance and also exploitation of sexual relations of every kind.

As far back as the middle of the century, converging challenges to the credibility of organized religion and to the authority of the Church had shaken the religious faith of many, if not most intellectuals. Darwin's *Origin of Species*, which cast doubt on the creation as a specific act of God at a moment in time, was published in 1859, Ernst von Haeckel's *Natural History of Creation* in 1868. Even earlier than that, textual criticism had cast doubt on the literal truth of the Bible. Strauss's and Renan's lives of Jesus, both of which treated Christ as a man, were published in 1835 and 1863 respectively. And the scepticism of the intellectuals, reached by reading and arguing about God, revelation, creation and philosophy, was reinforced by the prevalent popular atheism of the socialists, which identified religion with ignorance and oppression. By the 1880s, Friedrich Nietzsche could cry out, *Gott ist tot! Gott bleibt tot! Und wir haben ihn getötet.* ('God is dead! God remains dead! And we have killed him.') It was in the middle of the nineteenth century, more generally, that religion felt the impact of science and scepticism, and nowhere more than in rational, sceptical, cynical Paris. Torn up from their roots in stable (if horribly hard and intolerant) rural societies, crammed together in crowded and insanitary cities, no longer believing in king or priest, and deprived of the ancient private consolations and public rituals of religion, nineteenth-century men and women turned inward. They erected their own gods: social justice, science, art, sensibility, family and love. And the artists who appealed to them, who became in a way substitutes for the priests they had metaphorically unfrocked, were inevitably Oedipal, iconoclastic and irreverent. If artists, by the late nineteenth century, despised the bourgeois and their mercenary values, that was in part because they were now dependent, not on an aristocratic Maecenas, but on the collective patronage of the bourgeois as distributed through the market. No wonder they were intent on differentiating themselves from their competitors, while at the same time clinging together for mutual support in their various bohemias; obsessed with innovation, until the desperate search for the new became art's oldest and most stifling tradition. Finally, in these circumstances, it was natural that artists, no longer striving for the favour of patrons who did not care how the thing was done, so long as the effect was pleasant, but fascinated by the skills which differentiated them from their friends and competitors, should become obsessed with technique; and that too is one of the distinguishing badges of this centenary modernism.

Paris, the most revolutionary, the most ideologically daring, after London and New York the wealthiest and the biggest of the nineteenth-century cities, and the one where both the artist and his innovations were most sure of a welcome, was the natural capital of modernism, both psychological and technical. And modernism in all its manifestations arrived there first. That is why it is the starting-point for a new grand tour, just as it had been for the old.

CHAPTER III
ALL HUMAN LIFE

ON HIS SEVENTIETH BIRTHDAY, IN 1920, TWO
hundred guests assembled at a house in Carlton Gardens in London
to do honour to that quintessence of the man of letters, Sir
Edmund Gosse, the critic, diner-out and author of the classic
account of the Oedipal conflict between the high Victorian and
late Victorian generations, *Father and Son*. The scene was recorded
in a drawing by that malicious pixie of the *fin de siècle*, Max
Beerbohm.[1] The ceremony took place at the home of Lord Balfour,
himself a noted essayist, golfer and philosopher as well as an ex-
prime minister. Balfour paid an eloquent tribute to Gosse's long
career as a critic. As a birthday 'surprise' his friends and admirers
had clubbed together to present Gosse with a bronze bust of

himself, and Beerbohm wickedly portrayed the old man receiving it: starting backward, left leg thrust forward, right hand raised, palm forward, in a pose of affected astonishment and gratification – the astonishment, at least, affected, since he must have known for months that his head was being modelled.

Some of those depicted in Beerbohm's drawing were grandees with a literary turn of mind: John, Viscount Morley, who had been a journalist and an editor as well as Gladstone's biographer before becoming a cabinet minister; Lord Haldane, a classical scholar and student of German metaphysics as well as a politician; and George Nathaniel Curzon, that 'most superior person' who was a scholar and man of letters as well as foreign secretary and Viceroy of India, and was only barred from the prime ministership itself, as he complained bitterly, because the achievements of his ancestors had been rewarded with a peerage. But even those glittering talents, the very apex of the political, social and intellectual worlds of Edwardian England, were outshone by some of the writers whom Beerbohm caught in various attitudes of writerish abstraction and self-absorption: among them George Moore, Rudyard Kipling, G.K. Chesterton, Arnold Bennett, Joseph Conrad and Thomas Hardy.

A few years later the irrepressible Max drew from memory another group portrait, this time of 'some persons of the Nineties'[2]. Very different they were from the established literary lions of the 'Birthday Surprise'. Only George Moore was common to both groups. The men Beerbohm chose to represent the nineties were all more or less clearly members of the group known as the Decadents. Here is Oscar Wilde, tragic emblem of the mauve decade; here are Henry Harland, the editor, and Aubrey Beardsley, the art editor, of The Yellow Book. Beerbohm added the artists Will Rothenstein and Walter Sickert, who trapped in paint the vitality of the London music-hall, much as Toulouse-Lautrec and Degas had captured the dancehalls of Montmartre. Next to them he put four poets: Richard Le Gallienne, with his great shock of black hair; John Davidson, whose spruce military bearing and big cigar give him a deceptively prosperous air; Arthur Symons, the apostle of French Symbolism to the Anglo-Saxons and poet of the mercenary temptresses of the promenade and the pavement; and, towering over this tribe in talent though not in stature, the young William Butler Yeats. Finally, a nice touch, he added 'Enoch Soames', the imaginary decadent invented by Beerbohm himself, whose volume of melancholy verses, *Fungoids*, sold no more than three copies.

In those two jesting group portraits Beerbohm described two waves, almost two generations, of the London version of modernism: the decadent nineties and the confident Edwardians. Before the war changed the face of London and of English society for good, a third generation, uncompromisingly modern, was to make its appearance. But it was never likely that Max Beerbohm would catch D.H. Lawrence, Lytton Strachey, Virginia Woolf, William Butler Yeats, Ezra Pound, Wyndham Lewis and T.S. Eliot all in one room together.

Long before even the beginning of the nineties, modernism was the mainstream in Paris. The Impressionist painters burst on the scene as early as the 1860s. In poetry, too, the themes of Verlaine, Rimbaud and Mallarmé were already clearly enunciated by Baudelaire and foreshadowed by the Parnassians; and in the novel Zola's realism merely carried on, with greater brutality, from Balzac's.

By the 1880s, in Paris, these convergent enterprises in painting and literature were established, acknowledged. In London it was very different. Victorian attitudes were profoundly suspicious of almost every aspect of French modernism, and not least of its frivolity and libertinism. The famous row between John Ruskin and James McNeill Whistler, inconceivable in Paris at any time since the middle of the century, actually happened as late as 1878.

Whistler, an American who had caught the Impressionist fever in Paris, but had been settled in London for almost twenty years, brought a libel suit against John Ruskin, the acknowledged leader of British art critics. Whistler had painted a tender Impressionist canvas of the closing of the Cremorne pleasure garden, which he called *Nocturne in Black and Gold: the Falling Rocket*. 'I have seen and heard much of Cockney impudence before,' wrote Ruskin, 'but never expected to hear a coxcomb ask two hundred guineas for flinging a pot of paint in the public's face.'[3] Again, in 1866, when Algernon Charles Swinburne raised the banner of 'art for art's sake' in his *Poems and Ballads*, he was called 'unclean for the sake of uncleanness' by the *Athenaeum* magazine for his . . . pains.[4] Victorian moral earnestness, Victorian prudery and Victorian hypocrisy demanded a conformity and a reticence that permitted the artistic achievement of the great Victorians, Dickens and Thackeray, Browning and Tennyson, but stamped down savagely on anything that smacked of moral laxity, sexual libertinism or exposure. Revealingly, in 1886 no less an eminent Victorian than the ageing Lord Tennyson denounced such moral turpitude, after the great French realist novelist, as 'Zolaism'.

By the 1880s, though, the atmosphere was changing fast. The liberal champion was William Ewart Gladstone, whose hobby it was to swing the axe in his estate at Hawarden on the Welsh border; his great Liberal administration had cut deeply into the roots of the Victorian system. The change is symbolized by, among many other reforms, the Married Woman's Property Act of 1882, by which for the first time the patriarchal husband no longer automatically owned all that his wife had brought to the marriage. Victoria's reign was long, and it covered a period of hectic, racing change in attitudes as well as in the circumstances of British life. Historians break it into three roughly equal generations. The first, from the 1830s through the Hungry Forties into the boom years of the fifties, was the Steam Age. In it, Britain emerged from the social crisis, recorded in Dickens's novels, which also provoked the political upheaval around the Great Charter, and began to be the workshop and banker to the world. Then came the high Victorian period, the age of earnestness and reform from the late fifties to the middle seventies. That was a time of certainties, but also of doubt; it saw the triumph of the middle classes, but also witnessed the debilitating personal and ideological crisis caused for so many Victorians by the loss of religious faith. Under those broadcloth coats and silk top hats there were troubled hearts and puzzled minds. But the late Victorian period, beginning at the end of the 1870s, was the age of a new generation, irreverent, iconoclastic and Oedipal in its determination to mock the pieties and taboos of its parents. This was a generation of inheritors, eager to enjoy the wealth accumulated by the thrift and enterprise of its parents, and ready to adventure into new ground. 'The eighteen nineties were so tolerant of novelty in art and ideas,' wrote Holbrook Jackson, a survivor of those years, 'that it was as though the declining century wished to make amends for several decades of intellectual and artistic monotony.'

Just so. But another survivor, E.F. Benson, whose father was a thoroughly Victorian Archbishop of Canterbury and who had been a friend of Oscar Wilde and some of his set, was scathing about those who later saw the 1890s as the decade of decadence.

Before the dawn even of the nineties, the old idols had been quite toppled over, and the attempt to demonstrate that there was now marching out of the Bodley Head under the flying flag of the *Yellow Book* a band of April-eyed young brothers singing revolutionary ditties and bent on iconoclasm is disastrous to any clear conception of what was actually going on.[5]

For one thing, Benson explained scornfully, the rising had already been accomplished when *The Yellow Book* appeared in 1894. For another, the famous magazine 'had no point of view at all'. So far from being a revolutionary gazette, it was a 'highly respectable, almost highbrow organ' most of whose contributors, leaving aside only Aubrey Beardsley, were 'no more rebels against Victorian convention than the Queen herself'. The contributors to the first issue certainly included, besides Henry James, such pontifical critics as George Saintsbury, the well-known expert on French poetry and claret, and Sir Edmund Gosse himself, as well as a member of the French Academy.[6] The illustrators included John Singer Sargent and Sir Frederick Leighton, president of the Royal

Academy. As for Oscar Wilde, surprising as it may seem, not a single line either of his prose or of his verse ever appeared in *The Yellow Book*.

In London, in the last twenty years of the nineteenth century and the first quarter of the twentieth, there was little or no sense of a movement of literary or artistic modernism sweeping traditional styles and values away. There was no single district, like Montmartre before the war or Montparnasse after it, where an admiring student of the arts could go and stare at the lions and lionesses at play. There were no cafés, no salons in the French sense of the word, no restaurants with tables reserved for regular customers, only one major theatre – the Royal Court in Sloane Square – which regularly put on the plays of the avant-garde. Indeed, in the sense in which the word was used in Paris or St Petersburg, there was no avant-garde. Unsuccessful London writers, like George Gissing and the even more unfortunate intellectuals he describes in *New Grub Street*, lived in Camden Town if all went well, and in Islington if it didn't, both grimy quarters north of the Park and downwind from the City smoke. Successful writers and painters lived in arty Chelsea or in bluestocking Bloomsbury, or in bourgeois splendour in South Kensington if they could afford it; but increasingly, after the turn of the century, they moved out to the suburbs or the seaside. In the 1890s you could have found Kipling, Conrad, H.G. Wells, Ford Madox Ford, and Stephen Crane all clustered within a few miles of Henry James at Rye on the Sussex coast.[7] Yet if the literary and artistic world seemed drowned in the smug materialism of late Victorian and Edwardian society, the position of writers and intellectuals more marginal than in Paris or Vienna or even Berlin, the achievement of London in that period was no less than brilliant. The thirty years from 1890 to 1920, roughly speaking, saw two generations of post-Victorian writers come to maturity. They did so from no single standpoint. Some were Fabian socialists, others unapologetic élitists, some even spokesmen for something close to an anticipation of fascism. Some believed passionately in Art for Art's Sake, others rejected that as self-indulgent frivolity. But together, or separately, they produced an immensely rich and varied literature which boldly challenged the Victorian assumptions and laid the foundations for twentieth-century literature in Britain and elsewhere.

At the time, and for a while afterwards, the Decadent group, the poets of the 'fleshly school' and the 'Grosvenor gallery, greenery-yallery, foot-in-the-grave young men', the pupils of Pater and the admirers of Wilde, held the centre of the stage. But a lot else was going on in the nineties and in the Edwardian decade. Add to those who attended old Gosse's birthday party such different but undeniable talents as those of Henry James, William Morris (whose *News from Nowhere* was published in 1891) and George Meredith, George Bernard Shaw, Sir Arthur Wing Pinero, John Galsworthy (whose *Forsyte Saga* is an extended treatise on the progression of the generations), H.G. Wells and Hilaire Belloc; Robert Louis Stevenson (a modernist in many respects, though to be sure he went to the South Seas at the beginning of the period and died in 1894) and George Gissing; A.E. Housman, Ernest Dowson ('I have been true to thee, Cynara, in my fashion') and Gerard Manley Hopkins; D.H. Lawrence and Katherine Mansfield; Conan Doyle and Rider Haggard, Virginia Woolf and E.M. Forster – that list is incomplete, but surely it bears comparison with the writers living and working in London or indeed any other city, in any other quarter of a century, before or since.

To be sure, it includes writers who could not by any stretching of language be called modernist – Rider Haggard, for example, as well as William Morris. But as the end of a certain way of life approached, in the years immediately before 1914, London did indeed become the focus of a cluster of movements which were undeniably modern, and which prepared the way for the unmistakably modernist heyday of the 1920s. Though James Joyce cannot be claimed for London, Eliot emphatically must be counted among the greatest of London's poets; and Joyce, as much as Eliot, lived in a literary universe formed by the new world of London in 1914, when Ezra Pound lived in Church Street, Kensington, and

Wyndham Lewis was quarrelling furiously with Roger Fry over
the Rebel Arts Centre. What sort of city was it that brought these
astonishingly various talents together – or kept them apart?

Once upon a time, London, like Paris, was divided between the
court, the City and the Church. The king's court, which in the
twelfth century migrated between Winchester, Gloucester and
Westminster, eventually settled in the latter, around St Stephen's
Hall and Westminster Abbey. Two miles to the east, linked by the
road called the Strand along the curving northern bank of the
Thames, lay the City,[8] already established by the fourteenth
century as one of the major centres for shipping, banking and
trade in all northern Europe; the Hansa had its 'steelyard', or
trading depot, there, and London was intimately linked with the
merchants, weavers and cloth manufacturers of the Low Countries
as well as with the northern ports which provided 'naval stores'
and grain. Around and even within these two secular poles,
Westminster the seat of temporal authority and justice, and London
the realm of gold, the Church was by far the biggest landowner
and the principal influence on the way the future metropolis
developed.

The roads leading from the City's gates were lined with religious
houses: convents, hospitals, leprosaria, schools, almshouses and
priories of many orders, supported by the revenue from the farms
and house property around them as well as from distant estates.
Archbishops, bishops and abbots owned palaces in London, and
what would now be called commercial real estate as well; notori-
ously, My Lord Bishop of Winchester owned the Southwark
'stews', just across the bridges from the City, which were to
medieval London what the Algiers honky-tonks across the Missis-
sippi were to New Orleans. Inside the City walls, the ecclesiastical
property was rich and strategically sited; it included the buildings
and lands of St Bartholomew's Hospital next to Smithfield,
and the Charterhouse just to the north. Outside, ecclesiastical
foundations owned whole manors: the manor of Ebury belonged

to the abbot of Westminster, the manor of Bloomsbury to the Charterhouse, much property in what is now Soho to the Abbey of Abingdon, near Oxford.

Since the sixteenth century, however, London has developed in an utterly different way from Paris, and that difference reflects the whole divergent historical experience of England and France. It has been said[9] that by far the most important single event in London's history was the Dissolution of the Monasteries by Henry VIII in the 1530s. The king rewarded loyal courtiers with the palaces, or 'inns', as they were called, of bishops and abbots, so laying the foundation of princely dynasties. The Bishop of Exeter's inn went to the Earl of Essex, and is now commemorated by Essex Street, running down from the Strand to the river just west of the Inns of Court. The Bishop of Bath and Wells's inn, to the east, went to the Howards, Earls of Arundel and Surrey, whence Arundel Street and Surrey Street. The Bishop of Carlyle's property went to the Russells, later Earls and eventually Dukes of Bedford; the manor of Bloomsbury to Thomas Wriothesley, Earl of Southampton; and so on. In the early seventeenth century these lucky grandees made the first tentative moves to develop their properties by building houses on them to let. As early as 1609 James I's minister, Robert Cecil, Earl of Salisbury, sought permission to build on the plot of land near the modern Marquis of Salisbury public house in St Martin's Lane, and in the 1630s the Earl of Bedford was given a licence to build in Long Acre and Covent Garden. Before the Civil War, Inigo Jones had built what are the oldest surviving London terraced houses in Lincoln's Inn Fields, and had imitated the place Royale, which is now the place des Vosges, in the 'piazza' in Covent Garden. The Civil War interrupted these aristocratic speculations for a generation, but with the Restoration they began again, on a larger scale, and further west.

For centuries London houses were warmed, and London's industries fuelled, by burning coal. It was called 'sea coal', as distinct from charcoal, because as early as the twelfth century it was being brought down the North Sea coast from Durham and

Northumberland, where at the time it could be dug out of shallow drifts or even picked up on the shore. Far earlier than we usually imagine, a pall of coal smoke hung over the town, and since the prevailing wind in the south of England is from the south-west, the 'liberties' east of the city were always less desirable than the farmlands and villages to the west. As a result, over the centuries fashionable London has expanded to the west and south-west, and the social geography of the city has always reflected that fact.

At the Restoration the great courtiers set about turning the property which they had inherited or been granted in and around London into the princely incomes they needed to keep up their state at a court that was set on imitating, admittedly on a more modest and provincial scale, the splendours of Versailles. As early as 1662 Henry Jermyn, Duke of St Alban's, the lover and perhaps the secret husband of the Queen Mother, Henrietta Maria, received a lease on the plum site in London, due north of the royal palace. It ran from the Haymarket in the east to St James's Street in the west, and on the north it was bounded by the street that bears the duke's surname, and is still the preserve of aristocratic shirt-makers and other luxury goods shops.

Farther east, that remarkable character, Nicholas Barbon, whose father was the Puritan member of the Long Parliament Praise-God Barebones, and who had spent the war and the Commonwealth years in Holland, became the first modern property developer in London; he built houses as a speculation on land belonging to Rugby School, Bedford town corporation and many other proprietors. Perhaps his most ambitious speculation was on the site of the Duke of Buckingham's property at the west end of the Strand, where he laid out streets to commemorate the duke's names and titles: George Street, Villiers Street, Duke Street, Of Alley and Buckingham Street.

While development was going on all round the periphery of the City in the late seventeenth century, for example in Spitalfields, Clerkenwell[10] and Hatton Garden (another Barbon operation, once the garden attached to the mansion of the Elizabethan courtier, Sir Christopher Hatton), it was in the West End that the system of ownership, leases and building was being developed that would give London its characteristic aristocratic flavour as a city, and incidentally create some of the vast fortunes that preserved that patrician tone until the end of the twentieth century.

The West End was the frontier of London at the Restoration. After the fall of Charles II's first minister, the historian Lord Clarendon, his magnificent house and its splendid gardens fell into the hands of a banker called Sir Thomas Bond, who laid out the street that bears his name. Several marriages helped to draw the economic map of the West End. The richest heiress in London's history was Mary Davies, who had inherited the 'five fields' of Ebury, some 270 acres of land stretching like a sickle round the westward growth points of the city from Grosvenor Square through Belgravia to Pimlico. After an unsuccessful attempt by the Berkeley family (of Berkeley Castle in Gloucester and Berkeley Square) to marry Miss Davies off to their heir, she married the heir of the Grosvenors, owners of broad lands in Cheshire. In 1710 her son obtained an Act of Parliament which allowed him to grant leases for building on his fields.

At the same time two powerful consortia, each with a political allegiance, were developing large tracts to the north and east of the Grosvenor inheritance. A group of Whig lords, led by Lord Scarborough, developed the area round Hanover Square. In 1711 Henrietta Cavendish Holles inherited from her father, the Duke of Newcastle, and two years later she married Edward Harley, the son of the Earl of Oxford and Wigmore. Harley set about trying to build a Tory development which would match the Whig power base on the south side of the highway which is now Oxford Street. But in 1720 the bursting of the South Sea Bubble, a speculative venture promoted by the Scots financier John Law, ruined many merchants and landowners who had borrowed heavily to speculate, and it was only slowly and with great difficulty that Harley was able to complete the streets which bear his name and those of his titles: Harley Street, Wigmore Street, Mortimer

Street and the rest. In 1734, however, Harley's daughter Margaret married Hans Willem Bentinck, son of William III's friend who became Duke of Portland, and the descendants of the marriage inherited the great Portland estate.

As a result of the depression in trade and in the stocks, there was a break in the development of the West End of London from the 1730s until the 1760s. Then speculative building began again with a new impetus as the great boom, fed by industrial revolution in the North and Midlands, victory in the Seven Years' War and export trade, enriched thousands of English capitalists, merchants and landowners alike. In 1760, symbolically, the gates of the City of London were pulled down, anticipating by a century the liberation of Paris by Haussmann and of Vienna by the emperor's decision in 1857 to tear down the fortifications and build the Ringstrasse. New estates consolidated and developed their holdings. Lord Cadogan built on the lands he had inherited by his marriage to one of the daughters of Charles II's physician, Sir Hans Sloane: hence Sloane Square, Cadogan Gardens, Hans Place. The Portmans, Dorset squires from Bryanston, built Portman Square and Bryanston Square and the adjoining streets in Marylebone. In 1811 Marylebone Park reverted to the Crown, and the Prince of Wales became prince regent; he engaged John Nash to build Regent's Park, Regent Street with its curving Quadrant, pulled down in the 1920s, and Carlton House Terrace there.

The map of the great London estates was not filled in until the Ladbroke Estate (Ladbroke Grove, Clarendon Road, Elgin Crescent) was built on in the last great speculative project of the old kind just before the crash of 1873. But by that time a pattern had been established. There were dozens of estates, great and small. The greatest of all was the Grosvenor Estate, whose almost royal income had raised a family of Cheshire squires to a dukedom, the last created for an English commoner, in 1874. Some estates belonged to more modest (but still exceedingly wealthy) families, like the Gunter Estate on the western fringes of Chelsea. Not all estates were owned by individuals or families. Some were the property of City livery companies, medieval guilds which had evolved over the centuries into charitable foundations, like the Mercers, with their property in the West End and in Clerkenwell, or the Skinners near St Pancras, or of other charities, such as Smith's Charity, founded to buy slaves their liberty, or the Foundling Hospital. Some belonged to schools: Rugby School north of Theobald's Road, Dulwich in the south, above all Eton College, with its great holdings (Fellows Road, Oppidan's Road, King Henry's Road) on the southern fringes of Hampstead, which in turn belonged largely to the Eyre and Maryon Wilson families and to the Dean and Chapter of Westminster.

Long after the Dissolution, the Church still owned vast tracts of London, including the Bishop of London's princely property in the manor of Paddington; it was not until 1870 that all these estates were transferred to the Church Commissioners and their revenue appropriated to even up the stipends of all the Church of England clergy. There were great estates in north London (the Marquis of Northampton); in east London (Lord Tredegar, of Tredegar Square); and in south London, where the Duchy of Cornwall, traditional source of income for the Prince of Wales as heir to the throne, owned miles of streets of terraced cottages from Kennington to the Elephant and Castle.

Whatever their origin, most of these estates operated in the same way. The ground landlord let his land on building leases of ninety-nine years or even longer, sometimes retaining a site for his own town house. Often squares were laid out and planted. Houses of differing standards, according to the social status of the district, were built and the landlord then enjoyed both the ground rent (and Londoners grew used to paying a quarter or even more of their income in rent) and the reversionary bonus payable when the lease fell in; the property could then be passed to a new tenant for this consideration or relet to the old tenant at a higher rent. Sometimes the builder prospered under this system to the point where he, too, could become a ground landlord on a more or less modest scale. Thomas Cubitt, the 'Prince of Builders', who built the Grosvenor Estate's imposing properties in Belgravia in the early nineteenth century, became a speculator, developer and landlord in his own right.

The ground landlord system had a number of consequences which have shaped the life of London to this day, even though a Labour government in the 1960s brought in leasehold enfranchisement, compelling landlords to sell houses to sitting tenants on easy terms. The most obvious consequence of the system is that in London, and to a lesser extent in some other British cities, a class of proprietors, typically agricultural landowners with homes elsewhere in the country, nearly monopolized the ownership of residential property in the most desirable parts of the city. There are other European cities where aristocratic families were major landowners; the closest parallel is in Vienna, where noblemen with princely estates in Hungary or Bohemia owned much of the prime real estate inside the old walls. Only in London was aristocratic ownership the rule in the parts of the capital where people most wanted to live. Moreover, instead of spending most of the year in the capital like the Viennese grandees and only visiting their estates briefly for the hunting season, many London landlords preferred their estates in the country, or in Ireland or Scotland, except for a relatively brief London season.

There were less obvious consequences of this system, too, and they have directly affected the intellectual life of the city. The first is that the social tone has tended to be set in London by people who preferred fox-hunting to opera. Though there have been many brilliant exceptions, the English country gentry have not been conspicuous as a class for their passion for theatre, music, opera or literature, or indeed with a few exceptions for their taste in painting. English intellectuals, as much as English businessmen, have been seduced by the prestige of the country gentleman, and by the agreeableness of his life. From Tennyson in the Isle of Wight to Kipling at Bateman's in his beloved Sussex, Hardy at Max Gate near Dorchester, Conan Doyle at Hindhead, John Buchan at Elsfield, as soon as he could afford to, the best-selling London writer became a country gentleman.

This, in turn, has influenced London in other ways. In London, unlike Paris or for that matter Vienna or Berlin, the sons of the upper and the growing upper middle class were not educated, as a matter of course, in the city. By the middle of the nineteenth century, new 'middle-class' public schools, some of them expanded from sixteenth-century grammar schools, had been added to the ancient foundations such as Winchester and Eton. With a brazen lack of scruple, foundations and endowments set up by medieval church-men or Elizabethan merchants were appropriated to subsidize the education of the sons of the rich or the comfortably off. Some of these schools (Charterhouse, Christ's Hospital, Harrow, West-minster) were in or near London; most (Rugby, Shrewsbury, Tonbridge, Uppingham) were in small towns deep in the shires. From these academies, dedicated to cramming Latin and Greek, a smattering of mathematics and the teachings of the Anglican Church into the boys, the cleverest, the most ambitious and those with the most influential families were siphoned off for higher education at Oxford and Cambridge. But the ancient universities, too, were outside and in many ways culturally very far removed from London. It is often argued that this education of a non-commercial élite for a nation doomed to depend on what it could make and sell has been a lasting source of weakness for the British economy. Whether that is true or not, London certainly differed from other European cities in that, even after the foundation of the first component colleges of what later became London University (University College in 1836, King's College in 1829), London was not the academic centre of the country as it was its political and commercial capital. It was not until between the world wars that London University began to challenge the pre-eminence of Oxford and Cambridge. Cambridge especially, the home of the most advanced work in two of the intellectually revolutionary sciences of the early twentieth century, economics and physics, as well as the nursery of the Bloomsberries and many other literary talents in the early years of the twentieth century, could almost claim to play the role in British life that was played by the Left Bank in Paris.

Finally, the great London estates, strongly held by an interlocking network of some of the wealthiest people in the country, many of them in Parliament, formed a physical mould in which London developed. It was partly due to them that the West End remained, until the Second World War and after, the home of an aristocratic society and of its suppliers, its wine merchants, booksellers, tailors, couturiers, gunsmiths and clubs. In particular, the great landlords, with their power in Parliament, were able to keep out the trains. The great estates, in fact, contributed to the establishment of a class geography of London. Of course, there were rich districts, middling districts and miserable slums in every city in Europe in the nineteenth century. The Haymarket in St Petersburg, the Scheunenviertel in Berlin, the Goutte d'Or in Paris were every bit as poverty-stricken and degraded as Whitechapel or the Old Kent Road. But the sheer size of London isolated those districts from the West End. The great estates made it a point to exclude all but 'respectable' – which meant prosperous – tenants from their property. To this day the key to the mysterious concept of a 'good address' in London is that it is in general socially more acceptable to live on rather than off the former property of the great ground landlords. The railways respected this class geography. Three of them – the London & North Western Railway, the Midland and the Great Western Railways – all refused to introduce workmen's fares, 'thus neatly preserving a ninety degree arc of north-west London from working-class colonization'.[11]

By the 1860s, however, the railways were beginning to conduct the grand exodus into London's suburbia. That was when the Great Eastern Railway introduced a twopenny ticket valid for ten miles, and whole suburban cities, Tottenham, Leyton, Walthamstow, Edmonton, grew up to house the workers. In the same decade the North London Line, lobbing across the top of the city from Hammersmith to the City, created Pooterland, the domain of tens of thousands of respectable, indeed desperately genteel, clerks and tradesmen, immortalized by the hero of George and Weedon Grossmith's *Diary of a Nobody*. And from 1862, when the

Central Line was built as little more than a series of cut-and-cover tunnels for horse-drawn trams, the commuting habit began to develop. By the end of the century, fast, clean electric trains, either on the District or Metropolitan lines or on the Southern Electric, made it possible for literally millions of Londoners to achieve their ambition: a trim house with a patch of garden away from the grime and the fog.

The explosion of suburban living, rational and even idealistic in itself, nevertheless had deleterious effects on London as an intellectual capital. Not that the new suburban dwellers stopped going to the London theatres and music-halls, or reading the London papers. It was simply that the sheer physical expansion of London in the last quarter of the nineteenth century, an expansion which continued undiminished until the great depression of the 1930s and has not been completely checked yet, made it less concentrated, less urban and perhaps more placid than far smaller cities. Only the most successful writers could afford a home in Mayfair, Belgravia or Kensington. The days of the 1840s, described in Thackeray's *Pendennis*, when young writers could find convivial chambers close to one another in the Inns of Court, were passing, as the pressure of business and the growth of professionalism kept all but lawyers out, though William Butler Yeats shared chambers in Fountain Court, in the Temple, with Arthur Symons for a few months in 1895–6.[12]

After the 1850s, when there was a wave of commercial building, much of it in the ornate Italian manner, the City finally ceased to be – what it had been since Chaucer's time – a home for writers and artists. The Rhymers' Club, whose members included William Butler Yeats, Lionel Johnson, Ernest Dowson and others, many of whom shared Yeats's obsession with reviving the Celtic tradition, met at the Old Cheshire Cheese in an alley off Fleet Street, close to the court where Samuel Johnson once lived. But in general there were few places where a young writer could count on seeing the great men of the previous generation at play, as he could at the Griensteidl in Vienna or in the cafés of Montmartre. Prosperous, established writers, including Dickens and Thackeray, who had a nasty row there, used the open stacks and deep leather armchairs of the London Library. But its subscription kept out those with their reputation to make, or to keep. Again, literary clubs, like The Club, survivor of that founded by Johnson, of which Edmund Burke, Edward Gibbon, the actor David Garrick and the great musicologist Dr Burney were all members, or the Literary Society, had by late Victorian days turned into dining clubs, the preserve of comfortable men of letters and wealthy amateurs.

The theatre acted to some extent as a focus of shared intellectual excitement, though no London theatre could boast of anything like the central role played by the great state opera houses in Paris, Vienna or Berlin. The London theatre had been moribund during much of the Victorian age. Three movements breathed new life into it. The first was Wagnerism. London was almost incredibly slow to respond to the vogue for Wagner abroad. The composer himself first visited London in 1839, and made no impression whatsoever, beyond arousing a vague distaste for his anti-Semitism, which was particularly offensive to English music-lovers because of their worship of Mendelssohn. When the vogue for Wagner did arrive, beginning in the 1870s, however, it reached precisely those people who were to be the spearheads of modernism in London. The first major article about Wagner's art there appeared in the *Athenaeum* and was by Dr Hueffer, the father of Ford Madox Ford.[13] Wagner, perhaps surprisingly, appealed immensely to the Decadents, perhaps because he was so admired by their masters, the French Symbolists. Swinburne was a Wagnerian, as was George Moore. Aubrey Beardsley wrote an indecent version of 'The Story of Venus and Tannhäuser', subsequently published in bowdlerized form in *The Savoy*.[14] But perhaps the most important effect Wagner had in England was on George Bernard Shaw, who extolled him in *The Perfect Wagnerite*, and took many Wagnerian themes and ideas for his plays, notably *Candida* and *Man and Superman*. The influence of Wagner led to a whole new class of poetic drama making its way to the London stage, from Yeats's

The Countess Kathleen to Eliot's *Murder in the Cathedral*.[15] This was one enthusiasm Fabian socialists like Shaw shared with the determinedly apolitical Bloomsberries. Virginia Woolf was overwhelmed by *Parsifal*, and E.M. Forster went to Bayreuth as often as he could. But Virginia Woolf has also left an intriguing vignette of the 'strange men and women . . . to be found in the cheap seats on a Wagner night', who 'walk off their fervour on the Embankment, wrapped in great black cloaks'.[16] Such strange men and women, in Paris, their brains full of leitmotivs, would have headed for the boulevards and a café, rather than for the Embankment and the tube back to remote digs.

The second great new influence on the London stage, also heralded by Shaw, was Ibsen. *A Doll's House* was first produced in 1889, *Hedda Gabler* the next year and *Ghosts* the year after that. To be sure, the *Daily Telegraph* critic, on seeing the first production of *John Gabriel Borkman* in 1897, wrote, 'it was a treat to leave a grim and darkened theatre and to meet healthy, cheery, buoyant life again in the Strand, where it was all bustle and activity, and boys shouting about cricket and exhibiting postcards . . . the Ibsenites issuing forth in a mournful throng were not to be influenced by light or life, or air or nature.'[17]

Yet as early as 1893 Shaw persuaded J.T. Grein, the founder of the Independent Theatre, to put on his first play, *Widowers' Houses*, and by 1904 it was Shaw's *Candida* which persuaded John Vedrenne to partner Harley Granville Barker in putting on modern plays at the Court Theatre in Sloane Square. These included works by Ibsen, Gerhart Hauptmann, Maeterlinck, and Arthur Schnitzler, as well as by Yeats, John Galsworthy and John Masefield. But the core of the Court's programme was Shaw, eleven of whose plays were put on there.[18] The Court became the flagship of a new, serious modern theatre in London. Other more or less fragile craft were the Independent Theatre Society and the Stage Society. They were, however, only specks bobbing up and down on the broad bosom of the ocean of commercial theatre in the West End.

Even there, however, there were signs of intellectual life after the theatrically dormant decades. Pinero's *The Second Mrs Tanqueray*, in 1893, tackled what was thought of as the 'daring' subject of a 'fallen woman', and treated it, even more daringly, with sympathy. Shaw savaged the play, charging Pinero with flattering the West End audience by giving them plays they liked 'while persuading them that such appreciation was only possible from persons of great culture'. It is fair to question whether Pinero, an expert playsmith whose intentions were largely commercial, would have attempted anything even so moderately daring had it not been for the triumph of Oscar Wilde's society play *Lady Windermere's Fan*. Wilde's *Salome*, first written in French and produced in Paris before London, was unmistakably Wagnerian, and in 1895, on the eve of the catastrophe of his three trials and imprisonment, he did something even more daring. His society comedy *The Importance of Being Earnest* hid a savage satire beneath its social smartness and polished wit: for 'earnest', a slang word for 'gay', and also perhaps a reference to 'uranian', a euphemism for homosexual, was a triple pun.[19] In the theatre, as in literature and in painting, London was bubbling and fizzing with exciting and dangerous reactions as the acid of new ideas bit into the solid metal of Victorianism. They excited the intelligentsia, and even intrigued the governing class – when the Fabian socialist Beatrice Webb took the conservative prime minister, A.J. Balfour, to see Shaw's *John Bull's Other Island* at the Court, Balfour was so amused that he invited two liberal leaders to see it again with him – but such acid comedies were very far from eating into the fabric of middle-class society, or even ruffling the surface of the shiny Edwardian top hat.

Between 1851 and 1901 London's population had more than doubled, from under 3 million to 6.7 million people, spread over something like twenty miles from east to west and twenty miles from north to south. The city throbbed with the intellectual energy of new poets, new novelists, new dramatists and above all new journalists, not to mention commercial enterprise and technical innovation. A positive explosion of cultural and artistic activity was taking place, for every taste from the most esoteric to the new mass market. Yet to a Parisian, or a Viennese, the place was hardly recognizable as a city at all.

London was grimy; it was foggy. It was a place of harsh social contrasts, between the effortless superiority of the wealthy Philistines whom Matthew Arnold had denounced in the 1860s and Wilde caricatured in the nineties, and the dirt and degradation, rage and despair which Charles Booth charted in the seventeen volumes of *Life and Labour of the People in London* and Arthur Morrison discovered in the 'mean streets' around the Jago, the most brutally desolate slum in Bethnal Green. This was the London of legend, the London of Jack the Ripper in the East End and toffs and mashers in the 'Dilly.

Yet London was not all gaslight glitter and dark desperation. It was also, for a large and growing number of Londoners, an extremely pleasant and congenial place to live. Like a magnet, it drew to it talent not only from Ireland, Scotland and the English provinces, but from all over the world – Kipling from India, Conrad from Poland, Impressionist painters like Monet and Seurat from France – and especially from the United States. The London literary world in the 1890s and 1900s would have been far poorer without Whistler, Henry James, Stephen Crane, Henry Harland, and, in the second decade of the century, Richard Aldington, Hilda Doolittle, Ezra Pound and Thomas Stearns Eliot.

In those days London was a city, like New York in the 1940s and unlike London today, which ran round the clock. 'Ah, London, London, our delight,' wrote Richard Le Gallienne, 'great flower that opens but at night.' In the 1880s, in the Strand and the West End, public houses took down their shutters at seven in the morning and did not close until midnight. These were places where one could eat as well as drink, as in a Parisian café, and in the better establishments one could also find free newspapers, get a cup of coffee or even play a game of chess. What are now thought of as examples of the immemorial London pub, the tall red-brick houses clad with decorated earthenware tiles, with their cut-glass windows and brass and mahogany fittings, were put up in a little pub-building boom in the middle 1890s. When even these splendid establishments – the Marquis of Granby in Charlotte Street, for example, immortalized in Anthony Powell's novels as the 'Mortimer', or the Chelsea Potter and the World's End at the other end of the town – had thrown out the last sodden wit, there were other places to go on to: the 'cellars', 'divans' (from which our word 'dive' is derived) and 'singing-rooms'. Evans's, in Covent Garden, did not close until three or four in the morning, and Nicholson's Coal Hole made the customers pull their feet up off the floor just long enough to sweep under them before it opened up again for the morning drinkers, just as the saloons of Manhattan's Third Avenue did until recently. For those not content with drink and music, there were nightclubs where there were girls to be picked up, such as Kate Hamilton's, 'Mother' Edwards's and Alsatia. Half a dozen theatres, like the Tivoli in the Strand, the Empire in Leicester Square and the Pavilion at Cambridge Circus – now the home of Andrew Lloyd Webber's endless string of hit musicals, and opposite the inoffensive men's tailor's whose premises John Le Carré borrowed, without a shred of justification, as 'the Circus', head of his fictional British secret service – boasted other attractions. 'There distinguished representatives of art, literature and the law mingled nightly with city financiers, lights of the sporting and dramatic world, and a very liberal sprinkling of the "upper crust".[20] They also mingled with some of the most desirable and expensive prostitutes in London. The new music-halls put on ballets in which the actresses were scantily clad, as well as comedy acts; but at the back of the dress circle there was an open area, behind the seats, with a bar, known as the 'promenade', and there available beauties stood, usually but not always obeying the house rules that forbade them to make the first move, but happy enough to be approached by the perfect gentlemen in white ties and tailcoats who sought their company.

The ladies of the promenades were near the top of a pyramid of prostitution in which some 60–80,000 women and young girls, according to estimates made by editors and bishops, tried to find a niche;[21] outside on the streets of Piccadilly and the Haymarket were less fortunate women, but they in turn feared to fall to the squalid and dangerous life of the girls who worked in the crowded immigrant slums of the East End or around the docks. If the young gentlemen found themselves wearied by these various nocturnal pleasures, they had only to retreat to one of the many 'hammams', or 'hummums', the Turkish baths sprinkled round the pleasure quarters of the West End, which were all the rage from the 1870s on, where they could bathe, rest, smoke, and exchange gossip.[22]

For young men arriving in town, like the youthful George Bernard Shaw clip-clopping from the boat-train at Euston to Victoria Grove in a growler in 1876,[23] or the young Rudyard Kipling when he took lodgings in Villiers Street, off the Strand, in 1889, London could be a cosy place, and a comfortable life with occasional luxuries need not be prohibitively expensive. There were all kinds of lodgings, or 'digs', to be rented, from luxurious chambers with service in the West End, like Albany, where a number of writers lived, to the actors' digs in the Brixton Road remembered with affectionate disgust in the old doggerel, *The Pro's Lament*:

> You seek till you find
> A cosy 'combined',
> Furnished with old-fashioned grace.
> There's a po with no handle,
> A picture of Randall,
> And two ruptured ducks in a case.[24]

As with lodgings, so with refreshment. As well as 9,000 pubs there were in 1890 some 600 chop-houses and 900 coffee-houses. You could eat a chop or a steak there for a shilling, and for the same amount you could eat a three-course meal with a bottle of wine in one of the numerous Italian restaurants, which were to be found especially in Soho. In the 1880s George Bernard Shaw, having decided to become a vegetarian, found a dozen or more vegetarian restaurants within easy walking distance of his chair in the British Museum: Gatti's and Rosedano's in the Strand, the Orange Grove in St Martin's Lane, and the Wheatsheaf, later a pub where writers used to gather in the 1930s, in Rathbone Place.

The library's vast domed rotunda was open even to the half-starved denizens of New Grub Street. From 1880 to 1888 the young Shaw worked there every day, applying for more than 300 books a year.[25] It was his free university, with 'all the advantages of communal heating, lavatory accommodation and electric light, with a comfortable seat, unlimited books, and ink and blotting paper all for nothing'.

Gissing describes a humbler shelter for impoverished writers, a 'reading room' of a kind that was quite common by the 1880s, for which the admission cost only one penny. It was a poor man's replica of the London Library.

A flight of stairs brought them to a small room in which were exposed the daily newspapers; another ascent, and they were in a room devoted to magazines, chess and refreshments; yet another, and they reached the department of weekly publications; lastly, at the top of the house, they found a lavatory, and a chamber for the use of those who desired to write.[26]

Paper and envelopes could be bought on the premises, and an enormous basket full of waste paper suggested the scope of the efforts made, some by semi-literate job-seekers and some by the strivers on the lowest slopes of Parnassus.

Gissing devotes considerable space to the shifts the more desperate inhabitants of Grub Street went to. One writer, for example, was delighted by the quality of the bread and dripping at the local grocer's. Another swore by a pennyworth of pease-pudding and a third had discovered a bakery off the Hampstead Road where a half-quartern loaf of bread cost 2½d instead of the more usual 2¾d: well worth a long walk in leaking shoes.

Even gastronomy need not be so very expensive, however, for

writers in funds. The Carlton, which opened in the West End in 1899, was intended to be the very last word in luxury. It was managed by no less a hotelier than César Ritz, and the immortal Auguste Escoffier was in charge of the kitchens. Colonel Newnham Davies, a serious diner-out, has rescued from oblivion the bill of fare of one dinner there. It began with royal native oysters, and went on by way of *consommé* Marie Stuart, *filets de sole*, *noisettes* of venison, *suprême* of chicken, stuffed ortolans, salad, peach soufflé and sweets, washed down, as the colonel might well have said, with an excellent Pommery and of course champagne. The bill? Just under three pounds, or enough for a writer in seriously low water to live off for a week.[27]

It was still a dangerous city. As Londoners came to terms in the 1970s with muggings and IRA bombings and firearms, they had mostly forgotten that London had not always been the exceptionally safe and peaceful place it was from the end of the First World War until well after the end of the Second.[28] Gentlemen and ladies who strayed from the safety of genteel neighbourhoods could expect to be whistled at, called after, spattered on purpose with mud and horse dung, and, if the neighbourhood was bad and the night was dark, beaten and robbed. As a consequence, any man who carried a gold watch, and to do so was almost a badge of membership in the gentle classes, was likely to go out armed, with a lead-loaded 'life-preserver' or 'Penang lawyer' or brass knuckles (such items were openly on sale at Gamage's stores in Holborn) if not with a revolver, and Victorian men bought gas guns for self-protection just as women in American cities now buy Mace.[29]

For all its risks and the long odds against success, late Victorian and Edwardian London did act as a cosmic magnet, sucking in talent. Margaret Drabble, in her biography of Arnold Bennett, reaches across two generations to admit that 'the yearning of the provincial for London is a quite exceptional passion. It sets in early and is never satisfied.' So Bennett borrowed the train fare from his mother, and left the Potteries for a job with Le Brasseur &

Oakley, solicitors in Lincoln's Inn Fields, and digs looking at 'endless railway arches' in Hornsey; just as Shaw, and Gissing, and Wells, and so many more whose names are forgotten, had done before him.

Two characters in George Gissing's *New Grub Street*, both failed novelists, lament the power of London's magnetism for young writers. 'It's a huge misfortune,' says one of them, 'this will-o'-the-wisp attraction exercised by London on young men of brains. They come here to be degraded, or to perish.' Many were degraded, and some did perish. William Butler Yeats spoke of the poets of the 1890s as 'the tragic generation': and it is true that Wilde died in his fifties, a broken man unable to write; that John Davidson, after living for years in the miserable poverty evoked in his best poem, 'Thirty Bob a Week', took his own life; that Beardsley died in his thirties, Lionel Johnson at thirty-five, Ernest Dowson at thirty-three. It is also true that that generation, the generation of the 'aesthetes', lived to see its deepest beliefs discredited. After the Wilde trials, the English business classes, like the theatre critic of the *Daily Telegraph*, emerged for a while into the cheerful brightness of everyday life.

The aesthetic movement, with its self-conscious decadence, its obsession with the forbidden fruit of sexuality and especially of homosexuality, does not look much like modernism today; at the turn of the century it looked as though, for all the painful honesty and the talent of its most gifted adherents, it had failed. The nineties, in fact, bear more than a superficial resemblance to the 1960s in America. Young people, especially young, highly educated people, rebelled against what they saw as the complacency, insensitivity and sexual conformism of their parents. In this there was, in the 1890s as in the 1960s, more than a touch of Oedipal neurosis. The aesthetes of the nineties were groping after a kind of counter-culture. Fascinated by foreign influences, they challenged all the pieties and pomposities of a wealthy, powerful and troubled society. In the process, they aspired to a New Hedonism, a New Woman and a New Age.

The parallel must not be pushed too far. But just as the American counter-culture in the 1960s was deeply involved in, was in large part created by, a detested imperial war, so Britain at the turn of the century was involved in an unlovely and unloved war in a distant country, the Boer War, which deeply divided British intellectuals. Since the 1880s there had been a fault line in British intellectual life between Left and Right; between those who remained broadly loyal to the pillars of the status quo, Church and Queen, capitalism and Empire, and a radical minority, even among intellectuals, who were to a greater or lesser degree agnostic, republican, socialist and pacifist. Still, if such ideas were commonplace after the 1880s, before 1914 they were by no means dominant. Indeed, there was a strong strain in the emerging modernism of the time that was anti-socialist and élitist, and even anticipated some of the themes of fascism.

There were, in fact, two waves of modernism in Britain, as there were elsewhere in Europe. The aesthetic movement of the decadent decade was the first wave. The second hit the beach in the years immediately before the First World War. But in the meantime there was an extraordinary flowering of work which, as well as being of the highest literary quality in itself, and while certainly not aggressively modernist, nevertheless looks forward to the fully modernist work of the second wave. Between 1899 and 1905 London publishers offered Conrad's *Heart of Darkness*, *Lord Jim* and *Nostromo*, Henry James's *The Ambassadors*, *The Wings of the Dove* and *The Golden Bowl*, Samuel Butler's *The Way of All Flesh*, E.M. Forster's *Where Angels Fear to Tread* and Kipling's masterpiece, *Kim*. Moreover, these major achievements were not isolated peaks. They rose above a forest floor which has perhaps never been so full of original and varied writing talents. In part this was because the profession of letters had never been before, and would perhaps never be in London again, so well organized or so prosperous.

These were bumper years for the business of publishing in all its aspects. New forms were developing. The 'three-decker' novel, which had commanded so high a premium in financial terms that writers of fiction could not afford to ignore the convention, died in the middle 1890s. The three-volume novel, published at a guinea and a half (31s. 6d.) and followed up by a cheap edition for 6s., depended on circulating libraries like Mudie's. In the middle nineties the libraries, annoyed that the cheaper editions were cutting into their business, told publishers they would no longer order three-volume editions. The change, symptomatic of a new spirit of aggressive commercialism that was replacing the more orotund capitalism of the mid-Victorian period, was abrupt. In 1894 184 three-volume novels were published; in 1897 just four. Novels became shorter and cheaper, and instead of buying the rights outright, as they had done before, publishers began to pay authors a royalty. This coincided with the appearance on the scene of the first literary agents. The American J.B. Pinker, who represented Conrad, and A.P. Watt, who represented the young H.G. Wells, were among the first.

In this atmosphere of innovation, experimental forms of publishing and journalism were being tried. The Victorian dailies – *The Times*, the *Daily Telegraph*, the *Morning Post* and their peers – were joined by the new halfpenny papers, such as the *Daily Mail*, which before 1914 had reached a circulation of one million, and the *Daily Mirror*. The new papers had an inexhaustible appetite for features, reviews and fiction as well as for news. George Gissing has left a vivid impression of how a young man with a nimble mind and the capacity for work could take advantage of these boom years of the new journalism: 'I got up at 7.30 and whilst I breakfasted I read through a volume I had to review. By 10.30 the review was written – three-quarters of a column in the *Evening Budget* ... from 10.30 to 11 I smoked a cigar and reflected, feeling that the day wasn't badly begun. At eleven I was ready to write my Saturday *causerie* for the *Will-o'-the-Wisp*' and so on by way of a paper for *The West End* and 'a long affair I have in hand for *The Current*'.

'And what's the value of it all?' asks his sister.

'Probably from ten to twelve guineas.'

'I meant, what is the literary value of it,' said the sister, with a smile.

'Equal to that of the contents of a mouldy nut.'[30]

There was, however, more to it than that. The new journals were creating a New Journalism. 'Some time in the eighties,' wrote Shaw,

... the New Journalism was born. Lawless young men began to write and print the living English language of their own day ... They split their infinitives, and wrote such phrases as 'a man nobody ever heard of' instead of 'a man of whom nobody had ever heard' ... The interview, the illustration and the cross-heading, hitherto looked on as American vulgarities impossible to English literary gentlemen, invaded all our papers.

The centre of this New Journalism, in Shaw's opinion, was the *Pall Mall Gazette*, edited by the fearless investigative journalist, W.T. Stead, who went to jail for purchasing five young women as if for white slavery, just to prove they could be bought, and gave them one of the greatest headlines ever written: 'The Maiden Tribute of Modern Babylon'.[31]

The short story, already established in the United States, became more and more worth writing, commercially speaking, as the number of magazines proliferated. As fast as these noisy papers with unheard-of circulations made their appearance at the bottom end of the market, new periodicals for serious readers and for less serious enthusiasts for the arts were also being born. *The Yellow Book*, we have seen, published serious fiction by writers of the highest quality. It was also, during its brief life, a howling commercial success, selling its quarterly issues of more than 400 pages to more than 7,000 readers. There were older periodicals too – the *Pall Mall Gazette*, for example, and the *Cornhill*. To them, in 1891, was added the liveliest of them all, and the one that contributed the most to the emergence of a new commercial fiction, written for the intelligent reader, but to entertain, in a new crisp, racy style: *The Strand Magazine*. It was in *The Strand* that Arthur Conan Doyle published the first Sherlock Holmes stories, beginning with

'A Study in Scarlet' in 1887. Two years later, Rudyard Kipling, home from India, put up at digs in Villiers Street, which runs down immediately to the east of the tracks as they enter and leave Charing Cross station. A brick arch, now full of fast-food and costume-jewellery stalls, links it with the Northumberland Hotel, now renamed by the brewery which owns it 'The Sherlock Holmes' and fitted up as a little museum to the Great Detective, but once upon a time the place where Sir Henry Baskerville's boots were stolen.

There were twelve theatres in the Strand in the nineties, and close to a hundred places where you could eat or drink. Aside from the Savoy Grill, where John Buchan's hero, Sir Richard Hannay, made the acquaintance of his American ally John Scantlebury Blenkiron, and where you can now see press lords and their editors entertaining cabinet ministers, there is only one restaurant left in the Strand that preserves some of the flavour of that departed London (though Boulestin's and Rule's both do their best to catch its echo), and that is Simpson's. Like the Rhymers' Cheshire Cheese, it is largely a tourist place now, much changed from the days when it was frequented by Edwardian publishers and writers. The dumb waiter in the centre of the room, 'almost as tall as a catafalque', has gone, and so has the great bay window[32] opening on to the busy pavement where lawyers hastened from the Temple to join their wives at the D'Oyly Carte for Gilbert and Sullivan's wicked satire on the aesthetes in *Patience*, and the young men sauntered along, their hands in their pockets, wondering whether to go to a play at the Strand or just drop into the promenade at the Tivoli.

'Let's all go down the Strand!' How that street, London's equivalent in those days of the 'Great White Way' in New York, haunts the memory of that era! Today it is largely occupied by the London offices of the former white dominions. It is therefore dedicated to the melancholy business of subsidizing natives so frustrated by life in Britain for one reason or another that they decide their salvation lies in moving to Brisbane, or Auckland, or

Winnipeg: Bulawayo and Johannesburg find few takers now. It is a strange commentary on the bursting pride of Empire which young men felt as they clip-clopped along the Strand from the boat train at Euston or Victoria and registered at one of the big hotels in Northumberland Avenue. Those hotels, in turn, were expropriated by the government in the First World War, and have remained government offices ever since. Great mounds of bird droppings testify to the passing of the once vibrant commercial civilization that then washed round their walls, and a dusty Cerberus demands passes from visitors with the appropriate security clearance where once the revolving doors of gleaming brass and mahogany positively spun with the energy of the young men who burst through them into the maelstrom of London.

The first decade of the twentieth century has suffered from the fact that unlike the nineties or the twenties it has no name. In London, it was an apogee of commercial activity. Advertising, a craft in which London already lagged behind New York in audacity and invention, was nevertheless both more inventive and brasher than it had ever been before. Young men like Saki's Mark Spayley made enough money to propose to 'the daughter of an enormously wealthy man' on the proceeds of the name he dreamed up for a new wonder cereal, the Filboid Studge; and Lucas Harrowcluff got the knighthood that should have gone to his brother, who had 'put in some useful service in an out-of-the-way, but not unimportant, corner of the world',[33] by composing what would now be called a jingle, with 'big drum business' on the last two syllables:

> Cousin Teresa takes out Caesar
> Fido, Jock and the big borzoi.[34]

The Yellow Journalism, too, had crossed the Atlantic. It had nothing to do with *The Yellow Book*. Whelpdale, one of the starving writers in *New Grub Street*, finds that his prospects look up when he suggests changing the title of a magazine called *Chat* to *Chit-Chat*, and proposes to fill it with 'the lightest and frothiest of chit-chatty information – bits of stories, bits of description, bits of scandal, bits of jokes, bits of statistics, bits of foolery'. That, of course, was precisely the formula that made the fortune of George Newnes and his *Tit-bits*, and it was by imitating *Tit-bits* with his *Answers* that Alfred Harmsworth, later Lord Northcliffe, London's answer to William Randolph Hearst, got his start. Whelpdale's friend Jasper Milvain, the prodigious journalist we have already watched at work, was walking along the Strand – where else? – one afternoon when he ran into Whelpdale in a state of excitement so acute that Jasper at first thought it was alcoholically induced. 'I've got Lake's place on *Chit-chat*!' cries Whelpdale. 'Two hundred and fifty a year! My fortune's made!' That was almost exactly the experience of Arnold Bennett. He came to London in 1889, and was launched on 'the humiliating part of my career, the period of . . . freelancing' by winning a twenty-guinea prize for a parody in *Tit-bits*. After a couple of years of rejection slips and poor attempts to imitate Maupassant or Turgenev he landed a job as assistant editor of *Woman* at £150 a year – £50 less than he had been making as a solicitor's clerk – and sat down to write his autobiographical account of a provincial storming the gates of London, *The Man from the North*. The New Grub Street might be a far cry from the solemnities of High Victorian literary life (though Thackeray and Dickens were both working journalists, never forget); dashing off paragraphs for the *Pall Mall Gazette* or squibs for *Tit-bits* might seem an ocean away from the august world of the Olympians who gathered to honour Sir Edmund Gosse at Lord Balfour's house; but the new journalism offered a broad base of publications to be filled, readers to be reached and money to be earned, and the peak of the pyramid reached all the higher for it.

'On or about 1 December 1910,' wrote Virginia Woolf, 'human nature changed.'[35] It was a commonplace of the *fin de siècle* everywhere, and not least for Oscar Wilde and his friends, that with the new century a new age was beginning. Poor Wilde did not live to see the new century,[36] but if he had lived until the war

which destroyed almost everything and quite a few of the young
men he had loved, and emancipated the Ireland he had escaped
from, he would probably have seen that in England, as in fact
elsewhere, modernism arrived in two stages. There was, first of all,
that Oedipal rebellion against Victorian values and Victorian stuffi-
ness, of which Wilde and the aesthetes and the pupils of French
Impressionism and French Symbolism were the heroes. There was
then a period, associated with the real trauma and bogus triumph
of the Boer War, when some of the best writers, Kipling and
Conrad among them, responded to the sheer colour as well as
to the moral drama of the imperial enterprise. But that was also,
as George Dangerfield pointed out long ago in *The Strange Death
of Liberal England*, a time of national crisis even before the danger
of world war. Dangerfield identified four conflicts which were
woven together, like so many hanks of gun cotton, to lay an
explosive charge under the foundations of Edwardian order.
There was the constitutional question, and in particular the
intolerable anomaly of the veto power possessed by a House
of Lords whose members still owned what many felt to be an
unconscionable, a strangling share of the land and the mineral
wealth under it. There was the eternal 'social question', now made
urgent by the rising determination of organized labour, in association with the new Labour Party, to seize a fairer share of the
national wealth for the working class. There was Ireland. And there
was the rise of the women's movement, which was now moving
beyond discussing how a New Woman would behave and
beginning to press militantly for political power through the
vote.

It was only natural, in this atmosphere of political and social
turmoil and even menace, that the second wave of modernism
should begin to break long before the war. They did not all look
particularly ferocious, the members of this new avant-garde. There
is a contemporary vignette of T.E. Hulme, for example, the
Cambridge philosopher and art critic, reading the *Observer* over his
breakfast at Fleming's Hotel in Oxford Street, which 'had retained

quite a Victorian atmosphere, and so had most of the customers, whose appearance suggested they were food-faddists or Plymouth Brethren or Jehovah's Witnesses or something else a trifle odd'. Nor was there anything revolutionary about the basement of the Aerated Bread Company's ABC café in Chancery Lane, the meeting place for the editorial discussions, once memorably described as a 'skewbald witanegemot',[37] of A.R. Orage's *New Age* magazine, affectionately known to Orage and to his contributors alike by virtue of its minimalist payment policy as the 'No Wage'.[38] Nor would anyone who had come across a furious figure hanging upside down by his trouser turn-ups from the points of the high iron railings in Soho Square necessarily have thought him significant.

Yet Hulme's paper on 'Modern Art and Philosophy', read to the Quest Society in Cambridge, correctly predicted the downfall of a tradition of Romanticism in poetry and painting as old as the Renaissance.[39] Hulme was a close friend of the sculptor Jacob Epstein, and it was in the *New Age* that he published a series of articles on the new artists, including David Bomberg and Henry Nevinson, which argued that the new art would assume complicated forms associated with machinery. Orage, the editor, was a complex and in some respects a flaky figure. A poor boy, he had been sent to teacher training college, and descended on London after a stint as an elementary school teacher in Leeds, where he and a group of friends discussed Plato, Nietzsche, Shaw and socialism. (London, again, was drawing to itself a clever man from the most modest of provincial backgrounds, like Bertie Wells from the draper's shop in Southsea, and making writers of them, or rather rewarding them for making writers of themselves.) Orage later came under the influence of Major Douglas and his 'social credit' economics, and then of Gurdjieff, Madame Blavatsky and Theosophy – seers and a dogma that had an influence it is now hard to credit among the intelligentsia of the first two decades of the century. Spiritualism, mediums, theosophy and the occult recur like a leitmotiv in the early volumes of Anthony Powell's

Dance to the Music of Time, precisely because it is so accurate a recollection of the intellectual atmosphere of his childhood; while John Buchan has left a malicious but wickedly true-sounding group portrait of the crackpot idealists who congregated around the 'Moot Hall' of a high-minded garden suburb during the First World War, adding pacifism to their existing commitments to socialism, feminism, vegetarianism and the most decorous Free Love.[40] Still, Orage's *New Age* had the immense merit of being responsive to the new winds that were blowing across Europe. At first he was interested in Bergson and his Life Force as well as in Wagner and Nietzsche. Later he contributed to the mania for Russian art unleashed by the arrival of the Russian Ballet. He published the first articles in Britain about psychoanalysis, and he introduced both Cubism and Futurism to British readers.

In this atmosphere of cultural crisis and neophilia, London began to spawn new weekly magazines like mushrooms in a damp cellar. Groups argued, quarrelled, split and split again. Shaw, Wells and Chesterton, as well as a wealthy theosophist, were among those who helped found the *New Age*, but in 1913 Orage broke with the Fabians, who went off to found the *New Statesman* in its offices overlooking Lincoln's Inn Fields, where – until it was compelled to move by financial pressures in the late 1970s – H.G. Wells's raincoat still hung on a peg.

Roger Fry, a friend, if not a member, of the Bloomsbury Group, introduced the later Cézanne and more generally Post-Impressionism to London in two famous exhibition. The first, at the Grafton Gallery in November 1910 (it was this that cued Virginia Woolf's comment about the change in human nature) consisted of paintings by Cézanne and Gauguin. The second, in 1912, showed a wholly new generation of painters, including Braque and Picasso. Between those two shows, if anywhere, in London terms, lay the line of division between the first and second waves of change. Wyndham Lewis cooperated for a while with Bloomsbury artists such as Virginia Woolf's sister Vanessa Bell and Duncan Grant in a project called the Omega Workshop. But

Bloomsbury was too tinkling and effete for Wyndham Lewis. 'This family party of strayed and dissenting aesthetes,' as he called them, 'were compelled to call in as much modern talent as they could find, to do the rough masculine work without which they knew their efforts would not rise above the level of a pleasant tea-party.'[41] Wyndham Lewis broke with Fry and founded the Rebel Arts Centre in Great Ormond Street with the help of money from the artist Kate Lechmere. It was as a result of a quarrel over her affections with Jacob Epstein, whose great crucifix looms over Cavendish Square, that Lewis found himself upside down on the railings in Soho Square. Bombastic and hot-tempered as he might be, Lewis had talent and energy, both as a writer and as a painter. He made ceaseless propaganda for what he called Vorticism, and in 1914, on the eve, he published the first of only two issues of *Blast*, a periodical which was a manifesto for modernism. In addition to a great deal of tedious 'bombardiering', as he called it, on behalf of abstract art, *Blast* included 'The Saddest Story', a first version of Ford Madox Ford's masterpiece *The Good Soldier*. As the war began, Lewis wrote much later, 'it looked to many observers as if a great historical "school" was in the process of formation' in western Europe, but also in Britain, of which 'Expressionism, Post-Impressionism, Vorticism, Cubism, Futurism were some of the characteristic nick-names'.

Ezra Pound arrived in England in 1908 from America by way of Italy. For several years after 1913 he acted as secretary to W.B. Yeats at his cottage in Ashdown Forest, in the Sussex Weald.[42] Cocky and convinced that the modern movement would be his own road to fortune, Pound considered that Yeats was the best poet writing in English, but that his manner was sadly out of date. He therefore 'set himself the task of converting Yeats to modernism', and was not above altering Yeats's poems before he sent them to the publishers.

In 1914 he was joined by T.S. Eliot, who, after studying philosophy at Harvard, had intended to continue his studies in

Germany until his plans were interrupted by the war. Pound persuaded Miss Weaver to start the *Egoist*, which published work by James Joyce, Pound himself, D.H. Lawrence and Eliot. Modernism had finally arrived, and London received, by way of St Louis, Missouri, Harvard and Marburg, its poet laureate, poet of the office workers' round:

> Unreal City,
> Under the brown fog of a winter dawn,
> A crowd flowed over London Bridge, so many,
> I had not thought death had undone so many.
> Sighs, short and infrequent, were exhaled,
> And each man fixed his eyes before his feet.[43]

And of their pleasure, when a typist, clearing the ruins of breakfast in her bedsit, awaits the expected guest:

> He, the young man carbuncular, arrives,
> A small house agent's clerk, with one bold stare,
> One of the low on whom assurance sits
> Like a silk hat on a Bradford millionaire.[44]

After their love-making,

> When lovely woman stoops to folly and
> Paces about her room again, alone,
> She smooths her hair with automatic hand,
> And puts a record on the gramophone.[45]

Eliot knew how to tie these razor-sharp observations of a moment in the city's centuries, humdrum or sordid, to its mythical dimensions: to the historical dimension, with its memory of Shakespeare and Elizabeth and Leicester, and to its geography, with the barges and the logs drifting down the river, past the Isle of Dogs towards the open sea, where the golden stream of trade flowed in, and out to the suburbs with their 'trams and dusty trees', and back to the timeless classicism

> where the walls
> Of Magnus Martyr hold
> Inexplicable splendour of Ionian white and gold.[46]

In London, over the last twenty years of the nineteenth century and the first twenty of the twentieth, the intellectuals were not at war with a harshly repressive autocracy, as they were in St Petersburg. They were not detested but admired, as they were in Paris. Nor did they absorb the whole of a cultivated bourgeoisie as they did in Vienna. Instead, they were ignored with amused tolerance. But they were also free to find their place in the decorous but pitiless contest that was society. If they succeeded, they were valued as suppliers of a number of unusually valuable brands of luxury goods. London has often been labelled the dullest of the European capitals, and much has been made of the fact that some of the most prominent writers and artists in London were not English-born. But such comparisons with other cities miss the point of what late-Victorian and Edwardian London was like: a gigantic hive. It had little structure or centre beyond the remote and Philistine monarchy and the plutocratic hierarchies of society, with its occasional intellectuals and connoisseurs. There were comparatively few places where writers or painters or musicians felt among their own kind in this city of fogs and mud, still less in the leafy suburbs with their dusty trees and lace curtains.

One was Bloomsbury. Everyone knows now, as a result of the strange nostalgic Bloomsbury boom of the 1970s, that after the Victorian man of letters Sir Leslie Stephen died in 1904 his four children, Virginia and Vanessa, Thoby and Adrian, moved from Hyde Park Gate to 46 Gordon Square and that 'if ever such an entity as Bloomsbury existed,' as Vanessa's husband, the critic Clive Bell put it, 'these sisters with their houses in Gordon and Fitzroy Squares were the heart of it'. The Stephen sisters and the circle that gathered round them, Bell and Virginia's husband, the civil servant and publisher Leonard Woolf, the biographer Lytton Strachey (first attracted by the Uranian charms of Thoby), the art

critic Roger Fry, the novelist E.M. Forster, the painter Duncan
Grant and the writer David Garnett, to give simple labels to only
the best-known members of the coterie of friends, were certainly
distinctive. They had a style, an attitude, at once élitist and
irreverent, a passion for friendship, often sexual, and for gossip,
likewise, and – both metaphorically and literally – an unmistakable
voice, that was theirs alone. On the other hand, as biographers
have often pointed out, they worked in very different fields. They
quarrelled. They had no manifesto, no common programme.
They were ultimately a group of friends, not a movement. And
many other writers lived in Bloomsbury who had no contact with
them. They were not the first, and not even necessarily the most
talented. The second of the two houses Clive Bell mentioned, the
one he shared with Vanessa Bell in Fitzroy Square was bought
from . . . George Bernard Shaw.

There was also, in those days, Mayfair. Since 1945 the old
aristocratic quarter has been captured by advertising, Americans
and Arabs. But in the twenties and thirties there were Mayfair
writers. Michael Arlen's Bright Young Things lived in Mayfair. In
Aldous Huxley's *Antic Hay* the smart lost soul Myra Viveash
'stepped through the intricacies' of the foxtrot in Mayfair. That
was where the darling dodos of Evelyn Waugh's *Vile Bodies* drank
too many Martinis. But the novelist who, more than any other,
seems to me to have captured the social geography of London
from 1918 to 1960, Anthony Powell, actually lived in Shepherd
Market, in Mayfair, until he moved to Tavistock Square, in
Bloomsbury, in 1929. And what is perhaps the key scene of his
twelve-novel sequence, *A Dance to the Music of Time*, takes place in
the Ritz. In the palm court, the narrator, Nick, meets his raffish
City friend, Templer. Later that snowy night, he begins his affair
with Templer's sister Jean, who becomes the first great love of his
life. In the background, chattering like exotic parakeets, is a family
party of South Americans. Neither Jean nor he knows that she will
eventually move to South America and marry a general who
becomes a dictator. But who should walk in to this incongruously

luxurious scene but two of his Oxford acquaintances, the poet
Members and the left-wing critic J.G. Quiggin, clad in a leather
coat. Thirty years later, and thirty years earlier, such visitors to the
Ritz would have been unthinkable. In 1930, even left-wing writers
were occasionally to be seen in Mayfair; London still retained a
vestigial unity.

By the thirties, though, Anthony Powell's characters, like their
real-life originals, were more often to be found in Soho and more
particularly in what was to become perhaps the first and last
London equivalent of Montparnasse. That northern extension of
Soho, Fitzrovia, centred on the restaurants and delicatessens of
Charlotte Street. Powell himself hung out there quite a lot in the
Eiffel Restaurant and the Fitzroy pub, with his great friend the
composer Constant Lambert ('Moreland' in the *Dance*, I have
always presumed) and other chums. He also got to know artists: he
was sketched by Adrian Daintrey, Nina Hamnett and the then
legendary Augustus John, all of whom frequented the Charlotte
Street watering-places.

Fitzrovia was halfway between Broadcasting House, where the
BBC, in those enlightened days before the accountants took over,
used to pay contributors in cash, and the half-skyscraper Senate
House of London University, which in wartime was converted
into the Ministry of Information, briefly run by Sir John Reith,
the creator of the BBC, with the art historian Kenneth Clark as
one of his division heads. In his evocative account of wartime
literary London, *Under Siege*, Robert Hewison described how
London, at long last, acquired a real bohemia of its own. In the
territory bounded by Shaftesbury Avenue on the south, by Goodge
Street on the north, there gathered 'writers, poets, painters,
musicians, actors (plus the necessary complement of hangers-on,
mistresses, entrepreneurs, patrons and journalists), all of varying
talent and achievement, who collectively experience[d] a specific
set of emotional and economic conditions'. The economic circumstances of most of the denizens of Fitzrovia are simply described:
unglamorous poverty relieved only by a chance windfall in the

form of a publisher's advance or a BBC commission, or a lucky loan extorted in the Fitzroy or the Wheatsheaf. The emotional landscape was infinitely more complicated: Cyril Connolly called his war, largely spent in Bloomsbury, where he created, in *Horizon*, one of the most brilliant literary magazines London has ever seen, 'five years in gregarious confinement'.

Late in 1943 the enigmatic Sri Lankan editor of *Poetry (London)*, J.M. Tambimuttu, universally known as Tambi, introduced a new denizen, the short-story writer Julian Maclaren-Ross, recently discharged from the army. Tambi's popularity, at least among heterosexual poets, was assured by his twin attributes: he could get poems published, and he was always accompanied by a retinue of attractive and friendly muses. 'Now,' Tambi explained to Maclaren-Ross, outlining a typical Fitzrovia *soirée*, 'we will go to the Black Horse, the Burglar's Rest, the Marquis of Granby, the Wheatsheaf, then the Beer House and after 10.30 back to the Highlander which closes later at eleven.'

'Beware of Fitzrovia,' Tambi warned. 'It's a dangerous place.'

'Fights with knives?'

'No, a worse danger. You might get Sohoitis, you know.'

'No I don't. What is it?'

'If you get Sohoitis,' Tambi said very seriously, 'you will stay here always day and night and get no work done ever.'

Titanic spirits – Dylan Thomas, Francis Bacon, Lucien Freud – seemed to have an immunity to Sohoitis, or at least managed to achieve a great deal of very good work in the intermissions. Julian Maclaren-Ross succumbed. Anthony Powell lampooned him as X. Trampnel, whose unfinished masterpiece, *Profiles in String*, was dumped into the Regent's Canal by a psychotic girlfriend, and whose reputation therefore hung on a posthumous *conte*, *Dogs Have No Uncles*. Maclaren-Ross shared the same favourite pub with a man who equalled him as a talker and greatly surpassed him both as a drinker and as a writer, Dylan Thomas. In the years immediately after the war, when he walked into the Wheatsheaf in Rathbone Place, Thomas always turned to the right to join

Augustus John and his circle. Maclaren-Ross was never seen to walk in. He was always holding court at the left-hand corner of the bar. The two men saluted one another: but neither was willing to risk conversational competition.

Maclaren-Ross didn't literally stay in the Fitzrovia pubs all his life. Some time in 1944 he encountered a fellow contributor to *Penguin New Writing*, the New Zealander Dan Davin. After a misunderstanding due to the suspicion that Davin, who was wearing a major's uniform, might have been a militarist, the two men became friends. Eventually Maclaren-Ross followed Davin to Oxford, where the latter had become a publisher at the Clarendon Press. He died there of a heart attack in 1964, still without publishing the great novel everyone who had ever heard him talk expected from him. Davin remembered Dr Johnson's obituary on his friend Savage. 'There are no proper judges of his conduct,' Johnson wrote, 'who have slumbered away their time on the down of plenty, nor will any wise man presume to say, "Had I been in Savage's condition, I should have lived or written better than Savage." ' But it was not only in London, and not only in the twentieth century, that those who defeated what Cyril Connolly called 'the enemies of promise' had to be tough as well as talented.

Edwardian London was so vast, so opulent, so philistine and so tolerant, that it could accommodate turbulent creativity and radical innovation with only an occasional fluster. In London, under the amused superciliousness of real Englishmen, brokers or bankers or butchers or bakers, a Shaw or a Wells, a Yeats or an Eliot, could change the way the world thought without any danger of puncturing the urbane indifference of the suburban megalopolis. By the 1940s, the affluence of the Edwardian age was gone, and with it the self-confidence. It would be hard to imagine the wits of the Wheatsheaf gathered, in white tie and tails, to be celebrated and sent up by Max Beerbohm in a prime minister's mansion. Writers, peripheral victims of the long relative decline of London's wealth, found themselves back where they had been in Johnson's day, scuffling for guineas in journalism and broadcasting, the modern equivalents of the booksellers and actor-managers, and now uncomfortably aware that the man who is tired of London, or of whom London is tired, can always try his luck in Manhattan or Hollywood.

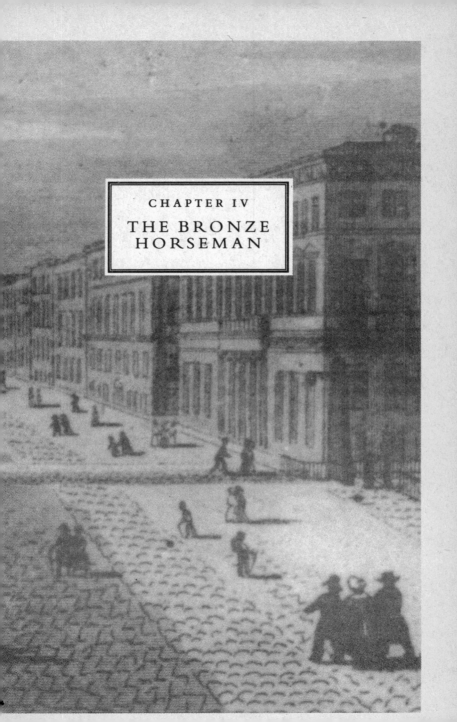

A FADED BOUQUET OF WHITE CHRYSANTHEMUMS
lies under the flying hooves of the Bronze Horseman. The emperor
sits astride his stallion, its hind legs rooted in Russian granite
and its flying hooves lashing European air. Today, after three
revolutions, after the nine hundred days and nights of starvation
during the siege, when the collapse of the Revolution which
began here in 1917 has brought freedom, but also renewed misery,
the young people of St Petersburg still leave flowers at Falconet's
statue of Tsar Peter after a wedding.

Almost three hundred years after his death, Peter has seen off his
great rival. The city is no longer Leningrad, the city of Lenin. It is
officially St Petersburg again. Unofficially, its people have always
called it simply 'Peter': not Pyotr, which would be the Russian for
it, but 'Piter', after the Dutch form of his name that he brought
back from his stay in the West.[1]

The locomotive which brought Lenin back to the city in 1917,
disguised as a fireman, still stands inside the Finland Station. His

statue, the first of thousands around the world, which are now being pulled over and smashed up, still stands in the square in front of the terminus. But no one would dream of giving *him* flowers now.

St Petersburg is still Peter's city. Rome, Paris, London, all grew street by street over centuries. St Petersburg was decreed by the will, the titanic vision, of a single man, and almost three hundred years later it is still trapped in the contradictions of Peter the Great's character and by the ambiguity of what he set out to do. The ancient capitals of Russia, Novgorod, Kiev and Moscow, lie deep in the birch and evergreen forests. Even Novgorod, the nearest, is a weary journey up long, sluggish rivers from the sea and from the reach and influence of Western Europe. Peter built his city on forty-odd muddy islands on the banks of the Neva, at the very westernmost tip of his vast empire. Or, as Alexander Pushkin, the greatest of all Russian poets, put it in the preface to his poem about the city called after the Bronze Horseman:

That young city, of northern lands the beauty and the marvel, from dank of forests, damp of bogs, rose up in all its grandeur and its pride; where once the Finnish fisher, Nature's sullen stepchild, had all alone beside the low-lying shores let down his ragged nets, today by bustling docks crowd, strong and shapely, bulks of tower and palace; ships swarm from all earth's ends to that rich port; Neva has clothed herself with stone; bridges have spanned her waters; her isles with groves dark-green are covered over; and now before the younger capital, old Moscow dims – as before the new Tsarina, the widow of the purple.

From Pushkin to the poets of the twentieth century, the greatest Russian writers have brooded over the double nature of Peter's city. They know that he sited it on the Gulf of Finland because he wanted to open Russia up to the western winds, bringing the trade and the ideas, the technology and the Enlightenment of the West. At the same time he built it to be the capstone and symbol of a system of ruthless autocracy, not the least of whose concerns was to deny the people freedom of speech and even thought. The whole history of the city has been the working out of that dualism, and of an overflowing basket of other contradictions. Because of the sheer vitality of the city's intellectual forges, hammering out ideas, books, plays, poems and styles with prodigal energy, St Petersburg's sharp contrasts, between the power of autocracy and the rebellion of the intelligentsia, the idle splendour of the nobility and the misery of the workers, eventually divided the entire world. Classic Russian literature may be said to begin with the Decembrist mutiny against Alexander I in 1825, the year Alexander Pushkin, a friend of the mutineers, published the first cantos of *Eugene Onegin*, and to end with the death of Chekhov in 1904, just before the first of the revolutions against the tsar. So, as Ronald Hingley has written, 'the great age of Russian literature ended as it had begun, with an attempt to overthrow the autocracy'.[2] Even after 1917, St Petersburg remained the literary capital of Russia, and four generations of supremely gifted St Petersburg writers, from Pushkin in the 1830s by way of Dostoyevsky in the 1860s, and the poets Aleksandr Blok in the 1900s and Anna Akhmatova in the years on either side of the Revolution, experienced the city as an ambivalent symbol of light and dark, hope and despair.

There is another dualism in the city's history: the three hundred years' rivalry with Moscow, inevitable from the moment Peter decided to transfer his affections from the 'widow' Moscow to the 'young tsarina' of the west. There was much more to it than that, however. Each city symbolized one face of Russia. St Petersburg was to be the window on Europe. It was to emphasize in its architecture – supplied in the first instance by foreigners, Italian, German, French – and in its whole style, the European character of the Russian Empire. But, as Peter well knew, there was another side to the Russian experience: the wanderings of peoples, Slavs, Scandinavians and Asiatics, over the vast spaces of Russia, the savage wars against Mongols and Tartars, the Eastern traditions of Orthodox Church and Muscovite autocracy. So, in the nineteenth century, when the great contest began between the 'Westernizers' and the 'Slavophiles' – feeble labels for the opposing camps in one of those Protean struggles in which the antagonists and the issues they are fighting over constantly take different, shifting forms – St Petersburg was always the natural home of those who wanted Russia to become more part of Europe, and Moscow, the third Rome, holy city of Orthodox Christianity, was the eternal home of the Slavophile tendency.

After the Revolution, Moscow had its revenge. Soviet Russia was born on the banks of the Neva, and born, moreover, of Western ideas, reintroduced from the West by Russians who had been driven into exile in the West. But with the new revolutionary state being threatened by the armies and navies of the West, Moscow was protected by many more miles of summer forest and winter snow. Supreme power, which had rested in St Petersburg for two centuries, moved back to Moscow. That was not the end of the rivalry, though. After the Revolution, as before, St Petersburg tended to think of Moscow as a holy fool, as crude, unsophisticated, lumbering and primitive. But Moscow despised Leningrad as corrupt, effete, perhaps in its secret heart unreliable in its support for the Revolution it had started. And now Moscow had the power.

Stalin in particular hated Leningrad. With his approval Sergey Mironovich Kirov, head of the Leningrad party, ruthlessly hunted down first the remaining Trotskyists, then the supporters of Zinoviev and Kamenev. It was not enough. The Great Terror of the 1930s began with the murder of Kirov himself, a Bolshevik of impeccable credentials, member of the Politburo and First Secretary of the Leningrad party. In the late afternoon of 1 December 1934, a dissatisfied young Communist, Leonid Nikolayev, who had been given a revolver and also a target, showed his pass to a guard outside the Smolny Institute, the aristocratic girls' school where Lenin had planned the October Revolution of 1917, and now the headquarters of the Leningrad party.[3] It was his third time lucky; twice before he had been turned away because his pass was not in order. This time he was not checked inside the building. Kirov was at home working on a speech, but at four o'clock he came to his office in Smolny, meaning to leave shortly for a scheduled speech at the nearby Tauride palace. Nikolayev shot him and collapsed next to him in the corridor.

It was, it has been said, 'the crime of the century', because it triggered off the whole orgy of purges by which Stalin cemented his grip on the Soviet empire. That in turn made a second world war more probable, and perhaps made it more likely that the Soviet Union would win it. Certainly it set off the Great Terror. It was on the day Kirov died that the secret police were given special powers, unknown to the tsars' *okhrana*, of executing people as an administrative process.

However that may be, the purger had been purged, and Stalin visited his hatred upon the city. He still feared it as the most logical place for opposition to his own autocracy to linger, the place where Western and bourgeois influences were most likely to penetrate the wall he had drawn round Russia. The great Putilov works, home of the shock troops of the Bolshevik Revolution, had just been renamed the Kirov works. Anything to do with Kirov was anathema. A T-28 tank was found with a bolt missing. The manager, Karl Martovich Ots, knew that it was an accident and had the courage to say so. No, it must be sabotage. In the end, anyone who had anything to do with the Kirov works, including Ots, was purged. Stalin's favourite, Zhdanov, was brought in to be the Leningrad boss. Leningrad's suffering was only beginning. Indeed, there is more than a suspicion that when the war came and Leningrad was blockaded by the Germans, Stalin delayed far longer than he need have done before relieving the city. It was, after all, no more than he had already done to the Ukraine, savagely visited in the great purges and famines of the 1930s, and no worse than he was to do to Warsaw when he deliberately halted the Red Army east of the Vistula and watched the Nazis get on with the job of smashing the Polish capital and massacring its people. Certainly, after the end of the war, Leningrad was the last of the war-smashed Soviet cities to be rebuilt.

★

The first thing you notice today is the contrast between magnificence and decay. The palaces loom out of the haze over the ubiquitous water in a wash of pastel colours: turquoise and ochre, mustard and plum. But behind the opulence of the baroque façades there are shabby courtyards and overcrowded tenements, and poverty, genteel and not-so-genteel. As the yellow winter dusk falls, the streets are full of citizens walking their dogs; if many of them are as big as Baskerville hounds, that is because these streets are no longer as safe as they were under two autocracies. Where once there were nobles and *raznochintsy*, literally, 'rankless ones', meaning commoners, then Communists and others, now there is a new and cruel social division, between those with access to foreign currency, who live like grand-dukes and commissars, and those compelled to work for a rouble which buys less food, less heat and less clothing every day. When a hard day's work hardly brings in a living wage, no wonder the streets are dangerous at night; and in real terms, the standard of living today is scarcely, if at all, higher than it was in 1914.

The Nevsky Prospekt is one of the half dozen noblest streets in Europe. It began as a wagon road, the Great Perspective Road cut through the woods in 1709–10 to bring naval stores from the Novgorod highway to the remote naval yard where Peter was building the fleet that would free Russia from the threat of Swedish invasion. By the middle of the nineteenth century it was lined with public and private palaces from the Admiralty at its western end to the monastery of Alexander Nevsky three miles to the east. In the 1830s Nikolay Gogol immortalized the street in his story, 'Nevsky Prospekt': 'What splendour does it lack, that fairest of our city thoroughfares? I know not one of the poorest clerks that live there would trade Nevsky Prospekt for all the blessings of the world.' And he describes the street's daily rhythm: the mornings, when 'Nevsky Prospekt is not the goal for any man, but simply the means of reaching it'; the hours from twelve to two, when 'tutors of all nationalities descend upon Nevsky Prospekt with their young charges in fine cambric collars'; the 'blessed period' between two and three, when 'everyone seems to be walking on Nevsky Prospekt'; three o'clock, when the avenue is like spring, so many government clerks in green uniforms are trying to look as if they had not been sitting in an office for the past six hours; and the hour after dusk when the street begins to stir, 'that mysterious time when the street lamps throw a marvellous alluring light upon everything' and the bachelors come out to peer under the ladies' bonnets, in search of adventures like those which befall the two protagonists of Gogol's story.

Today, at the far end of the avenue, in the monastery of Alexander Nevsky, which gives it its name, I heard bass voices sing the Orthodox funeral rite once again, after decades in which it was forbidden, but the street is seediness itself. Grubby windows in peeling buildings proclaim a pharmacy, an unhygienic-looking dairy or a *gastronom*, a grocery with only a few battered tins of Bulgarian jam or pickled gherkins on their shelves. These state enterprises seem half-empty and half-hearted, in contrast to the enthusiasm of the people selling vodka, bootlaces, newspapers or *matryoshka* dolls in makeshift kiosks or on the pavement.

As you pass the Moscow station, where Anna Karenina threw herself under the train at the climax of Tolstoy's novel, you are nearing the monumental centre. Here foreigners, and Russians with foreign currency, are thick enough on the pavements to keep foreign currency shops alive. The drabness recedes. The Nevsky shops may still be ill-stocked, but the pavements are crowded, and the House of Books, with its globe capping the roof, the offices of the Singer Sewing Machine Company before the Revolution, is crammed with buyers, especially for anything in English. I found my mind casting back to other descriptions in other times. I thought of the 'new city . . . forming in the air' dreamed of by the wretched clerk who is the hero of Dostoyevsky's first novel, *Poor Folk*: 'this whole world with all its inhabitants, strong and weak, with all their domiciles, the shelters of the poor or gilded mansions' which 'resembled at this twilight hour a fantastic magic vision'; that was the St Petersburg which Alexander Herzen likened to an army barracks: 'If you were to show an Englishman these battalions of tightly buttoned fops in identical frock-coats on the Nevsky Prospekt, he would think they were a squad of policemen.'[4] And in that same Nevsky of the nineteenth century a German visitor[5] saw policemen standing over the gangs of prostitutes they had rounded up to sweep the streets before the gentlefolk were awake.

In the heyday of the *fin de siècle*, and in the boom years just before 1914, the express trains thundered in from Paris in under two days, with the new fashions in socialism and hats. The International Wagon-Lits Company had its offices on the Nevsky, of course, where by 1911 there were no fewer than twenty-three cinemas.[6] If you didn't know Russian, you could speak French, English or German in Fabergé's shop on the Morskaya[7] and you could eat an Italian dinner at Privato's,[8] and smart society went in and out of the Nobles' Club and the Merchants' Club on the Nevsky. On the very eve of revolution, while the committee rooms 'buzzed and hummed all day and all night' in the Smolny Institute, and the heavy boots of soldiers and dark-smocked workers 'made an incessant thunder on the wooden floor'[9] where once princesses had danced the quadrille in silk pumps, John Reed, the American Communist, mingled with the crowds 'pouring in voluble tides up and down the Nevsky, fighting for the newspapers'.

Gambling clubs functioned hectically from dusk to dawn, with champagne flowing and stakes of 20,000 roubles. In the centre of the city at night prostitutes in jewels and expensive furs walked up and down, crowded the cafés . . . And in the rain, the bitter chill, the great throbbing city under grey skies rushing faster and faster towards – what?[10]

Towards many trials and many sorrows, which the Nevsky itself would not avoid. Anna Akhmatova, who had loved the city since her childhood, described it in the early 1920s:

All of the old St Petersburg signboards were still in their places, but there was nothing behind them except dust, gloom and yawning emptiness. Typhus, hunger, execution, darkness in the apartments, damp firewood, people swollen to unrecognizability. In the Gostiny Dvor [the eighteenth-century covered-market in the Nevksy Prospekt] one could collect a huge bouquet of field flowers. The famous Petersburg wooden pavements were rotting. The smell of chocolate still emanated from the basement of Kraft's. All the cemeteries had been vandalized. The city had not changed; it had simply changed into its opposite.[11]

Today the white and cream distemper is peeling from the arcades of the Gostiny Dvor, where one of Dostoyevsky's heroines haggled for a set of Pushkin's works.[12] The great library, which owns Voltaire's personal collection of 8,000 volumes, where half of Russia's great writers and scientists worked, and where Lenin himself researched his pamphlets, is badly in need of maintenance. But the Kazan Cathedral still stretches out the welcoming arms of its colonnade. There in 1877, on the day when Russia declared war on Turkey, Fyodor Dostoyevsky dashed in to join in prayer with the people. There, Alexander I and General Kutuzov, and incidentally also the future American president, John Quincy Adams,[13] who was the American minister in St Petersburg at the time, heard the *Te Deum* sung in thanksgiving after General Mud and General Snow had routed Napoleon and in so doing made Russia a Great Power.

Akhmatova lived for fifteen years in a tiny apartment in Fountain House,[14] the great baroque palace of the Sheremetevs, once the owners of no fewer than 300,000 serfs, on the Fontanka. This is the first of the man-made waterways, lined with palaces like Venetian canals, which curve away from the main stream of the Neva above the city centre to rejoin it further down. The Nevksy Prospekt crosses it on its dog-legged march into town at the Anichkov Bridge. Then, after the Gostiny Dvor, comes the second canal, the Griboyedova, which Dostoyevsky called 'the ditch' and which in his time was a stinking open sewer, and after that the Moyka. It was to his too-expensive flat at no. 12 Moyka, with its view of the back of the Winter Palace, that Alexander Pushkin was taken with a bullet in his stomach to die after he was shot in a duel

A NEW GRAND TOUR

defending his wife's honour. After loving, by his own account,[15] more than thirty women, many of them the wives of generals, high officials and even the wife of the minister of the interior whose secret police were following him, Pushkın was killed in a duel with his brother-in-law, a French officer, who had 'manifested his admiration for Mrs Pushkin to an extent that was completely inadmissible in the case of a married woman'. He also felt he had to give the lie to an anonymous flysheet which called him a cuckold; and the last twist in the tail of the story was that his wife is said to have promptly become the mistress of the emperor himself.

As you near the Neva, there are still blue signs to be seen, warning you to keep to the southern side of the street; it was safer from German shells during the great siege of 1941–4. (In 1949, during the 'Leningrad Affair', one of Stalin's purges, the city woke up to find workmen painting out these signs; they were restored in 1957 after Khrushchev's thaw!) The Nevsky Prospekt culminates in the most perfect of St Petersburg's great buildings, the Admiralty. Its gilt needle spire rises over the trees of a small park, topped by its weathervane, the golden ship that is the badge of the city. 'In the darkness of the green,' wrote the great poet Osip Mandelstam, who died in the *gulag* in 1938,

> a frigate or acropolis
> Shines from afar, a brother to the water and sky.
> Boat of the air, a touch-me-not for a mast,
> Serving as a yardstick for Peter's heirs
> It teaches; beauty is not the fancy of a demigod
> But the simple carpenter's predatory eye.[16]

In St Petersburg, you cannot get away from the tension between the demigod and the craftsman, or between Autocracy, massively stupid, deceptively cunning and ruthlessly cruel, and the intelligentsia. You can even argue that the intelligentsia as a class originated in St Petersburg. In Victorian England, intellectuals found opportunities in the City, in the Empire, in the universities and in Grub Street. In post-revolutionary France, they could earn their living in the service of the state and still feel free to say more or less what they wanted to say. But when a government allowed as little intellectual freedom as it did in Russia under the tsars, those who wanted to write, or to change Russia, had no choice but to band together, more or less conspiratorially. The autocracy sometimes reacted with surprising mildness, especially if the offenders came from the high nobility. It could also be petty, cruel, unrelenting. The Russian poet Yevgeny Yevtushenko has written that 'all Russian literature can be seen as the ordinary person's defence against the state's bronze hooves'.[17]

In any case, St Petersburg is the magnificent mausoleum of both Autocracy and intelligentsia. For, almost unnoticed by tsars and literati alike, another conflict was brewing among what were sometimes called 'the Dark People'. Rapid industrialization,[18] especially after 1905, brought capital in from western Europe to build engineering and textile factories on the 'Vyborg side' to the north of the city, where the Nobel company had its plant, and in the southern suburbs round the great Putilov heavy engineering and armaments works. Many of them were built by foreign capitalists: the Neva Thread company, for example, was owned by J. & P. Coats of Glasgow; Siemens of Berlin had a plant in the city; and the Neva Shipyards were largely owned by French interests.

Altogether in 1910, when the city's population was approaching two million, 238,000 worked in factories and construction, and another 51,000 in transport. The population increased by 39 per cent between 1890 and 1900 and by another 32 per cent between 1900 and 1910. The height of the boom, however, came in the years after 1910 and before the beginning of the war. Hundreds of thousands of workers were pulled in from the country, especially from the provinces of Yaroslav and Tver; in the three decades from Dostoyevsky's death in 1881 to 1910, more than two thirds of the inhabitants of the city were born elsewhere. Among these peasants-turned-workers, in the mills and foundries, fanned by professional revolutionaries, a new proletariat was forming. Once the failure of the imperial armies in Galicia, Poland and the Baltic

States had left the regime vulnerable and the people hungry, the last battle between tsar and people could begin. Revolution swept in from the grimy industrial neighbourhoods to the city of palaces until it reached the Winter Palace itself and rolled over the empire of Peter and Catherine as a wave on the beach idly destroys a sandcastle.

The achievements of the St Petersburg intelligentsia – poems, books, plays, ballets, operas – are imperishable. But the monuments of the autocracy are more visible. If you cross the Neva on the bridge between the Admiralty and the Hermitage, you come to a spit of land called the Strelka, 'the arrow', on the eastern tip of Vasilyevsky Island. It is decorated with two odd red columns, imitated from the 'rostral columns' of ancient Rome, with half-ships sticking out of their shafts; like the Bronze Horseman, the Strelka is a favourite place for wedding pictures, and for buskers, food vendors and even sometimes a man showing off a tame bear for the benefit of tourists, Russian and foreign. Turn your back to the pastel blue walls of what was once the world's most elegant stock exchange, and look to the north. Across an arm of the Neva steely with ice in winter, the slim golden spire of the church where all the Romanovs are buried, from Peter to the Grand-Duke Vladimir Kyrillovich, who died in Miami in 1992, rises above the low walls of the Peter and Paul Fortress, the very heart of the system Peter built: the woman who became the conservative novelist, Ayn Rand, worked there as a guide in 1918.

There, a short distance across the water, is the Trubetskoy Bastion. Inside is the casemate where Peter the Great was present when his own son, who rebelled against him, was tortured to death. Peter might want Russia to be opened to the liberal influences of the Enlightenment, but he was as cruel as his ancestor Ivan the Terrible, and when state criminals were to be executed, he sometimes wielded the axe himself. In 1825, on the same wall, the five ringleaders of the Decembrists, idealistic and aristocratic young mutineers, were publicly executed.[19] Nicholas I, the new tsar, whose accession they opposed, graciously spared them from being disembowelled and quartered, but insisted that they should be hanged. The nooses slipped, and the men fell from the gallows. One of them, Muravyev-Apostol, broke both his legs. 'Poor Russia,' he said, 'she cannot even hang people decently.' They took him back and hanged him all over again.

Look the other way from the Strelka, across the Neva, and you will see the crowning achievement of the same Autocracy: the gleaming green and white façade of the Winter Palace, now the home of the incomparable treasures of the Hermitage. It is an astonishing assembly: into it poured paintings, sculpture and furniture from all over Europe, including Sir Robert Walpole's collection from Houghton in Norfolk and whole palaces full of Dutch and French masterpieces from Berlin, Amsterdam and Paris. It was one of the duties of Russian ambassadors to the courts of Europe to swell what was, immense as it is, Catherine the Great's private museum. Most incongruous of all, the hoards of two pre-revolutionary Moscow millionaires, Morozov and Shchukin, found their way to the Hermitage too, so that this sanctum of tradition has the most extraordinary collection of the revolutionary art of the Impressionists and Post-Impressionists outside Paris: Cézanne, Degas, Monet, Derain, Picasso and the two great canvases by Matisse called *Music* and *Dance*, which epitomize the very spirit of modernism and free thought.

The whole city is a museum of the architecture of the Russian baroque, that theatrically opulent style made possible by the sheer wealth of the patrons, from the Romanovs on. It was brought to the highest pitch of elegance and grandeur by architects both Russian and imported. The names of the architects who built the Hermitage and the Winter Palace make the point: Bartolomeo Rastrelli and Giacomo Quarenghi, Yuri Felten and Vasily Stasov. Even more stunning in their grandeur and opulence are the summer palaces the tsars and tsarinas built for themselves in the suburbs. Peter the Great started Peterhof, known since 1944, when its ruins were recaptured from the Wehrmacht, by the Russian form of its name: Petrodvorets, with twenty palaces and a grand cascade intended to outdo Versailles. Oranienbaum, the orangery built for Peter by his favourite, the former pastry-cook Menshikov, was renamed Lomonosov under Stalin, after the greatest Russian scientist of the eighteenth century. Tsarskoye Selo – where Catherine the Great entertained her fourteen official and countless unofficial lovers, and which the last tsar and his family left for Siberia and death – was renamed Pushkin. It is Russian baroque to perfection: a riot of turquoise, gold and white outside, and inside long sequences of rooms richly decorated, including the famous amber room, most of which was looted by the Germans. Perhaps the most elegant of all is Pavlovsk, built by the Scots architect Charles Cameron in an exquisitely elegant blend of Adam and Palladio.

The Emperor Paul, who hated his mother Catherine and commissioned that lovely building in order not to live with her, was treacherously murdered in 1801 and succeeded by his son Alexander I. It was when Alexander died that the Decembrist conspirators took advantage of the confusion, hoping to overthrow Alexander's will, which left the throne to his son Nicholas, and to turn another brother, Constantine, into a constitutional monarch. The Decembrist soldiers were surrounded in Senate Square, the Bronze Horseman inside their hollow square, and their leaders taken off to be interrogated, first in the Winter Palace and then in the fortress.

Twenty-three years later, in 1849, a young reserve officer of engineers was taken in a closed carriage under escort of mounted Cossacks from the Peter and Paul Fortress, over the bridges, past the rostral columns to Semyonovky Square on the Fontanka Canal in the south of the city.[20] Only when a general began to read from a document did the young man and his friends realize that they had been sentenced to be shot immediately by a firing-squad. The general, who had been sadistically selected by the emperor himself because he had a stutter and would take longer to read out the sentences, droned on about 'criminal conversations . . . a felonious missive . . . impudent expressions against supreme authority and the Orthodox Church'. The first three convicts were dressed in white shrouds and tied to stakes. Suddenly an aide-de-camp galloped up with new orders. They were read, to a roll of drums. The death sentences had been commuted to terms of exile in chains and hard labour in Siberia. The whole sadistic comedy had been dreamed up by the emperor himself. The young engineer's crime was that of belonging to a circle of young intellectuals who had discussed political reform and the abolition of serfdom. His name was Fyodor Dostoyevsky.

The brutality of the tsarist system should not be exaggerated. The death penalty was abolished in 1763, except in cases of attempts on the life of the sovereign, though flogging was still permitted, and it was not unknown for men to be flogged to death with the knout. But by the 1820s, when liberal ideas were flooding in from Britain, Germany and France, many, perhaps most, educated Russians yearned for a constitutional monarchy at least, for parliamentary government and above all for the abolition of serfdom. To be educated, to be an '*intelligent*', almost invariably meant to be critical of Autocracy, to be more or less overtly alienated. In the first half of the eighteenth century, education was comparatively rare. Few but the children of landowners, officials or army officers received a thorough education, though a surprising number of the sons of priests became seminarists and later revolutionaries, Stalin himself among them. As a result, the disaffection of the intellectuals had about it something guilty, parricidal and sometimes ambiguous. Later in the century, as the repeated convulsions of revolution approached, proletarian revolutionaries and radical intellectuals from the lower middle classes made themselves heard – though it is often forgotten that Lenin himself was inscribed as Vladimir Ilyich Ulyanov in the book of the hereditary nobility. As the century wore on, indeed, there was among the *raznochintsy*, the 'other ranks' of the St Petersburg bureaucracy, a class of angry, half-educated clerks and impoverished students like Raskolnikov, the anti-hero of Dostoyevsky's *Crime and Punishment*, and many other characters in the novels of Gogol, Turgenev and Tolstoy. The heaviest blows against the autocratic, aristocratic system in nineteenth-century Russia were for the most part delivered by its own children. Dostoyevsky was technically a noble. His family, which originally came from the Lithuanian nobility, had sunk into the depressed ranks of the Uniate[21] clergy, but his father, having risen in the ranks of officialdom as an army doctor, was entitled to put Fyodor and his brother Mikhail down in the Moscow book of the hereditary nobility. Tolstoy was a great nobleman, scion of a family who owned tens of thousands of acres and hundreds of serfs, and Turgenev, too, was a big landowner.[22]

The life of the first great Russian writer, the man who can be said to have 'invented' literary Russian rather as Luther, three centuries earlier, invented High German, illustrates to perfection how disaffection spread from the very core of traditional Russian society. It also reveals how the Autocracy's strange style, compounded of ferocity tempered by unpredictable forgiveness and personal whim, contributed to the making of the bitter feud between the intellectuals and the empire. Alexander Pushkin's great-grandfather on his mother's side was unusual, in that he was an African slave called Hannibal. Captured by Turkish slavers, he was taken to Constantinople to be sold and was then freed and brought to Russia by a Russian ambassador. After serving in the French army he became a favourite of the tsar and married into the nobility. In the fourth generation, Pushkin had recognizably African facial traits and dark curly hair. On his father's side, Pushkin came from the highest nobility. Four of his ancestors signed the documents that elected the Romanovs to the throne.[23] Alexander was brought up in the Lycée, or Lyceum, attached to the imperial summer palace at Tsarskoye Selo. The boarders hated the Emperor Alexander I, because of the way he treated the empress, whom they admired; the emperor lived openly with his mistress. Pushkin was unpopular at the Lycée, but his talent was recognized; he wrote about 130 poems before he left school. When he graduated, into a job on the lowliest of the fourteen ranks into which Peter the Great had divided the imperial service, he lived in his parents' flat in the unfashionable suburb of Kolomna and threw himself into 'an uninterrupted round of Bacchanalian orgies'.[24] He was always passionately interested in women, starting with the headmaster's housekeeper at the Lycée, Maria Smith, and even as a schoolboy, when he danced with the serf actresses at Count Tolstoy's, 'his eyes blazed, he panted and snorted, like an ardent horse in the midst of a herd of young mares'. It seemed he was only interested in pleasure. 'The champagne, thank God,' he wrote to a friend soon after leaving the Lycée, 'is magnificent, the actresses likewise, the one gets drunk, the others get fucked, amen. That is how it should be!' Even this hedonistic young man, however, was soon a member of a literary society of army officers and gentleman-writers called the Green Lamp, whose members read aloud poems 'directed against the emperor and his government'. In the intervals between orgies he wrote an 'Ode to Liberty' which strongly implied that Alexander I had been involved in the murder of his own father, Paul I, because the assassins were not punished, but promoted. He also published an ostensibly innocuous poem, 'The Village', whose second half, not published in Russia until 1870, was an excoriating attack on the institution of serfdom. In 1820 the tsar personally ordered his rooms to be searched and told an acquaintance that he meant to exile Pushkin to Siberia. In the end he was exiled, first to the south, in the benevolent custody of a certain General Rayevsky, who had two pretty daughters, and then to his own family's estate, where his father agreed to inform on him to the secret police. In Bessarabia, newly conquered from the Turks, he was implicated in one of the two secret societies which were plotting the Decembrist uprising. All the while, in the intervals of amusing himself with love affairs with everyone from the wife of Count Vorontsov, the tsar's viceroy in the south, to a serf girl on his father's estate, including the wife of the minister of the interior, Pushkin was in constant trouble with the censor, with the secret police and with the emperor in person.

In September 1826 he was allowed to travel to Moscow and was taken straight to an interview with Nicholas I in the Kremlin. The tsar asked him if he would have taken part in the Decembrist rebellion. 'I most certainly would, sire,' he replied with characteristic bravado, and courage. 'All my friends were involved in the conspiracy, and I could not possibly have let them down.'[25] The tsar, who was never to forgive the Decembrists, was nevertheless convinced that Pushkin had no part in the uprising, and asked him why he did not publish more poetry. Pushkin complained of the censorship. Very well, said the tsar, I will be your censor, and on that extraordinary basis Pushkin was allowed to return to St Petersburg. It is revealing of the unanimity of anti-tsarist feeling in literary circles that the mere suspicion that even Pushkin, the most brilliant poet then writing, had done a deal with Autocracy was enough to destroy his reputation. Pushkin married, disastrously. Each summer he retired to his little estate at Boldino and wrote a stream of masterpieces – in 1832 four plays, including *Mozart and Salieri* and the last cantos of *Eugene Onegin*, and in 1833 'The Tale of the Fisherman and the Fish' and the story 'The Queen of Spades', which Tchaikovsky was to turn into a haunting opera.

When he was in St Petersburg, he took to hanging around Smirdin's bookshop, where the younger writers were to be found. One of them was Gogol, a neurotic young genius, newly arrived from the Ukraine, with an obsession about his comically big nose and a martyr to haemorrhoids. Pushkin gave him the idea for his great novel, *Dead Souls*, and also for his play, 'The Government Inspector'. By then Pushkin was writing to his wife, with angry casualness, 'I'm not a cuckold, am I?' If he was, his wife may have been unfaithful, not only with the vain young Frenchman D'Anthès, but also with the emperor himself, and though the emperor would not pass his poetry for publication, he did lend Pushkin 20,000 roubles, and he did make him a junior gentleman of the bedchamber, to keep his lovely wife Natalia near at hand. By this time Pushkin was humiliated, angry and desperate. No less an observer than Ivan Turgenev caught a glimpse of him at a Philharmonic Society concert. He was leaning against the door, and when he caught Turgenev's eye he shrugged 'as though with vexation' and walked away. A few days later he rode out along Stone Island Prospekt to fight D'Anthès and came back a dead man.

Gogol was not the only writer to carry on the flame Pushkin had lit. Mikhail Lermontov was a Guards officer, one of the tsar's military family.[26] He had never met Pushkin. Yet he was so outraged at the manipulations that had drawn the great poet into the fatal trap that he dashed off an angry poem, 'Death of a Poet'. After he had heard the details of the affair from the court doctor, who had treated the dying Pushkin, he added sixteen lines of savage diatribe against

> You, greedy crew that round the sceptre crawl,
> Butchers of freedom, genius and renown.

For good measure, he called them 'vile panderers of lewdness'. The lines raced from mouth to mouth, and it was not long before they came to the attention of the sovereign himself. Lermontov was exiled to the Caucasus, there to die in a duel as wasteful as and even more pointless than the one in which Pushkin got his fatal wound.

It was doubtful, it was said at the time, 'whether such a tremendous and universal impression had ever been created by verses in Russia'.[27] By the end of the 1830s, in fact, when Fyodor Dostoyevsky came to St Petersburg to attend the Engineers' School (in the sinister Mikhailovsky Palace, where Paul I was murdered), to be a writer, an intellectual, even within the officer corps and the highest aristocracy, meant as often as not to hate and despise the very Autocracy which officers, landowners and officials were expected to serve.

When Pushkin died, his reputation was tarnished by his association with authority. But within a very few years Vissarion Belinsky, who was until his death in 1848 the most influential of all St Petersburg's nineteenth-century critics, claimed for Pushkin the place he has never lost as Russia's greatest poet. Belinsky's circle of friends included Turgenev, other gifted novelists such as Nekrasov and Goncharov, the author of *Oblomov*, the celebrated satire on the idleness of the landed aristocracy, and – until they quarrelled – Dostoyevsky himself. Later, after his return from exile in Siberia, Dostoyevsky was to turn, like Gogol before him, into an arch-reactionary. His *Diary of a Writer* is openly anti-Semitic. He became the scourge of socialists. And in his prodigious fable of the Grand Inquisitor in *The Brothers Karamazov* he took the side of the Church, the side of order, even against Christ himself. But the young Dostoyevsky was a radical. The crime for which a police informer reported him to the authorities and for which he was exiled was reading aloud, with passionate emphasis, Belinsky's 'Letter to Gogol', a philippic against the evil of serfdom. And his first novel, *Poor Folk*, is set in a cheap boarding-house where impoverished clerks struggle not only for a living but for some shreds of dignity in the cruel city, and the hack writer, Ratazyayev, churning out his thousands of words a day, earns his crust by putting the other lodgers into his books. The hero, Makar Davush-kin, has come down in the world. Now he lives in a single room off the kitchen for twenty-four and a half roubles a day, and the backstairs are littered with eggshells and fish bladders: but once he courted an actress and mooned under her window; she lived on the third floor, where else but in the Nevsky Prospekt.

Dostoyevsky spent four years in chains in Siberia because the tsar in person refused a request by the provincial governor that his fetters should be struck off. Even after his term of strict confine-ment was over, he was obliged to remain in the east as a private soldier, and it was not until 1859 that he was allowed to return to St Petersburg. Still misfortunes showered on him. His wife died. So did his brother, the person who had been closest to him all his life. A magazine in which they had invested everything collapsed. There were mistresses, painful quarrels and eternal finan-cial problems, made worse by a crooked publisher who had bought up his promissory notes and used them to force the writer to hand over his copyrights.

He was also bullied into signing a contract for a new novel. It was *Crime and Punishment*. It is the story of the penniless student

Raskolnikov, who murders an old woman pawnbroker with an axe because he thinks that he, like Napoleon, is above the petty laws that govern common men. At one level it is a murder story; at another it is the story of Raskolnikov's redemption by the love of the prostitute Sonya. It is set in the district round the Haymarket,[28] now Ploshchad Mira, or Peace Square, on the south side of the city, near the central bus station. Dostoyevsky himself lived there both before his exile and in the 1860s. In *Crime and Punishment*, he painted from life

the crowds of people everywhere, the slaked lime everywhere, the scaffolding, the bricks, the dust and that distinctive summer aroma, so familiar to every inhabitant of St Petersburg who has not the means to rent a dacha in the country . . . the unbearable stench from the drinking dens . . . Next to the cookshops that occupied the lower floors of the Haymarket buildings, in the dirty and stinking courtyards, and most of all outside the drinking dens, there were jostling crowds of small manufacturers and rag-pickers of every sort.

Dostoyevsky himself knew the prostitutes and the drunks, smelled the smell of slaked lime and heard the song of the street singer with the hurdy-gurdy, who cut off her high note 'as if it had been cut with a knife'. Dostoyevsky had always written within a realist tradition, and now he put his characters in real buildings which are still standing. You can go and see for yourself the five-storey tenement which was Raskolnikov's house in Stolyarny Lane near the Haymarket. It is still standing, and so is the house of Alyona Ivanovna, the pawnbroker, just 730 steps away as Raskolnikov paced them out on his rehearsal of the murder. So is Sonya's house at no. 63, three storeys high, 'old and green-coloured', on the Griboyedov canal, then the Yekaterinsky canal.

In *Crime and Punishment* Dostoyevsky did for St Petersburg what Dickens had done for London and Balzac, Victor Hugo and Dostoyevsky's other early model, Eugène Sue, author of the *Mysteries of Paris*, had already done for Paris. (It was in his lifetime that St Petersburg replaced Paris as the capital of the revolutionary intelligentsia.) But he did more than that. He took the living city and transformed it into a symbol of man's alienation from God, as a representation of Hell.

Early in the nineteenth century the writer Nikolay Karamzin, a friend of Pushkin's uncle, already saw the city as a place of ill omen. He believed that it was tainted with original sin from the moment Tsar Peter decided to build his new capital on the marshy islands at the mouth of the Neva. 'The idea of establishing there the residence of our sovereigns was, is and will remain a pernicious one . . . Truly, Petersburg is founded on tears and corpses.' It is true that many thousands of those drafted to build the city – Russian serfs, Finnish peasants, Swedish prisoners of war – died in the process. It is also true that the city was always subject to devastating floods. There was a particularly severe one in November 1824. Hundreds of poor people who lived in basement flats were drowned when the Neva rose, and thousands more lost their homes. Alexander Pushkin, then in exile at his family estate of Mikhailovskoye, made a joke of it in a letter to his brother.[29] But the sheer scale of the disaster and its impact on the 'common people' made him change his tone. 'I cannot get this flood out of my mind,' he wrote to his brother. 'It is not as amusing as it seemed at first.' He asked him 'to help some unfortunate man' who was a victim of the flood with the money he had just been paid for the first cantos of *Eugene Onegin*. Eight years later he was to take that flood and make it the subject of the poem which has provided generations of later writers with their favourite symbol of the city and its ambiguous destiny, 'The Bronze Horseman'. He begins with his admiration for the city: 'I love thee, Peter's proud creation.' He recalls happy memories:

> And, at a bachelor's get-together
> The hiss and sparkle of iced champagne
> And punch bowls topped with bluish flame.[30]

He even says how much he loves the parades on the Champ de Mars when the tsar's young wife produces an heir or Russia celebrates a victory. He evokes the great flood when the river,

> like a beast for vengeance craving
> Enraged, upon the city fell . . .
> . . . a host of things comes drifting
> Logs, roofing, stalls, the wares of thrifty
> Tradesmen, a bridge and furniture,
> The prized possessions of the poor,
> Huts, coffins from a graveyard.[30]

But then he tells the story of Evgeny, the Little Man, who dreams that the bronze tsar on his bronze horse has leapt from his granite plinth and is chasing him through the streets. From that moment, it has been written, 'the dual image of the city, glittering and accursed, real and phantom, was established in Russian literature'.[31] At the end of the century Valery Bryusov modernized that image in the manner of the French Symbolist poets, transforming St Petersburg into a 'city of delirium'. He influenced a far greater poet, Aleksandr Blok, whose cycle of poems, *Gorod*, 'The City', was published between 1904 and 1908. Blok, too, took his inspiration from Pushkin's 'Bronze Horseman', but he portrayed St Petersburg as a 'night city' of 'drunken streets', not so much because of the cruelty of Autocracy, but because he saw it as a place of decadence and moral confusion.

In the eighteenth century, St Petersburg had been, like the Hollywood of the 1920s, a magnet for talent nurtured elsewhere. By the middle of the nineteenth century, it was producing talents that stood comparison with those thrown up by any other society on earth. The reign of Alexander II, from 1855 to 1881, exactly covers the ripest season of the Russian novel. It begins with the first of Turgenev's great novels, *Rudin*, published in 1856, and it covers Tolstoy's *War and Peace* and *Anna Karenina* and all four of Dostoyevsky's great novels, *Crime and Punishment*, *The Devils*, *The Idiot* and *The Brothers Karamazov*, not to mention other great achievements such as Goncharov's *Oblomov*, all, with the exception of Tolstoy, St Petersburg writers; and in *Anna Karenina* Tolstoy wrote what is, second only to *Crime and Punishment*, the archetypal

St Petersburg novel. At the same time, the four greatest Russian composers of the middle and late nineteenth century, Tchaikovsky, Borodin, Rimsky-Korsakov and Mussorgsky, lived and composed there. By the beginning of the twentieth century, St Petersburg was exporting books, ideas, fashions and talents, where once it had been a cultural importer from the West.

On 19 May 1919 Serge Diaghilev brought the Russian Ballet to Paris for the first time.[32] Although he had succeeded with the great Russian bass, Boris Chaliapin, singing *Boris Godunov* at the Opéra the previous year, the ballet had to be put on at first at the Châtelet Theatre, as the Opéra thought it was beneath its dignity. With a certain philistinism, Diaghilev had put together a season of tasters, ruthlessly eliminating anything that might bore a society audience. The very first night featured two ballets choreographed by Mikhail Fokine, *Le Pavillon d'Armide* and *Le Festin*, framing the Polovtsian dances from Borodin's *Prince Igor*. The second programme, on 2 June, consisted of *Les Sylphides*, choreographed by Fokine to arrangements of Chopin, with one act of Pushkin's *Ruslan and Ludmilla*, set to music by Glinka. Cleopatra, played by the stage-struck heiress Ida Rubinstein, was carried on to the stage horizontal, at head height, by a cortège of dancers, and wrapped in mummy cloths; these were then unwound to reveal the astonishing beauty of her body. A third offering included Rimsky-Korsakov's opera, renamed *Ivan the Terrible*, with Chaliapin.[33]

Diaghilev left nothing to chance, and the audience for that famous first night had been carefully chosen. It included half Proust's friends: the society poet Anna de Noailles; the Comtesse de Greffulhe, one of the origins of Proust's Madame de Guermantes; and Robert de Montesquiou, the model for the wicked Baron de Charlus; not to mention the composers Ravel, Fauré and Saint-Saëns, the sculptor Rodin and the dancer Isadora Duncan. But to make absolutely sure that the evening was a success, Diaghilev's local impresario, Gabriel d'Astruc, had given tickets to fifty beautiful actresses, half of them blonde, half brunette, and placed them alternately in the front row. The evening was one of the greatest sensations in the entire history of the theatre. The costumes, the designs, the colour, the quality of what seemed to Parisian palates barbaric opulence and the unmistakably explicit sexuality of the dancing took Paris by storm, though it has also been shrewdly suggested that what amazed Parisians was the higher production standards St Petersburg audiences were by now accustomed to. Whatever the reason, audiences and critics in Paris alike agreed with Serge Lifar, who said, 'There is no way to express the sacred flame, the frenzy with which the whole audience was seized.' That was 1909. In 1910 the mighty Opéra relented, and the Russian ballet danced on its august stage. That was the year of the first collaboration with a dazzlingly talented Russian of the new generation, Stravinsky, the year of his *Firebird* and Ravel's *Schéhérazade*. In 1911 there were seasons in London and Monte Carlo as well as Paris, with *Petrushka* added to the repertoire, then in 1912 *Daphnis et Chloë* to music by Ravel and *L'Après-midi d'un faune*, inspired by Mallarmé's poem and scored by Debussy, and in 1913 *Le Sacre du printemps*. Again the first-night audience was 'taken by surprise, excited to uproar' by the violent rhythmic drive of Stravinsky's music and the athletic energy of Nijinsky's dancing. The dancers, Nijinsky, Fokine, Pavlova and Ulanova became the early twentieth-century equivalent of superstars, and so did the designer Léon Bakst and above all Diaghilev himself. Here was St Petersburg bringing the avant-garde to Paris.

By 1914, with audiences in Paris and London lionizing their productions, and composers like Richard Strauss in Germany, as well as Ravel and Debussy in France, only too pleased to compose scores for them, the Russian Ballet and its creators had left St Petersburg behind and become one of the main currents of the modern movement, the common property of Europe and America. But the Russian Ballet in its beginnings was quintessential St Petersburg. Its opportunity came from the patronage of the imperial theatres, but the impulse came from the great conflict over the true role and destiny of Russian art set off by the publication of Chernishevsky's book, *The Relationship between Art and Reality*, which called for a revolutionary art in the service of the masses. 'It is time to create a Russian school,' he said.[34] This cause, too, got caught up in the rivalry between St Petersburg and Moscow, with a Moscow-based school of painters, the Peredvizhniki, or 'Wanderers', up in arms against the aestheticism of St Petersburg. They were nationalist, moralist, Slavophile and deeply didactic, and their star was the powerful painter Ilya Repin. The irony is that, though the Russian Ballet struck Western audiences as the epitome of oriental barbarism, it arose out of St Petersburg's preference for the culture of the West.

Son of an officer in the Chevaliers Gardes, Diaghilev was a dilettante. Even as a young man he wrote to his stepmother, with considerable self-knowledge, 'I am, firstly a charlatan, though rather a brilliant one, secondly a great charmer . . . I seem to have no real talent. Nevertheless I believe I have found my true voca-tion — to be a Maecenas. I have everything necessary except the money — but that will come.'[35] And so he flirted with music, organ-ized art exhibitions, founded a review, Mir Iskusstva, or 'World of Art', before he found his perfect métier as the ultimate impresario in the theatre. His friend the painter Alexandre Benois had been a balletomane all his life, but as so often happens, Diaghilev's great opportunity was reached only through great trouble. He was a homo-sexual. There was gossip. He was even presented with a powder puff. There was intrigue at court. Diaghilev gave as good as he got, and recovered enough to put on an epoch-making exhibition of two centuries of Russian portraits in the Tauride Palace, which Catherine the Great built for her lover, Count Grigory Potemkin, as his reward for conquering the Crimea — as well as for other more personal merits. But in the end he found it advisable to go to Paris, first to put on a Russian exhibition in the Grand Palais, then to bring Chaliapin to the Opéra and at last to stun the world with the total artistic experience of the Russian Ballet, in which dancing was blended with costumes, scenery, book and music to overwhelm all the senses at once.

While Diaghilev was conquering Paris and ultimately the world, a new burst of energy was exploding in the art which is least easily communicated across the barriers of culture and language: in poetry. In 1912 a café called the Stray Dog opened in St Petersburg. (It is still there, and indeed is being refurbished.) It had a basement with a small stage decorated by a leading set designer, Sergey Sudeykin. From this stage all the poets of the day used to read their work aloud.

There have been few gatherings of poetic talent to match those at the Stray Dog: Blok and Mayakovsky, Velimir Khlebnikov, Valery Bryusov and many others read from that tiny stage. So did Akhmatova and her first husband, Nikolay Gumilev, founder of the 'Acmeist' school of poets, arch-opponents of the Symbolists. Osip Mandelstam and Boris Pasternak were others who could be heard at the Stray Dog.

There is a painting of Akhmatova at twenty-five, painted just before the war by Nikolay Altman, which shows her at the height of her beauty. Her legs crossed, wearing a deep-scooped purple dress and a voluminous yellow scarf, she is half-smiling, under her proud, high-bridged nose, with mysterious, half-detached sensuality. On the last day of 1912 a banal tragedy took place there, which in retrospect came to seem to Akhmatova to be the beginning of the end of her happiness and of St Peterburg's, even the beginning of the end of a civilization.[36] One of Akhmatova's intimate friends was Olga Glebova, the wife of Sudeykin, the designer. A young officer of dragoons, who also wrote poetry, Vsevolod Knyazev, was in love with Olga. On New Year's Eve he shot himself on the staircase outside Olga's apartment after discovering that his rival for her love was none other than the great poet Aleksandr Blok.

As a young woman, Akhmatova had used the city as the background to her love poetry, 'the dark city on the terrible river', but also 'that city I have loved since childhood'. But she lived to be the poet of St Petersburg's long Calvary: of the Revolution, the Civil War, the Terror and the Blockade. She split up with her first husband, the poet Gumilev, in 1916. He was shot by the Bolsheviks in 1921. Apart from her personal feelings, this left her as a non-person; the Central Committee of the Communist Party itself decreed at one point that her work must not be published. She lived for a while with an Assyriologist and then with Nikolay Punin, who was arrested in 1935. Her intimate friends included the poet Osip Mandelstam, who was arrested in 1938 and died in a concentration camp in the Far East, and his widow, Nadezhda Mandelstam; and Lydia Chukovskaya, whose husband was also executed.

Worst of all, her only son, Lev, born just before the tragedy at the Stray Dog, was arrested in 1938 and sentenced to death for no other reason than that he was his father's and his mother's son, though the sentence was commuted to exile, when those who had sentenced him had been purged in their turn. It was then that Akhmatova wrote her *Requiem*. She recalls with surprise how little she would have thought, growing up as a happy, rebellious girl in Tsarskoye Selo that she would stand, three hundredth in the queue, with her food parcel, outside the Kresty prison. It is still there, just along the river bank on the Vyborg side from the Finland Station. It takes its name, Kresty, the Crosses, from its Victorian floor plan; but the name inescapably suggests the crucifixion that is the climax of Akhmatova's poem.

> Mary Magdalene smote her breast and wept,
> the disciple whom He loved turned to stone,
> but where the Mother stood in silence
> nobody even dared look.

Almost twenty years after the New Year's Eve tragedy at the Stray Dog, in 1940, Akhmatova took it as the theme of her greatest long poem, *Poem without a Hero*, and for more than twenty more years she worked at it, adding, rewriting, polishing, through the approach of war, the beginnings of the siege, and her exile in Tashkent, where she was evacuated in late 1941, and where she finished the first draft in 1942, 'seven thousand kilometres' away.

My city is still standing, but sewn up in a shroud
The tombstone lids are heavy
On its sleepless eyes.

★

Every day, long queues of tourists form outside the Impressionists section in the Hermitage. But when we visited the museum of the history of St Petersburg in its handsome palace, down the river, near the naval dockyard and the commercial port where Pushkin saw 'ships swarm from all earth's ends', we were alone. Elderly women dropped their paperbacks to take our tickets and switch the lights on for us. The museum is dedicated to the history of the city since the cruiser *Aurora*, still moored near by with its four funnels, fired its blank signal round and the Red Guards moved out of the factories in the southern suburbs and closed in, almost without a shot, on the provisional government, nervously watching behind the great windows of the Winter Palace. The story is told with maps that light up to show the path of the conquering proletarians, though to tell the truth it was more a *coup d'état* than a revolution that day, with less violence than many a modern metropolis experiences over a warm weekend. There is a fine collection of the bold, unquestioning poster art of the day, beefy proletarians, cringing capitalists, red sunbursts and everywhere the jutting chin of an idealized Lenin.

Heroic though their vision of the future was, those artists can hardly have imagined the cold agony of the city's crucifixion in the nine hundred days of the siege and blockade. First the heat went off, then the light, then the water. People could only stay alive by melting snow. A survivor, Lydia Ginzburg, remembers the small miseries of surviving.

The typical day started with a visit to the kitchen or the service staircase, where firewood had to be prepared for the temporary stove. Night was only just starting to disperse, and the walls of the building opposite did not yet carry even a hint of their yellow colour; they loomed darkly through the broken glass of the staircase window.

So one had to work by touch, driving the axe at an angle to the wood, and then striking. Hands were the greatest problem. Fingers tended to close and remain in some chance position. The hand lost its ability to grasp. It could only be used as a paw, a stump or a stick-like tool.[37]

Recollected in tranquillity, even that horrifying account has an almost chirpy sound, like memories of the London Blitz. The reality was infinitely more terrible.[38] The German ring closed tight round the city, and the only lifeline was over the frozen Lake Ladoga; all supplies had to be trucked in that way. The first priority went to ammunition. Within weeks, there was widespread hunger, then starvation. People ate horses, dogs – all but five of the city's police dogs were eaten – rats, mice. Akhmatova was fiercely attacked after the war because, in a poem written from Tashkent, she imagined the pigeons in St Isaac's Square. In reality there were no pigeons; they had all been eaten.[39]

In March 1943 the writer Pavel Kuknitsky, a friend of Akhmatova who had become a war correspondent, returned to the city. As he entered his street, a woman walked towards him in the dusk, chanting, 'Death! Death! Death!' As she came nearer, with staring eyes, he heard her say, 'Death by starvation will take us all. The soldiers will live a little longer. But we will die. We will die. We will die.'[40] The Communists boasted of having cleared up the haunts of criminals around the Haymarket. But by the winter of 1941, it was once again the liveliest place in the city. It was a market where anything could be bought, not for money, but for bread or for vodka. Everything was for sale, including 'Badayev earth' – ordinary soil from bombed warehouses which had been soaked in molten sugar. And it was in the stalls and the side streets around the Haymarket that the cannibals appeared, and even more repulsive human fauna, the traders who dealt in human flesh, not out of hunger, but for profit. Dmitri and Tamara,[41] two young friends of the writer Anatoly Darov, went to spend their bread ration in the Haymarket to buy a pair of warm felt boots. Dmitri was lured to a flat near by a giant of a man who called out as he rang the doorbell, 'I've got a live one here!' Through the door, Dmitri saw parts of human bodies hanging from hooks, including a human hand. He managed to escape down the stairs, found armed soldiers, and ran back to the flat. They burst in and found 'hocks' from five human bodies hanging there.

Official estimates said for a long time that 632,253 died of hunger in the city and that another 16,000 were killed by shells and bombs. A distinguished American journalist, Harrison Salisbury, after reviewing all the evidence and various estimates, calculates coolly that 'a total for Leningrad and vicinity of something over a million deaths attributable to hunger, and an overall total of deaths, civilian and military, in the order of 1,300,000 to 1,500,000, seems reasonable'.[42] More people died in the Leningrad blockade than ever died in any other modern city: ten times as many, for example, as died in Hiroshima.

The suffering was almost a presence in the chilly rooms as we stumped round them, thinking of that far greater cold. The old ladies knitting in the cloakroom and in the corners of the gallery must have been there as children, must remember what it was like. They must have survived. They must have been much the same age as Tatiana Savicheva, whose diary is preserved in a glass case. It records in a childish scrawl the death first of granny, then of Uncle Alyosha, then mummy. It ends 'Everyone's dead, only Tanya's left.' But unlike the ladies in the museum, Tanya did not survive. Perhaps her body was dragged across the ice, like the child in a photograph blown up in the exhibition, wrapped in a shroud, on a toboggan like the ones children were playing with in the snow outside.

The punishment dealt to St Petersburg/Leningrad in the Revolution, the purges and the blockade was appalling; and there are those who say that St Petersburg has never recovered from it, that it will never again rival Moscow as a cultural or political capital. There are others, though, who believe that as Russia looks for economic and political salvation, it can only look westwards, and that, as it does, St Petersburg must come into its lost inheritance again, not as the capital of the Russian state, but as its umbilical cord and its heart and brain. Certainly no other city burns with the same emotional intensity under its shabby–elegant exterior. No other city exhibits in itself, like this abandoned capital at the very edge of Europe, the same ambiguity, the same contrast between the nobility and the cruelty, the splendours and the miseries, that are the heritage of the European past.

CHAPTER V
SECESSION

IN 1908 A RELATIVELY OBSCURE ARTIST
called Theo Zasche[1] painted the *Korso*, the regular afternoon
parade at the Sirkecke, the corner of the Ringstrasse, outside the
Bristol Hotel and across the Kärntnerstrasse from the Opera in
Vienna. That was the place where the famous and the fashionable,
the social and the demi-reputable, all gathered between five and
seven to see and be seen. It is a crowded and animated scene.
Confident gentlemen in silk hats salute elegant ladies in fashionable
gowns and audacious millinery. Among them, the artist has painted
in real people. Some of them, however famous in their own day,
can no longer be recognized. But there, near the foreground on
the right, is Gustav Mahler, who has just returned from New
York. You would not guess from the picture that he was shattered
by losing his job as director of the Opera, by the death of a child
and by the knowledge that he had heart disease. Nor would you
know that in that year he completed *Das Lied von der Erde*, his

'Song of the Earth', and among all his masterpieces perhaps the most personal. And there, with a neat white beard, next to that new-fangled contraption, an automobile, is no less a personality of turn-of-the-century Vienna than Otto Wagner, the city's best-known architect: from his dapper appearance you would not guess that he had thrown in his lot, in his sixties, with the artistic revolutionaries of Young Vienna.

It is an unforgettable snapshot of a city, a culture, a whole civilization, at its zenith, but also at a poignant moment when the seeds of its destruction were already ripening. At that moment, Richard Strauss and Hugo von Hofmannsthal were exchanging letters about what was to become *Rosenkavalier*, their exquisite evocation of baroque Vienna, which was at the same time the subtlest psychological portrait of a woman who is facing the end of love. Ten years later, at the end of a war for which the government of Austria–Hungary must bear a large share of the responsibility, Vienna ceased to be the refulgent capital of an empire of 50 million people and became a backwater, the still pleasant but undeniably disproportionate head of a mountain republic of 6 million, a third of whom lived in its capital city. And at the very time when Zasche's watercolour captured the confident strollers in the Ringstrasse, the young Adolf Hitler was ranging the city like a hungry wolf. He was spending his way through his father's inheritance, day-dreaming of building palaces even more grandiose than those that lined the Ringstrasse, and listening more than thirty times to the *Liebestod* of Wagner's *Tristan und Isolde* at the very opera-house we can see in the background of Zasche's scene. That autumn, rejected a second time by the Academy of Art, he began his descent into the angry depths, copying picture postcards in the home for men in the Meldemannstrasse in the Twentieth District, and reading the obscene and bloodthirsty anti-Semitic fantasies of the defrocked monk, Jörg Lanz von Liebenfels, amid the 'garbage, repulsive filth' he would remember when he came to write *Mein Kampf*.[2] That, too, it should not be forgotten, was Vienna in the 1900s. Thirty years later Hitler had his revenge.

Three hundred thousand Viennese thronged the Heldenplatz in front of the Hofburg to greet his return to their city as its conqueror.

In 1908 the government of Vienna had been for over a decade in the hands of the energetic and creative but cynically anti-Semitic mayor, Karl Lueger.[3] His taking up office was delayed for two years after he first won control of the city council because of the emperor's reluctance to confirm his appointment. But in 1897 Franz Joseph, who had nothing but contempt for anti-Semitism personally, gave in and allowed Lueger to become mayor. His appointment, though delayed, was one more sign of the end of the thirty years of liberalism in which Viennese Jews had contributed so much to what has been called 'our century's nearest approach to the Athens of Pericles or the Florence of the Medici'.[4]

Many years later, after the catastrophe, recalling the mood of his youth from his exile in Switzerland, the Austrian novelist Robert Musil wrote that 'out of the oil-smooth spirit of the last two decades of the nineteenth century, suddenly throughout Europe there arose a kindling fever. Nobody knew exactly what was on the way; nobody was able to say whether it was to be a new art, a New Man, a new morality or perhaps a reshuffling of society.'[5] In the event, it was to be a bit of all of those. But Musil's recollection was at fault in one respect. As we shall see, the 'kindling fever' of change was already visible before the turn of the century. It will be worth going back in a while to look in more detail at why the liberal experiment collapsed. For the moment, the point is not just that in the first decade of this century Vienna was at its zenith as a centre of culture and creativity, but also that in the new climate of the turn of the century many of the most gifted of Vienna's creators turned inwards. It was as if they despaired of the liberal, bourgeois society that had built the Ringstrasse and the Opera, and had created the cultivated society that thronged around the nodal points of the city's life. Certainly they despaired of politics, in which as a matter of fact they had never been much interested:

the poet Hugo von Hofmannsthal once noted in his diary, with surprise, that he and a friend had talked politics the previous evening. What happened was that, despairing of the search for the public good, they looked for inner satisfaction, in art, in love and in dreams.

That turning inward took place in two more or less distinct stages. In the first stage, for example, the painter Gustav Klimt abandoned his great public commissions, like his murals in the Burgtheater, and began to paint his lusciously sensuous images of women, sometimes portraits of real women he knew, sometimes expressions of allegorical fantasy. In a later stage, under Klimt's friendly eye, wilder young painters like Egon Schiele and Oskar Kokoschka explored a second dimension of modernism, each in his own way. Similarly, towards the end of the century, musicians such as Mahler, Bruckner and Hugo Wolf consciously departed from the direct line of the Viennese classical succession which runs back unbroken through Schumann and Schubert to Beethoven, Mozart and Father Haydn, and which ended when Brahms died, in Vienna, in 1897. Then, in the early years of the century, a second generation, led by Arnold Schoenberg, broke far more radically with the whole tradition of Western music, which Mahler inhabited as much as Brahms or Beethoven, and ventured into dangerous emotional waters in the artistic exploration of sensation and experience. In 1908 Schoenberg, who was working on his revolutionary *Theory of Harmony*, to be published three years later, finished his song cycle, *The Book of the Hanging Gardens*, the work in which he rejected conventional tonality and achieved what he called 'the emancipation of dissonance'.[6]

In architecture and design, as in painting, modernism arrived in Vienna in two waves. First there was the appearance of the modern style in the hands of Otto Wagner, the best-known architect of his day, who moved away from what can be called a 'historical' style in the 1890s and began to experiment first with the flowing, uncorseted decoration of art nouveau and then with new materials and a plain, modular style that was the herald of the modern movement. Only in a second wave, in the hands of architects such as Adolf Loos, Josef Hoffmann and Joseph Olbrich, and of designers such as Kolo Moser and the Wiener Werkstätte did this sparer, modern style finally emerge. In 1908, as it happens, the Werkstätte received the accolade of imperial respectability; in that year one of its founders, Kolo Moser, designed the official postage stamps to commemorate the sixtieth anniversary of Franz Joseph's reign![7]

The 1890s was a time of turmoil everywhere and in many respects. Socialism, anarchism, industrial and nationalist unrest, from Chicago to St Petersburg by way of Dublin, expressed the impatience of those excluded from the high table of Victorian prosperity; and these political movements were echoed by troubling movements of rebellion against the accepted canons in literature, art and every department of thought. In the United States and elsewhere, this was a time of economic depression. In France, the decade was dominated by the Dreyfus affair, which revealed the deep cleavage concealed by the 'beautiful epoch' of the Third Republic. One of Vienna's most brilliant young journalists, Theodor Herzl, was the Paris correspondent of the *Neue Freie Presse*, the house organ, so to speak, of the cultivated and assimilated Viennese Jewish bourgeoisie. He saw Dreyfus condemned, as he believed from the start, unjustly. And he heard crowds, in that French Republic, which had always seemed the home of the liberal spirit, not least to Austrians and to Jews, screaming, '*À mort les juifs!*' 'In Republican, modern, civilized France,' he told a friend, 'one hundred years after the Declaration of the Rights of Man . . . the edict of the Great Revolution has been revoked.'[8] Herzl, the very model of the successful, assimilated Jew, drew from what he had seen and heard conclusions that were profoundly shocking, not least to his colleagues on the newspaper, assimilated Jews themselves,[9] and expressed them in his pamphlet, *Der Judenstaat*.[10] He became the founder of the Zionist movement. The first Zionist congress met in Basel in 1897.

In that same year, a group of artists, already calling themselves

Jung Wien, 'Young Vienna', left the traditional academy and held the first exhibition in the new style. Now they called themselves 'The Secession', and the name will do for much of the ferment of activity in Vienna in the last years of the old century and the first years of the new. It was in those same years around the turn of the century that Gustav Klimt evolved from a conventional, even dull painter into one of the most dazzling of colourists, the supreme explorer of sensuality, and a psychological investigator who took his rebellion against all forms of convention to the brink of personal psychological crisis.

The first Secession show was publicized by a poster by Klimt, depicting Theseus slaying the Minotaur, the monster who guarded the prison surrounded by the labyrinth. The painters, like the writers, of the *fin de siècle* were fascinated by classical myths and motifs; not for the first time in European cultural history, people were finding it easier to say new things in the language of the old. The next year, the Secession was able to move into the small, elegant gallery, purpose-designed for them by Olbrich, which still stands in the Friedrichstrasse, near the Karlsplatz and the heart of the city. It has an openwork dome of gilded floral tracery, which the Viennese, with their usual facility for nicknames, quickly called 'the golden cabbage'. In the basement, newly restored, you can see Klimt's masterpiece, the *Beethoven Frieze*, which he painted as an accompaniment to a statue of the composer in 1902. It concludes with a couple wrapped in a standing embrace, captioned with a quotation from Schiller's 'Ode to Joy', which Beethoven set to music in his Ninth Symphony: 'This kiss to all the world'. The Secession took as its motto the Latin *nuda veritas*, naked truth, a concept Klimt embodied in one of his most sumptuous nudes; and in German, *Wahrheit ist Feuer und Wahrheit reden heisst leuchten und brennen*: 'Truth is Fire and to speak the Truth is to light and to burn.'

That same new spirit was found in literature. Where the writers of the nineteenth century were concerned with the public and the external, and with morality, the writers of the 1890s − for example, the novelist and playwright Arthur Schnitzler, the poet, dramatist and opera librettist Hugo von Hofmannsthal, the journalist Karl Kraus – were more interested in psychological truth and freedom, especially sexual freedom. Schnitzler is best known outside Austria for his novel *Der Reigen*, or rather for the Max Ophüls film *La Ronde* based on it. His greatest novel, *Der Weg ins Freie*, 'The Way into the Open', is a study of the many responses of Jews of every kind, from wealthy bankers to struggling intellectuals, to the rise of anti-Semitism. It is pervaded by the sense that, for all these people, there is no 'way into the open'. If the public ambitions of the liberal era with its hopes of social progress are not to be fulfilled, then all that is left is art and self-knowledge. As one of the characters in Schnitzler's novel says, 'the only thing that matters is always how deep we can look into ourselves'.

That summer Count Franz Thun, a cultivated grandee with vast estates in Bohemia, took over the increasingly hopeless task of trying to hold the German-speaking lands[11] of the Austrian Empire together as minister-president. As the count was leaving the West Station to meet the emperor at Bad Ischl, a researcher from the university, not yet, to his bitter disappointment, a professor, was also leaving the West Station, taking his children on holiday.[12] It was Sigmund Freud, and that night he dreamed about Count Thun what he came to call 'the revolutionary dream'. (Characteristically for a Viennese, his revolutionary feelings took the form, in the dream, of humming Figaro's aria from *The Marriage of Figaro*, '*Se vuol ballare, signor contino*'.[13] Two years before Freud had dreamed the first of the dreams he analysed according to his new method; it was the one he came to call 'Irma's injection'.[14] Turning aside from his earlier work on cocaine and then on hysteria, he began his path-breaking explorations into personality. In 1896 he first used the term 'psychoanalysis'. In 1897 he first analysed himself, and the year after he saw Count Thun at the station he sent off to the printer what he already knew was the most profound, the most revolutionary book he would write, *On the Interpretation of Dreams*.[15] He tacked on to it as an epigram a phrase from Virgil which had been drawn to his attention because the Prussian socialist Ferdinand Lasalle used it in a book Freud took on holiday that year:

> *Flectere si nequeo superos, Acheronta movebo.*

> If I cannot bend the Gods above to my will,
> Then I will move the Underworld.[16]

It is a good motto, not only for Freud's own work, but for the whole inward-looking mood of Vienna at the turn of the century.

In the 1890s Otto Wagner, who was born in 1841, was at the height of his activity. In style, he was moving away from the *Ringstrassenstil*, the 'Ringstrasse style', as the Viennese call the Victorian historicism of the confident years of liberal ascendancy, when the Ringstrasse was being lined with palatial town houses. The art historian Egon Friedell described the Viennese interiors that made the Secession a necessity: 'These were not living-rooms but pawnshops and curiosity shops ... In the boudoir a set of Buhl, in the drawing-room an Empire suite, next door a Cinquecento dining-room and next to that a Gothic bedroom ... all purely for show.'[17]

No doubt it was revulsion against that kind of over-stuffed Victorian taste that turned Wagner towards the art nouveau charm of houses like the 'majolica house' or his own palace (later the Yugoslav Embassy) in the Rennweg. But Wagner was not just an architect in the conventional sense. He was also an entrepreneur, a property developer, and heavily involved in two vast new public works projects. He sat on the advisory committee for the Danube Regulation Commission and designed a lock and a lock house for the Danube Canal. He was also the chief designer for the Stadtbahn, the new suburban railway, and to this day you see the sun motif he chose on the wrought ironwork of bridges and embankments. He also built thirty-six stations for the new railway, and out of the

budget he contrived to scrape together the money for an idea of
his own: a private court station for the emperor and his family at
the gates of Schönbrunn. It is a jewel of a building, recently
restored: white, green and gold on the outside, and opulently
panelled and furnished for the imperial family inside. In the
octagonal waiting-room, with its sumptuous red and pink carpet
and wallpapers both patterned with giant cheeseplant leaves, between the numerous mirrors with which the emperor could check
his impeccable uniform, there is an unusual view of the city of
Vienna by the painter Carl Ott.

It is literally a bird's-eye view, for Ott painted it from a
Montgolfier balloon tethered over the Gloriette, a baroque folly
on the hill behind Schönbrunn palace. There is the city spread out,
from the crests of the Vienna Woods in the west, down through
the vineyards to the suburbs, past the Ring to the Old City, with
the mighty spire of St Stephen's as the boss on the shield, and out
past the Prater and the great river to the Hungarian plain. But in
the foreground the painter has placed two great eagles as a reminder
of the very reason for Vienna's being: the double eagle of the
Habsburgs.

There was a trading post, Vindobona, on this site in Roman
times, and a bigger Roman settlement at Carnuntum, halfway to
Bratislava some twenty miles away. This is, after all, the intersection of two important trading routes, the old amber road from
north Germany to Italy, and the Danube itself. But it was the
Habsburgs who made Vienna: to use a term for which there is no
exact equivalent in English, it was their *Residenzstadt*, the town
that grew up around their palace, and by the seventeenth century
the long-range trade routes had dried up or moved elsewhere. The
Altstadt, the inner city behind the great walls, was the most
crowded urban area in Europe, which is why people there split
single-family houses up into flats as early as the sixteenth century
and began to build blocks of flats for the purpose by the eighteenth
century, earlier than anywhere else. Rents were fiercely expensive,
which is why there are so many Mozart houses and Beethoven

houses to be seen: composers, like other Viennese, moved house whenever they couldn't afford the rent. The city lived off the court, and off the great landowners whose baroque palaces lined the Herrengasse.

Vienna's other function was as a fortress. In a sense it was *the* fortress of Europe, for it stood at the very edge of Christendom, and guarded it for centuries against its most dangerous enemy, the Turk. Twice, in 1529 and again in 1683, Turkish armies besieged the city closely. In 1683 the garrison's heroic commander, Count Ernst Rüdiger von Starhemberg, directed operations and signalled to the relieving army under Jan Sobiesky, King of Poland, from the tower of the cathedral. For many centuries, Hungary was part of the Turkish domains, and as late as the early eighteenth century Prince Eugene of Savoy thought it worth building new, outer walls, the so-called 'line walls', on the line where the *Gürtel* parkway and the city railway now run, to keep out Hungarian raiders, and in case the Turks should ever come back. They never have. But they have left Vienna with a psychological and a physical residue. The psychological trace is that of having been for centuries a frontier town, a city that is German, yet not in Germany, capital for the many peoples of eastern Europe, and for a minority only of German speakers. The physical trace is the irregular horseshoe shape of the old fortifications.

Inside them was, and is, the city: aristocratic, expensive, luxurious and pleasure-loving, centred on cathedral and court. Outside are two rings of suburbs: the *Vorstädte*, or inner suburbs, and the *Vororte*, beyond the 'line walls'. For centuries, the social geography of Vienna has been simple. The closer to St Stephen's, the better. There are distinctions even within the inner city itself. The princely town houses cluster most thickly along the Herrengasse, 'the Street of Lords', and between it and the palace. The smartest shops are still on that side of the town. Over on the other side is the Danube Canal, which is really the canalization of what was originally one of several streams that the Danube is divided into at this point in its course. (That is the explanation of the fact, which surprises and disappoints visitors at first, that, unlike its twin Habsburg capital Budapest, Vienna is not 'on' the Danube.) Near the canal lies the ancient Jewish ghetto and a Greek district and what is now a pleasant neighbourhood of restaurants and nightspots round the Ruperts-platz, known locally, perhaps rather hopefully, as the 'Bermuda triangle'.

The Habsburgs succeeded the Babenbergs as dukes of Austria in 1282,[18] but at first they did not single out Vienna among their vast domains – there are the arms of more than twenty Habsburg provinces, great slices of Europe like Flanders, Burgundy and Bohemia among them, in the armoury in the Hofburg. It was not until after the first Turkish siege that Charles V, the wealthiest heir in the whole history of Europe, preoccupied with the affairs of Spain, of the Low Countries aflame with Protestantism and rebellion, with Italy and the Indies, sent his brother, the Archduke Ferdinand, to administer his Austrian domains, which included the kingdoms of Hungary and Bohemia. And it was not until Charles retired to a monastery in 1547 and Ferdinand succeeded him as Holy Roman Emperor, that a Habsburg emperor was firmly settled in Vienna, as was to be the case (including Maria Theresa, the only woman to sit on the throne) until 1918.

Ferdinand was a Catholic, and a Spanish Catholic at that, and he came from Spain at the time when the Inquisition was putting down heresy with a ferociously heavy hand. He was also a dynast who had taken part in the equally savage repression of the *comuneros*, the Spanish townsmen who had dared to rebel against the House of Habsburg. It is hard to believe now, but when Ferdinand entered Vienna in 1527, it was a Protestant city. Not only that, it was a city ruled by Protestant merchants. All classes were predominantly Protestant – perhaps four fifths of the city's population – particularly the wealthier and more powerful citizens. Ferdinand visited upon the heretics the full force of the Inquisition and, later, of the Counter-Reformation. The Jesuits arrived at his invitation in 1551. From the start, terror was reinforced by subtler pressures. It was illegal after 1527 for Protestants to be witnesses in court, to establish a business, to enter into an inheritance or to make a will. One Viennese writer[19] records a tiny trace of the savage religious conflict, surviving in Viennese nurseries into this century. Staunch Viennese Catholics would say to their children, when threatening them with dire punishment, 'I'll make you a Catholic!' It took a century, but the Habsburgs were utterly victorious in the end. By the 1620s, they felt strong enough to insist that every Viennese must become a Catholic or emigrate, and the last lingering remnants of what had once been a Protestant population left for less frightening cities. In the process, the Habsburgs had also transformed the city socially and economically: from a thriving, independent city, growing wealthy through trade and craft manufactures and ruled by a Protestant merchant oligarchy, into a *Residenzstadt* utterly controlled by the imperial court, the imperial bureaucracy and the great territorial aristocrats, Liechtensteins and Schwarzenbergs and Esterházys, whose estates might be in Hungary or Poland or Bohemia, but who lived and spent their princely revenues in Vienna.

Thus the Vienna of the baroque, the city of churches and palaces, celebrating in luxuriant plaster and marble and in even more luxuriant music the glory of God and of his representatives on earth, the House of Austria, stands on the ruins of an older, Lutheran culture, which has disappeared without trace. Or rather it has left behind only displaced, hidden traces of forgotten suffering, not altogether unlike those repressed experiences which Sigmund Freud hunted in the lower depths of his patients' subconscious.

It is even arguable that the forgotten Protestantism of the Viennese, and the long and painful struggle for their religious allegiance, may have contributed two traits to that indefinable but unmistakable amalgam, the 'Viennese character'. The triumph of the Habsburgs and the Counter-Reformation certainly seems to have endowed the Viennese with an enduring love of pleasure, ceremony, beauty, art and – especially – music.

Servants of a glorious but selfish and ruthless court, the Viennese acquired over the centuries Figaro's sly contempt for his masters. Ilsa Barea, whose long years of exile gave her a shrewd insight into the faults as well as the glories of her native city, says this distrust of authority amounted almost to anarchism. 'Behind it,' she adds,

lay not only the experiences of three or four generations with a succession of lip-servers, turncoats and spurious converts, but the much older legacy of the border fortress: a familiarity with civic muddle, military blunders, weakness of rulers, with camp-followers and racketeers, half-victories, half-defeats and with the willy-nilly toughness of those not important enough, rich enough or lucky enough to get away from dangers.[20]

A century earlier, the most famous of Austria's classic playwrights, Franz Grillparzer, put a startlingly similar thought into the mouth of one of his Habsburg characters:

> Das ist der Fluch von unserm edlen Haus:
> Auf halben Wegen und zu halber Tat
> Mit halben Mitteln zauderhaft zu streben.

(This is the curse of our noble House: to be stuck, half-hearted, halfway, half-done, with half what's needed.)

The modern history of Vienna begins with the imperial edict, signed on Christmas Eve 1857, permitting for the first time building on the glacis, the space cleared for artillery in front of the fortifications.[21] Ironically, just because Vienna had waited longer than any other major European city to get rid of its medieval fortifications, it now found itself with a unique opportunity to join the old city and its suburbs with a memorable architectural statement. Liberal Vienna, in the optimistic atmosphere of the boom produced by capitalism and the railways after the abortive revolution of 1848, reacted with energy. In 1865 the Ringstrasse itself, the magnificent avenue that followed the outline of the walls, was officially opened by the emperor and empress. By the time of the stock-market crash of 1873, 40 per cent of the avenue had been lined with private palaces, most of them *Mietpaläste*, or apartment houses of the greatest splendour. And in the early 1880s, the great street was crowned with whole series of imposing public buildings in a bewildering variety of pompous historical styles: the neo-classical Parliament, the Flemish Gothic city hall, the French Gothic votive church, the baroque university, the museums, the Burgtheater and, by no means least, the Opera.

In Britain, by the third quarter of the nineteenth century, the liberal middle class was already in the ascendant.[22] It had long established its practical equality with the old aristocracy, which indeed it had penetrated and almost coopted. In France, the old aristocracy had been defeated by the Revolution, its privileges abolished, and by the Second Empire the bourgeoisie were likewise triumphant. Not so in Austria. The Austrian Revolution of 1848 had been ignominiously defeated. Constitutional government arrived more as a series of concessions offered by the emperor after 1848 and after the defeats in foreign wars by the Italians, helped by the French, in 1859, and by the Prussians in 1866. Moreover, the Liberals only clung to power because of a restricted franchise which contradicted their own principles. Still, the Liberals' achievement should not be underestimated. It was hardly their fault if the upsurge of nationalism within the ramshackle multinational Habsburg empire jammed the works of parliamentary government and brought the Liberal age to an end.

In 1880 the emperor called on a singular man to be his chief minister. This was Count Taaffe,[23] an Irish-Bohemian. His family was descended from an Irish Catholic soldier of fortune who prospered under Wallenstein in the Thirty Years' War, and it did not surrender the Irish peerage until 1917. A tolerant, moderate man, Taaffe was at his wits' end balancing the demands of German and Czech nationalists. In 1890, more or less in desperation, the emperor made the mistake of adopting the proposals, startling in the Habsburg context, of his finance minister, Baron Steinbach. They were nothing less than universal suffrage, coupled with social reforms so advanced that if they had been adopted, Austria would have been the most progressive state in Europe. In October 1893 –

see how the threads of political and cultural disintegration persist in marching step by step – the crunch came over the Bill that would have legislated this reform programme. Instead of appeasing discontent, it united everyone, Czech nationalists, German nationalists, even the Galician Poles, against it. For the first time Taaffe, and Franz Joseph, confronted a hostile coalition. Taaffe resigned. And then, in an incident that might have been invented by the great satirical novelist, Robert Musil, the coalition in its turn fell apart over the affair of the grammar school at Cilli. This was a little town in what is now Slovenia – it is called Celje now – but was then part of Styria. The townspeople spoke German, the country people Slovene. The Germans bitterly resented the Slovenes' demand for classes in Slovene in the grammar school. In the end, the Slovenes got their classes, with no trouble. But in the meantime the affair of the grammar school at Cilli had dominated Austrian politics through the year 1894. It had set Germans against Slavs and led to their withdrawing from Parliament, which in turn made parliamentary government impossible. The emperor turned to a new minister, Count Badeni. He promptly introduced a series of language ordinances, intended to conciliate the Czechs. By making Czech, a language few Germans in Bohemia spoke well, the language for all but communication with Vienna, it gave the Czechs an outrageous advantage. The government tried again, and again. In the end, the emperor gave up. He ruled by emergency decree under Article 14 of the Constitution. And he shrugged his shoulders and allowed Karl Lueger to become the mayor of Vienna after all. Lueger, 'Handsome Karl', was a cynical anti-Semite, rather than the red-eyed, Lanz von Liebenfels variety. 'Who is a Jew,' he once announced, 'I shall decide.'[24] His political tactic, and that of the Christian Social party he led, was to portray the Liberals as 'the Rothschild party', and as time went on it is true that the Liberals, lacking support among lower-middle-class and working-class German-speakers, did become more and more the party of capitalism, and also of the cultivated Viennese Jewish upper middle class.

★

Lueger was also, however, an energetic administrator and ambitious for his beloved Vienna. One of the key figures in his plans for the city was that complicated man we first glimpsed lounging near an automobile at the Sirkecke, and then saw building a private railway station for the emperor: Otto Wagner, who managed to be both the Crown Prince of the Ringstrasse, and the revolutionary who overthrew what it stood for; and even that contrast understates the contradictions of his personality.[25] After the best education at the Polytechnic and in Berlin, then at the Vienna Academy under the two architects who designed the Opera, ultimate ikon of Ringstrasse society, finally in the office of the Ringstrasse's main planner, he embarked on a brilliantly successful career as a practising designer who also developed property and speculated in it successfully. His widowed mother told him, he liked to say, 'to strive for independence, money and then again money as the means thereto'. Although he showed some early signs of original-ity, until the 1890s he remained a traditional architect. Two things changed that. First he became involved in the public-works projects mentioned above, the Danube Canal project and the *Stadtbahn*. And then he became involved in the Secession movement. The railway project encouraged him to break new ground, using an iron trestle as a decorative feature of the Unter-Döbling Station, for example, and a rich art nouveau decoration for the elegant Karlsplatz Station in the middle of the town. In his canal work, too, he began to experiment with using structural elements in a decorative way.

It was not until 1898, though, that he broke with traditional buildings and developed a true *Jugendstil* manner – at the age of fifty-seven! In that year he designed two apartment houses on the left side of the covered-over Wien river (*Linke Wienzeile*), opposite the modern *Naschmarkt*, or food market. Both are richly orna-mented, the second with a façade in majolica tiles across which a stylized rose tree meanders upwards. In subtler respects, too, the design marks a departure from the Ringstrasse style. The windows are simpler, almost flush with the walls. Above all, the buildings make no claim to descend from any historical school whatever; they are themselves, a young style from a middle-aged architect. And Wagner went on to develop what was in many respects the forerunner of the modern style as it was to be developed, after the war, by Walter Gropius and the Bauhaus school. His apartment house at 4 Döblergasse, or 40 Neustiftgasse, has all the marks of the modern style: clean, functional lines, almost wholly free from external decoration though, interestingly, in Wagner's own apartment the decor, in the modern style, is nevertheless quite ornate. Past fifty, perhaps, personal taste changes less readily than professional judgement about the right way forward. In the twenty years before the war, Wagner completed a number of buildings in this new, simplified style, among them his great church Am Steinhof on the western approaches to Vienna, in which a spare exterior rises to a cupola, originally meant to be gilded, and a bare white interior is decorated with rich mosaics, predominantly in gold, by Kolo Moser, a designer closely associated with the Secession. But in many ways the most significant of all Wagner's later individual buildings was one which came to terms with the new politics.

One of the ways in which Karl Lueger appealed to the anti-Semitism of his Christian Social followers was by attacks on the Liberals as the 'Rothschild party'. The post office savings bank was created by one of Lueger's henchmen with the express purpose of calling in the small savings of the lower middle classes, to free them of dependence on 'Jewish finance'.[26] For this movement, dedicated to the overthrow of all that liberal Vienna stood for, Wagner designed in the early years of the century what is perhaps his most influential building. In external form, it is plain, and the interior is a model of elegant design. What makes it so important is the originality Wagner brought to every technical detail of its construction. Outside, the walls are covered with thin marble slabs anchored to a frame with aluminium bolts. Inside, the partitions are movable so that internal spaces are free, and aluminium is used again in the heating system of the banking hall. Altogether,

Wagner had made the transition from the historicist opulence of the Ringstrasse palaces to a new architecture, appropriate for a new ideal of urban, business culture. In his great novel, *The Man without Qualities*, Robert Musil describes one aspect of the whirl of change in turn-of-the-century Vienna: the longing for modernity, American-style.

For some time now such a social *idée fixe* has been a kind of super-American city where everyone rushes about, or stands still, with a stopwatch in his hand . . . Overhead trains, overground trains, underground trains, pneumatic express-mails carrying consignments of human beings . . . The various professions are concentrated at different places. One eats while in motion. Amusements are concentrated in other parts of the city. And elsewhere again are the towers to which one returns and finds wife, family, gramophone and soul.[27]

Otto Wagner had grown up in an earlier age, the age of Ringstrasse liberalism. He made the break and identified with the young who wanted to break away from the cluttered style and stuffy Victorianism of that age; that was why he joined the Secession and helped some of its younger artists. But he also hankered after the dream metropolis of the future. In his later years he proposed a whole series of ambitious projects, a gigantic academy of arts, a remodelling of the Karlsplatz – the gracious drawings are now framed and used to furnish contemporary living-rooms. But the most ambitious scheme of all was for a modular plan to expand Vienna into a megalopolis that would have covered the Vienna Woods with brick and concrete; luckily the plan could not be carried out before the war, and after the war Vienna was too poor even to contemplate fulfilling Otto Wagner's dreams for it. Indeed, to this day the population of Vienna, at 1.5 million, is 25 per cent lower than in 1910.

If Otto Wagner was a convert to the spare idiom of the modern style, Adolf Loos needed no conversion. Brought up in Brno, he went to the United States at the age of twenty-two and stayed abroad, there and in London, for about five years.[28] When he came back he began to publish articles in *Ver Sacrum* ('Sacred Spring'), the journal of the Secession. One of them was an uncompromising attack on the Ringstrasse style, called 'The Potemkin Town'. In 1908 he designed a miniature masterpiece which you can still see: the American bar, just off the Kärntnerstrasse, which is only 15 × 8 feet, but is made spacious by Loos's ingenuity. The next year he got the commission that made his name, in the Michaelerplatz, opposite the Hofburg and bang in the middle of the aristocratic district of baroque palaces. The house on the Michaelerplatz, originally an expensive tailor's, now a bank, scandalized Vienna. It was called 'the house without eyebrows', the 'horror house' and much else. It remains as a confident, elegant essay in early modernism. Loos went on to build plain, modern villas in the suburbs for many of the younger generation of cultivated upper-middle-class Viennese, who were just beginning to move out.

The Secession building, next to the Wien River, now covered over where it runs under the Karlsplatz, was designed by Joseph Olbrich, a pupil of Wagner and a draughtsman in his office. Only two years later he accepted an invitation to work in Darmstadt and worked for the rest of his short life in Germany. Another of Wagner's pupils was Josef Hoffmann, who, in 1903, with the designer Kolo Moser and the financier Fritz Wärndorfer, set up the Wiener Werkstätte. Strongly influenced by the great Scots designer, Charles Rennie Mackintosh, the WW created furniture, fabrics and objects of every kind of the greatest beauty, in a style that evolved from the vegetative whorls of art nouveau to the rectangular chastity of art deco. But Hoffmann also worked as an architect, designing, like Loos, chaste but luxurious suburban villas in the modern manner on the leafy hills surrounding the city, where the upper middle class, now that Wagner had provided them with a suburban railway, were just beginning to settle. One of these was on the Hohe Warte, the crest of the hill beyond Döbling, with views of the Leopoldsberg and the Kahlenberg in the Vienna Woods, and out across the river. The client was the painter Karl Moll, who had recently married the widow of a successful landscape painter called Schindler, and in so doing had taken on the rather heavy burden of responsibility for Schindler's daughter, Alma.

In November 1901, when Alma was twenty-two, she was walking along the Ring with some friends when she ran into her friend Berta Zuckerkandl, a journalist and later a courageous pacifist who was married to the dean of the medical faculty at the university. 'We've got Mahler coming tonight,' said she. 'Won't you come.' Alma had already been involved in a serious flirtation with the composer Alexander von Zemlinsky, then her music teacher, and her stepfather had felt obliged to warn off Gustav Klimt, the most famous painter in Vienna and a dedicated womanizer. When the Mahler dinner was finally arranged, Klimt was there, and so was Max Burckhard, who as director of the Burg-theater held the only post with comparable status to Mahler's as director of the Opera. Mahler's attention was caught by this beautiful young woman, a student of composition, what was more, who seemed so much at home with such powerful figures in the world of art. Alma never forgot the pick-up.

There was just time before we parted for a quick question:

'Where do you live?'

'Hohe Warte –'

'I'll take you –.'

But I did not want to go on foot. It was late and I was tired.

'Well, you'll be at the Opera? For certain?'[29]

The wedding took place four months later. As a marriage, it was not a great success. It launched Alma on her career as one of the most egotistical and successful sexual scalp-hunters of the twentieth century: apart from Zemlinsky, Klimt and Mahler himself, not to mention many less eminent lovers, including, if her biographers are to be believed, one distinguished Monseigneur, she subsequently married the great architect Walter Gropius, the poet and novelist Franz Werfel and was involved in a prolonged, public and passionate relationship with the great painter, Oskar

Kokoschka. For Mahler, the marriage was painful. He had fought his way up from a large, modest Jewish family in Moravia by sheer effort as well as by his musical genius. He found Alma's upper-middle-class arrogance hard to handle. But he also took it for granted that the function of a wife, his wife, was to subordinate herself, however great her own talent, to him. 'You have only one profession from now on,' he actually wrote to her, and early in their courtship at that, '*to make me happy!*'

Mahler's musical style was set, his reputation established, before he met Alma. Yet Mahler, too, was affected by the 'kindling fever' of Vienna in the 1890s. Moreover, in Mahler, as in Hofmannsthal, the Oedipal rebellion against the liberalism of the Ringstrasse era took the form, not of the modernism of the second wave, but of a return to love of the baroque.[30] Mahler, for all the private scars he bore, was a man of the new generation, conscious of the rising of new wells of creativity beneath the 'oil-smooth' surface of the last decade of the nineteenth century and the first decade of the twentieth. His own work is the best proof of it. He transformed the Opera, demanding and getting higher standards not only of playing and singing, but also of acting and design, than had ever been seen before, either there or anywhere. The dramatic improvement in the costumes and decor was a direct result of Mahler's contact, through Alma, with the Secession; for it was at Alma's parents' house that he met the painter Alfred Roller, whom he invited to become the Opera's permanent designer. This is not the place to attempt an analysis of Mahler's musical development. There are elements in his music, however – the mingling of symphonic composition with the human voice, the obsession with the folk songs of *Des Knaben Wunderhorn*, the insistent interruptions of street songs, military bands and other snatches of popular music – which unmistakably share the impulses of Young Vienna, even if he, like Otto Wagner, belonged to an older generation.[31] But Mahler, like Wagner, was a transitional figure, a member of the first, not the second, wave of Viennese modernism. While his career was reaching its tragic climax – resignation from the Opera in 1907 after a hostile press campaign that was at least in part anti-Semitic in character, illness, exile to New York and death in 1911 – an even sharper revolution was taking place in painting.

At first sight, Otto Wagner's admiration for Gustav Klimt might seem surprising. Wagner was a man of business, a survivor from the Victorian age, a confident, capable person who was the master of practical questions such as how to make a fortune or how to build a railway. Klimt was almost a caricature of the sort of nineteenth-century artist who might have stepped out of the pages of Murger's *Scènes de la vie de Bohème* fifty years earlier. He wore a monk's robe. He lived with his mother all his life, even while having innumerable affairs. (Viennese legend says that he fathered more than a dozen illegitimate children.) Yet Wagner called him 'the greatest artist who ever walked on this earth'.[32] Only half in jest, Klimt expressed to Wagner the modern artist's eternal resentment of *them*: 'They won't let you build the walls they won't let me paint on.'[33]

Klimt, born twenty years later than Wagner, began, like him, in the Ringstrasse, literally and metaphorically.[34] His father was a craftsman, an iron-worker, and he started out with one of his brothers as an artistic team. They soon got two prestigious commissions to decorate major buildings in the Ringstrasse: panels in the staircase of the Burgtheater, and in the Kunsthistorisches Museum (the Museum of the History of Art). In 1892 both his father and his brother Ernst died, but his bereavement did not immediately affect his style, which remained sugary and romantic. Indeed, a painting like *Love*, in which two lovers stare into one another's eyes, might have been a caricature of the art from which the Secession wanted to secede. Yet such was the recognition of Klimt's talent by his contemporaries that they chose him as the Secession's first president. The first sign of his mature ability, and of his breaking away from sentimentality to a more psychologically perceptive manner, came in a portrait of Sonja Knips in 1898. A pair of paintings for the music room of a Ringstrasse millionaire, Nicholas Dumba, shows Klimt in transition from his old manner to the new. In one, interestingly enough the later to be executed, he painted Schubert playing the piano, surrounded by society ladies in beautiful gowns, in the manner of the early Impressionists. But in the other he deployed the symbols, drawn from Nietzsche, of the inner world of instinct, sexuality, irrationality and terror.

For the next few years Klimt painted, and drew, women, not as individuals, but as mythological figures of sensuality. In *Fish Blood* he drew young naked women, their faces apparently showing physical pleasure, floating away from a great fish. In *Nuda Veritas* he represented truth as a woman with flaming red hair, and flaming red pubic hair; and this same image appears as a miniature statuette in the hand of Pallas Athene, in his third representation of the goddess in the same year. He was approaching the confrontation with conventional taste and public authority that would lead to the crisis.

As long ago as 1894 Klimt had been commissioned to paint three big and ten little pictures to decorate the great hall of the university. These were commissions like those of his uncontentious youth, but the paintings he produced to fulfil them infuriated the academic establishment of the university and precipitated both a blazing public row and a psychological crisis for Klimt. His first picture was entitled *Philosophy*. It depicted naked figures, mostly female, floating up through a starry night sky in what might almost be a parody of a baroque altarpiece. It has been said that the painting echoes Nietzsche's great poem, 'Drunken Song at Midnight', at the end of *Also Sprach Zarathustra*: '*O Mensch! Gib acht: Was spricht die tiefe Mitternacht?*' ('Oh man! Give heed! What says the deep midnight?')

This is the poem Mahler had already set to music in his Third Symphony, and it is possible that Klimt was consciously identifying philosophy with the world-view that Richard Wagner and Nietzsche, the intellectual gods of his generation of artists in Vienna, derived from their interpretation of Schopenhauer, the

German philosopher, or anti-philosopher, who saw the universe as a cosmic arena of the will and its eternal, purposeless striving. It was not on technical philosophical grounds, though, that the professors criticized what Klimt had done. For one thing, he had departed by a wide margin from what he had said, in his preliminary sketches, that he would do. For another, the vision of their trade was just too wild, too negative, too nihilistic.

If the philosophers did not like Klimt's conception of philosophy, the doctors liked his *Medicine* even less. On the right-hand side of his canvas a hieratic female figure, Hygeia – Greek goddess of health – holds the serpent of Asclepius, while behind her a column of naked figures, including a pregnant woman and a skeleton, rise in a column of emblematic humanity. To the left, a single female figure, naked, desirable and backward bowed, floats past them.

The painting is troubling, with unmistakable sexual allusions, no concessions to academic piety and no recognizable reference to the healing craft. It set off a full-dress row within the university and Vienna's cultural universe. The professors accused Klimt, not altogether unfairly, of expressing 'hazy ideas in hazy forms': the rector of the university made the point that at a time when doctors, even Dr Freud, very much thought of themselves as scientists, it was insulting to represent medicine as nebulous. But what is interesting is that Klimt was defended by Franz Wickhoff in a highly polemical lecture at the Vienna Philosophical society under the title, 'What is ugly?' Wickhoff was one of a group of art historians in Vienna who had been revolutionizing the study of art. In 1895 he had published (jointly with the Greek scholar Wilhelm von Hartel, who became minister of culture and another of Klimt's defenders) an edition of the early Christian codex, the *Vienna Genesis*. His point was that late Roman painting – including the illustrations to the codex – was not 'silver' or decadent compared to Greek painting, as it had been traditional to maintain, but represented an adaptation of classical tradition to the beliefs of the new, Christian age. In other words, Hartel and Wickhoff were proposing a new, relativistic standard of artistic value that was bound to be shocking to the children of the Ringstrasse.

Klimt's third painting, *Jurisprudence*, showed signs that he was not just angry with the professors, his critics; he was also deeply troubled in himself. The painting is not far short of an open satire on the whole idea of criminal jurisprudence, but of a bizarre kind. Above, three female judges, one of whom holds a cloth covered with symbols which does not quite hide her body. Below, three naked female figures, Furies, perhaps, their heads surrounded by something like the haloes of Christ and the saints in Byzantine paintings, surround a naked old man who is enveloped by an obscene octopus and holds behind his back a cruel, curved knife. The picture has nothing to do with jurisprudence; it reeks of psychotic fantasies, of sexual sadism, perhaps castration. The spirit is that of Franz Kafka.

The symbolism is imprecise, but hardly obscure. Klimt is rejecting the rational world of law, the foundation of bourgeois liberalism. Instead he invokes terrifying, subterranean fancies. Like Freud, only two years earlier, the greatest painter of his generation, having failed to move the Olympian gods of reason and justice above, turns to the gods of the underworld within, to the secret world of fears and fantasies. '*Flectere si nequeo superos, Acheronta movebo.*' Klimt survived this personal crisis. The year after *Jurisprudence* he painted what for me is his masterpiece, the *Beethoven Frieze* in the basement of the Secession building. Its symbolism and mood are closely related to those of *Jurisprudence*, but where the earlier painting is troubling, even sick, a symptom of a personality struggling against emotional crisis and perhaps mental illness, the *Beethoven Frieze* is the work of someone who has fought his way triumphantly – along the 'way into the open'? – towards the light.

In the *Beethoven Frieze* and in his later work, Klimt found his salvation in a new, more resolved and harmonious sexuality. In the frieze, he has already begun to evolve his characteristic device, clothing women with cloaks richly decorated with symbols. Between the *Jurisprudence* crisis and 1908, he combined naturalistic portraits of women's faces with this rich decoration, sometimes with gold leaf, sometimes with flowers, sometimes with abstract symbols, in a manner that recalls the adjective applied by Aeschylus to night: *poikileimon*, 'night painted like a meadow'.[35] He used this utterly original, yet strangely satisfying technique in a series of flattering portraits of women from the Jewish upper middle class, one of them the sister of the philosopher Ludwig Wittgenstein. He also used it for two of his finest paintings, *Danaë* and *The Kiss*. The first, a naked, red-haired girl curled up like a kitten, echoes the sexual magnetism of the terrifying furies of his crisis, but transformed into an image of peaceful satisfaction. The second follows the kissing couple of the *Beethoven Frieze*, but now the two kneeling figures, draped with the richest profusion of colour and symbol even Klimt ever devised, meet in a happy, even decorous embrace. After the crisis of *Jurisprudence*, Klimt came to terms with sexuality, with women, and with himself; but in the process he turned his back on the conflicts of the public arena.

At this stage in his life, Klimt helped two younger painters of immense talent and unsublimated rage. Egon Schiele, an angry young man who died at only twenty-eight, worked with 'a painful intensity, a frightening wildness and, occasionally, a blood-curdling indecency'.[36] Schiele's paintings reflect a tormented existence. He came from a prosperous middle-class family. His father, a railway official, went mad and burned the family fortune in railway shares; he died while still young.[37] Schiele was helped by patrons, including Klimt; even when he was called up into the army his officers bought his pictures. He was deeply shaken by the 'Neulengbach affair' in 1912, in which he was accused of abducting and raping a minor, and he was lucky to get off with a short prison sentence for a lesser offence. Schiele shared Klimt's contempt for the surface preoccupations of academic painting, but he went much further in his investigation of the squalor and suffering of life, including sexual life. Although his work is pervaded with anger and sadness – in not one of his three hundred paintings and thousands of drawings does the subject smile or even appear relaxed – his technique was impeccable and the psychological insight of his portraits probes deep beneath the surface of life.

Born four years before Schiele, the other great painter of the second wave of Viennese modernism, Oskar Kokoschka, outlived him by sixty-two years.[38] Kokoschka trained at the commercial art school in Vienna, and he began by designing brightly coloured postcards for the Wiener Werkstätte, and illustrations for its Fledermaus cabaret. In 1908, still for the Wiener Werkstätte, and still in the same naïve style, using bold primary colours, he produced his first illustrated book, *The Dreaming Boys*. But this was not a pretty children's book. In the text, Kokoschka explored the auto-erotic frustration and Oedipal anger of puberty. And in his next work, *Murderer, Hope of Women*, a play, he plunged deeper still into sexual psychopathology, exposing raw aggression between men and women in the most unrestrained Expressionist manner. There was a row. Kokoschka was expelled from the Arts and Crafts School and his grant withdrawn by none other than Alfred Roller, one of the founders of the Secession and Mahler's talented designer at the Opera. Nothing could have marked more clearly the transition from the first to the second wave of Viennese modernism, the secession from the Secession.

For a while Kokoschka lived by hawking paintings in the majestic neo-Gothic Café Central in the Herrengasse. But not for long. He was taken up by Karl Kraus, by the Berlin publisher, Herwarth Walden, who put a savage illustration out of *Murderer* on the front page of his magazine, and by, of all people, Adolf Loos, the dandified architect of coolly simplified villas for the new migrants to the suburbs.

Kokoschka turned at last from graphics and poetry to painting in oils. He painted a series of brilliant portraits, one of the best of them of Loos. And, as the war approached, he became involved in a wild affair with Alma Mahler. They travelled together to Italy. He begged Alma to marry him. She said she would do so only when he had painted a masterpiece. And he did. It is called *Die Windsbraut*, which in German means both 'the tempest' and 'the

wind's bride'. It is characteristically indiscreet, shocking, even –
given Alma's relationship to Walter Gropius at the time – reckless.
It shows a naked woman, Alma, afloat in a cockle boat in a wild
sea, next to a naked man, Oskar. The tones are stormy blues,
greens, thick impasto of white. She is asleep, her expression is
tranquil, relaxed; he is awake, and stares past her, tense and
unrelenting. A year later, Kokoschka was seriously wounded at the
front. (Adolf Loos had got him a commission, incongruously, in a
smart cavalry regiment.) He survived, but the rest of his life
belonged to Germany and then to America. In 1918 Klimt, Schiele
and Kolo Moser all died of the Spanish influenza. The two
generations of Viennese modernism in the visual arts had lived
their short, butterfly lives.

Alma Mahler is the most striking evidence of how tightly wound
the world of Viennese culture was. Wife of Mahler, mistress of
Kokoschka, pupil of Zemlinsky, stepdaughter of Karl Moll,
brought up in a house designed by Hoffmann, pursued by Klimt,
her life is a scarlet thread interwoven into the fabric of Vienna
1900. But she was only a special case of a general proposition: this
was a small, an intimate élite, where in an almost literal sense,
'everyone knew everyone'. The valencies run in every direction.
Start to unravel the web wherever you like, and the threads will
run back to the Sirkecke, the corner of the Ringstrasse opposite
the Opera, down the road from the gorgeous concert-hall of the
Musikverein, a short stroll from the Secession, and not much
further from the Café Griensteidl, almost under the walls of the
Hofburg, where Arthur Schnitzler and Stefan Zweig used to meet.
Its demolition in 1897 caused Karl Kraus to fear that the end of
literature itself was at hand. Klimt tried to seduce Alma Mahler,
helped Kokoschka, decorated Hoffmann's masterpiece the Palais
Stoclet in Brussels, introduced Egon Schiele to the wealthy patron,
August Lederer, and when Mahler, after his resignation from the
Opera, left for America, Klimt was at the West Station to wave
him goodbye. And so you could go on. Anton Bruckner gave

piano lessons to the philosopher, Ludwig Boltzmann. Young Dr Freud fought a duel with Viktor Adler, later the great Social Democratic leader;[39] Freud, Adler and Arthur Schnitzler were all assistants in the clinic of Dr Theodor Meynert, a luminary of the salon of Mrs Wertheimstein, where Hugo von Hofmannsthal shone as a schoolboy.[40] Adler, the social democrat, went to school with Arthur Seyss-Inquart, later the Nazi *Gauleiter* in Holland, and with the last emperor, Karl.[41] The cultural life of Vienna in the last years of the Habsburg dynasty, in fact, was the non-sexual equivalent of Schnitzler's play *Der Reigen*, or rather of the film Max Ophüls made of it; a social and cultural merry-go-round in which, sooner or later, everyone rode on the back of everyone else's hobbyhorse. Strangest, perhaps, of all these interconnections, but hardly surprising in view of this intimate interlocking of lives, Mahler was psychoanalysed by Freud;[42] to be precise, at a crisis in his relations with Alma in 1910, Freud, who was on holiday in the Baltic, met Mahler in Leiden, in Holland, and 'spent four hours strolling through the town and conducting a sort of psychoanalysis'. This unusual analysis, Freud's biography concluded, 'evidently produced an effect, since Mahler recovered his potency and the marriage was a happy one until his death, which unfortunately took place only a year later'.

One does not have to accept all the quasi-magical claims that have been made on behalf of Freud's powers as an analyst and healer to see that he was a titanic figure in the development of the modern mind.[43] The body of work on which he built his daring theories was skewed because the clients who climbed to his consulting room in the Berggasse were overwhelmingly upper-middle-class neurotics. (Freud more than once suggested that if a child saw its parents making love this would be traumatic; in the crowded tenements of working-class Vienna this must have been an everyday occurrence, yet Freud simultaneously argued that the working class were less likely to become neurotic than the middle classes.) He had what can only be called a pre-modern attitude to women. He had far less experience of psychosis than Jung, and as a consequence his psychopathology was based on neurosis, not psychosis. His theories are based on a surprisingly small number of full analyses – there are no more than six accounts of extended treatment in his voluminous collected works, and perhaps only one of all his patients can be said to have been successfully treated by Freud.[44] He was arguably far more interested in ideas than in patients, and he persisted in maintaining that his theories were 'scientific', even though he produced no evidence, only ingenious rationalizations for them, and indeed, though he would not allow others to modify his ideas, he himself frequently revised or abandoned them himself.

Yet, when all these criticisms of Freud have been driven home, his towering intellectual achievement remains essentially unscathed. He remains one of the handful of thinkers who, by the force and attraction of his ideas alone, actually changed the way we think of Man. As one of his patients, known as the 'Wolf Man', put it, 'Freud was a genius, there's no denying it. All those ideas that he combined into a system . . . Even though much isn't true, it was a splendid achievement.'[45]

Freud himself saw his work on the interpretation of dreams, not just as an aid to therapy, but as 'a royal road to a knowledge of the unconscious activities of the mind'. Others had explored the unconscious before him. His achievement was to 'carry the lamp to the back of the cave', to dare, Prometheus-like, to investigate the fiercest impulses lurking in the darkest recesses of the mind, and to use his brilliant literary gifts to fit his theories into a gigantic structure, almost a modern synthesis of science and religion. Much later, when he had decided to assume the existence of only two instincts, Eros and the 'destructive instinct' or 'death instinct', he wrote that 'the meaning of the evolution of civilization is no longer obscure to us. It must present the struggle between Eros and Death, between the instinct of life and the instinct of destruction as it works itself out in the human species.'

Anthony Storr comments, 'Who would have supposed that a doctor striving to comprehend the neuroses of the Viennese upper classes would have derived from his researches so majestic a concept of the human condition?' And he adds, 'Whether or not such a vision is true is another matter. It has nothing to do with science.'

What it does have to do with is the predicament of the great Viennese middle class of *Bildung und Besitz*, of 'education and property', confronted with the rising challenge of the classes who had been excluded from liberal society under the Austrian empire. For it was not only the search for a new art and a New Man, not to mention a New Woman, that was disturbing the 'oil-smooth' surface of Viennese civilization in what Karl Kraus called 'the last days of humanity', which of course were really the last days of his kind of humanity, Café Griensteidl humanity. The challenge came also from Slavs, excluded by a German-speaking civilization which they often identified with Jews, and from lower-middle-class and proletarian German speakers who were all too ready to rally to anti-Semitic leadership, whether it came from the haughty feudal-ism of Georg Schönerer, the 'Knight of Rosenau,[45] or from the bustling demagoguery of Karl Lueger.

Sigmund Freud saw himself as a victim of anti-Semitism. He attributed to 'denominational considerations'[47] the seventeen-year delay in his being given a professorship. There can be no doubt that anti-Semitism was involved. But the position of Jews in upper-middle-class Vienna in 1900 was both more complicated and more subtle than might be imagined. It was, for example, significantly different from the situation in Berlin. The emperor disapproved of anti-Semitism, and made his distaste plain. In the cultivated salons of the 'Second Society', the world that Freud frequented, it was 'not done' to admit to anti-Semitic feelings,[48] though Alma Mahler, who made it her business to shock in more than one way, openly used anti-Semitic language, even though she married two Jewish husbands, Mahler and Werfel.[49] Nor was it true, as has been assumed, that Freud's professional career was blocked by crude or envious nonentities. In June 1897, two years after his studies on hysteria had appeared, but before *The

Interpretation of Dreams was finished, let alone published, the medical college of the University of Vienna, acting on a report by Professor Krafft-Ebing, the author of *Psychopathia Sexualis*, that Freud's researches 'prove an extraordinary gift', voted by twenty-two votes to ten that he should be made a professor *extraordinarius*.[50] It was five years before the ministry acted on that recommendation. The fact remains that Freud did not, as the myth would have it, experience nothing but prejudice and jealousy from his colleagues. There was anti-Semitism in cultivated upper-middle-class Vienna. It fuelled the campaign, fed by other causes as well, that led to Mahler's resignation from the Opera. But the real damage was internal as much as external; and it was in the past and in the future more than in the present.

For Freud, Mahler, Karl Kraus, Herzl and Josef Hoffmann came from Jewish families which had struggled up to at best a modest prosperity in the provinces: in Herzl's case in Hungary, in Kraus's in a small town in Bohemia, in each of the other three cases, and in many, many others among the cultivated bourgeoisie of Vienna, in Moravia. Vienna was a melting-pot. The population quadrupled between 1860 and 1910. People swarmed in from every province of the empire, from Trieste in the south to northern Bohemia, from the Tirol to Galicia. Those who were Jewish – and by 1910, when the population of the city was over two million, as many as one in ten were of Jewish origin[51] – had the memory of persecution in the past and the fear, the justified fear, of persecution in the future.

The achievement of liberal, bourgeois Vienna between the repression of the revolution of 1848 and the 1890s was a modest one compared to the astonishing vigour and expansion of Britain, the United States and Germany in that same period. Austrian liberalism, by comparison to the boisterous creeds of Manchester or of Republican America, was a vulnerable and apologetic plant, and it flourished only on the sufferance of the dynasty. Still, its achievements were real. It was when those achievements were threatened by the breakdown of the parliamentary system, the rise of socialism among the working class and of anti-Semitic nationalism in the lower middle class, that the Viennese intelligentsia turned away from its involvement in public and political life, which had always been pretty tenuous anyway. There was something, as Freud was to put it, very Oedipal about this change of temper. The sons of the liberals turned against their fathers. In the first wave, they turned from business to art, and from art as a business to art for art's sake. In the second phase, they turned inward and explored what lay below the surface of their world and, especially, beneath their skins.

Not that Vienna was uninterested in skin. Stefan Zweig, the poet, who was one of the regulars, with Schnitzler and Hofmannsthal, at the Café Griensteidl until it was pulled down, said that prostitution 'constituted a dark underground vault over which rose the gorgeous structure of middle-class society with its faultless radiant façade'. To be sure, there was prostitution in Paris, too, and in London and Berlin. But the intellectuals in Vienna were unusually preoccupied with sex, partly as an Oedipal rebellion against the constraints of a bourgeois society that still functioned in the lee of the Counter-Reformation crowned and triumphant in the Hofburg. The Crown Prince Franz Ferdinand, persuaded to visit an exhibition of Kokoschka's paintings, stood in the middle of the room, shouting, 'Pig's muck! Pig's muck! Somebody should break every bone in that man's body!' The painters rebelled against restrictions on how they could paint sexuality, the writers explored it, Freud listened to the dreams of middle-class women driven hysterical by the repressions of their sex lives. Again, something similar happened in France and in Britain. The intellectuals of the nineties in both countries explored their visions of sexual liberation in the generation of Oscar Wilde and Aubrey Beardsley, Pierre Louÿs and Maeterlinck – though we have seen how much earlier the revolt against 'bourgeois' values came in France than elsewhere. Rimbaud's *Une Saison en enfer* was published in 1873, Mallarmé's *L'Aprés-midi d'un faune* in 1876. But to join the avant-garde there, as we have seen, was to drop out of bourgeois society.

What was different in Vienna was that, because of the failure of political liberalism, the upper middle class as a whole had joined the intelligentsia. People who in London or Paris would have been concerned with politics, speculation, real estate and colonization, with dances and dinners in Paris, and weekends and sport in England as their recreation, were in Vienna obsessed with art and above all with music.

There was a sort of revolution in Vienna in 1918, but compared to the events in St Petersburg or Berlin it was a very Viennese revolution. The social democratic leader, Viktor Adler, said of the Habsburg empire that it was *Despotismus gemildert durch Schlamperei*, 'despotism softened by muddle'. What was true of the Austrian autocracy, it turned out, was true of the Austrian revolution as well: it was a revolution mitigated by muddle. After it had run its course, Vienna continued to give a lead to Europe in many respects. In the seventeenth century the leading troops of an army were sometimes called the 'vanguard', sometimes the 'forlorn hope', and it was not clear which the new music of Arnold Schoenberg and his disciples, Alban Berg and Anton von Webern, was. The Wiener Kreis, philosophers of the stature of Ludwig Wittgenstein and Rudolf Carnap, political thinkers like Karl Popper and Friedrich Hayek on the Right and the 'Austro-Marxists' like Karl Renner and Otto Bauer on the Left, kept the lustre of Vienna alive until it was extinguished, and they were driven into exile, by Adolf Hitler, the wolf man of the Home for Men in the Meldemannstrasse. That, it turned out – not the adolescent fantasies of sexual aggression of a Schoenberg or a Kokoschka – was the dark secret hidden in the European underworld.

Civilization is always a precarious thing. The fifty years of the Periclean Age were the prelude to catastrophe for Athens. Karl Kraus once said, with his inimitable acid, that 'the sphere of action of Viennese liberalism [is] restricted to the stalls of theatres on opening night'. Austria in the last days of the Habsburgs presents perhaps the only example from modern European history where a governing class, almost as a whole, gave up governing, and devoted itself to the pleasures and the arts of life. Their greatest achievement, ironically, was not the opera, or the literature, nor yet the art and architecture of the Secession; it was that dangerous inward secession that explored the inner spaces of psychological Man.

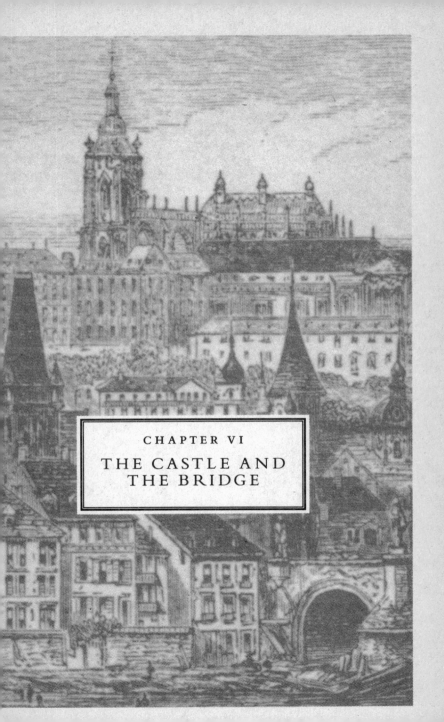

CHAPTER VI

THE CASTLE AND
THE BRIDGE

WALK TO THE MIDDLE OF THE CHARLES
Bridge before you look back, and the view will take your breath
away. Under the bridge there are noisy weirs, swans and an
immemorial inn. Against the western sky lie the churches and
palaces of Malá Strana, the Lesser City, the most unspoiled memorial this side of Rome to the age of the baroque. Above all there is
the long bulk of the castle, crowning the ridge with its towers and
palaces, and itself crowned with the three great Gothic spires of St
Vitus Cathedral, soaring black above the floodlit white walls and
the western sky.

It is a footbridge, and all day it is thronged with Czechs
and tourists: buskers and high-school students, young women
selling the most beautiful marionettes you have ever seen, artists
and craftsmen, hustlers and drop-outs. Only at nightfall is it
empty, and you can look back at the castle at your leisure, before

you plunge through the winding alleys of the Old Town to emerge in the wide cobbled space of Old Town Square, with its statue of Jan Hus, its ancient clock tower, its pastel palaces and its twin churches, the Gothic and the baroque.

The parapets of the bridge are a gallery of sculpture silhouetted against the sky. One is of St John of Nepomuk,[1] patron saint of the Habsburgs, who was martyred in 1393 by being thrown from the bridge into the River Vltava; in the Counter-Reformation the Habsburgs and their Jesuit confessors and advisers built that St John up to challenge Jan Hus, the hero of the Bohemian Reformation. Here are baroque crucifixions and saints, most of them in place by the early eighteenth century. The earliest has an inscription in Hebrew: the legend is that a Prague Jew was made to pay for it for speaking slightingly of the Cross.

It is easy to see Prague today as the most opulently beautiful of all Europe's tourist destinations, luxuriant in its wealth of architecture, from the flamboyant late Gothic of the Vladislav Hall in the castle, by way of the baroque splendours of the Strahov Monastery or the Clementinum to the art nouveau mosaics and caryatids of Wenceslas Square and the Masaryk Embankment. But that is to miss the dense history of religious conflict and bitter struggle those princely buildings bear witness to, and in particular to miss the two great divisions that have created the city. The first affected the 'Czech lands', Bohemia and Moravia, as a whole. It was a religious, national and dynastic struggle between the Czech people, 'the most Protestant people in Europe' since the Hussite wars at the beginning of the fifteenth century, and their German-speaking overlords, the Habsburgs. The second was the division of Prague itself between German lords, German merchants, Czechs and Jews.

In the beginning[2] there were two eminences: the Hradcany, on the great bend of the Vltava or, as it was called in German, the Moldau, and two miles further south, the rock of Vyšehrad, now the site of a national cemetery, the Père Lachaise or Westminster Abbey of the Czechs. By the tenth century, both had been crowned with fortifications by the Přemyslids, Slavic chieftains who were converted to Christianity in the ninth century, shortly before the lifetime of the shadowy figure we sing about as Good King Wenceslas. Historically, he was not King but Duke of Bohemia, murdered by his brother Boleslav the Cruel.

Opposite the Hradcany there grew up the Old Town – Staré Mešto in Czech, the Altstadt in German – around what is now Old Town Square. But in the very inside of the river's elbow, just north of Old Town Square, was the Jewish ghetto, one of the oldest in northern Europe, settled in the tenth century by Jews coming over the Alps from the south and from the Byzantine empire. Jewish Prague, the Josefov in Czech, Josefstadt in German, begins only a couple of hundred yards behind Old Town Square.

The Přemyslid dynasty died out at the beginning of the fourteenth century. In their place, thanks to an opportune dynastic marriage, came the House of Luxemburg, and under them Bohemia enjoyed what came to be remembered as a Golden Age. Charles IV became King of Bohemia in 1346 and Holy Roman Emperor in 1355. He it was who built the Charles Bridge, to replace the twelfth-century Judith Bridge, which had been swept away by a flood. He built the New Town, curving around the landward side of the Old Town, and the great fortress, Karlstejn, twenty miles to the south-west of the city. Most important of all, he founded the Charles University, and although he spoke French and German as well as Czech, he encouraged teaching and preaching in the Czech language.

That paved the way, two generations later, for the man who was to the Czech nation, a hundred years earlier, what Martin Luther was to the Germans: Jan Hus. He was a man of learning as well as an inspired preacher, professor of philosophy and rector of the Charles University. He put himself at the head of the movement for reform of the Church in which resentment of Rome

and of the wealth and remoteness of the Church were blended
with the early stirrings of Czech nationalism, much as John Wyclif
and the Lollards in England prefigured the Reformation that was
to come a century later. (In fact, Hus and the Hussites were
specifically much influenced by Wyclif's teaching, a reminder of
how medieval Europe was a cultural and intellectual unity, which
it ceased to be after the Reformation and the Counter-Reformation.) The Czechs rallied round one theological issue in particular.
Bohemia had received Christianity in the first place, back in the
ninth century, from St Cyril and St Methodius, Byzantine mis-
sionaries who taught the Slavs the Cyrillic script. The Czechs later
claimed they were used to receiving communion in both bread
and wine as in the Eastern church, or in Latin *sub utraque specie*, 'in
each kind'. They resented the Roman discipline, which denied the
laity the blood of Christ. Their badge, which you will find carved
on the Týn Church in Old Town Square, was the chalice, and
sometimes they called themselves Calixtines, from the Latin for a
chalice, sometimes 'Utraquists'.

At the height of the dispute Hus was lured to the Council at
Constance under a safe conduct, and there betrayed by the future
Emperor Sigismund and burned at the stake. In July 1419
Utraquists from all over Bohemia gathered in Prague. As they
were processing through the New Town they were greeted
with a shower of stones from the new town hall. Enraged, they
stormed the building and threw the mayor and sixteen of his
councillors out of windows into the street, where they were torn
limb from limb by the infuriated Utraquist crowd. This was the
first 'Defenestration' in Prague. It established a long tradition of
summary violence against those seen as the enemies of the Czech
people.

The Defenestration led to the bloody Hussite Wars. King
Wenceslas had a seizure when he heard the news and died shortly
afterwards. The followers of Hus soon divided into a moderate
wing, the Utraquists, and the more fanatical Taborites, called after

their stronghold in southern Bohemia, who accepted only the two sacraments of baptism and communion and rejected much of the teaching as well as the authority of the Roman Church. The Hussites were brilliantly led by the man who had led the mob in the storming of the new town hall, Jan Žižka, a charismatic preacher and inspired military leader. He successfully defended Prague against the army of Wenceslas's brother Sigismund, the champion of Rome. Žižka died of the plague in 1424, but the Hussites fought on. What came to be known as the Hussite Wars did not end until 1436, and for a time Bohemia was actually ruled by a king who was both a Czech and an Utraquist, George of Podebrad.

In 1526 Louis, who was King of Bohemia as well as of Hungary, was defeated by the Turks in the great battle of Mohacs and died shortly afterwards. After considerable confusion the crown of Bohemia fell at last to Archduke Ferdinand of Austria. He set about stamping out the prerogatives of the towns and also the heresy of the Bohemian Brethren, successors to the Hussites. In the middle of the sixteenth century over three quarters of the population of Bohemia were Protestants or Hussites, and in 1561 Ferdinand brought the Jesuits in to convert its heretic people. The great territorial nobles – most of whom had been Roman Catholic all along – began to rally to Rome. So lines were being drawn, never absolute or hard and fast, but sharp enough to define the essential political realities, between a Protestant Czech people and a Catholic German aristocracy.

The Clementinum, the great ochre mass that dominates the foreground of the view from the Charles Bridge towards the Old Town Square, was the headquarters of the Jesuits, the theological sharpshooters of the Catholic reconquest, from their introduction in the middle of the sixteenth century until their expulsion in 1777. In the late sixteenth century, under Rudolph II, Prague became the capital of the Habsburg Empire. Rudolph was a strange, withdrawn man. Some think that he had inherited a strain of madness from his grandmother, the Spanish queen Juana la Loca, Joan the Mad. He was interested in astrology as well as astronomy, but he attracted great astronomers to Prague including Tycho Brahé, Giordano Bruno – later burned as a heretic in Rome's Campo dei Fiori for his heretical views on the age of the creation – and Johannes Kepler. Challenged by his brother Matthias, Rudolph turned to the Bohemian Estates, or parliament, which extorted from him concessions of liberty of conscience and other freedoms set down in the 'Letter of Majesty'. But quarrels over the meaning of this obscure charter led to the outbreak of the final conflict between the House of Habsburg and German Protestantism. All Germany was set on fire in the terrible Thirty Years' War, which ended, so far as Prague was concerned, in the total triumph of the Habsburgs. After the death of Rudolph, the Archduke Ferdinand, who had been educated by the Jesuits, became King of Bohemia, though he moved his court to Vienna.

Once again matters came to a head with a defenestration. Two leading Catholics, Jaroslav of Martinic and William of Slavata, and one of their followers, were hurled from the windows of Prague Castle sixty feet into the courtyard. (Luckily for them, they landed on a heap of dung and were hardly injured.) The Protestant Diet expelled the Jesuits and invited the Calvinist elector-palatine, brother-in-law of Charles I of England, to take the throne of Bohemia. But in November 1620 the elector and the Protestants were routed at the White Mountain, just outside Prague. Twenty-seven leaders of the revolt were executed with great cruelty in Old Town Square. By 1627, when Ferdinand imposed a new constitution, the victory of the Habsburgs and the Jesuits was complete. Bohemia, still nominally independent, was absorbed into the Austrian monarchy. The towns were compelled to convert to Catholicism, and 30,000 Protestant landowners emigrated. Before the war the great Catholic German-speaking nobles owned one third of the land; after it they owned two thirds. German became the official language, at first alongside Czech; later Czech became little more than a peasant dialect. The Czech peasants were reduced to misery by being forced to work several days a week for the lords, and the population fell, according to some accounts, by as much as 30 per cent. Worst of all, the intellectual leaders of the Czech people had either been killed or had emigrated abroad.

In the eighteenth century, under Maria Theresa and her 'enlightened' son Joseph II, the harshness of the Austrian conquest was relaxed and prosperity returned. The triumph of Austria brought the glories of the baroque to the *Kleinseite*, the 'little side' or 'lesser town' on the castle side of the Vltava, which the Czechs now call Malá Strana. Great aristocratic families like the Liechtensteins and the Waldštyns (in Germany, Wallenstein), the Lobkowitzes, Thuns and Schwarzenbergs built and ornamented superb palaces in the gardens and streets below the castle ramparts. In the closing years of the seventeenth century, great churches went up in an ornate baroque style to complement these private palaces. Finest of all is St Nikolas in Malá Strana, designed by Prague's two greatest masters of the baroque, Krystof Dientzenhofer, originally from Bavaria, and his son Kilian Ignaz Dientzenhofer. Their particular skill was to gather around them teams of painters, sculptors, cabinet-makers and metalworkers to undertake every detail of their conceptions. By the seventeenth century there was a whole quarter in Malá Strana occupied by Italian craftsmen and builders. The Dientzenhofers also worked in the Clementinum and at the great monastery of Brevnov, just outside the city near the site of the battle of the White Mountain.

The churches and palaces of the Prague baroque compose an incomparable ensemble, arguably as fine an architectural treasure as can be found anywhere between Rome and St Petersburg. Yet, beautiful as they are to our eyes, they had and perhaps still have a different, more sinister significance for the inhabitants of the city. For they were built as conscious trophies of the triumph of the House of Austria and its allies, the German-speaking nobility, over the defeated Czechs and Protestants. One of the proudest palaces in

Malá Strana, for example, is that of the Liechtensteins, descendants of the prince who governed Prague after the Habsburg victory at the White Mountain. Another is that of the Waldštyns, heirs of that Count Albrecht von Wallenstein who was the ruthless champion of the Catholic cause in the Thirty Years' War; it was his troops who perpetrated the sack of Magdeburg, a by-word for cruelty. The villa Hvězda, in the shape of a star, outside the city, and the Belvedere palace near the castle were built in the mid-sixteenth century by the first Habsburg ruler of Prague, Archduke Ferdinand: to a visitor they are light, elegant pleasure palaces; to a Czech they look like the arrogant assertions of the Austrian ruler who brought the Jesuits to Bohemia. And one of the masterpieces of K.I. Dientzenhofer, the church of Our Lady of Victories at Bila Hora, the site of the catastrophe of the White Mountain, is literally intended to celebrate the Habsburg triumph there.[3]

Across the river from the aristocratic palaces and monasteries of Malá Strana, the ghetto, known as the Josefstadt, survived and even from time to time prospered. Although the first Jewish inhabitants of Prague came from the south and the east, they were reinforced by Jews who came east from the Rhineland, Franconia and Bavaria along with the Christian Germans who were called in by the early Bohemian rulers and were later attracted by the city's prosperity, fed by the silver mines of the Bohemian mountains. The ghetto begins only a few hundred yards from the modern statue of Jan Hus in the Old Town Square. Walk a couple of blocks down Pařížská, a street of turn-of-the-century buildings in Parisian art nouveau, and you are in a neighbourhood where Jews have congregated for a millennium. Turn left after the kosher restaurant, and you can see the Old-New Synagogue, which dates from the second half of the thirteenth century. One century sounds much like another in guidebook prose; but the Old-New Synagogue has been celebrating the God of the Hebrews as long as there has been a Parliament at Westminster. The extraordinary Jewish cemetery near by, with memorial stones piled up and leaning on

one another like souls in an overcrowded heaven, was in use from
1439 to 1787; that is, from before the fall of Constantinople to the
Turks to the year Mozart's *Don Giovanni* got its first performance
a few hundred yards away. In this neighbourhood the Rabbi
Loew invented the Golem, a magical servant/monster that could
perform miracles; and to this crowded corner, at the end of his life,
came none other than the Wandering Jew, who in real life was
Joseph Solomon ben Elias del Medigo, who was born in Crete,
studied at Palermo and under the great Galileo, and practised
medicine everywhere from Cairo to Spain.[4]

Only once, as late as 1741, were the Jews expelled from Prague,
by the Empress Maria Theresa; she suspected them of sympathy
with the Prussians, who shelled the city and captured it under
Frederick the Great in 1757. But her son, Joseph II, brought the
Enlightenment to Prague, and with it the beginnings of emancipation for the Prague Jews. (If you want to catch the spirit of the
Austrian Enlightenment, there is no better place than the great
Strahov Monastery, at the top of the hill beyond Prague Castle. Its
twin glories are the theological and philosophical libraries, magnifi-
cently housed in rococo panelling, gilding and allegorical painting;
the canny abbot of Strahov was able to pick up those thousands of
volumes, sumptuously bound in calf, on the cheap, because the
enlightened emperor was closing so many other monasteries.) In
1781 the emperor decreed that the Jews need no longer wear the
yellow star. Jews were allowed to learn crafts and trades and even
to join the learned professions. The first Jewish doctor in the
Habsburg dominions graduated in 1788, the first Jewish lawyer in
1790; soon a pent-up, unstoppable drive for professional advancement and social improvement had been unleashed among Jews all
over the empire and beyond, with profound consequences for
Prague and for Europe. Now Jews were allowed to practise their
own religion. Nevertheless, for a time many cruel restrictions on
their freedom remained. The *numerus clausus*, or fixed limit on the
number of Jews permitted to reside in a given city, was maintained;
and at first only the eldest son in a Jewish family, the *familiant*, had

the right to marry and bring up children. But the essential step was taken under Joseph II: Jews were allowed to leave the ghetto. The remaining disabilities were removed, under the influence of the French Revolution, in 1848, and in 1860 Jews became full and equal citizens in all respects. Jewish families, ambitious to improve their own and their children's prospects, migrated into the city from smaller communities in Bohemia and beyond. By the middle of the nineteenth century there were 125,000 people in Prague, and 8,500 of those were Jews.

One consequence of emancipation was that the more prosperous Jewish families moved out of the ancient ghetto to newer suburbs that were springing up beyond the New Town. The Josefstadt became a slum for poor Jews and poor Christians as well. According to one contemporary description, the streets were covered with filth and children ran around half-naked. Many of the houses were the homes of poor but pious Jews; others were brothels.

What a fantastic mixture there was of riotous living and strict Jewish orthodoxy! Cheek by jowl with the haunts of vice and debauchery were the austere houses of believing Jews who locked their doors at nightfall, kept the Sabbath and observed the high festivals in traditional style. While the taverns and coffee-houses rang with the crazy mirth of Saturday night revellers, the synagogues and houses of prayer, of which there were some forty in the Jewish quarter of Prague, would be filled with the monotonous chant of their congregations.

In 1893, the decision was taken by the city authorities to clear the ghetto, and the sentence was carried out between 1897 and 1917.

In the years when the heart of the old city was being thus ruthlessly brought up to date, two small boys were already running around the streets of the Old Town and the scarcely less ancient fourteenth-century New Town next door. They were to grow into respectively the most important writer in the German language to come out of Prague (though that title is not wholly unchallenged) and the most influential and beloved of all writers in the Czech language.

The similarities and the differences of their lives could hardly be more striking, and together they stake out a strange, shared claim to have made Prague the capital of a certain spirit, a certain challenge to the orthodoxies of respect for nation and authority that have deeply marked the twentieth century, far, far beyond the tiny world of city streets, schools and cafés where they grew up. Both were born in 1883. Both died young, one in 1923, the other in 1924. Their families both came to Prague from small towns in Bohemia in the 1860s. They actually knew each other slightly; there are witnesses who put them in the same café at the same time on more than one occasion, though we have no record of what impression either made on the other. Kafka attended some meetings, it seems, at the Klub Mladych,[5] or Club of Youth, a place where the Anarchists met under cover of a mandoline club, of all things, in an inn called Zum Kanonenkreuz. Hašek, as a boy, was the ringleader of a gang of Czechs who went around beating up 'Germans', many of whom were in fact Jews;[6] Kafka had a close Jewish friend, already blind in one eye, who lost his other eye to a stone thrown by a Czech boy in a street fight.[7] Long before the final catastrophe, Prague was a city divided by bitter, if half-repressed, racial hatreds and conflicts.

Franz Kafka was a Jew, Jaroslav Hašek a Christian, or to be more precise a post-Christian Czech. Kafka wrote in German, Hašek in Czech. Kafka was skinny, neurotic about food, detested noise and lived all his life – except for a few brief holidays or visits to sanatoria – within the narrow compass of a few streets immediately around the Old Town Square and Prague Castle, and loved nothing so much as to explore the labyrinths of ancient houses in the very oldest parts of the city. He had few close friends, indeed perhaps only one true friend, the equally withdrawn boy who was to be a leading Zionist and his friend's literary executor, Max Brod. He was obsessed with the idea that he could, or should, never marry, and his love affairs, most of them largely on paper, were an endless sequence of neurasthenic games in which he teased any woman who showed interest in him by endlessly telling her how impossible he was.

Hašek, on the contrary, was fat, drunken, rowdy and confident, a cheerful psychopath who travelled compulsively, tramping all over Slovakia and Bavaria, and, after escaping across the Ukraine to Siberia with the Czech Legion, would have stayed in Soviet Russia if he had not been sent back to Prague as a secret agent by the Comintern. In a characteristically alcoholic replay of Prague's oldest myth, the martyrdom of St John of Nepomuk, Hašek drunkenly tried to commit suicide by throwing himself from the Charles Bridge. He was a bigamist, but a loyal one. He remained reasonably faithful to his first wife until he had gone to war, been taken prisoner, had spent years in Russia and met his second wife. Then he got back together with Jarmila, the mother of his son, and ended his life on would-be friendly terms with both of them.

Kafka was a capitalist, of a sort, an efficient and successful official of the (state-owned) Workers' Accident Insurance Institution; Hašek was an anarchist first, and not just a café anarchist, but an agitator who really attracted the attention of the secret police for his activities in the northern Bohemian coalfields, while the blameless Kafka was imagining police persecutions in Prague. Then he was a Bolshevik, and again not of the Bollinger variety; he was the political commissar of the Red Fifth Army and an agent of the revolution. Hašek scribbled his sketches and short stories with drunken facility and only finished his masterpiece when a friend dragged him down to the country and sat him down to work. He died expansively, weighing 300 lbs, of heart failure and cirrhosis of the liver brought on by his gargantuan self-indulgence. Franz Kafka, after a lifetime of fussing about his food, finally gave in to the tuberculosis that had made him a real invalid after years when he behaved like one.

'A great epoch calls for great men.' So begins, in the mock heroic Ercles' vein[8] which the book follows, the author's preface to *The Good Soldier Svejk*.[9] 'There are,' it goes on,

modest unrecognized heroes, without Napoleon's glory or his record of achievements. An analysis of their characters would overshadow even the glory of Alexander the Great. Today, in the streets of Prague, you can come across a man who himself does not realize what his significance is in the history of the great new epoch.

Jaroslav Hašek scribbled those words with tongue in cheek, no doubt sharing that cavity with a quantity of Budweiser. The fact is that the words apply even better to Svejk's creator than they do to Svejk. To the casual eye Jaroslav Hašek was as ordinary a man as you would meet downing Pilsners in the Prague pubs, just the kind of seedy journalist – with half-serious left-wing loyalties and a talent for satire – whose insignificance seems painfully obvious, a man who looked as if he was all set to drink himself to death and did just that before he was forty years old. Yet before he went he had performed an anabasis into central Asia which could compare respectably, for adventure if not for glory, with that of Alexander himself.

What Napoleon did for military glory, Hašek did for dumb insolence. Infinitely more effectively than any prophet of Czech nationalism could have done, his sly buffoon expressed the resentment and contempt the Czechs felt for their Austrian overlords. No man, the French say, is a hero to his valet. Like the English with the Irish, the Austrians had treated the Czechs as servants; and like the Irish of George Bernard Shaw's generation, the servants knew their masters' weaknesses better than the masters did themselves. Mercilessly, Hašek pins down the Austrian officers' petty vanity about ranks and uniforms, their half-baked sense of cultural superiority and their doomed effort to convince the world that a ramshackle collection of provinces flung together by dynastic accident added up to a great power. In doing so, and without meaning to, Hašek also helped to define the newly independent Czechs' picture of themselves. He endowed his countrymen with a sense of identity and a sense of humour that were to give them courage to resist far more savage oppression than the comic-opera strutting of the Austrians. He may also have encouraged them to set too low standards of expectation for their country and its public life; but more of that later.

In the compromise of 1867 the Habsburg empire bought off the smouldering discontent of the Hungarians by elevating the Hungarian crown into equality with that of Austria in the Dual Monarchy. The emperor was duly crowned in Budapest. But it should have been a Triple Monarchy. The crown of St Wenceslas of Bohemia was as old and as honourable as that of St Stephen of Hungary. But the Emperor Franz Joseph repeatedly put off his coronation in Prague, and the Czech people of Bohemia and Moravia, bursting with a new national pride and conscious of the wealth the industrial revolution was bringing to their provinces, resented it. They felt, one historian has written, 'no sympathy for the Germans and little loyalty for the Crown',[10] or for the German-speaking aristocrats with their huge estates in Bohemia. Hašek's mother's father, for example, was a water bailiff on the great carp ponds of the Schwarzenberg estate at Krc, which supplied half Prague with the fish that is the traditional Bohemian Christmas dinner. Hašek's father was well educated, but when he moved to Prague the best job he could get for a time was teaching mathematics in a private school. Later he got a job as an actuary in one of the new insurance companies. He died when Jaroslav was thirteen, a tough, restless boy who was active in a Czech street gang that fought Germans – many of them Jews.

Eventually he became so rowdy that he was expelled from the gymnasium, the classical school that prepared pupils for the university and for careers in the bureaucracy. Instead he went to the Commercial Academy, also an excellent secondary school that gave a good general education. There too he was a tearaway, with a sense of humour. One day he was sitting in Schäffer's café when he noticed that, during some rioting by Czechs against the Germans, a number of senior police officers had come into the café to refresh themselves, leaving their long military great coats, cloaks, feathered helmets and sabres on the hooks in the passage; the rector of the Commercial Academy, a pompous gentleman who loved to be known by his title of *Hofrat*, or 'court councillor', was also in Schäffer's at the time. Young Jaroslav disguised himself in uniform, slung on a sabre and, in a deep, official voice summoned the *Hofrat* to the police station, refusing to give any explanation. Once there, he left the wretched headmaster awaiting interrogation, skipped back to the café, slipped off his uniform and went back to his beer, looking as if butter would not melt in his mouth.

At seventeen he went on a walking tour in Moravia, Slovakia and down as far as Hungary and sold some articles about his adventures to a leading newspaper. That set a pattern. He became a wanderer, exploring much of south Germany, central Europe and even parts of the Balkans in long hikes with or without friends. He became an expert scrounger. He discovered, for example, that in any Slovak village you could get a bed for the night from the priest if you said the Protestant pastor had refused you. At the same time he became part of a group of young writers who belonged to a literary club called Syrinx and hung out in a pub called U Fleku. It was first built in 1499, a warren of panelled rooms with a curious old clock for an inn sign. (Though it still exists, it is crowded with German tourists, and it is difficult to recapture the atmosphere of Hašek's day.) At the time, Hašek found the tone a little too literary; his fellow members included serious-minded writers, one of whom later wrote the libretto to Janáček's famous opera *The Cunning Little Vixen*. But Hašek's special friend was a young man called Ladislav Hájek.

Hašek was constantly in minor trouble with the police for such offences as pissing up against the wall of the police station. But in 1904 he got into company that could have led to serious trouble. He went to work with the anarchists who were trying to agitate among the coal miners of the Brux basin in northern Bohemia. The miners were what was called 'Anarcho-syndicalists'; they had been politicized by the famous anarchist Johann Most. The Prague intellectuals, on the other hand, who met at a café in the prosperous middle-class Prague suburb of Vinohrady, and included young poets like Fráňa Srámek and Karel Toman, later to be well known as a left-wing union leader in Vienna, were influenced by the gifted writer S.K. Neumann. They called themselves 'anarcho-communists'. Their slogan was 'the revolutionary liberation of the individual', a cause that was entirely compatible with Jaroslav's penchant for talking and drinking the night away in cafés.

In the summer of 1906, however, Hašek fell in love with one of a little band of girls he had met. She was Jarmila Mayerova, daughter of a plasterer/contractor who was prospering as a result of the vogue for art nouveau decoration in the new quarters of Prague. Even so Hašek did not give up his anarchist activities – and this was at a time when a whole series of anarchist outrages had shocked and frightened the bourgeois like Jarmila's parents from one end of Europe to the other.[11] In 1907 he was arrested for beating up a policeman in a demo. When the case came up in court, with typical cheek, he tried to defend himself by reading out loud a Dostoyevsky story called 'The Double'. The magistrate joined in the laughter in court, but sent him down for a month just the same.

In 1910 Hašek put himself up in the local elections as the candidate of a spoof party called 'The Party of Moderate Political Progress within the Bounds of the Law', of which he later published a spoof history, after the usual confusions about rights, publishers and royalties which attended all of his writing ventures. As the Screaming Lord Sutch of Habsburg Prague, Hašek was a rather genial figure. But there was a darker side to his mocking humour. His friend Hájek had got a job as the editor of a periodical called *Animal World*. In a dispute with the owner, Hájek resigned, assuming that Hašek would resign in sympathy. But he didn't; instead, he took his friend's job.

That enabled him to get married, and in May 1910 he married Jarmila at the church of St Ludmila in Vinohrady. But no sooner had he got a steady job than he began to risk it with wild hoaxing. *Animal World* reported that 'dangerous herds of Scottish collies' were terrorizing Patagonia, and that the Vltava was alive with musk rats that had escaped from the grounds of the Princess

Coloredo's palace. One of his hoaxes, which involved setting up a bogus 'Cynological Institute' to sell pedigrees for mongrels, seems to have verged on downright fraud.

These wild practical jokes built up to what seems to have been a serious mental breakdown in February 1911. Possibly he had quarrelled with Jarmila over his behaviour. Certainly he was extremely drunk. For whatever reason, he climbed over the parapet of the Charles Bridge, apparently intending to commit suicide. He was rescued by a heroic hairdresser, one Eduard Bauer, who handed him over to k.u.k.[12] policeman František Melech, who in turn handed his prisoner over to Sergeant Hlinka, and he took Jaroslav straight to the k.u.k. mental home. At first, Jaroslav said he had seriously meant to kill himself. Later, he claimed he had merely wanted to attract attention. Whether or not the suicide attempt was genuine, however, there is little doubt that the mental crisis was real enough. Yet three months later, he was back with Jarmila, and in May he scribbled down the idea for a short story called 'The Booby in the Company'.

It has been speculated by scholars that the germ of that idea came from a joke in the Munich comic paper, *Simplicissimus*, which was translated into Czech and appeared in a paper in Prague. 'Who is the senior officer in the German army?' the private is asked. 'You are, my lieutenant!' he answers. Whether or not Hašek saw the story, that is the essence of the spirit of Svejk, the fool who is wiser than the wise. Soon afterwards, at any rate, Hašek wrote the story that has come to be known, in irreverent parody of Goethe and his *Urfaust*, as the *Urschweik*, the original Svejk.

That year, too, his first son was born. He remained, however, a deeply troubled and unpredictable young man. There are stories – the whole of Hašek's life is surrounded by an aura of apocrypha – that he was so proud of his son Richard (Ríša) that he dragged the baby round the pubs to show him off. But there is not much doubt that when Jarmila's family arrived for a visit, Jaroslav slipped out to bring in some beer, and never came back. For the next two years, until the beginning of the war, he became obsessed with cabaret, which was a new craze in central Europe. He wrote sketches for some of the most talented directors and actors in Prague, but then he took to going on endless pub crawls, from which he would return to clamber on to the stage at the Montmartre, take off his boots to reveal disgustingly dirty feet, and drone obscene monologues until the management banned him from the theatre.

When the war came, his first response was to check into a Prague hotel as Ivan Fyodorovich Kuznetsov, giving his profession as 'Russian spy'. Not long afterwards, though, he was called up, passed fit and, surely the most uncharacteristic act of his life, actually joined the 91st regiment as a volunteer so that he could become an officer. In July 1915 he went up to the front. Little he or Svejk knew or cared about the deliberations of general staffs. But Svejk's creator arrived at the front after the fortunes of war had already swung both ways. By the time Hašek and the 91st arrived in the line, the Austro-Hungarian armies had taken a severe beating, but had then been rescued by their German allies and had tasted success. The Czechs in the Austro-Hungarian army were ambivalent about the whole enterprise, however. Most of them disliked Germans in general and German militarism in particular. What was more, they were under the influence of Czech nationalism, which was strongly tinged with pan-Slav sentiment. They were far from sure they wanted to fight for the House of Austria; even less sure they wanted to fight for Austria against their Slav brothers in Russia. Many of them, nevertheless, fought loyally and well for Austria. Still, by September 1915, in spite of the Russian reverses, there were 200,000 Czechs and Slovaks in Russian prisoner-of-war camps. They had expected to be welcomed as prodigal sons by the Russians. Instead, they were treated less well than the Germans or even the Hungarians. Conditions in the camps were terrible, with minimum facilities, rampant disease, including typhus, and guards with whips who seemed not to have heard of the brotherhood of the Slavs.

On 24 September, Jaroslav Hašek was captured on a patrol. In captivity he found himself in an intensely politicized world in which the new Czechoslovakia that would emerge from Austrian defeat was already being hammered out. Specifically, the Czechs and Slovaks in Russia, who included emigrants and settlers as well as prisoners of war, were deeply divided between a conservative, slavophile group, led by Václav Vondrak, which was centred in Kiev; and a pro-Western group, led by Jan Masaryk. The February Revolution in Russia in 1917 was to put the Masaryk group in a strong position, as Masaryk was close to several of the moderates and liberals in the provisional government that emerged from that first upheaval.

A number of rudimentary political institutions were already in place when Jaroslav Hašek was made a prisoner. There was the Družina, the nucleus of the famous Czech Legion, ready and willing to fight for the Russians and against the Austrians. There was the League of Czech Clubs, and there was a Club of Associates of the League. There were also several shrilly political newspapers. Jaroslav plunged in with a characteristic lack of caution. He started out by taking a reactionary position, supporting the Romanovs and denouncing Masaryk. He wrote a number of articles which made him a wanted man for treason in Austria-Hungary. And on top of everything, after he had got out of the camps and was writing as a journalist for Czech papers in Kiev, he was sent back to camp for telling a Russian officer that if he, Jaroslav Hašek, stuck his finger up his arse he could run the war better than the Russian general staff.

On 2 July, meanwhile, the Czech Legion won a great victory over the Austro-Hungarian army at Zborov. It was to be part of the national legend of the new Czechoslovak republic. But the Czech Legion was in an exposed position. After General Brusilov's desperate offensive, the Russian front in the Ukraine was crumbling. The Legion could only get home if Austria-Hungary ceased to exist. Its leaders played with the idea of fighting their way out and going round by sea to fight in France, first by way of

Constantinople and later by going all the way to Vladivostok. That, in the end, is what they did. In one of the strangest and most heroic feats of arms in history, the Czech Legion, led by Masaryk, fought its way along the Trans-Siberian Railway to Vladivostok. At one time, in the chaos of the Russian civil war, the ten thousand Czechs controlled a territory thousands of miles across.

By that time, though, Jaroslav Hašek was no longer with them. At first, he saw the Bolsheviks as the allies of Austria. He was reinstated, and made a lance-corporal in the Legion. But then he moved sharply to the left. Probably he was influenced by a Communist journalist on the exiled Czech newspaper *Čechoslovan*. He wrote excited articles calling for a popular uprising in Prague. In April, at Samara on the Volga, which was where the Legion had got to by then, Hašek broke with the Legion and joined the Reds. On the three-hundredth anniversary of the Defenestration of Prague in 1618, the breach between the Bolsheviks and the Czech Legion became open, unbridgeable. Jaroslav Hašek, one little lance-corporal with a badly blotted copybook, was stranded in the middle of revolutionary Russia as the tides of civil war ripped in and out. Yet, surprisingly, Hašek survived. He did more than survive. As Comrade 'Gashek' – Russians can't manage Hs – if we can believe his own version in a short story published long afterwards, he ousted his boss, manoeuvred craftily between two factions, escaped hours ahead of Admiral Kolchak and the avenging White cavalry with the printing machinery for his party newspaper on a cart. What is undoubtedly true is that he rose to be the secretary of the Communist Party cell in the headquarters of the Fifth Red Army, and that in May 1920, in Krasnoyarsk, he married a comrade, Alexandra 'Shura' Lvova.

Married! But he was still married to Jarmila. In Krasnoyarsk, that might seem a remote and irrelevant fact. But Jaroslav did not remain in Krasnoyarsk. In December 1920 he arrived in Prague as a Comintern agent. He did not know it at first, but while he was travelling from Moscow by a circuitous route, Masaryk had smashed a Bolshevik rising in Prague. 'We've come too late,'

Jaroslav told Shura. 'The people I was supposed to get in touch with are all in jail.' In Russia, he had settled down, stopped drinking, turned himself into a disciplined and even ruthless party agent and bureaucrat. Now he went out and got so drunk that he didn't come home for three days.

In truth, that was not such an irrational response to the situation Jaroslav now found himself in. He was, after all, a deserter from the Czech Legion, which had returned as the praetorian guard of the triumphant Masaryk. He was an agent of the Comintern. And he was a bigamist. In April 1921 he was summoned by the police, not for political offences but, under Article 206 of the constitution, for bigamy. Oddly enough, in the two years of his life that remained, Jaroslav started to see Jarmila again and became, in an emotional as well as a technical sense, a bigamist.

He was also drinking, worse than ever. When anyone tried to help him, he raged at them. Yet a kind of salvation, even a strange canonization was at hand. In the Ukraine, when he was sent back to the camp, he started adding to the adventures of Svejk. In February 1921, at the end of his tether, he had the idea of writing a new and longer version of the story. He knew he would get no help from conventional publishers. Instead, he published it himself with a friend called Franta Sauer who, among other activities, ran an underwear shop. They inveigled Jaroslav's old friend Josef Lada into doing the drawings. They were exactly right for the text: coarse but robust and very funny. Svejk is instantly recognizable by his stubbly chin, whether he is 'administering extreme unction' by kicking a pompous gentleman downstairs, or cheeking Lieutenant Lukasch. 'It's a very funny thing, Schweik,' said Lieutenant Lukasch to his uncouth but ever resourceful batman, 'but, as I've told you several times before, you've got a strange way of poking fun at officers.' 'Oh, no, sir,' replied Svejk breezily. 'I only wanted to show you, sir, how people get themselves into trouble in the army.'

This is a burlesque view of the disasters of war. Hašek portrays the Habsburg Empire lurching into its last campaigns half-cut, unshaven and essentially ridiculous. There are beery parsons, thieving squaddies, cunning peasants. If there are also outrageous military blimps, like Colonel Kraus von Zillergut, who says, 'What's the good of taking prisoners? Shoot the lot. No mercy. And finish off the babies with bayonets,' in the 1920s that could still be played for laughs; a quarter of a century later it no longer seemed a caricature, still less a joke. Now Svejk's adventures were pouring out of Jaroslav's head, a distillation of all he had seen in peace and war, and he was planning to tell Svejk's story, which was also his own, from his call-up to Russia, in six volumes, if only he could stay sober and alive long enough to finish them. The first was published, amid oceans of beer, rivers of rum, lashings of frankfurters, onions, vinegar and potato dumplings, appropriately enough in a pub.

At this point, a strange fairy intervened and saved Jaroslav Hašek long enough to save Svejk for the Czech nation and eventually for the world. The fairy was Jaroslav's friend, the painter and illustrator Jaroslav Panuška, a man of the same gargantuan bulk and appetites as the writer, but with a kinder heart and a shrewder head. He spirited Hašek away from Prague to Lipice, gave him some money and installed him in the inn. Hašek continued to drink on an epic scale. His favourite tipple was what he called 'sailors' punch'. It was made with six bottles of white wine, two pints of cognac, and two allspice corns, six peppercorns, ten cloves and a piece of lemon. First you boiled the spices in half a litre of water, then you added the wine and the cognac and brought the whole heroic mixture to the boil.

Hašek was ill now, and grossly overweight. He hoped to get Svejk on the stage, and there were the usual quarrels with producers about money and rights before he succeeded. But now he had a small regular income, paid by an impresario. At first he used to sit toping and writing in the old castle hall. Then he bought a small house, knocked together from some of the castle outbuildings. By the time it was ready for him to move in, he was so ill that he could only use one room. But at least in Lipice he was

able to write. By the time he died, on 3 January 1923, four months
short of his fortieth birthday, he had finished four of the six books
of what has become one of the greatest comic masterpieces in any
European literature, a book which epitomizes the character of the
Czech nation as Don Quixote.

In October 1910[13] Franz Kafka went to see a troupe of travelling
Yiddish actors at the Savoy Café theatre in Prague. It was a
revelation. At one level he was perfectly capable of understanding
that the actors were mediocre and that the plays they performed –
Der Meshumed ('The Apostate') by Joseph Lateiner, *Shulamith* by
Avraham Goldfaden – were by all accounts creaking melodramas.
But at another, and for him deeper, level he was profoundly
stirred. He fell in love, at a respectful distance, since she was a
married woman with a child, with one of the actresses, Mania
Tschissik. And he entered into a fascinated friendship with the
leader of the troupe, Yitshak Löwy, a young man who had quit a
strictly Orthodox family to practise the forbidden craft of the
theatre. Kafka's feelings for Mania Tschissik were complex, because
she both fascinated him sexually and reminded him strongly of his
mother.

Although both his father and his mother were Jewish, Kafka
had not been brought up in Jewish orthodoxy. '*Nichts von der
Judentum*', his father used to say: 'Nothing from Jewry'. He seems
to have been relatively ignorant about Judaism: for example, he
did not know what a *yeshiva*, a traditional rabbinical school, was
until Löwy told him about a visit to one. He was indifferent to
Jewish ritual, which he once called 'a slothful routine of ritual
observance'; and he found the ceremony of circumcision distaste-
fully primitive.[14] His infatuation with Mania Tschissik led him to
say, in the privacy of his diary, that 'I did not always love my
mother as I should, only because the German language prevented
it.' To call a Jewish mother *Mutter*, he thought, made her a little
comic.[15] His friendship with Löwy stimulated his curiosity about
Judaism, and he began to read voluminous books about the history

of the Jews in French as well as German. Above all, the Yiddish actors seem to have provoked a sort of envy. Short of money, professionally struggling, marginal they might be. But they had no doubts about who they were. He recorded in his diary a little Yiddish rhyme he had presumably learned from his new friend Löwy: '*Os mir seinem, seinem mir, Ober Jüden seinem mir*' ('What we are, we are, But Jews we are').[16]

Some of Kafka's innumerable critics and biographers have laid heavy stress on his Jewishness, and so have seen in his encounter with the Yiddish actors an episode of absolutely crucial importance to his development because it stripped away a false, German consciousness and enabled him to come to terms with who he was. This is probably too simple. For one thing, to be a Jew in Prague was to be a member of a double minority. To be a German-speaker was to belong to a minority, but to be a Jewish German-speaker was to be a member of a minority within a minority, and one, moreover, which was rejected by German Christians and by Czechs, and which rejected and despised both. As Pavel Eisner points out, the German Jews in Prague belonged to a ruling class. The Germans were a ghetto consisting of the nobility, high officials, the officers of the garrison, industrialists and the wealthy bourgeoisie; the German Jews were wealthy businessmen, lawyers and industrialists, most of whom had moved far from the Josefstadt to the newer suburbs, as the parents of another Prague Jewish writer, a friend of Kafka's, Franz Werfel, had done. 'Jews had only Czechs working for them, both in their businesses and at home. The children of German Jews were suckled by Czech wet-nurses, waited on by Czech servant girls, received their first sexual initiation from Czech women.' What is more, this prosperous German Jewish class was dwindling. When Hitler finally marched in, some 60,000 out of the total population of Prague, which was about one million, were German speakers; and about half of those were Jews. Prague Jews had been leaving for decades, to seek their fortunes in Vienna, Berlin or other German cities, or in the United States. Franz Kafka, in his neurosis, was perhaps more typical of Prague Jews than he was of central European Jews generally.

He was certainly neurotic. As he spelled out near the end of his life, he hated his father, a moderately successful shopkeeper with a sturdy body and a bullying manner. He complained bitterly in his *Letter to My Father* that his father did not keep the rules he himself laid down for table manners for his children, but clipped his nails and cleaned his ears with a toothpick at table. Kafka was always preternaturally squeamish about bodies, his own and other people's. He was put off Rudolf Steiner, whose teachings interested him, because Steiner picked his nose. Kafka himself was fairly tall, and good-looking, though with a whimsical, vulnerable look; but he saw himself as hollow-chested and, though he loved to go swimming, he suffered agonies if he had to expose his half-naked body to the inspection of strangers. From a very early age he was neurotic about food. His diaries and letters are full of expressions of his disgust at eating, teeth, digesting and excreting. One sits at table talking and laughing, he said, or others did, for he neither spoke nor laughed at table, and meanwhile 'the teeth produce germs of decay and fermentation no less than a dead rat squashed between two stones'.[17]

Not surprisingly, Kafka was equally squeamish about sexuality, though he did have at least a few sexual experiences with Czech prostitutes whom he picked up in the streets of the Old Town. He was horrified by the sound of his father and mother making love, which he could hear in at least some of the apartments he lived in with them. Yet not until he was past thirty did he move out of his parents' apartment and rent a room of his own. Although the family had moved out of the ghetto, physically as well as emotionally, before he was born, he spent virtually the whole of his life within an astonishingly enclosed space in what is now the heart of the Prague beloved by tourists. He was born in the house next to St Nicholas Church in Old Town Square. The family moved repeatedly, to Wenceslas Square and back to Old Town Square, as Hermann Kafka sought to better himself; at one point, the family lived in a house next door to the Týn Church on the other side of the square, with a window inside the apartment that looked down into the church itself.

The whole of Kafka's early life, in fact, centred on Old Town Square. Hermann Kafka's shop was on the ground floor of the pink-stuccoed Kinsky Palace, the other side of the Týn Church, and Franz attended the German gymnasium on the first floor. The teaching was excellent, and the curriculum classical; Kafka studied Latin and Greek for ten hours a day. From there he went on to the Karl-Ferdinand-Universität, the German half of the ancient Charles University. The way that came about was in itself an illustration of how German culture, and with it German-Jewish culture, was being squeezed by the rise of Czech nationalism. In 1882 two separate Universities were set up, both successors in law of the Charles University. In one, the teaching was in German, in the other in Czech. They had different entrances, but they shared the Aula, the Great Hall, and they had access to the library on alternate days![18] His father, ambitious for him, wanted him to study law, which would open the way to careers in the Austrian administration as well as in the practice of law or in business. Kafka tried chemistry and German literature before settling on law. He graduated with little difficulty, and spent a year acquiring practical experience in the courts before he took a dead-end job as a clerk in the Prague office of the Italian insurance company, Assicurazioni Generali. The next year he got a better job, with the state-owned Arbeiter-Unfalls-Versicherung-Anstalt, or Workers' Accident Insurance Institute. It is worth remembering, as one reads his stories, elegant yet fantastical creations of a mind seemingly on the very frontier of paranoia, that the writer kept office hours as an ultra-correct, indeed – until physical illness interfered – highly successful insurance executive. Writers, after all, have to keep body and soul together, even if they hate their bodies as much as Franz Kafka did, and so Kafka worked in an insurance office, as James Joyce worked at a language school, Italo Svevo in a marine paint company and T.S. Eliot in a bank.

From very early on, Kafka knew that he wanted to write. In 1908 his early prose pieces were published as *Meditation*, and by 1910, when he began to keep a diary, you can see him painstakingly polishing his writing technique. He writes six different versions, for example, of a paragraph about his own education and the harm he considers it has done him. Yet very early he seems to have realized that, for him, salvation could only be attained by writing. 'I write this,' he noted soon after he started keeping a diary, 'very definitely out of despair over my body and over a future with this body.' Yet on the next page he was admitting that 'finally after five months of my life during which I could write nothing that would have satisfied me . . . it occurs to me to talk to myself again. Whenever I really questioned myself, there was always a response forthcoming, there was always something to catch fire.'

It was on the night of the 22–3 September 1912 that his writing caught fire. In a single sitting, from ten o'clock at night to six o'clock in the morning, he wrote the story 'The Judgement'. It was 'a fearful strain', as if he were 'advancing over water'. As the maid walked into the flat, he wrote the last sentence, and he rushed into his sisters' room and said with the pride he usually kept to himself, 'I've been writing until now.' Later in the day he wrote with the certainty, the pure joy of a man who knows he has found his way: 'Only in this way can writing be done, only with such coherence, with such a complete opening out of the body and the soul.' The story, though, is hardly joyful. On the contrary, it is a grim, paranoid tale of a young man whose father, after a trivial argument about a friend and his fiancée, goes mad and passes judgement on him: death by drowning. At which he rushes across the road to the river and throws himself in, as an unending stream of traffic was crossing the bridge. As Jaroslav Hašek had attempted to do, the fictional *Doppelgänger* of Franz Kafka re-enacted the martyrdom of St John of Nepomuk.

Now Kafka had found the manner of his mature writing, a strange, dream-like mixture of realism and sinister fantasy, the language of nightmare, and in the next two years he used it to write a series of works of haunting power. There was 'Metamorphosis', the story of a young salesman, Gregor Samsa, who wakes up one morning transformed into a giant insect. There was the horrible, undeniably powerful 'In the Penal Settlement'. This is the report of an explorer who visits an island prison, like Devil's Island, where an officer has invented a machine for torturing condemned prisoners to death by tearing their flesh with needles which write the nature of their crime on their body. By writing with absolute detachment Kafka transforms this horrible idea into a fable, a metaphor for life itself, that is almost noble.

Rereading the proofs of 'The Judgement' a few months later, Kafka subjected his own story to a sort of psychoanalysis. 'The story came out of me like a real birth, covered with filth and slime, and only I have the arm that can reach to the body itself and the strength of desire to do so.' And he proceeds to identify the characters: his father with the father, himself with the young man, and the young man's fiancée with Félicie Bauer, whom he called Félice. She was a sensible, strong-minded Jewish woman whom he subjected to endless neurotic doubt, agonizing over his feelings, about his desire to get married, his terror of marriage, his horror at the physical aspect of marriage. 'Coitus,' he wrote in his diary at the height of his hesitations, '[is] punishment for the happiness of being together.'[19] Twice they were engaged, twice they broke it off, the second time after Kafka was diagnosed, in 1917, as having tuberculosis of the lung.

There were to be other relationships, other attempts to reconcile Franz's horror of the flesh with his yearning for love and companionship. There was an engagement to a Jewish woman, Julie Wohryzek; a love affair, much of it conducted through the medium of passionate letters, with a Czech woman, Milena Jesenka; and a final affair, more that of a patient with a loving nurse, with a German-Jewish woman, Dora Dymant. Kafka went to live with her in Berlin, but his illness drove him back to Prague. He spent time in various sanatoria. In 1924, he died in a nursing home at Kierling and was buried in Prague.

Max Brod, Kafka's closest friend, who had grown up with him in the Old Town, was appointed his literary executor. Kafka laid it down that all his unpublished work must be destroyed. Happily,

Brod ignored this request. In 1925, he published *The Trial*. In 1926, *The Castle*. In 1927, the story he had begun as *Der Verschollene* ('Missing, Presumed Dead') but which Brod called *Amerika*. That is the weakest of the three. But in *The Trial* and *The Castle* Brod rescued from the dustbin of history two of the most powerful and resonant novels of the twentieth century. *The Trial* is the story of Joseph K., who works in a bank as Franz K. worked in an insurance company; one morning, as suddenly and inextricably as Gregor Samsa was turned into an insect, K. is arrested. The book is the story of his futile attempts to clear himself. It reaches a magnificent climax in St Vitus Cathedral in Prague, in a scene with echoes of Dostoyevsky's Grand Inquisitor's speech; in it, a priest, mysteriously appearing to pass judgement on K., expresses the indifference of Kafka's world, the world in which God has died. 'The court wants nothing from you,' says this priest, or anti-priest. 'It receives you when you come and it dismisses you when you go.' A few days later, two men come for Joseph K. They drag him to some waste land beyond Prague Castle. And there they stab him to death. 'Like a dog', is his last conscious thought.

The hero of *The Castle* is also K. He is a 'land surveyor', and he has been sent for by 'the Castle', domain of German princes, perhaps, like the castle at Lipice where, in the very same months in 1922 when Kafka was writing in Prague, Jaroslav Hašek was racing against death to finish Svejk. Like the leaden-booted self in a frustration dream, K. flounders through the village at the foot of the castle hill. No one is expecting him. His assistants turn into mysterious, malevolent figures. He becomes involved with women. One of them, Frieda – which means 'peace' in German – seems to be a symbol of carnality. The other, Amalia, has earned the enmity of the Castle by refusing the advances of one of its minions; she appears to be a symbol of morality, or at least of the heroism of resistance to 'arbitrary power'. The novel is unfinished, and Kafka has teased us by telling Max Brod that in the end, K. would find 'partial success'.

He was not to relax his struggle, but to die worn out by it ... From the Castle itself word was to come through that though K.'s legal claim to live in the village was not valid, yet, taking certain auxiliary circumstances into account, he was to be permitted to live and work there.

But of course by then he was dying! Nothing could better sum up Kafka's art, and his view of life: that it is puzzling, cruel, but also absurd. His stance is tragic, ironic, but also witty and above all courageous. Understandably, Kafka's writing has been seen as somehow prophetic of the Holocaust, and as somehow a metaphor for a specifically Jewish anguish. Irving Howe has pointed out, though, that by Kafka's time the themes of estrangement, isolation, terror before men without pity in a world without God, had ceased to be specifically Jewish concerns, but had become 'quandaries for all mankind'. One peculiar trick of Kafka's style is to supply so little detail about his central narrators that they become Everyman, and everyone can therefore identify with them. His literary achievement in fact was to make every reader identify with the man in the maze, waiting for the brazen rush and hot breath of the minotaur. His philosophical contribution was to understand that we are all in the maze, and that the brazen monster is waiting for us all; it is in the way that he faces up to the maze and the monster that a man is justified. Together, *The Trial* and *The Castle* are nothing less than the last will and testament of that central European society, Gentile as well as Jewish, that was to be consumed, twenty years after Kafka's death, by the brimstone and the fire.

The bumbling bureaucracy that provided Franz Kafka with his metaphor for human life, and the incompetent militarism satirized by Jaroslav Hašek, were soon to be succeeded by something infinitely worse. The Prague which Kafka carried in every cell of his body and brain was exterminated. The tragedy was described with pitiless precision and stark humour by one of the few survivors, Jiři Weil, in his great novel, *Life with a Star*. For once again, two hundred years after the reforms of the Enlightenment, Jews in Prague were obliged to wear a yellow star, and it was the Jewish community itself which took responsibility for dishing out these marks of humiliation. Altogether 77,000 Jews from Bohemia and Moravia were killed on German orders, 36,000 of them from Prague. In the old fortress at Theresienstadt, in Czech Terezin, only an hour's drive north of Prague, the Nazis enacted a sinister comedy that might have eluded even Kafka's imagination. Terezin was a sorting office from which the Jews of Czechoslovakia were sent onwards in those terrible trains to their final destinations. But in the meantime, because Terezin was the prison shown to visitors from the International Red Cross, a kind of Potemkin village of the Final Solution, the Prague Jews were allowed to continue to express, right to the end, their extraordinary passion for the high culture of the society that was about to exterminate them. Several string quartets, even a full symphony orchestra, performed in the fortress. There was even a jazz band, named, almost incredibly, the Ghetto Swingers. With savage restraint, the obscenity of Terezin is commemorated in a small exhibition in the gatehouse to the Old Cemetery in the heart of the Josefstadt, displaying the talents of the children locked up with their parents in the fortress. Where little English children drew Spitfires and tanks, their guns belching orange flame at Jerry, the children of Terezin crayoned their own experience of war: gallows and firing squads.

For almost half a century, darkness descended on Kafka's Prague and on Hašek's. The brief flicker of hope at the liberation was extinguished by another defenestration: Jan Masaryk, the son of the founder of the Republic, who was foreign minister, threw himself to his death from the windows of the Cernin Palace, on the castle hill, not far from Karl Ignaz Dientzenhofer's church of St John of Nepomuk. Nobody knows for sure why Jan Masaryk died; probably he killed himself because he was being intolerably chivvied and perhaps blackmailed by the Communists.

At first the Communist regime exceeded Kafka's worst nightmares. In 1948 Stalin ordered a purge of the Czechoslovak-

Communist Party. Under the supervision of sinister Soviet security agents, called 'teachers', non-Communist Czechs were tortured into confessing every kind of treason. The show trials were orchestrated by the party's secretary-general, Rudolf Slansky. Hundreds were executed and thousands sent to prison or to labour camps. But Stalin was still not satisfied that he had crushed the independence of Czechoslovakia. In 1951 he turned on the party. Thirteen senior members of the government and party were put on trial. They were tortured into humiliating, incoherent confessions. In 1952 eleven were executed, eight of them Jews. One of them was Rudolf Slansky.

The Prague Spring of 1968 was a false spring, and if under Gustav Husak the repression was not quite so harsh as in the Stalin years, it was hard enough for those who had to bear it, and especially for the writers and intellectuals who defied it. It was not until the Velvet Revolution of 1989 that Prague emerged, blinking, into freedom, though freedom with severe political and economic problems.

One candle had shone throughout the dark years; the light of literature. Between the Nazi invasion and the Velvet Revolution, Prague had become the centre of perhaps the most vigorous and interesting literature in Europe. The novels both of writers like Josef Škvorecký and Milan Kundera, who went into exile, and of those like Václav Havel, Jaroslav Seifert, Ivan Klíma and Ludvik Vaculík, who stayed behind, were published at first by the 'Padlock Press', as the samizdat writing was called. After 1989, as everyone knows, Havel became the president of the Czechoslovak republic and, after an interval, of the Czech republic. Nowhere in the West was literature accorded so high a place by ordinary people as it was in the Communist lands. Sir Isaiah Berlin has recorded the astonishing outpouring of response to Russian poets such as Boris Pasternak and Anna Akhmatova when the Stalin regime, in the years immediately after the war, allowed them to read their work in public; if they hesitated for a moment over a word, even in unpublished poems, eager voices from the audience of soldiers and workers would supply it.[20] It was like that in Prague too.

After 1968 repression was less brutal, more subtle and sly than in the Stalin years. That did not mean it was not real. Havel was twice sent to prison, and so was the 'jazz section' of the Musicians' Union. Jazz, as Josef Škvorecký explained in a notable essay, had a special meaning for the dissidents, in that it was at once intellectual and popular, American and proletarian, if not intrinsically subversive.

Some writers used to frequent the Slavia, a handsome art nouveau café now being restored to its former glories on the Vltava embankment, with a glorious view of the Castle, where the arch-enemy Gustav Husak sat. Here Jaroslav Seifert, the Nobel Prize poet, wrote, poets gathered and looked across to the miniature Eiffel Tower on the hill opposite, and at the Vltava, and 'it was the Seine, yes, it was the Seine'. The Slavia boasts of a misty emblematic figure dressed in green, known as the Green Goddess. In the good old days, so to speak, she was supposed to appear in the hallucinations of those who had drunk too much absinthe; under Husak, the Slavia served only *turecka*, Turkish coffee, and *becherovka*, a gingery vermouth, watched by slit-eyed spooks at the neighbouring tables. Havel preferred to meet friends in a little restaurant near his apartment called the Paraplavba. Karel Pecka, an older writer who had been sent to the uranium mines for a long stretch in the bad years, used to drink in the Black Ox on the castle hill, the pub patronized by his STB interrogator, to whom he would occasionally lift a silent glass across the room. Some writers got together in the Viola nightclub, not far from the opera house. Bohumil Hrabal, who wrote *Closely Observed Trains*, used to drink at Hašek's favourite pub, U Fleku, though you would see more German tourists than Czech writers there now.

The commonest hang-out for dissident get-togethers, however, was their own homes: that was cheaper, more discreet and, up to a point, safer. Older intellectuals who had come to prominence before 1968 often had surprisingly spacious flats and even country cottages. Younger people, for example those expelled from university for writing or speaking of the party in a critical way, often had a far harder life. The leading Slovak intellectual, Miroslav Kusy, a bulldozer driver under the Husak regime and now rector of the Comenius University in Bratislava, used to invite a regular group for sessions of chess and politics at his home in the suburbs. At one session attended by, among others, the much mourned Slovak writer and dissident, Milan Simecka, the intellectuals pounded the table until its legs became wobbly. When they got down to repair it, they found a small metal object screwed to its under surface. This they removed and placed on the mantelpiece. A little later a police car drew up and a poker-faced official, announcing that they were in illegal possession of state property, pocketed the bug and left.

Prague, Brno and Bratislava were full of window-cleaners, stokers and cleaning ladies who had been philosophers, playwrights and poets. If manual work was hard for previously sedentary intellectuals, it had its compensations. It left a good deal of time for discussion and writing 'for the drawer'. There were two quite elaborate dissident arrangements for higher education, the 'underground university', conducted by Czechs who met in each other's flats and read each other's work, mostly politics and fiction; and the 'flying university', taught in part by Western academics such as the Oxford philosopher Anthony Kenny and the sociologist Steven Lukes, who came to Czechoslovakia on holiday and disappeared for long enough to bring their Czech opposite numbers up to date on what was happening in the West. Moreover, under Communism manual workers were not badly paid, and some dissidents managed to supplement their wages as stokers or cleaners with smuggled royalties from the West. Of the two leading exiled writers, Milan Kundera, who lived in Paris, was resented by the dissidents in Prague; but there was gratitude for Škvorecký, who went to Canada and set up a press there which published a lot of Czech writers. A steady and discreet flow of books, whisky and royalties somewhat cushioned the harsh realities.

Music, both classical and popular, was important. Top of the pops was Marta Kubisova, who got into trouble in 1968 for kissing

Alexander Dubček, the hero of the Prague Spring, in front of TV news cameras on his return to Prague from the Soviet Union. Sex, too, enlivened the bored, hothouse atmosphere of the dissident scene. If Philip Roth's *Prague Orgy* exaggerated matters, it was not by much. Milan Kundera described the Prague of the years before 1968 as a sexual paradise, and others have observed a pervasive eroticism in Czech life as well as in Czech writing. Helena Klimova, the wife of the novelist Ivan Klíma, told an English friend that 'one of the oddest results of persecution was how political frustration boiled over into a preoccupation with sex'.

If the repression had its consolations, the persecution was real enough. Some dissidents tried to opt out by going to live in communes in remote corners of the country; the Communists sent bulldozers and knocked down the little houses they had built with their own hands. A cruel punishment for central European intellectuals, who cared more about education than about almost anything else, was the regime's refusal to allow the dissidents' children to go to university. Some of the dissidents challenged the regime openly. Nothing was more highly prized than an unregistered typewriter, and lovingly the dissidents typed eleven copies each of samizdat articles, because that was the most carbons you could use and still type a legible copy, and then start again; lovingly these articles about the politics of repression and the ethics of resistance were distributed to a tiny audience. And if you were caught you went to prison. Every intellectual of any standing had his own personal interrogator, like the man to whom Ludvik Vaculík dedicated his *Letter to My Interrogator*. Vaculík was one of several people jailed for taking Jaroslav Seifert's work abroad.

There was no mass resistance in the 1970s and 1980s like Solidarnosc in Poland. Charter 77 was not a broad working-class movement, but a stand made by a few thousand people who consciously thought of themselves as 'intellectuals' in the classic central European tradition: fewer than 2,000 signed the Charter in its first year. Instead, many people retreated into what they called 'inner exile', 'living the truth', as Havel put it in a famous essay.

That, too, could be dangerous. Helena Klimova, a psychotherapist, was not allowed to work for some years. When she at last got a job again, she found she was expected to pay a monthly subscription to a charity. The amount was small, but Klimova believed some of the money went to support international terrorism, and she refused to pay. So she lost her job again until she finally decided that she could help people more by doing her job than by refusing to pay. She calls this 'living by example'. It remains to be seen whether writers will be able to maintain the same position in freedom that they were given in the dark years. What, after all, will they find to write about?

When you stand on the bridge, and look up at the castle, it is easy to imagine a golden age when these domes and spires echoed to the music of Haydn and Mozart. That is to misunderstand the nature of Prague, and of that central European civilization of which Prague is one of the supreme ornaments. It was a place of beauty, of laughter and music. It was also, always, a place of conflict and pain and anger.

The Reformation and the Counter-Reformation clashed with peculiar sharpness in Prague, which had bred, in Hussism, a precursor of Protestantism that answered to the deep individualism and 'bloody-mindedness' of the Czech people. Catholicism, the Reform and Judaism were in conflict there, and so were Germans, Czechs and Jews. For centuries, the Germans worked closely with the Jews while repressing and persecuting them; in the end, abruptly, they annihilated them. Over centuries, the Germans succeeded in reducing the Czechs to a status not much higher, with a few exceptions, than servitude; over the last century, the Czechs have recaptured Prague and made it once again what it was before the later Middle Ages, a Czech city. Glorious it is. But it is not the effortless glory of Augustan equilibrium and untroubled grace. It is the glory that celebrates centuries of heroic strife, the recollection of countless martyrdoms, celebrated and forgotten.

CHAPTER VII
MEMORIES OF THE FUTURE

THE FIRST TRAFFIC LIGHT IN EUROPE WENT
up in the middle of Berlin's Potsdamer Platz.[1] It was a proud
symbol. Greater Berlin was formed that same year from two
dozen suburbs. Now it had four million people, the third largest
city in the world. It was the capital of modernism, the World
City, determined to catch up and surpass London and New York.
Around the 'traffic tower' an endless swirl of cars, buses, trams and
people, pouring in and out of banks, hotels and the entrances of
the U–bahn, the underground railway, thronged what Berliners
called 'the busiest crossroads of Europe'.

Berlin itself was a crossroads. In 1927 it was a great industrial
metropolis employing hundreds of thousands in engineering. There
was Siemensstadt, newly decorated with the latest ideas in modern
housing by a team of architects including Walter Gropius, and

AEG, the great electrical combine. It was a communications ganglion with the most modern airport in Europe at Tempelhof, the most modern film studios, UFA, at Babelsberg, three major newspaper groups; it was a centre of entertainment and intellectual life in publishing, music, theatre, sport and cabaret. It was the home of the avant-garde in every field from nuclear physics to nudism, of Bertolt Brecht and Marlene Dietrich, Max Reinhardt and Albert Einstein.

The contrast between the fabulous vortex of activity in the Potsdamer Platz in the 1920s and the scene there today is telling enough. For a start, you literally can't see that there ever was a square there at all. When you climb out of the U-bahn today, you are in a sea of mud. Scraps of the infamous wall are still standing. Refugees are crammed into a ramshackle caravan park. A tatty anti-war exhibition offers a Cruise missile scrawled with tawdry hip-hop graffiti. A crassly commercial museum commemorates the rise and fall of the Berlin Wall, and Russian deserters, the former conquerors, hawk fur hats and Soviet cap badges to German tourists for a few marks.

The crowds will come back to the Potsdamer Platz. Daimler Benz, Sony and other world corporations are committed to investing billions of D-marks in office and shopping projects.[2] The Wall is down. Traffic moves once more through the Tiergarten, under the Brandenburg Gate and past the once imperial buildings of Unter den Linden. Berlin is again the capital of a united Germany. A new Federal Chancery will go up next to the refurbished bulk of the Reichstag, burned by the Nazis in 1934, and the next president of the Federal Republic will move into what is now the Opera Café, where old ladies meet for coffee and cakes, but was once the palace of the Crown Prince.

Unlike Prague, physically if not psychologically unscathed by the twentieth century, Berlin was flattened, first by British and American bombs, then by the Russian guns. Then it was divided by the Wall, as if a frenetic Western world of neon and nightlife still flared in Kensington High Street, but the equivalents of

Whitehall and Westminster, the City and Whitechapel, lay dark under the orders of a dreary Stalinist government in Walthamstow. In the 1960s the historian Gerhard Masur, who was brought up in Berlin and attended the Kaiser Wilhelm Gymnasium and Berlin University before fleeing, like so many of the most talented of his fellow citizens, to California, revisited the city and spent some time at the new Free University. He soon realized, he said, 'that the city of my boyhood no longer existed ... What is now called Berlin bears no resemblance to the old imperial city.'[3]

Berlin has many interests and pleasures for a tourist now that the Wall is down: great museums in Charlottenburg and Potsdam, three opera houses and the raunchiest nightlife in Europe. But its fascination, for a visitor who can see beneath the surface, is that this was not only a focus of talent and creativity on an extraordinary scale; this is also where some of the greatest wickedness and folly of the twentieth century took place. Half of the buildings where the most terrible nightmares of our time were dreamed are as if they had never been; the other half still stand as if butter wouldn't melt in their mouths.

The house where Otto Hahn and Fritz Strassmann first split an atom of uranium is a suburban villa in leafy Dahlem: 83 Thielallee.[4] Not far away are the Glienicke Bridge, where the CIA and the KGB swapped spies in the Cold War;[5] and another handsome villa where the Wannsee conference in January 1942 decided on the 'final solution' of the 'Jewish question'.[6] This is the banality of evil indeed.

The Schloss, the Hohenzollerns' great palace on the Spree Island, was so badly damaged by Allied bombing in 1944 that it had to be blown up in 1950. Symbolically, the space it once occupied is now the Marx-Engelsplatz, complete with lumpish sculptures of Karl and Friedrich. Many of the fine classical buildings along Unter den Linden still stand, including the Zeughaus,[7] once the arsenal and then the museum of Prussian militarism; the New Watch, an exquisite miniature by the great neo–classical architect, Karl

Friedrich Schinkel, where East German sentries, until the Wall came down, did their drill like Prussian grenadiers; and the prancing statue of Frederick the Great. Here we are among the very hearthstones of Prussian militarism, fountain and origin of so much harm.

The very elegance of the architecture, though, reminds you that there was another side to Prussianism, a taste for style and a passion for learning; and so do the buildings on the museum island near by. The Pergamon Museum holds the treasures brought back by German archaeologists under the two kaisers between 1871 and 1914 in a conscious bid to challenge the archaeological imperialism of the British Museum and the Louvre. Whatever the motive, the collections of Greek, Hellenistic, Near and Far Eastern art are extraordinary, especially the reconstructed gate of Babylon and the Pergamon altar itself. Next door the Old Museum, with another of Schinkel's cool colonnades, is being restored.

Schinkel's greatest masterpiece in Berlin, though, is the Schauspielhaus, the theatre, famous for its performances of Schiller's classics. It stands between the twin French and German cathedrals, in the Gendarmenmarkt. Walk a few blocks west to what was called the Otto-Grotewohl-strasse for forty years, and has now reverted to its old name, the Wilhelmstrasse. Turn south and look for the Chancellery, the nerve centre of imperial Germany. It has gone, like the Schloss. In its place is a hideous complex of Stalinist buildings which once housed East German ministries and are now occupied by the Treuhandanstalt, the organization that is privatizing East German industry.

In the winter of 1918–19, with numbing speed, the pompous edifice of imperial Germany melted like a snowman; and Germany's near-revolution happened in this same small quadrilateral of streets between the Brandenburg Gate in the west and the Alexanderplatz, with its 1950s television tower, in the east. It was in the Reichstag building, still standing, that the Social Democrat minister, Philipp Scheidemann, rose from his lunch and casually announced the coming of the republic from a window. It was in the Schloss that the revolutionary Karl Liebknecht, in his long johns, climbed into the kaiser's bed and piled his dinky bedside table so high with revolutionary texts that it snapped.[8] The Schloss has gone.[9] In its place there stands the dismal modern Palace of the Republic in bronze-tinted glass erected by the German Democratic Republic, which cannot even be safely demolished because it contains so much lethal asbestos. But the Marstall, the imperial stables, where the Red sailors from the North Sea fleet were shelled by the future Nazis of the Freikorps, still stands. The Eden Hotel, where Rosa Luxemburg and Liebknecht were interrogated by the Horse Guards, was bombed in 1945, but the wooded rides of the Tiergarten, where they were shot, are bright with azaleas in spring and cheerful with children and lovers.

It is the same with the monuments of the crazy years between the great inflation of 1923 and the coming of Hitler ten years later: some have disappeared as thoroughly as if they were in ancient Babylon, others are still banally in use. The Scheunenviertel, the ghetto north-west of the Alexanderplatz where the immigrant eastern Jews congregated after the First World War, has gone without leaving a trace of its *yeshivas* and its old-clothes men, its prostitutes and its Hebrew publishers. The Romanisches Café, where in the 1920s you might have seen Thomas Mann or the young Bertolt Brecht, was in the Tauenzienstrasse, in the tacky 'showcase of the West' near the 'decayed tooth' of the Memorial Church and the ice-rink in the Europa Centre. The transvestite clubs of Isherwood's Berlin have gone; but there are plenty of shady bars in the Lietzenburgerstrasse in the west and the Prenzlauer Berg in the east.

In 1900 imperial Berlin was to all intents and purposes the youngest of the world's capitals. To be sure, there was a settlement of Slavic Wends near the sandy island on the Spree, and the twin settlements of Berlin and Kölln were established there in the middle of the thirteenth century in the course of the *Drang nach Osten*, the crusading thrust of the Christian Germans to the east. Berlin lay in the territory of the Brandenburg March, which by a dynastic accident fell into the hands of the junior branch of a remarkable family, the Hohenzollern, and in the middle of the fifteenth century they built their chief castle there. It remained the unremarkable seat of one among many German princes until the eighteenth century, when first Frederick William I – the soldier king – and then his grandson, Frederick the Great, transformed the kingdom of Prussia, as the Hohenzollern fief had become, into a military power to rival Austria and even France. Frederick also transformed Berlin physically. He planted the Tiergarten with trees and flowering shrubs, and he endowed the centre of his capital with the complex of churches, palaces and opera-house he called the Forum Fridericianum, the essence of which still survives in spite of all the disasters of the past seventy-five years. From the time of Frederick Berlin acquired a recognizable architectural idiom, a sober classicism which has been called 'the Prussian style'. And it was in his time, too, that Berlin, the home of a flourishing colony of French Protestant émigrés since the end of the previous century, began to develop as a centre of crafts and industry and also of university and intellectual life, all, however, strictly under the patronage and authority of the Hohenzollern court.

Berlin and its university played an important part in the explosion of German nationalism which followed the French Revolution and responded to Napoleon's victories by resolving to build a Prussian state that could defeat revolutionary and republican France. Even so, in 1870, when the task had been triumphantly completed and the new German empire, with its foot on the neck of prostrate France, extorted an indemnity of five billion gold francs, Berlin was still no great European capital. The transformation came with astonishing speed in the *Gründerjahre*, the 'founders' years', as Germans called the 1870s. The 'bliss of billions', one historian has written, 'transformed Berlin from a second-rate residential town into an industrial metropolis'.

It was a time of roistering economic growth. The city's population shot up, from 657,000 in 1865 to 964,000 in 1875. By 1920, when twenty surrounding communities were merged into Greater Berlin, it reached four million. Berlin, in fact, was the only great European city to grow at the explosive pace of American cities like New York or Chicago. Hundreds of new companies were founded, 780 of them in Prussia in the two years 1872–4 alone, the majority of those in Berlin. The great new banks had their headquarters there, the Deutsche Bank, the Dresdner Bank, the Diskont Bank and the House of Bleichröder, Bismarck's own Jewish banker, all in the Behrenstrasse,[10] and so did the double structure of government, for Berlin was the capital of Prussia, the biggest and wealthiest German state, as well as of the empire. In 1896 the Gewerbeausstellung, or Industrial Exhibition, consciously rivalled such exhibitions as the Universal Exposition in Paris in 1881 and the Chicago exhibition of 1893. A whole new exhibition ground with its own S-bahn station was purpose-built at Treptower Park, specially lit with electricity provided by Berlin's own electrical giants, AEG and Siemens und Halske, not to mention a Borsig steam engine, locally built. With eighteen brass bands a Festival of Labour claimed for Berlin the title of 'the first industrial city in the world'.[11]

This economic expansion had profound consequences for Berlin and indeed for Germany. It created for the first time a wealthy bourgeoisie, whose genteel adulteries are described with insight and elegance in the novels of Germany's best nineteenth-century novelist, Theodor Fontane.[12] There was a wave of real-estate speculation and whole new districts were developed. The wealthy classes, as in London, Paris, Brussels and other European capitals, moved out to the west. The new millionaires lived either around the Tiergarten park or in the Grünewald in the far west. The older intellectual upper middle class, the professors at the university and the upper civil servants, lived in what was called the Old West, closer to the centre and their beloved opera and subscription concerts. The prevailing wind in western Europe is from the south-west, so that the smoke of the steam age was blown over the eastern districts, and there a swollen proletariat crowded together in *Mietkasernen*, 'rent barracks', as the tenement blocks were called. Typically, a family of workers would live in a two-room flat. Rents were high and hours were long, ten or twelve hours a day. But conditions were 'dismal, rather than desperate', and these were in many ways years of hope and progress for the Berlin working class, which looked on itself as the vanguard of the European working class. The vote for the Social Democrats rose steadily over the thirty years before the war and the Berlin workers proudly claimed '*Berlin gehört uns*' ('Berlin belongs to us').

It didn't, though. It belonged, almost as firmly as in Russia, to the monarch. The empire had universal manhood suffrage for the lower house of Parliament, the Reichstag, from the start. But this was what the Social Democratic leader, Wilhelm Liebknecht, father of Karl Liebknecht, the Spartakist leader of 1919, called 'pseudo-constitutionalism' and 'the figleaf of absolutism'. For the Reichstag had no power over the monarch or over his ministry. There was no doctrine of ministerial responsibility to parliament and the Reichstag could not get rid of a chancellor; only the emperor could. As late as 1878 Bismarck, as chancellor, tried to suppress the working-class movement as a whole, party, trade unions, marching bands and all, with his anti-socialist law, which would have enabled him to declare a state of siege in case of strikes.

The Austrian ambassador, Graf Paul Vassili, who must have known what he was talking about, observed that 'nowhere is there a greater differentiation between the classes which compose the nation than in Berlin', and the police president, von Madai, agreed. 'The antagonism between the classes has sharpened,' he wrote in an official report in 1889, 'and a gulf separates the workers from the rest of society.'[13]

Another gap separated Jews from the rest of society. The roots of anti-Semitism in Germany go deep into the medieval past. Thirty Jews were burned alive in Berlin in 1500, accused of ritual murder, and it was not until 1671 that a stable Jewish community was allowed to settle there. Between 1871 and 1910 the Jewish population in Berlin tripled in size, from 47,000 to 150,000, by far the largest concentration in Germany, though smaller than Vienna's. There were Jewish proletarians, and after the First World War a large migration of impoverished Jews arrived in the city from Poland, Lithuania and other parts of eastern Europe, concentrating in the slums of the Scheunenviertel, immediately north of the Alexanderplatz, the centre of working-class and lower-middle-class Berlin, rather as the Jewish immigrants in London settled in Stepney and in New York thronged to Brooklyn and the Lower East Side.[14] Many Berlin Jews, however, were highly educated, successful in business and many professions, and assimilated, although they did encounter both social exclusion and various forms of discrimination, for example in promotion at the university. Although at no time did they amount to more than around 4 per cent of the population, Jews were highly visible. They were prominent in banking, in the press, both as the owners of the three big Berlin newspaper companies and as journalists, and in every kind of entertainment from the theatre and classical music to the music-hall.

Although Berlin had long been tolerant towards Jews, anti-Semitism was on the increase there as elsewhere from 1875 on. It was given a boost by the failure of a prominent Jewish financier, Henry Bethel Strousberg, in the crash of 1873, and stimulated by the anti-Semitic politician, Adolf Stoecker, a former prison warden, from 1880 on. What was equally dangerous was that in the later years of the century anti-Semitism was becoming respectable, both in court circles, and even among such intellectuals as the eminent Prussian historian, Heinrich von Treitschke, who went so far as to write, in a serious book, '*die Juden sind unser Unglück*' ('the Jews are Germany's bad luck').

There was another group, far smaller than the Jewish population, but far more powerful, that escaped criticism. By the end of the century it was calculated that 57 per cent of the population of Berlin were 'workers', 42 per cent were 'bourgeois', ranging from wealthy millionaire bankers to modest shopkeepers and clerks. Just

1 per cent belonged to the aristocracy.[15] Yet such was the conservatism of the Prussian polity, and such was the prestige of the imperial house of Hohenzollern after its triumphant victories over Austria in 1866 and France in 1871, that the aristocracy held an extraordinarily disproportionate share of power. It dominated the army, and the army, in Prussia, claimed to dominate the state, under the emperor, *Allerhöhest Kriegsherr*, All-highest Warlord. The highest prestige within the army went to the Guards regiments, and these were an aristocratic preserve. In one regiment stationed at Potsdam, near the end of the pre-war period, there were no 'bourgeois' officers at all, but thirty-four princes and fifty-one counts![15]

Berlin was an intensely complex urban structure, with considerable opportunities for men (much less so women) to acquire an education and improve their position. At its apex, though, there stood a political control mechanism of exceptional rigidity, steeped in conservatism of every kind, political, social and intellectual. And at the very tip of that, perched above the dangerously whirring wheels of a society modernizing itself at breakneck speed, there stood, head high, chin firm, and mind closed, the emperor himself.

Wilhelm, after whom the whole era was rightly called, personified many of its traits, but most of all he embodied, to a degree that bordered on caricature, the sheer arrogance of the society he ruled. He was given to absurd outbursts which his unfortunate ministers, relatively sensible bureaucrats like Bülow or Bethmann-Hollweg, had to clean up after. He ordered his troops, departing to help quell the Boxer rebellion, to behave like Huns. He gratuitously took the world's 300 million Muslims under his protection without consulting a single one of their leaders. He insulted the Russians, the French and the British, and could then never quite understand why they were annoyed. And the trouble was that, after the stunning victories of 1866 and 1870, the prestige of his house and of its surrounding aristocracy was so great that the middle classes were increasingly aping their feudal betters: their manners, their monocles, their prejudices and their dreams of empire. As the century opened, a Berlin poet apostrophized it in upbeat doggerel:

> *Dich du zwanzigstes nach Christi, waffenklirrend und bewundert,*
> *Wird die Zukunft einst dich nennen das germanische Jahrhundert?*

('Oh, thou twentieth after Christ, rattling with weapons and bewildered, will the future call you the German century?')[16]

As long ago as 1871, when the coming of empire had just launched Berlin on its dangerous trajectory, the newspaper publisher Rudolf Mosse, founder of the *Berliner Tageblatt*, announced that 'Berlin will and must become Germany, a metropolis, a world city.' Privately, as on so many questions, the kaiser, like his people, could express doubts that he, in his greatcoat and plumed helmet, would never admit to the world: 'The glory of the Parisians robs Berliners of their sleep. Berlin is a great city, a world city (perhaps)?'[17] Sooner than he dreamed, and in a very different way, Berlin was indeed to become, first the wonder, then the terror of the world.

The ninth of November 1918 was the longest day the city of Berlin had lived through.[18] Six weeks earlier General Ludendorff, who had been for two years to all intents and purposes the supreme leader not only of the German military machine but also of Germany, had told the kaiser that the war was lost. He did not tell the kaiser or anyone else, but he had in fact decided that the only way out for the General Staff, the office corps and the military tradition they served was to deny the reality of defeat, to blame it on others, and to propagate the *Dolchstosslegende*, the legend of the stab in the back.

Events were in any case already out of the control even of such a meticulous planner and gifted strategist as General Ludendorff, and now they began to race with dizzying momentum, nobody knew to what frightening conclusion. The kaiser appointed the liberal Prince Max of Baden as the new chancellor. On 23 October a note arrived from Woodrow Wilson which undercut Prince Max's hopes of negotiating peace by saying the Allies refused to deal with the 'military masters and monarchial autocrats of Germany'. On 24 October a proclamation that the army refused to surrender was drafted but never made public, and the next day the kaiser demanded Ludendorff's resignation. Four days later the High Seas Fleet, ordered to sea for a do-or-die assault on the British Grand Fleet, mutinied, and before long trainloads of mutinous sailors, led by Workers' and Sailors' Councils on the St Petersburg model, were arriving in Berlin to make the revolution.

On 9 November, there was a vacuum of power in Berlin. The kaiser had slipped away to the Western Front's advance headquarters at Spa, in Belgium. Philipp Scheidemann, the senior of two Social Democrats in the government, told Prince Max that he would resign if the kaiser did not abdicate, and a group of Social Democratic leaders, led by the party leader, Friedrich Ebert, called on Prince Max and bluntly told him to hand over power.

The Social Democratic party, which for decades had been the largest party in the Reichstag and had pressed for a constitutional revolution, now found itself in the situation its members had dreamed of since the beginning of the empire. All it had to do, it seemed, was to reach out and pluck the fruits of defeat, as the Bolsheviks had done in Russia. But for the past two years the great Social Democratic party had been split, and not into two but into three parts. On the far left were the die-hard revolutionaries, led by Karl Liebknecht, son of a veteran party leader, and by the remarkable Rosa Luxemburg, who with her energy and intellectual brilliance shrugged aside the triple disadvantages of being a woman, a Jew and a foreigner; she was born in Poland and only enjoyed German nationality as a result of a marriage of convenience. This group were called the Spartakists, after the Roman gladiator who led a slave rebellion in 71 BC, and were eventually to develop into the Communist Party of Germany. Next came the Independent Socialists, still a minority of the party, but one which included many of the most gifted socialist intellectuals in the party, including the father of revisionist socialism, Eduard Bernstein, who provoked some of Lenin's most furious pamphlets. The Majority Social Democrats constituted the solid, working-class, trades-union leadership of the party. Its leaders had risen from skilled working-class jobs: Friedrich Ebert was a saddle-maker, Gustav Noske a basket-maker.

Now the Spartakists had called a general strike, and the streets were full of the Kiel sailors, driving around with rifles, and of demonstrating workers. Philipp Scheidemann was enjoying a bowl of potato soup in the restaurant of the Reichstag when they came to him and said that a crowd was gathering outside the windows. A roly-poly little man with a pointed white beard, he waddled to the window of the reading-room, overlooking the Victory Column that celebrated the battles of 1871, and confirmed that Ebert had become chancellor. Then, almost as an afterthought, he added, 'Long live the German Republic!' Up to that moment, no such thing had existed. Ebert was furious, but he could not put the cat back in the bag.

Meanwhile, a quarter of a mile to the east of the Reichstag, a shopkeeper called Schlesinger, anxious to prevent the crowds from vandalizing the Schloss, had hung a red blanket over the balcony from which the kaiser used to harangue orderly crowds of soldiers and courtiers. At four o'clock in the afternoon, with snow beginning to fall, the Chicago reporter Ben Hecht was watching outside the Schloss.[19] The crowd cheered a 'black-eyed, quick-moving little man' who got out of a taxi and, saluted by the tall mutineer marines on the gate, marched into the Schloss. Hecht followed the little man into the palace and eventually into the emperor's bedroom. He started to undress to his long johns, which were missing some buttons. He took four large reference books out of his briefcase and placed them and the case on a spindly-legged bedside table. There was silence in the room. The springs creaked as Liebknecht stretched out. There was a sharp crack as the table collapsed under the weight of revolutionary literature. The lamp fell to the floor and the light bulb shattered. This was the way the empire ended, not with a whimper, but with the small bang of a broken light bulb.

At the Chancellery, in the Wilhelmstrasse, halfway between the Reichstag and the palace, Prince Max handed over to Fritz Ebert. 'Herr Ebert,' said the prince, 'I commit the German Empire to your keeping.' And Ebert replied, 'I have lost two sons for this empire.' Late that night, Ebert was in the chancellor's office, his jacket off, finding his way around. A telephone rang.[20] It was a special line, number 988, which connected with army headquarters. Ebert picked it up, and a voice said, 'Gröner here': General Wilhelm Gröner, who had taken over the supreme army command from Ludendorff. The conversation was short and to the point. Ebert asked what the army was going to do. Gröner said the kaiser was asleep in his private train, but had decided to go into exile in Holland, and had handed over the command to Field-Marshal Hindenburg. They exchanged a few civilities. The key statement came from the hyper-efficient Gröner. 'The officer corps expects that the imperial government will fight against Bolshevism, and places itself at the disposal of the government for such a purpose.' Ebert asked Gröner to convey his gratitude to the field-marshal. The first phone call Ebert took as chancellor determined his and his government's fate. A deal had been struck. Without saying so, the army had accepted the legitimacy of a civilian, socialist government, by no means a foregone conclusion. And it had offered its help to destroy the revolution.

For there was a revolution in Germany at the end of 1918 and the beginning of 1919, and although there were insurrections in Munich, Kiel, Hamburg and many other cities, the fate of the whole country was decided, as you might expect, in the capital, Berlin. But Berlin was also the scene of a counter-revolution. In a nutshell, what happened was that the army accepted the fall of its master, the kaiser, but did not accept defeat. Instead of taking over and leading Germany towards a more or less revolutionary process of change, the great Social Democratic party split. The general staff threw its weight into the scales on the side of the Majority

Christian Democrats, and against the revolutionary Independents and the Spartakists. The Majority Social Democrats installed a constitutional Republic, called after the town where the constitution was drafted, Weimar. But, and that is why the events in Berlin in 1918 and 1919 were so important, and so disastrous, not only for Germany, but for Europe, the generals and their agents, the Freikorps, recruited from the toughest and the most fanatical of the young front-line officers and non-commissioned officers, and many businessmen and ordinary Germans of many kinds, refused to accept Weimar. Four years were to pass before Hitler came to power. But Hitler's spirit was already on the streets in Berlin and other German cities in the brief, bloody civil war of 1918–19 as the Freikorps roughed up the poor eastern Jews in the Scheunenviertel and murdered socialists in the streets.

On 11 December, in fulfilment of Gröner's promise, three crack divisions under General von Lequis began to march into the city. Ebert met them at the Brandenburg Gate with words that were to have disastrous echoes: 'As you return unvanquished from the field of battle' . . .[21] They were not unvanquished. Worn out by four years of war, eroded by casualties, pushed almost to the point of rout by the great Allied offensive of the summer of 1918, and faced with the collapse of their allies on other fronts and with the prospect of inexhaustible American reserves being thrown into the front line to relieve the French and British, the German army had no fight left in it. Ludendorff knew that. The generals knew that. But they had not told the soldiers, for fear of sapping their morale. And no one had told the German civilian public, because of wartime censorship. So it became possible to believe, and to persuade others to believe, that Germany had never been beaten in a fair fight but had been stabbed in the back, by socialists, revolutionaries, traitors, foreigners, Jews. Berlin, and the world, were to suffer much from the legend of the stab in the back, and from the Social Democrats' unwillingness, dependent as they thought they were on the army for their own survival, to nail the lie.

A week before Christmas a revolutionary National Council of Workers and Soldiers on the Russian model met in the Prussian Parliament in Berlin and called for the abolition of ranks in the army and the creation of a *Volkswehr*, a people's army. When Gröner and his deputy, Major Kurt von Schleicher, a sinister figure who was to be Hitler's rival for the chancellorship, got together with the six commissioners appointed by the new government, the two Independents broke the meeting up, saying 'Ebert has betrayed the revolution to the officer corps.'[22] It is not easy to say what alternatives Ebert had, nor is it possible to say that the Independents had got it wrong.

The most immediate problem for the Ebert government was the sailors from Kiel, who called themselves the People's Naval Division. They had occupied the Schloss, and they kept asking for more money before they would leave. Moreover they took hostages. In desperation, Ebert called Major von Schleicher. 'General von Lequis's trusted troops, who are at Potsdam, will march on Berlin to set you free.' In the early hour of Christmas Eve they began to arrive. At 7.30 in the morning, Rittmeister Waldemar von Pabst[23] of the Horse Guards told the sailors they had ten minutes to leave the building. Then, after a brief artillery bombardment and heavy machine-gun fire, the Guards stormed the palace. When they got in they found the sailors had escaped through an underground tunnel to the Marstall, the former stables, next door. But in the next twenty minutes, the fortunes of revolution were reversed. Spartakist agitators roamed the city, screaming to everyone to gather in the Schloss Square. Veterans of Verdun drew the line at using heavy machine-guns in a square crowded with civilians. For the time being, 'the Horse Guards melted away'.[24]

The showdown came in 'Spartakus week'. It began on the streets on Sunday, 5 January. The immediate issue was the government's attempt to get rid of the police chief, a left-wing social democrat called Emil Eichhorn. On Saturday leaders of the Left met and planned a demo for Sunday. That same day Ebert and Noske were driven out to Zossen, 35 km out of the city, where they found four thousand well-armed, well-disciplined Freikorps men, including artillery and machine-gunners, drawn up on parade under the command of General Ludwig Märcker. The Freikorps[25] – their full name was Freiwillige Landesjägerkorps, or 'Volunteer Regional Rifle Corps' – were the general's response to the melting away of the field army once it reached the civilian and revolutionary atmosphere of Berlin.

On the Western Front, the German army had developed units of a new kind for assault operations. Commanded by young, bachelor officers under twenty-five years old, they abandoned the conventional discipline and spit-and-polish uniform culture of the Prussian tradition. These Sturmbataillone marched with unslung carbine . . . 'he sticks his cartridges in his pockets . . . he moves from shellhole to shellhole . . . like a robber . . . full of confidence in himself'. The young commanders were supposed to be 'the élite of Mittel Europa . . . a completely new race, cunning, strong and packed with purpose'. When the war ended, and in defeat, these soldiers and their officers were spoiling for a fight, rather like their British opposite numbers, the Black and Tans who volunteered for service in revolutionary Ireland. Later, they were to earn an evil reputation in the Baltic states and to provide the core of Hitler's Sturm Abteilung ('Storm Section') and of the SS (original Schutzstaffel, or 'Protection Service') of the Nazi party. For the moment, they were exactly what the army high command, and the Majority Social Democratic government, needed as an instrument to sweep the streets of Berlin. They succeeded, where Kerensky's Cossack regiments failed, in destroying a revolution.

On Sunday hundreds of thousands of men and women poured into the city from the working-class districts. The crowd stretched from the police headquarters in the Alexanderplatz all the way back past the Reichstag into the Tiergarten. Exhilarated by the demonstration, the leaders of the Left called another for Monday morning. Confident that the soldiers and sailors would support them, they also voted 'to take up the fight against the government and carry it on until its overthrow', and to issue a proclamation calling on 'Workers! Soldiers! Comrades!' to 'up and into battle for the power of the revolutionary proletariat'.[26] By Wednesday it looked as if the revolution had won. There were rumours that several army units were about to march on Berlin. Lenin sat down to write an open letter praising the Spartakists for their uprising against 'the imperialist robber bourgeoisie of Germany'. The Spartakists took over most of the city's public buildings, and on Monday Noske fled the city to establish his headquarters in a girls' school, the Luisenstift, in Dahlem.

On Thursday, 40,000 workers from AEG and other factories met in a mass meeting. Resolutions were passed calling for unity among the working-class parties. They had realized the mortal dangers implied by the split between the Majority Social Democrats and the two parties, or factions, of the Left. But it was too late. That same night the Freikorps struck with the panache and ruthlessness they had learned on the Western Front. Blocking off the streets to prevent the crowd coming to hamper them as it had on Christmas Eve, 1,200 veteran soldiers under Major von Stephani, with machine-guns, flame-throwers and even a tank stormed the offices of the Socialist newspaper, *Vorwärts*. Some of the defenders were shot out of hand. The next evening, 11 January, the Freikorps marched on Berlin in earnest, with the Social Democrat minister, Noske, literally marching at their head. With military precision the Freikorps entered the city as a wedge and fanned out from there, reducing opposition street by street. By midnight on 15 January the Spartakist insurrection was over.

That night a patrol from the Garde-Kavallerie-Division, the Horse Guards Freikorps, broke into a flat at 53 Mannheimerstrasse in middle-class Wilmersdorf, near the Freikorps headquarters at the Hotel Eden, and arrested Rosa Luxemburg, Karl Liebknecht and the young Communist, Wilhelm Pieck. After being questioned by Captain Waldemar Pabst and roughly treated in the hotel, Liebknecht and Luxemburg were taken out of the hotel separately.[27] As each came out they were clubbed with a rifle butt by a giant private called Runge. Liebknecht was taken by car to the nearby Tiergarten. The car stopped and he was shot, 'while trying to escape', by an officer called Lieutenant-Captain Horst von Pflugk-Hartung. Rosa Luxemburg was shot in the head by her escort, Lieutenant Vogel. He then threw the body off the Liechtenstein Bridge into the Landwehr Canal, where it was found days later, washed up against a lock. Wilhelm Pieck was unharmed, and there are suspicions that he betrayed his colleagues.[28] He was certainly a survivor: he survived to become the first president of the German Democratic Republic.

The Freikorps assault of January 1919 was not quite the end of the revolution, either in Germany or in Berlin. Appropriately, in view of Marx's dictum that history repeats itself, the first time as tragedy, the second time as farce, the extreme Right made an attempt to overthrow the Social Democratic government again, in March 1920. The immediate cause was Defence Minister Noske's disbanding of the Ehrhardt Freikorps brigade. This was a unit which marched under the red, black and white flag of the empire, with swastikas on its helmets. Noske, hearing rumours of a coup, summoned police and army units into the government district, but when the Ehrhardt brigade marched on Berlin, the supposedly loyal soldiers refused to fire on the Freikorps, and the generals not only refused to support Ebert and Noske, but actually placed them under arrest. For a single day, it seemed that the government had fallen. An obscure right-wing official called Kapp was installed as chancellor; after him, the coup came to be known as the 'Kapp putsch'. But behind Kapp were Ehrhardt, General von Lüttwitz and other conservative officers, and no less a figure than General Ludendorff. As they fled from Berlin, though, the Ebert cabinet ordered a new general strike, and the working class, first in Berlin and then all over Germany, responded with remarkable unanimity. Kapp was left with the levers of government in his hands, but unattached to the wires of control. After a single day he was ousted by the generals, and General von Lüttwitz tried to make himself a military dictator. He too was obliged to admit defeat, and the generals reopened negotiations with the Ebert government.

The person they chose to handle this delicate task was none other than Waldemar Pabst, newly promoted major in recognition of his handling of Liebknecht and Luxemburg.

As a result of this truly astonishing sequence of events, in which a real revolution, and a real counter-revolution, ended in a semi-farcical stand-off, Berlin was left the capital of a German republic, indeed, but one whose many enemies, to the Left and even more dangerously to the Right, were so far from regarding the constitutional issue as closed that they treated the republican government with open derision and evinced an unconcealed determination to avenge themselves on those whom they blamed for their defeat and the national dishonour, by any means whatsoever. There are extant photographs of Lüttwitz's Freikorps, steel-helmeted and mustachioed, and with death's heads painted on their armoured cars, 'cleansing' the Scheunenviertel of Spartakists, many of whom, of course, just happened also to be Jews. And there are also photographs of armed police hunting 'foreign' Jews in the Grenadierstrasse in 1920. Early the next year, 'undesirable foreigners' were being rounded up in the Grenadierstrasse and sent to what were already called concentration camps at Stargard and Cottbus.[29] So Berlin headed towards the most liberated, the most exciting and the most nostalgic time in its history, with ghosts at the feast and a fox in the attic.[30]

At one o'clock one morning, Count Harry Kessler took a call from his friend Max Reinhardt, the great producer, who was at the apartment of Kurt Vollmöller, the author of the spectacularly successful religious play *The Miracle*. 'Come on over,' Reinhardt said. 'Josephine Baker is here, and the fun is just starting.' By the time Kessler got to what he called Vollmöller's 'harem' in the Pariserplatz, the party was going strong. The women were naked, except for 'the little Landshoff girl' – Vollmöller's incumbent mistress, who was dressed up as a boy in a dinner jacket, like the men. Josephine Baker was dancing alone, wearing nothing but a pink muslin apron, and it seemed to Kessler that she danced as the women had done before Solomon or Tutankhamun in their glory. The naked girls lay or skipped about among the four or five men in evening dress, and then Josephine Baker and Fräulein Landshoff were lying in each other's arms 'like a pair of rosy lovers'. Kessler was inspired to suggest to Reinhardt that he would write a mime on the theme of the Song of Solomon, for Josephine Baker as Shulamith and the Landshoff girl as Solomon. Music by Richard Strauss. Reinhardt was enchanted, but nothing came of the idea so far as anyone knows.[31]

There was nothing especially decadent about Count Harry Kessler. Elegant, certainly: that much is clear from the portrait by Edvard Munch, in which he wears a broad-brimmed hat with a distinctly raffish look about it. But he was also a decent and courageous man, who on one occasion had the guts to march into a Freikorps headquarters and complain that he had seen a soldier outside beating a prisoner with a whip. But his description of the party at Max Reinhardt's fits perfectly with the stereotype that has been handed down of the decadent Berlin of the Golden Twenties. To this day, the very name of the city conjures up for many people, not technological skill or academic achievement, not the imperialist policies of the Wilhelmstrasse or the cruelty of the Prinz-Albrecht-strasse, but the wild bohemian dissipation, the sexual licence and sheer uninhibited partying described in so many memoirs of the time.[32] This is the Berlin of novels like those of Vicki Baum,[33] the professional harpist who worked as a chamber-maid for two months at the Eden to get the atmosphere right for her bestseller *Grand Hotel*; the Berlin of Irmgard Keun's *The Girl in Artificial Silk*[34] or Alfred Döblin's *Berlin Alexanderplatz*; of Brecht's early plays; and above all of Christopher Isherwood's two autobiographical novels, *Mr Norris Changes Trains* and *Goodbye to Berlin*. They were turned into a play, *I am a Camera*, and that in turn was turned into a movie and finally into the musical *Cabaret*. Perhaps the strongest, and the most deceptive, image is that produced by the film version of *Cabaret*.

It is not that the sexual high jinks in Berlin were imaginary. On the contrary, there was something for everybody who wanted to misbehave. There really were smoky low-life cabarets like the White Mouse (so called because it was opposite the Black Cat) in the Friedrichstrasse. People crowded in to see a dancer called Anita Berber: she danced quite naked, and she was known to have had several husbands and many lovers, and to be an alcoholic and addicted to both morphine and cocaine. There really were dancehalls like the Eldorado where the men dressed as women and the women dressed as men. And there were certainly armies of prostitutes, of both sexes, on the streets, from the 'fierce amazons, strutting in high boots made of green, glossy leather' and waving canes, who frightened the young Klaus Mann in the smart streets off the Tiergarten, to the pathetic women, and men, driven by hunger and other compulsions to sell their bodies in the wretched streets round the Alexanderplatz.

What is misleading about the popular image of Berlin wickedness is that it utterly fails to understand the catastrophic social and historical context of the feverish search for gratification. There had always been pleasure to be found in Berlin, including sexual pleasure and specifically homosexual adventures. In 1906 the journalist Maximilian Harden created a spectacular scandal by accusing two members of the kaiser's most intimate circle, his 'camarilla', as even his friends called it, of homosexual behaviour. He named Prince Philipp von Eulenburg and Count Kuno von Moltke, aide-de-camp to William and commanding general in Berlin. Germany had lived through four years of war, of austerity and sacrifice, of 'turnip winters'. Soldiers who had faced death and wounds and survived wanted to let off steam. Women and men both instinctively felt, as their contemporaries in London and New York felt, that the war had discredited the society which had blundered into it, that Victorian world with its 'thou shalts' and its even more numerous 'thou-shalt-nots'. And Germany had lost the war. The disillusion and the hunger for escapism were so much the stronger. On top of defeat, Berlin had experienced revolution, counter-revolution and vicious street fighting. Perhaps most important of all, Berlin had experienced inflation.

Historians have uncovered, what the people of Berlin understood all too well at the time, that inflation, and certainly hyper-inflation of the kind that raged in Berlin from 1922 to 1924, has corrosive effects, not only on the economy, but on society as a whole. Golo Mann, for example, reminds us that as a result of the inflation 'the rich became richer and the poor became poorer ... most people suffered real misery, the old, the pensioners, those who did not know how to speculate and all those who worked for a wage and owed nothing'.[35] The depreciation of the currency, Mann points out, in effect produced a second revolution after that of the immediate postwar period. 'Whole sections of the population were expropriated and an age-old confidence was destroyed and replaced by fear and cynicism.' It was worse than a revolution, says Alan Bullock.

The savings of the middle classes and the working classes were wiped out at a single blow with a ruthlessness which no revolution could ever equal ... The result of the inflation was to undermine the foundations of German society in a way which neither the war, nor the revolution of November 1918, nor the Treaty of Versailles had ever done. The real revolution in Germany was the inflation.[36]

Yes, adds an elderly woman journalist interviewed by Otto Friedrich in the 1970s, but those are just words.

You have to realize what they *meant*. There was not a single girl in the German middle class who could get *married* without her father paying a dowry. Even the maids – they never spent a penny of their wages. They saved and saved so that they could get married. When the money became worthless, it destroyed the whole system for getting married, and so it destroyed the whole idea of remaining chaste until marriage ... What happened from the inflation was that the girls learned that virginity didn't matter any more. The women were liberated.[37]

The context of sexual liberation in Berlin in the twenties, in other words, was the prevailing misery. For those few who had access to foreign currency, or who were in a position to buy assets, including flats and houses, at depreciated prices, the years from the stabilization of the currency in 1924 to the Wall Street crash of 1929 were indeed *die goldene Zwanzige*, the Golden Twenties. But for most people it was a hellish time. Unemployment was 20 per cent higher in Berlin than in the rest of Germany in 1924–5 but by 1927 it was twice as high as elsewhere. In December 1928 164,000 Berliners were out of work; by July 1932, 865,000 Berliners were out of work, as against 2,184,000 in work; or in other words 28.4 per cent were unemployed.[38] Even for those with a job, life was bitterly hard. Between 1927 and 1932, it is said that wages were below the official poverty level, and in 1932 they didn't reach half that level.[39]

It was not just that daily life was hard. All the values Berliners had been brought up to cherish – God, kaiser, country, morality, family, savings and respect for the conventions – had been swept away. A special anger was reserved for those on the Left, and for intellectuals of every stripe, who seemed pleased at this hecatomb of moral values. Ordinary people in Berlin looked back to the immediate past with shame and anger, and they looked forward to a future that seemed to belong either to chaos or to anarchy, with fear tempered only by animosity against whatever group they blamed for their plight: the Allies, the Left, the industrialists, the bohemians, the refugees, the Jews.

Work of the greatest creativity and originality was being done in Berlin in the 1920s in almost any field you choose to name. This was, for example, a golden age in the history of the Zeitungsviertel, the newspaper district south of the Leipzigerstrasse, where the three great houses of Ullstein, Scherl (taken over after the war by the conservative financier Hugenberg) and Mosse continued to fight it out, each publishing an upmarket daily, at least one mass circulation paper, and illustrated weeklies as well. Altogether around a hundred daily papers were published in Berlin in 1925, and something like four hundred titles altogether. The big Berlin dailies spent money to send their reporters all over the world, and their *feuilletons* vied with one another to hire the best writers and the most authoritative critics.[40]

In architecture, Martin Wagner, the city architect, was a passionate socialist and an admirer of the modernist style. He took advantage of the commitment in the Weimar constitution to provide 'decent lodging' for every citizen to commission Walter Gropius and a team of talented modernist collaborators to design workers' housing on the grand scale and in the modern idiom at Siemensstadt. But that was only one of Wagner's projects, and there were other excellent modern architects working in Berlin, including Richard Neutra and Erich Mendelssohn. It would be a mistake, however, to see Berlin as being transformed into a modernist metropolis. The modernist architects were commissioned to do public housing, because their work was extremely cheap, and to build private homes for each other and for their friends in the cultivated upper middle class; Mendelssohn also carried out a number of commercial commissions (Columbus House in Potsdamer Platz, the Universum Cinema in the Kurfürstendamm). Otherwise Berlin remained a city of palaces in the Wilhelminian version of the pompous Beaux Arts style.

On the surface, too, this was a golden period for the University of Berlin. Both the Quantum Theory and the General Theory of Relativity were propounded there, and it was there that Otto Hahn split the atom in 1938. In the 1920s such demigods as Max Planck, Werner Heisenberg and Albert Einstein were all working there. Planck won the Nobel Prize for physics in 1918, Einstein in 1921, their colleagues Hertz and Franck in 1925, Heisenberg in 1932 and Schrödinger in 1933. The record in chemistry was almost as splendid. Yet a closer look reveals that the atmosphere at the university was not quite so favourable to intellectual achievement as those names might suggest. Even before 1914, one historian noted, 'there was a deep-seated complacency in the University of Berlin which played down the flaws of authoritarianism, militarism and thinly veiled absolutism that characterized the second empire'.[41] In 1915 Einstein wrote to a friend, 'In Berlin, it's bizarre. The scientists and the mathematicians are, as scholars, strictly internationalist. But the historians and philologists are for the most part enraged chauvinists.' That remained true throughout the Weimar period. Students and scholars alike encountered an astonishing degree of class prejudice, anti-Semitism and ultra-conservatism, epitomized by the German literature scholar Gustav Roethe, who is said to have begun his lectures by saying, 'We who are ruled by the Jews and the proletarians . . .'[42]

Two of the glories of Berlin in the Golden Twenties were its cinema and its theatre. Looked at closely, however, each tells the same story: each reveals the shallowness of the popular image of Berlin in the 1920s as a carefree boom town. The German film industry[43] was stimulated by the war, which cut off supplies of (predominantly French) imports. The number of film production companies in Germany, most of them in Berlin, shot up from twenty-eight in 1913 to 245 in 1919. In the early years of the Weimar Republic, UFA alone produced more films than the whole of the rest of Europe combined: 646 in 1921 and over 200, longer and more expensive films on the whole, in each year from 1924 to 1927.[44] The rise of the German film industry was to some extent the consequence of deliberate government policy. Aware of the magnetic attraction of Allied propaganda films, the Reich government started two agencies, the Deutsche Lichtspiel Gesellschaft (Deulig) and then the Bild- und Filmamt, to supply films for soldiers. After the United States entered the war in 1917 it became even more important to counter the appeal of American films, and the high command, in conjunction with the existing film industry and with backing from the banks, started Universum Film Aktiengesellschaft, soon to be known as UFA, with the state owning eight million out of twenty-five million shares. The Reich sold its shares to the Deutsche Bank late in 1918. Long before that, UFA was exporting its films to promote German culture, for example in the newly occupied Ukraine.

The first product of the new German film industry was escapist. One producer had the bright wheeze of getting the backing of the Society for Campaigning against Sexual Diseases, and turned out a whole series of pseudo-medical epics, ostensibly warning against the danger of venereal disease, with titles like *Lost Daughters* or *Hyaenas of Lust*. Another recruited the pre-war apostle of German colonialism, Karl Peters, to crank out adventure films purporting to be set in exotic locations, but in fact filmed in sandy, but not particularly sunny, Brandenburg. More important were the historical films directed by Ernst Lubitsch for UFA, some of them featuring the beauty of Pola Negri. But the decisive film, which set the pattern for the best German silent films of the decade, was *The Cabinet of Dr Caligari*. The story of how the film came to be made is odd enough. Originally intended to convey the revolutionary message that those in authority are insane, and only the inmates of a lunatic asylum are sane, it was 'framed' in a scene in the lunatic asylum in such a way as to reverse its message, by suggesting that those trying to propagate such revolutionary messages are themselves insane! In spite of this perversion of its authors' original purpose, however, *Caligari* was an immensely powerful and original film which was an instant success in New York and indeed everywhere it was shown. Its moral universe, however, was very far from a liberated or revolutionary one. It laid bare, with immense artistic power, the stark idea that there was no alternative between authority, conceived as tyranny, and freedom, identified with chaos. And *Caligari* was the first of a long series of brilliant silent films from the UFA studios at Babelsberg and from other Berlin production houses, that hammered home the same moral, and all the more effectively for doing so more or less unconsciously. *Nosferatu*, a version of Bram Stoker's Dracula story, directed by F.W. Murnau; *Vanina*, a story about a mad prison governor; *Dr Mabuse*, by the brilliant Fritz Lang; *Das Wachsfigurenkabinett* ('Waxworks'); and two sequels by Fritz Lang, *Der Müde Tod* ('Destiny') and *Die Nibelungen*, which would have an immense influence on Nazi propaganda: all seemed to take it for granted that there was no choice except tyranny or anarchy, unless perhaps it was a combination of the two.

In the second half of the 1920s, that fragile period of prosperity between the stabilization of the mark and the onset of the world crash, the German film industry continued to turn out films of compelling talent and interest, such as the so-called 'instinct films' written by Carl Mayer and directed by Lupu Pick, such as *Scherben* ('Shattered') or *Der letzte Mann* ('The Last Laugh'). The world-view they imparted, though, was uniformly pessimistic and depressing. It expressed the feeling of the 'little people' that life was a cruel farce, in which there was little chance of anything good happening, and all too great a likelihood of some dirty trick played by an arbitrary and uncaring fate. There was, too, a morbid undertone of self-pity mingled with sadism to many of these films. The only upbeat films were in two genres, both unmistakably associated with the *völkisch*, right-wing nationalist political tradition. One was an oddity: the remarkable mountaineering dramas made by Dr Arnold Fanck and a team of collaborators, including Leni Riefenstahl, chosen equally for their cinematic talents and their skill as skiers. The other was all too predictable. It was the series of costume dramas about the life of the supreme hero of Prussian militarism, Frederick the Great, or *Fridericus*, as he was called in the films. The militarist undertone was so heavy that the left-wing press urged its readers to boycott the *Fridericus* series. But when two thousand extras were assembled in the courtyard of the Schloss in one scene, they cheered as no mere extras ever cheered. 'Here,' said an eyewitness, 'the people act themselves!'

In the late 1920s, the economic circumstances of the German film industry reinforced these currents of popular feeling. Film companies had done well out of the inflation, both because there was an entertainment boom, and because they earned substantial foreign exchange. As soon as the mark was stabilized, UFA and the other companies (one of which, Phoebus, turned out to be secretly owned by the Reichswehr!) were in trouble. In 1925 UFA itself would have gone bankrupt if it hadn't been rescued by Paramount and Loew's/Metro-Goldwyn from Hollywood. Two years later UFA was in debt again, and the lion's share of the German film industry fell into the hands of Alfred Hugenberg, the steel and newspaper baron of extreme conservative politics. By then, the talent had begun to drain away to Hollywood: actors and actresses like Ernst Lubitsch, Pola Negri and Marlene Dietrich; directors like Pick, Murnau and E.A. Dupont, not to mention cameramen, editors and other technicians. Erich Pommer left for the United States under a hail of criticism for his bad management, notably for the huge overspends on two ambitious productions, Murnau's *Faust* and Fritz Lang's *Metropolis*.[45] But it is impossible to disagree with the verdict of the historian of the German silent cinema that the decline of the German screen was the consequence of 'a widespread inner paralysis'.

The path of the Berlin theatre was different.[46] There the enemy was not within, but in front of the footlights. Leading writers, directors and actors were committed to left-wing politics, and they went down shaking their fist in the faces of their political enemies; but down nevertheless they eventually went. Max Reinhardt was a liberal rather than a man of the committed socialist Left, though in the 1920s, as we shall see, he leaned in the Left's direction. His rival for the title of the most admired and influential director in the Berlin theatre, Erwin Piscator, though he started the war as a loyal nationalist, became a Communist and in 1919 started the 'Proletarian Theatre'. He did a Red revue for the Communist party's election campaign for the Reichstag in 1924 and a whole series of plays, some classics like Schiller's *Robbers* reinterpreted with a heavy Marxist spin, others provocative pieces like *Schweik*, with sets by George Grosz, which was prosecuted for blasphemy, and Alexis Tolstoy's *Rasputin*, which drew libel actions both from a Russian financier and from the kaiser himself!

The most extraordinary talent of the Berlin theatre arrived in the city from Augsburg by way of Munich in 1921. Bertolt Brecht was a young man, so undernourished he once had to be taken to the Charité Hospital; he loved to strum complicated chords on a guitar and, so his enemies said, to wear silk shirts under his proletarian leather jacket. When he first came to Berlin he had already written *Baal*, a play which combines the nihilistic despair of the postwar period with a flair for shocking the bourgeois and an apparently effortless gift for writing German lyric verse of a purity hardly seen since the age of Schiller and Heine. A Berlin critic who journeyed, at Brecht's request, to see his play about the Spartakus days, *Drums in the Night*, said he had 'changed the literary face of Germany overnight'. That was not so gross an exaggeration as such critical judgements commonly are. Back in Munich at the time of Hitler's 'beerhall putsch', Brecht conceived the idea of a play about *der Stadt Mahagonny*, the brown-shirt city. In 1924 he settled in Berlin with a job as joint house writer at Max Reinhardt's Deutsches Theater. In the late 1920s he moved to the Theater am Schiffbauerdamm, later in a different world to be the home of the Berliner Ensemble, and it was there that he put on his version of John Gay's eighteenth-century London *Beggar's Opera*, the *Dreigroschenoper*, with unforgettable music by Kurt Weill enchantingly sung by Lotte Lenya. When the second version of *The Rise and Fall of the City of Mahagonny* was produced in March 1930, Brecht, and Germany, were in a far less sunny mood. The first night, in Leipzig, was a snarling confrontation between Left and Right. The actors waved defiant placards from the stage. The bourgeois, someone said, demonstrated inside the theatre, and the Nazis demonstrated outside. Fights broke out in the aisles, and the riot reached a crescendo as God, dressed as a caricature of a German capitalist, with fur coat and big cigar, came on stage and shouted '*Gehet alle zur Hölle*' ('You can all go to hell!'). Hitler's arrival in power was then still three years away. But the Golden Twenties were over. It was Brecht who, in one of the choruses of the *Threepenny Opera*, coined a slogan for the Germans confronting the economic crisis and the deeper crisis of values: '*Erst kommt das Fressen, dann kommt die Moral*' ('First you have to eat; morality can come later'). By that stage, a majority of Germans were prepared to put their trust in men who would take from them, first their morality and then their food and everything else that they had.

Imperial folly and grandeur were the first act, revolutionary black comedy the second. There was metropolitan glamour, bohemian exaltation and proletarian misery in the third act, but the fourth was the theatre of cruelty. Walk a couple of blocks further south along the Wilhelmstrasse, past blocks of high-rise flats as in any south London estate, and you will reach the corner of what is now the Niederkirchnerstrasse, but was once the most feared address in Europe: Prinz-Albrecht-strasse 8, headquarters and interrogation centre for the Gestapo.

A whole city block looks like a bomb site. A small notice on the street side, headed '*Topographie des Terrors*', explains that here were the offices, not only of the Gestapo, but of the SS and Himmler's Reichssicherheitsamt as well. All that remains is two cellars – not, as it happens, Gestapo torture cells, but something to do with the canteen where bureaucrats like Eichmann could have eaten their lunchtime sausage while planning mass extermination.

In the cellars there are photographs of the flower of Germany: pastors, professors, soldiers, civil servants and trade unionists who had the unimaginable guts to join the Resistance. To Prinz-Albrecht-strasse, to be interrogated and in many cases to be tortured, came the pastor Dietrich Bonhöffer and his brother-in-law Hans von Dohnanyi; Count Peter Yorck von Wartenberg, whose hero-ancestor's statue stands next to Field-Marshal Blücher's in Unter den Linden and Adam von Trott, the diplomat, who had been a Rhodes scholar;[47] Ernst Thälmann, leader of an International Brigade in Spain, and Admiral Canaris the head of military intelligence. Under most of the photos, in which they look incongruously young, there is a laconic note of the date of their execution. But some survived, and went on to be the builders of both Germanies. Erich Honecker survived, and now he is sought for murder because as head of state of East Germany he ordered the guards on the Berlin Wall to shoot to kill. Kurt Schumacher survived to be one of the founders of the European Community.

Among those who were brought to Prinz-Albrecht-strasse were the members of the left-wing network, Rote Kapelle, the 'Red Orchestra'. Miraculously, a piece of paper was found in the ruins after the war on which one of them, Harro Schulze-Boysen, had written a poem. Its last verse says:

> *Die letzten Argumenten*
> *sind strang und fallbeil nicht,*
> *und unsere heut'gen Richter sind*
> *noch nicht das Weltgericht.*

('The noose and the guillotine are not the last arguments; and our judges of today are not yet the world court.')

Not far north of Unter den Linden, workmen are finishing the restoration of the great synagogue in the Oranienburgerstrasse. The domes have been gilded, and so has the Star of David on top. Two plaques explain that the building was finished in 1888 and burned to the ground by Nazi stormtroopers on Kristallnacht in 1938, and that it is being rebuilt with the help of 'friends from all over the world'; the world court, so to speak, has reversed the judgement of 1938. The other plaque says tersely: 'VERGESST ES NIE', 'Never forget it'; no one needs to be told what is meant by 'it'.

From 1947, when relations between the Allied governments broke down, until 1989, when the Wall came down, the history of Berlin splits into two. That of the east is a part of the larger, depressing story of the failure of Communism in the Soviet empire. That of the west, superficially happier, is also a sad story. For Berlin, the *Weltstadt* which Kaiser Wilhelm II dreamed of, the World City which Berlin really did become for a brief, hectic moment in the 1920s, had been pulverized by British and American bombs and Russian guns. The shiny 'shop window of the West' of the news magazines and the politicians' speeches was not much more than a Potemkin village. The Mercedes taxis, the neon lights in the Kurfürstendamm, were real enough in themselves, and the West German government did what it could to see that Berlin continued to be a major industrial city. But Berlin was fast becoming a backwater shared by the old, the students and the Turks.

By the 1980s immigrants made up a quarter of the population, but in spite of them and their babies the average age of Berliners was higher than that of any other German city. And with births each year among native Germans lower than deaths, the population of the country was failing to reproduce itself naturally. Berlin, with its major university and numerous other institutions of higher education, was a magnet for students, and they played a leading part in the ebullient youth unrest of the 1960s and the darker alienation that succeeded it in the 1970s. Unlike Hamburg, Munich, Stuttgart, Berlin looked like a great city, in the unflattering sense that it looked like London or New York; it had graffiti, dirt, ruins, sleaze of many kinds, and – unlike newer German cities – there was a pervasive awareness of class differences, of ideological irreconcilables, of racial tension lurking under the surface. In the middle of this only-half-reconstructed metropolis, the occupying powers followed their military rituals, painted up their trilingual signs, and pursued devious plots in the name of 'intelligence'. The Berliners came to call their city the *Agentensumpf*, the agent swamp. The British and Americans even dug a two-metre-diameter tunnel for a third of a mile to tap communications between East Berlin and the Soviet headquarters at Karlshorst.[48] John Le Carré himself, the Tolstoy of the Cold War, is said to have received his induction into the murky tradecraft of intelligence and its 'wilderness of mirrors' in Berlin, working from the British headquarters in what had been Hitler's Olympic stadium. Sometimes, in hasty nocturnal dramas like scenes from *The Third Man*, they swapped agents at the Glienicke Bridge in the west or at Checkpoint Charlie in the centre. The common herd of Berliners visiting their relatives on the other side of the grim, snaking wall that divided the city, and Western tourists or journalists wanting to sniff the unfree air of Unter den Linden and stare at the Stalinist architecture of the Marx-Engels-allee and the Alexanderplatz, waited more or less patiently to go through the hyper-suspicious procedures in the Friedrichstrasse Station.

Now that is all changed. The Friedrichstrasse Station, a barn-like structure built to go with Berlin's earliest elevated railway as long ago as 1877, is thronged with Berliners going every which way as they please. The city is reunited. Except that it is not. Physically, the streets of the former East Berlin are dilapidated, the shops dowdy, the people dressed like Western workers in the 1950s. Psychologically, the gap between Ossis and Wessis still gapes. Resentments, cultural misunderstanding and mutual suspicion abound. For the time being, Berlin is truly what Tacitus said of the Roman emperor Galba, *capax imperii, nisi imperasset*,[49] a city that could have been imperial, if it had never had an empire – a city, as some wit translated Tacitus' epigram, with a great future behind it. From the explosive boom of population, of economic activity and of intellectual innovation that followed the declaration of the German empire with its capital in Berlin in 1871 up to the hubris of 1914, and again in the Indian summer from 1919 to 1933, Berlin truly seemed to be capital of the future. London, Paris, New York were bigger, wealthier. But Berlin seemed to be catching up. Berlin seemed to be not only the most modern of capitals, but the capital of modernism, the metropolis of the future. So as we look back over the short hundred years of Berlin's experience since its first heyday of Wilhelminian Germany, we are truly looking back at memories of the future.[50]

As, once again, the capital of the most powerful state in Europe, Berlin now has a future as well as a past. But, for the time being at least, it offers the visitors something they cannot find in Paris or New York. Other great cities can match Berlin's museums and palaces, its opera-houses and its legendarily tolerant nightlife, and even its truly metropolitan mixture of vitality and humour. No other city can show quite so rich a gallery of object-lessons in the ironies of history.

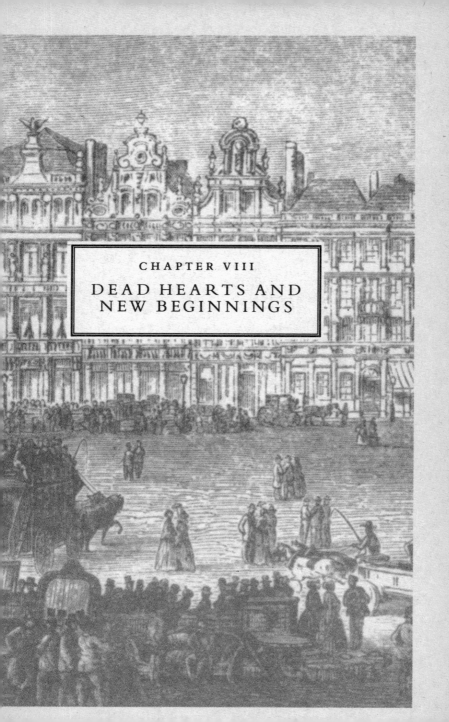

CHAPTER VIII

DEAD HEARTS AND
NEW BEGINNINGS

AT THE TOP OF THE DUKE OF YORK'S STEPS,

which lead down from Carlton House Terrace to St James's Park in the heart of London, there stands the statue of the Duke of York, that soldier-prince who has become a byword for indecision because of the nursery rhyme:

> The Grand Old Duke of York,
> He had ten thousand men.
> He marched them up to the top of the hill,
> And he marched them down again.

There are two rust stains on the stone pediment of the duke's statue which may be read as a history of the parliamentary question, that cherished protection of British rights – or indeed of the moral development of Victorian London. The duke stands on guard over a walk which many great and good men have taken over the last three centuries between the world of business and the world of pleasure. Below, across the park, lie Westminster and Whitehall, the Houses of Parliament, Downing Street, the Foreign Office and the Treasury. Above are the haunts, respectable and disreputable, to which generations of servants of Crown and empire betook themselves of an evening: the clubs of Pall Mall and St James, the drawing-rooms of St James's Square and Mayfair beyond, and the theatres, restaurants and less respectable places of entertainment of Soho and the West End.

If only the statue, like the Commendatore in *Don Giovanni*, could come to life and speak, he might tell many tales out of school. No doubt he would recall grave legislators and dedicated bureaucrats striding in one direction and staggering in the other. This particular story, though, involves not an indiscretion by one of the great and good, but an outrage upon such a personage. It was just after the Crimean War, in 1856, that an elderly general, who was also a member of the House of Commons, was descending the steps, having dined at his club, when two young cavalry officers on horseback, having dined all too well at theirs, reached the bottom of the steps. One of the two officers dared the other to ride his horse up the steps, and the other accepted. The general was given a nasty fright; it was a serious breach of good order and military discipline. In those days, a member could ask a parliamentary question without notice. The general was so incensed that he rose in his place, that very same evening, and asked the minister of war what steps he intended to take to prevent untoward incidents upon the Duke of York's Steps. The minister replied that he had every sympathy with his honourable and gallant friend, and that a sentry would thenceforth be posted on the steps to prevent a recurrence.

For twenty years, a soldier of the queen, with fixed bayonet and pipe-clayed belt, was duly posted against the granite wall on the west side of the steps, halfway up, until some time in the 1870s when a radical Member of Parliament, of a humanitarian temper, asked the First Commissioner of Works why soldiers were being asked to stand out in the fog and rain without protection from the elements. The First Commissioner agreed to cover the sentry with a handsome lead canopy, fastened to the granite wall with iron stanchions. In the 1890s, however, a mood of economy having returned to fashion in public finance, a question was asked in the House about why it was necessary to keep a soldier standing around doing nothing on the by now well-lit steps, and the sentry was duly moved.

In 1907 the story moves from the darkness of myth into modern times, for it was the liberal, W. Wedgwood Benn, who asked a question in the House about the useless canopy disfiguring the Duke of York's Steps, and the First Commissioner of the day sent a couple of workmen to go and saw off the stanchions. They did not do a very good job, though; when my informant was told this story by Wedgwood Benn, then the first Lord Stansgate, the stumps of the stanchions could still be seen. Only some time in the 1960s, with rising interest in conservation, was the iron prised from the stone and the cavities filled with mortar. But on the left-hand side of the steps as you go up from the Mall, about six foot above the step, you can still see two tell-tale marks of rust.[1]

The story makes the point that a great European city is a living, organic thing. If you know where to look, you can read the ancient settlements of Europe like a book. Each great stage of European history, from the Roman Empire by way of the Crusades, monasticism, the rise of the merchants, every great movement of the European mind – Reformation, Counter-Reformation, Enlightenment, revolution, liberalism, industrialization and war – has scored its traces on the fabric of the streets and buildings. So too have the little changes of fashion, the trivial events: like a young officer's prank, and the irritation of a powerful old gentleman who did not like to be upset on his way from dinner to the House of Commons.

Quarters, streets, buildings have a stubborn life that survives through successive transformations of a city, like the genes that transmit the shape of a chin, the wave of a lock of hair, through the generations of a family. Trastevere, we have seen, has been the poor neighbourhood in Rome since Jewish settlers, some of them converts to Christianity, made their homes there in the first century. Schools and colleges still congregate around the Montagne St-Geneviève in what has been the Latin Quarter of Paris since Latin was spoken there by the monks and scholars of the twelfth century. And there is an example in Vienna that is even more intriguing, even moving in its way.

In 1643, as the Habsburgs were emerging on the winning side in the Thirty Years' War, the Emperor Ferdinand III gave a piece of land in the Wieden, just beyond the River Wien, then outside the walls of Vienna, to Conrad Balthasar von Starhemberg, and four years later Starhemberg bought out the emperor's remaining rights to rent, tax and feudal obligations, so that when the Starhembergs later built a house on the property, it was called the Freihaus. It burned down, but they rebuilt it, this time as a palace with its own chapel. By then the Starhembergs, after four generations as Protestants, had converted back to Catholicism. In the great Turkish siege of 1683 Count Ernst Rüdiger von Starhemberg was the commander of the beleaguered city's heroic garrison. To deny the Turks cover and to give his own guns a field of fire, he had all the houses beyond the walls pulled down, his own house among them. From his command post in the cathedral tower he could easily see its ruins.

After the siege, and again after a fire in 1759, the Freihaus was rebuilt. But in the late eighteenth century, with the city's population growing, the Starhemberg of the day, now a prince, converted his suburban palace, superfluous to his requirements because of the family's other home in the city and its estates in the country, into flats for rent as an investment. From that time until the First World War, the Freihaus was the biggest tenement building in Vienna, with 1,500 tenants living in three hundred apartments around six courtyards. Over those decades candles were replaced by oil lamps, oil by gas and finally electricity was wired into the more expensive dwellings. In the late nineteenth century the

Starhemberg of the day sold the Freihaus to a bank, and the bank eventually sold it on to an industrial company. The Starhembergs' place as the Freihaus's aristocratic protector passed unofficially to the Marsanos, a family of Genoese immigrants who had made their fortune as oil merchants. They first hung out their signboard in 1662. The oil-press they installed in the seventeenth century was still in use in the twentieth, by which time they too had became a patrician family, Viennese of the Viennese. By the early twentieth century the Freihaus was a world of its own, inhabited by shrill housewives who spoke the purest Viennese patois, and their gutter-snipe children.

In 1786, however, a troupe of strolling players set up a small theatre in the third courtyard of the Freihaus auf der Wieden, and after a few years it came into the hands of a struggling theatre operator – writer, actor and man of business – called Emmanuel Schickaneder, who happened to be a Freemason. With some encouragement from the emperor, Schickaneder was trying to produce musical plays, *Singspielen*, in German, to compete with the vogue for Italian opera. Desperate for a commercial success, he sent a strange libretto, of his own composition, to one of his brother masons who was a musician. The libretto was a crude mishmash of magic and fairy story, knockabout, sentimentality and religiosity with a strong flavour of masonic deism. But the musician was Wolfgang Amadeus Mozart. The play, duly given its first production in the Freihaus, was *The Magic Flute*.[2]

In his delightful book *Invisible Cities*, the Italian novelist Italo Calvino imagined strange oriental cities with the names of women: Adelma, Diomira, Isidora, Sophronia, Zenobia. In Anastasia the craftsmen worked in agate, onyx and chrysoprase; in Dorothea the parents of brides and their grooms exchange presents of bergamot, sturgeon roe, astrolabes and amethysts. Some Calvino calls cities of desire, some trading cities, some cities of memory, and one of these last is Zaira, which soaks up the past and expands with it like a sponge. 'A description of Zaira as it is today,' Calvino says, should contain all Zaira's past. The city, however, does not tell its past, but contains it like the lines of a hand, written in the corners of the streets, the gratings of the windows, the banisters of the steps, the antennae of the lightning rods, the poles of the flags, every segment marked in turn with scratches, indentations, scrolls.

So the past of Vienna is contained in a suburban tenement, the past of London in the rust stains on a stairway. From such signs, and from reading their history, the observant traveller in the cities of Europe can see and comprehend their history. The purpose of this book has been, not to supply signs complete enough for the reader to achieve that perfect reconstruction of the past Calvino imagined for the visitor to Zaira – that would be too ambitious a project for a book many times the length of this one – but to sketch some rough hints so that readers could enjoy the pleasure of attempting their own reconstruction.

A place-name – the Strand, the Linke Wienzeile, the Marais, the Haymarket – can be a clue to changing use of land and water. It can bring to life earlier periods when noblemen and bishops built their palaces along the bank of the Thames, before the River Wien was enclosed in a culvert, before kings and convents drained the marshes on the Right Bank of the Seine, and when the neighbourhood where summer hay was sold for the droske horses of St Petersburg had not yet become the slum where Dostoyevsky found and redeemed the lower depths of humanity. The shape of a building, its angle to the street, its age, can all supply clues. The sudden juxtaposition of eighteenth-century houses round an older convent, for example, can reveal the traces of an urban speculation centuries old.

Some of the great European cities are older than others. Rome was founded some time before 753 BC, St Petersburg not until nearly two and a half millennia later. In the Latin Quarter in Paris, near the Barbican in London, under the Michaelerplatz in Vienna you can see substantial traces of Roman walls, while in Rome they are still a major obstacle to traffic. Even the 'newer' cities, Berlin,

Prague and St Petersburg, have a very ancient, fundamentally Mediterranean tradition of city life. People have been crowding together in their markets and churches for centuries, sharing their joy at coronations and festivals, their horror, or glee, at public executions, their passions for politics, theatre, music, and conversation. That shared, crowded life is the essence of European civilization. It is now under attack, both from technological innovations and from new conceptions of what a city is and ought to be.

Italo Calvino's imaginary cities were described to the great khan, Kublai, by that greatest of travellers, Marco Polo. Every now and again the khan interrupted Marco, saying, 'Does your journey take place only in the past?' Marco explained that as he journeyed in each new city he found a new past. He cannot stop, but must go on to another city where another of his pasts awaits him, 'or something perhaps that had been a possible future of his and is now someone else's present'; for, he says, 'futures not achieved are only branches of the past: dead branches'.

In that respect, Calvino's imaginary Asian cities of the past resemble our real European cities of the present. Each city's future will be chosen from possible alternatives, and at least in part those futures will be chosen from the past of other cities. London's characteristic squares were borrowed from Paris's place Royale, which in turn had models in the piazzas of northern Italy. The Georgian houses that made a Danish writer call London 'the unique city' were copied from the town houses of Bruges and Amsterdam, while Vienna and St Petersburg both borrowed from the past of Paris and from baroque Italy. But in the last fifty years, for the first time, both the stylistic models and the technological forces driving change in the city have been coming, not from other parts of Europe, but from outside Europe altogether, and especially from the quite different cities of the New World.

Every now and again it happens that a business newspaper or an airline in-flight magazine asks its readers to name their favourite cities and publishes lists of them. Typically, cities like Winnipeg, Adelaide, Denver or Houston rate very high in these businessmen's preferences. Often European cities do not figure there at all, or at best barely scrape into the top twenty. The impression is left that shrewd judges think that Atlanta, Brisbane or Miami have outstripped London or Paris or Rome and left them behind as cities.

The truth more nearly is that these conurbations in the new countries, of nineteenth-century foundation and twentieth-century growth, while undeniably extremely attractive as locations for offices and as places for families to bring up their children, are not cities at all in the European sense of the world. They did not need, like Vienna or Paris, to free themselves in the age of the railways from fortifications which had girt them in since the Middle Ages; they have space, and can afford to spread themselves at their ease over the surrounding prairie or woodlands. Over a few generations, their prosperous citizens have equipped them with handsome public buildings and with excellent schools and universities, libraries and art galleries. They are not yet, however, places where generations have grown up in a great tradition: musicians, actors, writers feeling that they are treading in the footsteps and standing on the shoulders of the immortals. The new cities of the new countries offer spacious housing on sizeable plots, surrounded by parks, tennis-courts and golf-courses, and convenient for opulent shopping centres with generous parking space. It is revealing that where in Europe 'suburban' has a flavour of second-best, in the United States the word has now acquired an aura of social prestige. American suburbs are linked by multi-lane highways to a concentration of office buildings in the central city, and to industrial facilities, tastefully landscaped, far out into the surrounding hinterland. Such 'cities', in reality clusters of suburbs increasingly independent of the central city, scarcely have a communal life. Their citizens meet, if at all, at great sporting events: a horse race, a football final, a tennis championship. Unused to crowds, except in a shopping mall, and therefore almost uneasy when surrounded by strangers, they drive from home to office, and home again, rarely meeting strangers. They generally entertain at home. To enter a bar, the closest equivalent to the European pub or café, carries an unmistakable suggestion of raffishness, except in New York and a few other metropolitan cities. The suburbs have long surpassed the central cities in population and therefore in political power. And now the process of suburbanization has gone one stage further. Increasingly, Americans travel to work, not from the suburb to the city, but from one suburb to another.

There is nothing distinctively American about the forces which have produced these transformations, however. The great cities of western Europe are already subject to them, and it can only be a matter of time before the changes that have transformed New York or Boston, and are now at work in Munich or Milan, will be felt in Prague and even St Petersburg too.

The first of these, indeed, the desire to escape from the dirt, the crowds, the physical and emotional squalor of the city centre into the green and leafy suburbs, first manifested itself in European cities like London as early as the middle of the nineteenth century. By the First World War, networks of trams and railways were bringing commuters in from the suburbs of Berlin and other big German cities, Vienna and Budapest, Paris and even St Petersburg, as well as London. Copenhagen developed delightful suburbs along the Sound, Brussels in the surrounding forests.

After 1918 the spread of the automobile began to make possible a new kind of suburban development, on a far bigger geographic scale. And there the European cities simply could not compete. Land around London or Paris, where income levels and car ownership most closely approached American levels in the 1920s, was far more expensive than land around Chicago or Melbourne. Tough structures of land ownership, historical association and local sentiment made it a far more formidable task simply to drive modern highways through the suburban landscapes of Europe. By 1940, as motorized German divisions tore up the political map of Europe, the motorized suburbs of New York and Chicago and most of all Los Angeles began to transform the whole conception of what a city is in a far more radical way than the suburban trains shuttling into nineteenth-century cities had done.

New York, hemmed in by the waters of the Hudson and the East River, Long Island Sound and Hell's Gate, did face the problems the automobile posed for European cities. It was repaid by preserving the feel and the amenities of a European city longer and more completely than any other large city on the North American continent, with the exception of San Francisco or Boston, both equally penned in by water on three sides. Around the newer US metropolitan cities land was cheap. The real estate industry was politically powerful, and not restrained as it was in Europe either by the state or by old-established landowners with political power. The majority of the well-to-do in the United States (as in England) had long moved out of town to the suburbs. But to the Parisian, the Viennese, the Berliner and the Roman, until the last quarter of the twentieth century, exile from the city and its pleasures, except for a brief holiday, was a kind of amputation, almost a living death.

Essentially the changes that threaten the survival of the European city as it has appeared in this book derive from technology. The most important of the new technologies in its implications for the structure of the city everywhere after the mid twentieth century was of course the car. But it was not alone. Radio, recorded music and above all television accustomed people to be entertained at home. By the 1960s, from Bruges to Bologna, the city centre after nightfall was abandoned to teenagers, tourists and tired businessmen. In every window in suburban streets the bright eye of the television screen brought to newly prosperous Europeans the politics and the entertainment, the sport and culture they had once sought in the square, the café, the theatre and the stadium.

By the 1970s, the density of car ownership in northern Europe approached that in the United States. The pressure of the automobile was far greater, and the resources of land, public money and political will to carry through the road-building programmes that could ease that pressure were far scarcer.

That was not all. By the very nature of their historical experience, the new countries – Australia and New Zealand, Canada,

Argentina and Brazil as well as the United States – were more flexible. To the great majority of their people, movement and change were the essence of life. Many had migrated to their new countries, or had a living family tradition of parents or grandparents who had done so. These immigrant forebears had adapted their whole way of life, learning a new language in the process. They lived where the 'standard of living' looked like being highest, not where their families had always lived. Europeans, fiercely attached to their homes, and especially if that home were in no mean city, were defined by their experience, their ways of speaking and living, their past. Suddenly they had to come to terms not only with six-lane highways and skyscrapers, but with immigrants, new languages, a whole new way of living in and thinking about cities. The impact of this new world on the ancient structures of a European city is nowhere more painfully illustrated that in the city which was chosen, largely for the very reason that it had not been one of the great imperial world cities in the past, to be the new political capital of Europe: Brussels.

The boulevards built, as in Paris and Vienna, on the line of the old fortifications, trace around Brussels the shape of a heart. Over the past century the pursuit of progress has come close to tearing the heart from its body. Right in the middle is what the Bruxellois call the Îlot Sacré, the Sacred Island, round the Grand' Place, one of the most beautiful squares in Europe. It is an oblong cobbled marketplace ringed with ornately carved and gilded merchants' houses, and dominated by the flamboyant Flemish Gothic belfry of the town hall, more than 300 feet high. Here and there in other parts of the inner city other great churches rise above the roofs, Gothic or baroque, old and new. But the 'Sacred Island' is just that: a remnant surrounded by modern office buildings, commercial or administrative, and by acres and acres of car parks. Hard as it is to believe, the Grand' Place itself was a car park for years, and one side of it was actually demolished before the Bruxellois woke up to what was being done to their city in the name of progress.

For more than a century, Brussels has been hit by successive waves of modernization, each of which has inflicted more damage than the infamous cannonade by the French in 1695. In 1867, the city of Brussels covered over its river, the Senne, and knocked Haussmann-style boulevards through the medieval centre. Then, in the full tide of imperial confidence, King Leopold II, business-man, builder and sole proprietor of the Congo Free State, turned his attentions to his own capital. He caused fifty-two streets, many of them of ancient houses, to be torn down near the southern tip of the heart to make room for his Palace of Justice, green-domed, eclectic and elephantine. It looks across Brussels from its hill to the equally elephantine and green-domed modern basilica on the Koekelberg hill, twin symbols of bourgeois state and national Church. But the worst damage came later, with the underground rail link between the north and south stations, which was not finished until the 1950s. A trail of lumpish office buildings scars the middle of the city along the line of that link, like so many molehills over the tunnels below. The exhibition of 1958 sprinkled the city with high-rise car parks, scored it with underpasses, hardened the arteries around the heart into motorways. It was already plain that real-estate speculation to provide offices for business and for the new-born European Community came first. Next came the convenience of car-borne commuters. Last by a long way was any idea of conserving the life of the inner city.

The worst, though, was yet to come. In the 1960s a real-estate developer conceived a monster of a plan. He proposed to pull down the entire north end of the city, 117 acres of it, and put up no fewer than fifty-eight tower blocks, each on a forty-foot high pediment, lining a motorway that would plunge right into the very vitals of Brussels in the boulevard Adolphe Max by the Opera. The authorities welcomed this grotesque scheme of vandali-zation, which was called, with a cultural cringe that was to be replicated everywhere in Europe at the time, the Manhattan Plan. Twenty-eight streets were razed to the ground, and 11,000 inhabit-ants moved out. In 1967 it was called 'the biggest project ever conceived in Europe'. More recently it has been called 'the greatest fiasco of contemporary town-planning'.

Fifty-odd of these towers were never built because of one of the first and most successful grass-roots rebellions ever mounted against brutally insensitive development. The uprising was coordinated by a nest of interlocking organizations led by ARAU, the Atelier de Recherches et d'Action Urbaines, or Urban Research and Action Workshop. ARAU's pungent criticisms and the skilful way it coordinated opposition in the neighbourhoods frightened off would-be investors and tenants; the over-building of office space in more salubrious districts along the avenue Louise and the recession of the 1970s delivered the *coup de grâce*.

The moving spirit of ARAU is Professor René Schoonbrodt, a sociologist with shoulder-length white hair who lives in an apart-ment bright with modern paintings in the elegant early-nineteenth-century quarter, close to the centre, behind the baroque church of the Béguinage. Schoonbrodt's theory of the city is based on a simple idea. Diversity and coexistence are healthy; specializa-tion and separation are death. 'The street is a way of coexistence,' he says. 'The motorway is a way of separation.' He is now 'relatively optimistic' about Brussels because the exodus from the city has stopped there. 'People don't want to live in slums,' he says, 'but if they can live well in the city, that's where they would choose to live.' In Europe, he says, 'there is a terrible nostalgia for what the city once was'. Not only in Europe. One of the founding fathers of modern American conservatism, Albert Jay Nook, cited the civility of Brussels, its opera and its cafés, as his example of what American cities had lost.

There are places in Europe where architects and town planners have been able to build on the same scale as in the new countries, either on green-field sites or in city neighbourhoods cleared by bombing or the bulldozer. Many of the residential neighbourhoods of the 1960s, both east and west of the Iron Curtain, fall into this category: great parks of tower blocks, remote descendants of the workers' housing put up by the architects of the Bauhaus school in Germany just after the First World War. So too do a handful of government developments like Mussolini's EUR on the outskirts of Rome or the United Nations City across the Danube from Vienna, and such business office projects as La Défense at the western tip of Paris or Docklands in the east of London.

At first, the skyscraper was seen as the very symbol of modernity, a phallic symbol asserting the potency of cities. Actually the skyscraper is a special case of a general development in architecture: the discovery of modular methods of design and prefabricated manufacture. Then, in the 1890s, after the discovery and improvement of the electrically operated elevator, architects such as Louis Sullivan discovered the advantages of building upwards. These advantages were specially great in city centres like Manhattan Island or the Loop between the Chicago River and Lake Michigan. Probably from the beginning the prestige element was more important than the saving of expensive central real estate. In any case, by the 1920s, in the United States, tall buildings were seen as the badge, almost the condition, of modernity. Remote, middle-sized cities in the middle of the prairie, sited by the hazard of a railway junction or a river bridge, had to have their multi-storey bank buildings, insurance company offices and a couple of tall hotels.

Before 1939 tall buildings were rare in Europe. There were plenty of seven- or eight-storey office buildings, swollen versions of models derived, at some distance, from the Italian Renaissance or from Flemish town halls, and the odd campanile ventured a couple of hundred feet into the grimy sky of the Ruhr or Lancashire. Essentially, though, the skyscraper office building was an American import, even if some of the masters in the genre at mid-century were transplanted Europeans like Marcel Breuer or Mies van der Rohe. The rush to build tall in Europe in the 1950s and 1960s was a spontaneous tribute, by architects and commissioning patrons alike, to the powerful imagery and perceived modernity of the United States, the victor and saviour of the Second World War.

By the 1960s, however, the reaction against the skyscraper was well under way in the United States itself. Although purely commercial developers continued and continue to build high in the United States, for hotels and apartment buildings as well as for offices, especially (interestingly enough) in places like Los Angeles and Atlanta that were anxious to boast that they are 'catching up' the commercial dominance of New York and Chicago, by the 1970s the high-rise building was no longer the modern style. It was increasingly replaced by variants of the 'post-modernist' idiom, some emphasizing the industrial technology of the new architecture, some concealing it in plastic designs or more or less successful pastiches of traditional styles.

The skyscraper, therefore, was on its way out in its native America soon after it became established in Europe. It was to have a profound (and usually negative) effect on the new residential districts that sprouted on the edge of almost every city in Europe, from Moscow to Manchester. Postwar governments rebuilt high on the outskirts of cities because they were determined to wipe out the slums that had bred dangerous and potentially revolutionary workers. Socialist city councils wanted nothing less than the best for their people, and saw gleaming towers in green parks as their ideal city. Architects dreamed of building the serried ranks of 'high houses', as they were called in Germany. Only gradually did all three realize that, unless expensively maintained, the tower blocks became unsightly, unhygienic and dangerous, that they were quite unsuitable for families with small children and that if you asked the majority of their residents they would rather be in an individual house with a garden.

Still, in most European cities, by providing alternative supplies of relatively high density housing, the tower blocks helped to preserve the city centres. In Milan, Turin and Bologna, the high-rises were at least equipped with ground-floor spaces for shops, bars and workshops, so that something of the old life of a neighbour-hood was preserved. In Edinburgh or Manchester, working-class clans were tipped out of the supportive humanity of the old slums into bleak estates scattered on bare moors far from jobs or public transport. With a lavishness and a loving care surprising among régimes dedicated to tearing down every vestige of the old societies, the men of power in Russia and in Eastern Europe spent princely sums on rebuilding the shattered centres of Warsaw, Cracow, Dresden. In the West, while some tall office blocks were built in many cities, there were comparatively few places where the sky-scraper produced the dramatic transformation it had worked in Manhattan, Chicago or Philadelphia.

Profound as were the changes high-rise building brought to cities in every corner of Europe, from Stockholm to Madrid, and from Glasgow to Belgrade, its effects were trivial compared to those wrought by the most influential technology of the century: the automobile, and the highways, car parks, shopping centres and suburbs built to serve and exploit it. The automobile was originally a European invention. But it was exploited far more swiftly and with more imagination in the United States. In 1915, Detroit, as the automobile industry continued to be called long after its assembly plants had been scattered all over the North American continent, first turned out one million cars in a year. By the late 1920s, the United States was producing some four million cars a year, while Britain, France and Germany were producing roughly 200,000 a year each. It was not until the 1960s, when the US industry was hopelessly stuck with ponderous, fuel-extravagant designs, that first the European, then the Japanese manufacturers equalled and ultimately surpassed the volume of American production.

By then the automobile was profoundly affecting every city in western Europe in at least five ways. First, it jammed streets and parking places, transforming ancient spaces built to the measure of man into stationary reservoirs of cars or near-stationary channels in which their circulation slowed to an angry walking pace. Second, the cars demanded traffic engineering. Great new multi-lane roads radiated from the cities, severing neighbourhoods and sometimes isolating them from open space or shops by a lethal river of traffic.

Hangar-like car parks disfigured some city centres. Inner ring roads and other urban motorways slashed through ancient quarters, squares, parks. Paris boulevards, the Vienna Ring, the alleys of the Berlin Tiergarten, and the Puerta del Sol in Madrid were all jammed with snarling traffic. Only a ninny would walk down Piccadilly after the 1950s with a poppy or a lily in his medieval hand: the vegetables in question would wilt even sooner than the most aesthetic of their apostles.

Third, exhaust fumes polluted the city air. '*Stadt Luft*,' said the ancient German proverb, '*macht frei*' ('City air makes you free'). Now it is truer to say that '*Stadt Luft macht Blei*' ('City air makes lead'). Now a traveller flying over Milan could see an oval mat of what looked like grubby cotton wool, through which there poked skywards only the jagged spires of the cathedral and the tower of that basilica of the motor civilization, the Pirelli building. Athens, a dream of the city beautiful for almost a hundred generations of Europeans, turned out to have the same configuration of inversions as Los Angeles, so that a polluted miasma of acid hydrocarbon poisons, trapped by hills whose mere names had been an inspiration to poets for centuries – Hymettus, Lycabettus – blanketed the Acropolis and ate into the marble of the Parthenon, Athena's no longer virginal shrine.

Perhaps most deadly of all was the exodus which the coming of these ever-growing herds of cars both stimulated and facilitated. Because cars were making inner-city neighbourhoods ever less attractive as places to live, especially for people with families, city dwellers moved to the suburbs. At the same time cars freed these fugitives from dependence on trains and trams and made it easier – at least until the growing streams of traffic overwhelmed the road system – to 'commute'[3] to purpose-built residential neighbourhoods or expanded villages further and further from the historic city. Ultimately, like most social changes, this exodus was self-correcting. After a certain time, the districts people escaped to began to resemble the cities they had escaped from. Beginning with the relatively young, relatively prosperous, people began to nose timidly back into the inner city, sniffing out elegant or lively neighbourhoods where beautiful old houses could be converted and brought up to date. Like the changes to which the flight to the suburbs was a response, this counter-flow, too, happened first in the United States. By the 1960s, the artistic grandchildren of upwardly mobile immigrants who had fled lower Manhattan were reinvading, looking for walk-up flats and industrial lofts to convert into apartments and studios. In the heart of Philadelphia, young professionals began to move back into town houses in Society Hill: in Boston they recolonized Beacon Hill. Before long something similar was happening in Europe too. By the 1980s, young professionals were 'gentrifying' streets in London's Islington which the hacks of New Grub Street, three quarters of a century before, had moved to as a last resort. By the 1980s, the Marais in Paris, the once-beautiful neighbourhoods around the baroque church of the Béguinage in central Brussels, the early eighteenth-century houses round Spitalfields Market in the City of London and the Piazza Navona in the historic centre of Rome were all firmly in the hands of the restorers, if not the speculators.

Even so, these were only partial offsets to the overwhelming social fact that was the principal impact of the automobile age on the cities of Europe: dispersal threatened the decline and eventual death of the city's heart because it destroyed the coming together, for work and pleasure, which was the historic *raison d'être* of the city. There was nothing mysterious about the form this threatened death might take. The car would kill the heart of the city because it would destroy the patterns of behaviour that had made men and women citizens. Even in Paris, where massive investment in public transport made it possible for a higher proportion of workers than elsewhere to travel to work by Métro, people saw their lives as divided into three parts: *Métro, boulot, dodo*, or tube, work and kip. People who drove into the city in the morning, parked their cars, and then drove home again to their homes in the suburbs in the evening, would not be citizens like their parents and grandparents. They would not go to school in the city, nor necessarily to the university. They would not eat there, at least not in the leisurely way that their forebears had done, nor would they drink there, or at least if they did they had lost the art of spending a whole evening over their wine or their beer in conversation artistic, political or general. They would no longer lounge along the city's boulevards, or pry into its alleys. They would not shop there. Gradually the habit of dropping into its cafés or pubs would die out. In a post-pedestrian society the Roman Corso, the Viennese Korso are already the merest relics of their former glory. The days when you could be sure of finding poets, novelists and painters in the Tauenzienstrasse, in Montparnasse or Fitzrovia are over. Some cities, especially in Germany, have rescued something of the old urban atmosphere by creating pedestrian precincts in the city centre. Elsewhere, a particular glory has departed.

Railways concentrate, it has been said, automobiles disperse. The late nineteenth century, after the coming of the railways, was in many ways a golden age for the European city. Railways made it possible for them to grow several times bigger than they had been in the eighteenth century, yet without losing their ancient sense of community. It is true that they also brought with them new slums, as bad as, and far larger than, the poor neighbourhoods of the old cities 'within the walls'. City populations grew, but the cities grew physically even more. Many of them – Paris, Berlin, Vienna, Brussels, later Rome – literally burst free of the walls that had protected but also contained them. But in spite of growth, sprawl, slums, the tensions brought by new wealth and poverty on a new scale, in spite, too, of angry and sometimes violent political conflicts, the cities of the nineteenth century retained cohesion, a specific civic personality and a culture of their own. The crowds in the Nevsky, Pigalle, Unter den Linden, Piccadilly or the Ringstrasse consciously shared in the collective life of the city, whistling its tunes and chuckling over its characters.

The skyscraper and the private car, with its attendant public works, are not the only technologies that tend to disperse the citizens from the city. That is also the implication of the computer, and more specifically of several recent developments. Technological innovations produce social consequences. Then in turn those social consequences dictate which further developments of innovative technology will be profitable, and that selection has further consequences. So it was not the computer itself which changed working habits. The massive mainframes of the 1950s and 1960s tended, if anything, to concentrate employment, though admittedly not usually in city centres. It was the improvement in the personal computer after the breaking of the IBM monopoly around 1980, and the subsequent fall in its price, that first made it realistic for thousands, then millions of people to work at home at many of the highly skilled jobs, from creative writing to all sorts of design, that had once been the characteristic trades of the central city. The subsequent development of the modem made it perfectly feasible for such typical citizens to move to Vermont or Wales. This dispersal of highly visible skills from the inner city to the so-called electronic cottage has been much noticed. The earlier dispersal of other city activities is less well understood. It was already happening before the computer became widespread, and owes more to the car, the van, the telephone, the television set and high city rentals than to electronics.

If you walk at dusk through the streets of Ghent or Rotterdam, Hamburg or Rome itself, the streets are already less crowded than they were a generation ago. In every window there flickers the screen. In some countries only a few channels are available, and the same music can be heard from house after house. In others, there is more variety. Everywhere, the box in the corner of the living-room is a deadly challenge to the cultural institutions of the city: to the opera, the stadium, the concert-hall and the café.

If you cross the river Hooghly from Calcutta to Howrah you will plunge into a warren of streets full of sweating men pulling, pushing, beating, polishing, greasing and painting everything from gearboxes to hotel furniture. Before the coming of the internal combustion engine every great European city had its Howrah. In the Quartier du Temple in Paris, in Clerkenwell just north of the

City of London, small businesses clustered together and created something greater than the sum of their individual capabilities. Within a few streets you could find firms performing every stage in the chains of textile production, light engineering, food processing, printing, brewing, jewellery, furniture-making. Precisely those same clusters of enterprise that had emerged in Berlin and Vienna and to a lesser extent in Prague in the 'founders' years' were beginning to appear in St Petersburg after the revolution of 1905. Out of those vulnerable and at the same time fiercely competitive businesses, innovations and entrepreneurs emerged. And at the same time out of these trades, with imperceptible gradations, there emerged crucial elements of the high culture of the city. Out of print shops came journalism, publishing, advertising. Out of textiles came the needle trades, fashion, new styles. Great restaurants swarmed round food markets, wig makers, costumiers and musical-instrument makers around the theatres. The line between the applied arts and fine art was not fixed, and the craftsman's son could and often did become an artist.

The rich, untidy fecundity of that urban life has been mortally threatened, if not yet killed, by all the changes of the twentieth century. Already, in even the greatest cities of western Europe, there is legitimate doubt whether any authentic spark of the true city life survives. In Paris, Rome, Vienna, you can hire a horse-drawn carriage to tour the monumental centre, and so recreate for an hour, however imperfectly, the world of the fiacre, the droshke and the hansom cab. It is a pleasant way to spend an hour. But it also a reminder of how far the cities of Dostoyevsky, of Proust, of Kafka, of Conan Doyle, have faded into the past. Soon they will be as invisible as the fantasy cities with which an imagined Marco Polo regaled an imaginary Kublai Khan.

Indeed, to a far greater extent than we like to admit, the traditional mores of London and Vienna, Prague and Paris, are kept going, not for the sake of the living citizens of those real cities, but for the benefit of tourists. Vienna's opera, London's West End theatres, the great Paris restaurants and Berlin's nightlife are already heavily dependent for their survival on the tourists' patronage. What was once the heart of the communal life of great cities is now suspiciously reminiscent of a theme park, or at least a survival, artificially preserved for the benefit of the tourist industry.

The great cities of the East have not yet enjoyed the luxury of this subtle process of decay. Cars are still relative rarities on the streets of St Petersburg and Moscow, though already far less so in Prague. Plenty of people in Prague, like some Muscovites, have a cottage in the suburbs, but it is not yet an option for many to travel into the city centre to work. The electronic village is still a pipedream in eastern Europe. When I worked for a newspaper in London it was a common experience for journalists from eastern Europe to offer to buy our computer terminals secondhand, not realizing that the terminals were only leased and were in any case useless without a central computer that was infinitely beyond their pockets. Still, this will change, and perhaps more quickly than we imagine. Within ten years, no doubt, Prague, Warsaw, Budapest and other cities in eastern Europe will be experiencing densities of car ownership comparable to those that transformed the cities of western Europe in the 1950s. Soon perhaps they will be ringed with suburbs, and soon after that they will experience the dispersal of population and economic activity that has blown out the yolk of Manchester or even Rome. And once political and financial stability have been achieved, who can doubt that St Petersburg, Kiev and Moscow will go the same way?

Some European cities are consciously and courageously fighting this degeneration. Berlin, newly reunited, is attempting to become once again the national capital, the 'world city' which Wilhelm II dreamed of in 1900. The Reichstag, the Crown Prince's palace, perhaps the Schloss itself, are to be renovated at what could prove a literally ruinous financial cost. Paris has invested huge sums in its future, both in subsidizing a superb system of public transport, and in building a new generation of 'great monuments' to rank with the Arc de Triomphe and the Eiffel Tower.

For successive presidents, De Gaulle, Pompidou, Mitterrand, Paris was so vital to the very survival of the nation that no resources were spared to make sure of its survival as a great city: as the vibrant, living heart and brain of France. Fifteen years ago the rebuilding of the central markets, Les Halles, and the opening of the Pompidou Centre created a new vortex of energy on the Right Bank, which then spread down past the Marais to the once-derelict neighbourhood of the Bastille, where a new opera-house was built in 1989 to celebrate the bicentennial of the great Revolution.

There are nine Great Works, all but one of them firmly in the public sector, and all but two of them unapologetically cultural. The first of these new monuments was the Orsay railway station, converted into a magnificent showcase for French Impressionism, among other things, on the Left Bank of the Seine. But the key to much of this bold cultural refit is *le Grand Louvre*. To the chagrin of the French architectural profession, I.M. Pei was chosen to design the new approach to the museum through an elegant half-buried glass pyramid. The ministry of finance, a formidable lobby-ist by any standards, was finally extruded from one wing of the Louvre, throwing the whole palace open for the first time to be used as a museum. The ministry of finance was found a new home, and 5,000 civil servants were decanted from the Louvre to a gigantic new building which reflects the style of the modern French state painfully well: it is overwhelming in its ambition, but grievously short on both elegance and charm. The same can be said of Carlos Ott's Bastille opera-house, the sort of building for which human beings less than six feet tall seem to have been carelessly designed to be too small, and of the 'very big library' in the rue de Tolbiac. The Institute of the Arab World, on the contrary, which occupies an admirable site opposite the apse of Notre-Dame, is comparatively small, but it is an architectural jewel. Far out in the once miserable district of La Villette, Paris's nineteenth-century slaughterhouses have been transformed into a cultural park, including a science museum and the Paris music conservatory. This gigantic development pulls the modern city towards the north-east, towards the new economic activity – warehousing, factories, office complexes – generated by the *autoroute* to Lille, Brussels and Cologne, and to the Charles de Gaulle airport at Roissy. The countervailing pull to the west, still on the right bank of the Seine, comes from the even more enormous office development at La Défense which sits across the great axis which links the Louvre, the place de la Concorde, the Champs-Élysées and the Arc de Triomphe at the Étoile, the grandest ceremonial perspective in any city in the world, with the possible exception of Washington.

There is a sharp ideological contrast between the Anglo-Saxon suspicion of government, and consequent commitment to leave it to private enterprise to shape the city, and the French faith in the capacity of the republican state, heir of monarchy, to create both architectural beauty and civic grandeur. It is hard to imagine either Margaret Thatcher or John Major writing, as Mitterrand has done: 'The world moves, the city changes, under the impulse of forces which, left to themselves, would end up with the disorderly juxtaposition of nothing but private interests.'

There have been attempts to conserve or protect London against the impact of the automobile and the unregulated pressure of commercial development. There was the Abercrombie plan of 1947, the Buchanan Committee's proposal, in 1963, to price most motor traffic out of central London. Since a succession of Conservative governments have held power, beginning in 1979, these attempts to defend London's future have been abandoned. The Greater London Council, the only municipal government for the city as a whole, was simply abolished, with little attempt to pretend that this action was not politically motivated. Public services, especially the Underground, have been starved of investment and at the time of writing are degenerating to Third World standards. The only public building of any consequence to be built since 1979 is the architecturally unfortunate new British Library.

The only visionary architectural schemes are purely commercial projects, such as shopping centres and those two beached whales, the office buildings, primarily intended for international financial corporations, at Broadgate in the City of London and Canary Wharf on the site of the largely abandoned London Docks.

The other cities of western Europe fall between Paris and London on the political spectrum. Some, like Brussels, Stuttgart, Seville, have completed impressive public building projects. Several – Munich, Brussels, Rome, Stockholm, Newcastle and, in the East, Prague – have built more or less impressive mass transport systems. Most have invested more than London in capital schemes of one sort or another to tame the motor car: urban highways, underground car parks, pedestrian precincts. There are many cities in Europe – big ones such as Munich, Amsterdam, Hamburg, Turin, Copenhagen and Barcelona, middling ones such as Nuremberg, Toulouse, Dublin, Geneva, Edinburgh or Cologne, small cities like Cardiff, Luxemburg, Oxford, Verona, Leiden, Aarhus, Bonn or Strasbourg, to cite names almost invidiously at random – which have retained some of the charm, the sense of well-being, dignity and significance that a true city should have. There are several among them – Seville, Lille, Stuttgart come to mind – that have even recovered a dynamism that seemed long lost. A new grand tour, to appreciate what is left of the urban civilization of Europe, would take in all those cities and many more.

Yet no visitor even to those cities that have worked hardest to hold off decay can deny that all are now threatened by what certainly looks like a rising tide of troubles. These are many. There is the congestion and pollution brought by the automobile, and in the richer European cities there are now as many cars as people. There is the dispersal of their populations into far-flung suburbs, to satellite towns, to the rural retreat and the electronic cottage. That is also a largely unanticipated consequence of automobile culture. There is de-industrialization, pauperization, crime; a great influx of refugees and immigrants at a time when the host population is neither well organized nor of a mind to receive them with understanding and generosity. There is the rise of mass culture, destroying the audience and so the financial support for 'high culture', and at the same time there is a certain failure of will, a cultural panic, if you like, within the high culture itself. Underlying that panic there is a real and pervasive sense of disgust and self-hatred among Europeans when they contemplate the crimes and cruelties that European culture committed or was at least powerless to stop: war, economic crisis, unemployment, fascism, persecution, genocide, more war, and now once again more crisis, more unemployment, and the dismal recognition that, like the Bourbons, we Europeans have learned nothing and forgotten nothing.

All European cities, in one way or another, face the temporal and spiritual consequences of these tragic failures. But there have been tragedies before in European history, and the great European cities have survived them. The question now concerns their inner strength: do they, which is to say their inhabitants, have the will and the faith to rebuild urban civilizations as London did after the Great Fire, as Vienna did after the siege, or Paris after the Commune? Berlin, certainly, is determined to forget the last sixty years and to make itself once again the World City of 1914 and 1930. Prague, helped as well as hindered by the floods of tourists who have converged on the castle and the bridge, is determined to recreate its unique urban culture. Vienna, like Paris, has made great efforts to cherish the glittering achievements of its past and, perhaps less successfully, to open new doors in the wall which seemed to block the future of Austrian culture after the Viennese washed their hands of the Jewish fellow citizens who had given them so much. London remains as elusive and inscrutable as ever: infuriatingly indifferent to public culture, yet obstinately rich in cultural institutions which work and in the talents to use them. As for St Petersburg, most of its citizens can hardly be blamed if they spend more time thinking about their own mere survival than about the glories of their city.

The proof of tours, after all, grand or less grand, has always been in the coming home.

Heureux qui, comme Ulysse, a fait un beau voyage . . .
Et puis est retourné, plein d'usage et raison,
Vivre entre ses parents le reste de son âge!

Happy, said Du Bellay, is he who, like Ulysses, has made a beautiful journey and then come home, full of experience and wisdom, to live among his own for the rest of his life. Back from our own tour, we must chiefly hope that the great cities of Europe will not be transformed into theme parks for tourists inspecting their past. If that past is anything to go by, after all, we can be sure that, in new environments but with the same spirit, their citizens are even now creating the books and the music, the buildings and the poems, the ways of thinking and the ways of living that will make them worth visiting by the tourists of the future. 'What is the use,' the khan asked Calvino's Marco Polo, 'of all your travelling?' And Marco answered that the more one was lost in unfamiliar quarters of distant cities, the more one understood the other cities he had crossed to arrive there. That is the point of tours, after all, old or new, grand or not-so-grand: by exploring a new past the traveller gives himself, even only by ever so little, a new future.

NOTES

1. To the City, to the World

1. Jeremy Black, *The Grand Tour in the Eighteenth Century*, Stroud and New York, 1992, p. 7.

2. ibid., p. 9.

3. On Englishmen travelling in Europe before the Restoration of 1660, see J.W. Stoye, *English Travellers Abroad 1604–1667*, Oxford, 1952, rev. edn, New Haven, 1989.

4. ibid., pp. 17ff.

5. Philip Francis, ed., *John Evelyn's Diary*, London, 1963, selected from E.S. de Beer, ed., *John Evelyn's Diaries*, Oxford, 1953.

6. Stoye, op. cit., p. 450.

7. Black, op. cit., p. 192. Black's chapter 9, 'Love, Sex, Gambling and Drinking', is a fascinating compendium of facts about the Grand Tour as a search for pleasure.

8. Frederick A. Pottle, *James Boswell: the Earlier Years 1740–1769*, London, 1966, pp. 137–45 (Belle de Zuylen), 150–51 (the Guardsman's wife), 162–83 (Rousseau), 184–97, 255–7, 521–2 (Paoli).

9. William F. Monypenny, *The Life of Benjamin Disraeli, Earl of Beaconsfield*, London, 1990, vol. 1, p. 108.

10. Black, op. cit., p. 70.

11. Verse XVIII.

12. Lindsay Stainton, *Turner's Venice*, London, 1985, pp. 13–14.

13. G.M. Trevelyan, *Garibaldi's Defence of the Roman Republic*, London, 1907, p. 1.

14. E.V. Lucas, *A Wanderer in Rome*, London, 1926, p. 9.

15. *The Life of Benvenuto Cellini Written by Himself*, London, 1949.

16. *The Memoirs of the Life of Edward Gibbon with Various Observations and Excursions by Himself*, ed. George Birkbeck Hill, London, 1900, p. 167.

17. Thomas Babington, Lord Macaulay, 'Essay on Von Ranke's History of the Popes', in *Critical and Historical Essays contributed to the Edinburgh Review*, London, 1885, p. 542.

18. For these and other details of Roman sites, museums and *objets d'art* I have used the Guide Bleu, *Italie*, Paris, 1968.

19. The classic account is in Gregorovius, *History of Rome*, book XIV, chapter 6. Bourbon died just before the Sack.

20. *Breve guida di Roma della Camera di Commercio di Roma*, Rome, 1875, quoted in Valentino De Carlo, ed., *Roma dei nostri nonni*, Rome, 1992, p. 137; the same source gives the population as 226,000 in 1870 and 256,000 in 1874.

21. The temple, of the first century AD, is wrongly thought to have been dedicated to Vesta.

22. This account of the papal government is based on G.M. Trevelyan, op. cit., pp. 54–61.

23. 'If one may judge from appearance, he would appear strange to political intrigues ... Nevertheless, as some imagine that he may belong to the class called "Thinkers", I consider it my duty to acquaint your Eminence with it, in order that he may be prudently watched.' Letter of the Cardinal Legate of Bologna to Cardinal Lambruschini, quoted in Trevelyan, op. cit., p. 56.

24. Luigi Palomba, 'Gli ultimi dieci giorni del governo papale', in Valentino De Carlo, ed., *Roma dei nostri nonni*, Rome, 1992, p. 95.

25. It is reproduced twice in Black, op. cit., as the endpaper, and on p. 99 as 'The arrival of a young traveller and his suite during the carnival in the Piazza di Spagna, Rome', by David Allan. The drawing belongs to Her Majesty the Queen and is in the Royal Library at Windsor.

26. Malcolm Bradbury and James McFarlane, eds., *Modernism: A Guide to European Literature 1890–1930*, London, 1993, pp. 20–21.

27. Palinurus [Cyril Connolly], *The Unquiet Grave*, London, 1945, p. 40.

28. Norman Lewis, *Voices of the Old Sea*, Harmondsworth, 1984.

29. This distinction is shrewdly discussed in Paul Fussell, *Abroad: British Literary Travelling between the Wars*, Oxford, 1980, p. 40.

2. Left Bank, Right Bank

1. See Herbert Lottman, *The Left Bank: Writers in Paris from Popular Front to Cold War*, p. 31.

2. Gallimard missed Proust at first. He went to Grasset, who published the first volume of *À la recherche du temps perdu* in 1913. But Gallimard got him in the end. See George D. Painter, *Marcel Proust*, London, 1989, pp. 191, 278–81.

3. See Humphrey Carpenter, *Geniuses Together: American Writers in Paris in the 1920s*, London, 1987.

4. Carpenter, op. cit., p. 100, quoting Frederick Kohner, *Kiki of Montparnasse*, London, 1968.

5. Richard Ellmann, *James Joyce*, London, 1982.

6. See his memoirs, Ambroise Vollard, *Recollections of a Picture Dealer*, London, 1936, *passim*.

7. On the Lapin Agile and Montmartre in 1900, see Francis Carco, *From Montmartre to the Latin Quarter*, London, 1929, *passim*.

8. For the early history of Paris, I have used extensively Jacques Hillairet, *Évocation du Vieux Paris*, 3 vols., Paris, 1952, and the same author's one-volume *Connaissance du Vieux Paris*, Paris, 1956.

9. I am indebted to James Billington, *Fire in the Minds of Man*, pp. 23–32, for much of the detail in this account of the Palais-Royal on the eve of Revolution.

10. See Walter Benjamin, 'The Paris of the Second Empire in Baudelaire', in *Charles Baudelaire: A Lyric Poet in the Era of High Capitalism*, London, 1973, p. 18.

11. Henry Murger's book was published in 1856. Giovanni Puccini's opera based on it, *La Bohème*, was not written until 1896, though the time of the opera is 'about 1830'. This in itself suggests the continuity of the Parisian student life it celebrates.

12. Louis Chevalier, *Montmartre du plaisir et du crime*, Paris, 1980, pp. 63–4.

13. Chevalier, op. cit., p. 65. There follows a learned disquisition on the 'moral topography' of the different grades of prostitute in the world of Balzac.

14. Chevalier, op. cit., p. 77

15. Chevalier, op. cit., p. 88.

16. Chevalier, op. cit., pp. 99–100.

17. Chevalier, op. cit., p. 83. Charcot, the greatest neurologist of the nineteenth century, lived in the boulevard St-Germain, close to the Salpêtrière hospital where Freud was to study with him in 1885. But as a young bachelor he lived in Montmartre.

18. Chevalier, op. cit., p. 150.

19. Enid Starkie, introduction to Charles Baudelaire, *Les Fleurs du Mal*, Oxford, 1942, pp. xvii–xviii.

20. *Encyclopaedia Britannica*, 'Villon'.

21. Charles Baudelaire, *Les Fleurs du Mal*, LXXXIX, 'Le Cygne'.

22. Jean Bruhat, *La Commune de 1870*, Paris, 1970, p. 24.

23. Haussmann's achievement is expertly described and discussed in Donald J. Olsen, *The City as a Work of Art*, New Haven and London, 1986, esp. pp. 44–57.

24. Raymond Escholier, *Le Nouveau Paris: la vie artistique de la cité moderne*, Paris, 1913, pp. 1–2.

25. See, for example, the photographs by Nicholas Breach, with a commentary by Richard Cobb, in *The Streets of Paris*, London, 1980.

26. This view was put forward by Amédée de Cesena in a guidebook published in 1864, *Le Nouveau Paris*, pp. 3–4, quoted in Olsen, op. cit., p. 44.

27. Walter Benjamin, 'Paris – the Capital of the Nineteenth Century', op. cit.

28. Norma Evenson, *Paris: A Century of Change, 1878–1978*, New Haven and London, 1981, p. 20.

29. Lenard Berlanstein, *The Working People of Paris 1871–1914*, Baltimore and London, 1984.

30. The following account of the siege and the Commune is largely based on two sources: Jean de Bruhat, *La Commune de Paris*, Paris, 1970; Robert Tombs, *The War against Paris*, Cambridge.

31. E.H. Gombrich, *The Story of Art*, London, 1950, p. 381. See also Phoebe Pool, *Impressionism*; Caroline Mathieu, *Musée d'Orsay: Guide*.

32. Chevalier, op. cit., p. 152.

33. According to Bernard Grun, *The Timetables of History*, London, 1975, p. 440.

34. Philip Stephan, *Paul Verlaine and the Decadence 1882–90*, Manchester, 1974.

35. Stephan, op. cit., p. 50.

36. ibid., p. 40.

37. ibid., p. 67.

38. The following account of Mallarmé's infatuation for Méry Laurent is based on Robert Goffin, *Mallarmé vivant*, Paris, 1956.

39. Goffin, op. cit., p. 44.

40. The question of what favours Méry may or may not have bestowed on the poet is discussed in great, if chastely metaphorical detail, by Robert Goffin, op. cit. His conclusion, if I may be so crass as to summarize it thus, is that if she did allow the poet a liberty or two, it was not much and it was out of kindness, but it was enough to inspire his grand passion and his poetry, notably *L'après-midi d'un faune*.

41. Ambroise Vollard, op. cit., p. 15.

42. Aristide Bruant, *L'Argot au XXme Siècle*, 2 vols, Paris, 1901. Bruant achieves seventy-five synonyms for *derrière*, for example, complete with etymological illustrations, each more vulgar than the last.

43. Stephan, op. cit., p. 11.

44. Claude Monet, *Les Déchargeurs de charbon*, Collection Durand-Ruel, reproduced in Pool, op. cit., p. 79.

45. Carco, op. cit., pp. 46ff.

46. Guillaume Apollinaire, *Alcools: poèmes 1898–1915*, Paris, 1947, p. 16.

47. Chevalier, op. cit., p. 280.

3. All Human Life

1. The drawing is reproduced between pp. 162 and 163 in John Gross, *The Rise and Fall of the Man of Letters*, London, 1970. The presentation is described in Evan Charteris, *Life and Letters of Sir Edmund Gosse*, London 1931, p. 444.

2. Reproduced in Karl Beckson, *London in the Eighteen Nineties: A Cultural History*, New York, 1992, as frontispiece.

3. Beckson, op. cit., p. 258.

4. Swinburne's habits were indeed peculiar. As Karl Beckson concisely puts it, 'his life could indeed be charged with decadence. In addition to chronic alcoholism, he frequented a brothel in St John's Wood in order to be whipped: he also had a well-publicized affair with an American circus performer, who later revealed she hadn't been able to get him up to the scratch, and couldn't make him understand that biting's no use', Beckson, op. cit., p. 38.

5. The publishing house at the sign of the Bodley Head in Vigo Street, between Regent Street and the north entrance to Albany, published *The Yellow Book* and a number of the fashionable writers associated with it. It was founded by John Lane and Elkin Matthews.

6. José-Maria de Hérédia (1842–1905), one of the Parnassian school of poets. His sonnets were collected in a volume called *Les Trophées*, published in 1893.

7. Miranda Seymour, *A Ring of Conspirators*, London, 1988, is about this exodus and Henry James's friends.

8. In the first part of this chapter I have used the 'City', with the initial capitalized, to designate the 'square mile' within the walls, from Temple Bar to Aldgate, and the 'city' to refer to the whole metropolitan urban area.

9. By Simon Jenkins, *Landlords to London*, London, 1975, p. 17. This whole description of the development of London owes a great deal to Mr Jenkins's admirable account.

10. Both district names, of course, commemorate ecclesiastical lands expropriated at the Dissolution.

11. Simon Jenkins, op. cit., p. 133.

12. Richard Ellmann, *Yeats: the Man and the Mask*, Harmondsworth, 1987, p. 160.

13. Ford Madox Hueffer, the grandson of the pre-Raphaelite painter Ford Madox Brown, changed his name to Ford Madox Ford during the First World War, when German names rendered their owners unpopular.

14. As 'Under the Hill'.

15. First produced in 1930, not in the West End, but in a festival in Canterbury Cathedral itself.

16. *The Times*, 24 April 1909, quoted in Beckson, op. cit., p. 289.

17. Beckson, op. cit. p. 178.

18. Beckson, op. cit., pp. 181–2.

19. Beckson, op. cit., p. 186. In 1892 a schoolmaster called John Gabril Nicholson wrote a series of poems to a fourteen-year-old schoolboy, William Ernest Mather, which contained several references to the pun, e.g. 'Some lightly love, but mine is love in earnest.'

20. Charles D. Stuart and A.J. Park, *The Variety Stage*, London, 1895, quoted in Beckson, op. cit., p. 111.

21. Michael Harrison, *In the Footsteps of Sherlock Holmes*, Beckson, op. cit., p. 110.

22. For a learned disquisition on Turkish baths, see Michael Harrison, op. cit., p. 19.

23. Michael Holroyd, *Bernard Shaw*, vol. 1, *The Search for Love*, London, 1988, p. 60.

24. I owe this magnificent verse, and much of the other detail about life in the 1880s to Michael Harrison, op. cit., an irreplaceable guide to what London *felt* like in the late Victorian age.

25. Holroyd, op. cit., p. 84.

26. Gissing, *New Grub Street*, Harmondsworth, 1968 (first published 1891), pp. 413–14.

27. Harrison, op. cit., p. 150.

28. As late as the early 1970s, the author saw Edward Heath, then the prime minister, eating at a restaurant in St James's with his father: they had walked alone across the Park from 10 Downing Street, with no apparent security.

29. Harrison, op. cit., p. 130.

30. Gissing, op. cit., p. 213.

31. Holroyd, op. cit., p. 290.

32. Harrison, op. cit., p. 22.

33. H.H. Munro ('Saki') – 'Filboid Studge, the Story of a Mouse that Helped' and 'Cousin Teresa', *The Penguin Complete Saki*, Harmondsworth, 1982, pp. 158, 306 and 308.

34. ibid., 'Cousin Teresa', pp. 342–3.

35. Beckson, op. cit., p. 380.

36. He died in 1900, and it was generally reckoned that the new century began with 1 January 1901.

37. The *Witanegemot*, or 'moot of wise men', was the council of the Anglo-Saxon kings. A skewbald horse is brown and white.

38. See Paul Selver, *Orage and the New Age Circle*, *passim*; and John Gross, op. cit., pp. 228–31.

39. For Hulme, see Erik Svarny, *T.S. Eliot and the 'Men of 1914'*, Milton Keynes and Philadelphia, 1988, pp. 17ff.

40. The 'Garden City of Biggleswick', with its 'Moot Hall' and 'about ten varieties of Mystic', its socialists, its New Movements, including 'a terrible woman who had come back from Russia with what she called a "message of healing"', 'a great buck nigger who had a lot to say about "Africa for the Africans"' and a 'jolly old fellow who talked about English folk songs and dances', is described in John Buchan, *Mr Standfast*, in *Four Adventures of Richard Hannay*, pp. 468–88. The description was no doubt intended to poke somewhat rancorous fun at the high-minded fads of the day: many may feel that it is Buchan who now comes off worse than his fictional targets.

41. Svarny, op. cit., p. 14.

42. Ellmann, op.cit., p. 215.

43. T.S. Eliot, *The Waste Land*, ll. 60–65.

44. ibid., ll. 231–4.

45. ibid., ll. 253–6.

46. ibid., ll. 263–5.

4. The Bronze Horseman

1. The Dutch, of course, would be 'Pieter', but this is rendered in Russian Литер, which sounds like 'Peter' in English.

2. Ronald Hingley, *Russian Writers in the Nineteenth Century*, London, 1977, p. 8.

3. Robert Conquest, *The Great Terror*, revised edn, Oxford, 1990, p. 37.

4. Hingley, op. cit., p. 115.

5. Edward Jerrmann, *Pictures of St Petersburg*, trans. by Frederick Haardmann, London, 1852, cited by Laurence Kelly, *St Petersburg: a Traveller's Companion*, London, 1981, p. 176. Kelly reproduces an engraving of this 'degrading and deplorable spectacle' from F. Lacroix, *Les Mystères de la Russie*, 1845.

6. Robert B. McKean, *St Petersburg between the Revolutions*, New Haven, Conn., 1990, p. 1.

7. Now Herzen Street, or Gertsena Ulitsa, it runs into the Nevsky Prospekt just on the Neva side of the Moyka. David McDuff, trans., *Crime and Punishment*, London, 1991, p. 643.

8. Beverly Whitney Kean, *All the Empty Palaces*, London, 1983, p. 31.

9. John Reed, *Ten Days that Shook the World*, Harmondsworth, London, 1966, p. 55.

10. Reed, op. cit., pp. 61–2.

11. Sharon Leiter, *Akhmatova's Petersburg*, Cambridge, 1983, p. 60.

12. Varvara Alekseyevna Dobrosolyova, in Fyodor Dostoyevsky, *Poor People*, trans. Olga Shartse, Moscow, 1988, p. 69.

13. John Quincy Adams, *Memoirs of John Quincy Adams, Comprising Portions of His Diary from 1795–1848*, ed. Charles Francis Adams, Philadelphia, 1874–7, at 28 October 1812.

14. Leiter, op. cit. p. 152. See also the moving account of a meeting with Akhmatova in Sir Isaiah Berlin, *Personal Impressions*, London, 1982, pp. 189–208.

15. It is known as the 'Don Juan List', Magarshack, *Puskin: A Biography*, London, 1967, p. 220.

16. Osip Mandelstam, 'The Admiralty', in *Selected Poems*, edited and translated by David McDuff, London, 1983. The poem's symbolism is dense. For example, 'the Admiralty . . . incarnates the original ideology of Petersburg and its dual, synthetic and paradoxical nature; the "northern capital" that is touched by the "demigods" and "acropolis" of the Mediterranean world. Peter's will alone (he ordered that the tower and the arch beneath it convey the form of the Cyrillic, and Greek initial of his name: π.) In the same way the ship is both figurative, the "ship of state" that carried Peter to empire, and literal; the wind-vane on top of the spire is a three-masted ship, the city's badge.' See Clarence Brown, *Mandelstam*, Cambridge, 1973.

17. Yevgeny Yevtushenko, essay on 'The City with Three Names' in Wilhelm Klein, ed., *St Petersburg*, Hong Kong, 1992.

18. Robert B. McKean, op. cit., pp. 1–29.

19. Anatole Mazour, *The First Russian Revolution*, Stanford, 1961, quoted in Kelly, op. cit.

20. This account is based on Ronald Hingley, *Dostoevsky, His Life and Work*, London, 1978. For the background of Dostoyevsky's relations with the Petrashevksy Circle and other more or less conspiratorial literary groups, see Joseph Frank, *Dostoevsky*, vol. 1, *The Seeds of Revolt*, New York and London, 1977, pp. 199–287.

21. Uniate Christianity was introduced into Ukraine and adjoining regions in the seventeenth century by the Jesuits.

22. According to a report by Helen Womack in the *Independent*, 25 February 1993, Tolstoy's estate at Yasnaya Polyana now consists of more than 400,000 hectares.

23. David Magarshack, op. cit., pp. 11ff.

24. The source is Modest Korf, who knew him at the time. He is quoted in Magarshack, op. cit., p. 60.

25. Hingley, *Dostoevsky*, London, 1978, p. 201.

26. Laurence Kelly, *Lermontov: Tragedy in the Caucasus*, London, 1983, pp. 59–60.

27. A. Stasov, quoted in ibid., p. 65.

28. Hingley, op. cit., p. 109; and the notes to David McDuff's translation of *Crime and Punishment*, London, 1991, pp. 633–47, which are especially useful because they give the tsarist equivalents of Soviet place-names.

29. Magarshack, op. cit., p. 195.

30. Alexander Pushkin, *Selected Works*, trans. Irina Zheleznova, Moscow, 1974, 'The Bronze Horseman'.

31. Leiter, op. cit., p. 5.

32. Charles Spencer, Philip Dyer and Martin Battersby, *The World of Serge Diaghilev*, London, 1974; see also Beverly Whitney Kean, op. cit.

33. Denis Arnold, ed., *New Oxford Companion to Music*, London, 1983, article on 'Ballet and Theatrical Dance' by Noel Goodwin.

34. Spencer, Dyer and Battersby, op. cit., p. 15.

35. Spencer, Dyer and Battersby, op. cit., p. 43.

36. I have followed closely the account of this incident in Max Hayward's Introduction to the Collins Harvill edition of Anna Akhmatova, *Selected Poems*, London, 1989, pp. 13–14.

37. Lydia Ginzburg essay in Klein, op. cit., pp. 63–4.

38. I have relied in my account of the siege on the Museum of the History of the City of St Petersburg, but also on the classic account in Harrison E. Salisbury, *The 900 Days*, London, 1986.

39. Salisbury, op. cit., p. 569.

40. Salisbury, op. cit., p. 601.

41. Salisbury, op. cit., p. 569.

42. Salisbury, op. cit., p. 608.

5. Secession

1. The painting is in the Kunsthistorisches Institut der Universität Wien, and was reproduced in Reinhard E. Petermann, *Wien im Zeitalter Kaiser Franz Josephs I*, Vienna, 1908. It is reproduced twice, in black and white and in colour, in Donald J. Olsen, *The City as a Work of Art*, New Haven and London, 1986.

2. Joachim Fest, *Hitler*, London, 1974, pp. 36–55.

3. Pronounced in three syllables, not as *Lüger*, which would mean 'liar' in German.

4. Donald J. Olsen, op. cit., p. 239.

5. Robert Musil, *Der Mann ohne Eigenschaften*; English trans., *The Man without Qualities*, London, 1955, vol. 1, p. 59.

6. Christian M. Nebelhay, *Wien Speziell: Musik um 1900*, Vienna, 1984, p. VI/15.

7. Carl E. Schorske, *Fin-de-Siècle Vienna: Politics and Culture*, Cambridge, 1981, p. 325.

8. Schorske, ibid., p. 162, quoting Alex Bein, *Theodor Herzl: Biographie*, Vienna, 1934, p. 189. Any reader of Schorske will understand how much this whole chapter owes to his brilliant study, not only for its overall thesis about the political context of Viennese modernism, but also for a rich haul of individual perceptions.

9. They included Moritz Benedikt, the editor of the *Neue Freie Presse* and the journalist, editor, essayist and satirist Karl Kraus, who was to satirize Benedikt savagely in his book, *Die letzten Tage der Menschheit* ('The Last Days of Mankind') in 1919. See the essay by Walter Obermaier, 'Karl Kraus', in *Wien 1870–1930: Traum und Wirklichkeit* ('Vienna 1870–1930: Dream and Reality'), Vienna, 1984. This is the catalogue of an exhibition at the Historical Museum of the City of Vienna, and it is an invaluable mine of facts, images and ideas for the student of Vienna in the period.

10. Theodor Herzl, *Der Judenstaat* ('The Jewish State'), Vienna, 1896.

11. Meaning those parts of the empire, including Bohemia, Moravia and Galicia, which belonged to the Vienna-based empire, as opposed to the Budapest-ruled Kingdom of Hungary, into which the imperial and royal domains of the House of Habsburg had been divided by the compromise of 1867 after the defeat at the hands of the Prussians in 1866. A substantial proportion of the populations of these lands, of course, were not German-speaking. They spoke Czech or Polish at home and from preference, though they spoke German in the education system and in their dealings with officialdom.

12. Sigmund Freud, *The Interpretation of Dreams* (Penguin Freud Library, Vol. 4), trans. James Strachey, London, 1991, p. 299.

13. 'If you want to dance, little Mister Count, I will play the guitar for you', meaning that if the Count wants to flirt with Figaro's fiancée, Susanna, Figaro will play the game with him.

14. ibid. pp. 80–199.

15. 'Insight such as this,' Freud wrote in the preface to the third English edition of the book, 'falls to one's lot but once in a lifetime', ibid., p. 43.

16. Virgil, Aeneid, VII, l. 312. See also Freud, ibid., p. 769. See also footnote, citing Freud as having said in a note in the German edition of his Collected Works that 'this line of Virgil is intended to picture the efforts of the repressed instinctual impulses'.

17. Allan Janik and Stephen Toulmin, *Wittgenstein's Vienna*, London, 1973, p. 96.

18. The last of the Babenbergs, Friedrich II, 'the Quarrelsome', was killed in battle against the Magyars at the battle of the Leitha in 1246. It was not until 1278, after a generation of 'the terrible Interregnum', that Count Rudolf of Habsburg, already crowned 'German king' at Aachen, defeated Ottakar Přemysl of Bohemia at the battle of the Marchfeld. This began the six and a half centuries of Habsburg rule. Four years later, in 1282, Rudolf and his brother Albrecht of Habsburg were awarded the duchy of Austria.

19. Ilse Barea, *Vienna: Legend and Reality*, London, 1966, pp. 43–57. I would like to pay tribute to this remarkable book, written with vast knowledge and empathy by a native Viennese driven into exile first in Czechoslovakia, then in republican Spain, finally in London.

20. Barea, op. cit.

21. See Olsen, ibid., pp. 58ff.

22. Edward Crankshaw, *The Fall of the House of Habsburg*, London, 1981, pp. 65ff.; Ilsa Barea, op. cit., pp. 244ff.

23. Crankshaw, ibid., pp. 299ff.

24. '*Wer Jude ist, bestimme ich*', Schorske, op. cit., p. 145.

25. For Wagner, see Schorske, op. cit., pp. 62–110; Nebelhay, op. cit., pp. IV/2–IV/24; Otto Antonia Graf, 'Otto Wagners Aufstieg zur Zukunft', in *Wien 1900*, op. cit., pp. 101–*109*.

26. Schorske, op. cit., p. 90.

27. Robert Musil, *The Man without Qualities*, vol. I, p. 30.

28. Nebelhay, op. cit, pp. VIII/1–VIII/23.

29. Alma Mahler, *Gustav Mahler: Memories and Letters*, London, 1968, p. 5; see also Françoise Giroud, *Alma Mahler: or the Art of Being Loved*, London, 1991, p.25.

30. See Schorske, op. cit., p. 191.

31. Mahler was born in 1860.

32. Schorske, op. cit., p. 84, quoting an unpublished letter in a dissertation by Hans Ostwald, ETH Zürich (Baden, 1948), p. 24.

33. Nebelhay, op. cit., p. IV/2, says the ubiquitous Berta Zuckerkandl preserved this remark.

34. Nebelhay, op. cit., p. I/2.

35. Aeschylus, *Prometheus*, l. 24.

36. Ernst Buschbeck, quoted in Barea, op. cit., p. 325.

37. Biographical information from Nebelhay, op. cit., pp. II/2–II/23.

38. Nebelhay, op. cit., pp. III/2–III/23. See also Werner J. Schweiger, 'Der junge Kokoschka', in *Wien 1870–1930*, op. cit., pp. 157–60.

39. Janik and Toulmin, op. cit.

40. Barea, op. cit., p. 299.

41. Janik and Toulmin, op. cit.

42. Ernest Jones, *The Life and Work of Sigmund Freud*, New York, 1961, p. 279.

43. The following summary of the criticisms that can be made of Freud owe much to the excellent short study in the 'Past Masters' series by my friend Dr Anthony Storr, *Freud*, Oxford, 1989, especially pp. 95–107.

44. Seymour Fisher and Roger P. Greenberg, *The Scientific Credibility of Freud's Theories and Therapy*, quoted in Storr, ibid., p. 107, conclude that 'Freud never presented any data, in statistical or case-study form, that demonstrated that his treatment was of benefit to a significant number of the patients he himself saw.'

45. Quoted in Storr, op. cit.

46. For Schönerer (1842–1921), see Barea, op. cit., pp. 300ff.; Schorske, op. cit., pp. 123–33. Schönerer's father, Matthias, was ennobled for his work as a railway director, of a Rothschild-controlled railway, and in the 1880s Schönerer himself professed an anti-Czech German nationalism which attracted some Jewish followers, including the Social Democratic leader, Viktor Adler himself. Only later did Schönerer turn towards a personal ideology in which anti-Semitism was a prominent part: he was admired by, and influenced, Hitler.

47. The phrase was attributed by Freud to a high official, who had given this as his excuse for not promoting one of Freud's (Jewish) colleagues. 'He told me that on this occasion he had driven the exalted official into a corner and had asked straight out whether the delay over his appointment was not due to denominational considerations. The reply had been that in the present state of feelings, it was no doubt true that His Excellency was not in a position, etc., etc . . . the same denominational considerations applied in my own case', Freud, op. cit., p. 218.

48. Barea, op. cit., p. 302. Barea, whose father was Jewish, is not denying the reality of popular anti-Semitism in Vienna. She makes the point that in the 1890s it was still not *salonfähig* – respectable in drawing-rooms – to admit to anti-Semitism or even to take notice of whether people were Jewish or not.

49. See, for example, Giroud, op. cit., p. 138, quoting Elias Canetti, who was in love with Anna Mahler, but was horrified to hear Alma saying that Gropius was 'Aryan to his fingertips. The only man who matches me racially. The others who fell in love with me were all little Jews, like Mahler.' Of course it is possible that Alma was irritated by Canetti. But she actually wrote of Hitler that he was 'a genuine German idealist, something which is unthinkable for the Jews', Giroud, op. cit., p. 139.

50. Barea, op. cit., p. 304. The full documents in the matter of Freud's promotion, or delayed promotion, were published by Professors Dr Joseph and Renée Gickelhorn, *Sigmund Freuds akademische Laufbahn im Lichte der*

Dokumente, Vienna, 1960. Barea finds their conclusion 'very peculiar, unwarrantable'.

51. It was characteristic of Vienna, and especially of the cultivated bourgeoisie, that there was a great deal of intermarriage, so that there were many who were – like Hugo von Hoffmannsthal, for example – partly Jewish. Estimates of the Jewish population therefore run from 100,000 to 200,000.

6. The Castle and the Bridge

1. Professor Zbynek Zeman believes that the tradition commemorates the wrong person. It was Jan Z. Pomuku, Vicar-General to the Archbishop of Prague, who was drowned in the river on the orders of Václav IV in 1393 because he had helped to frustrate the king's design of founding a new bishopric in western Bohemia. After 1620 one Jan Nepomucky was canonized as a martyr.

2. The standard work is R.W. Seton-Watson, *The History of the Czechs and Slovaks*, London, 1943. See also F. Dvornik, *The Making of Central and Eastern Europe*, London, 1949; E. Wiskemann, *Czechs and Germans*, London, 1938; S.H. Thomson, *Czechoslovakia in European History*, Princeton/Oxford, 1953; M. Spinka, *John Hus and the Czech Reform*, Chicago, 1941; Cambridge Mediaeval History, vol. X. For this general historical section, I also found the following essays in *Encyclopaedia Britannica* by E. Wiskemann and O. Odlozilik useful: Bohemia, Jan Hus and Hussism.

3. On the architecture of Malá Strana, I have followed Lucy Abel Smith, *A Guide to Prague*, London, 1991, as well as the *Blue Guide: Czechoslovakia* (ed. Michael Jacobs), London, 1992.

4. On Jewish Prague, I have used Johann Bauer, *Kafka and Prague*; Pavel Eisner, *Franz Kafka and Prague*, New York, 1950; Frederick R. Karl, *Franz Kafka: Representative Man*, New York, 1991, *passim*.

5. Karl, op. cit., pp. 194–5, 242.

6. Sir Cecil Parrott, *Bad Bohemian*, London, 1978, p. 37.

7. Bauer, op. cit., p.48.

8. William Shakespeare, *A Midsummer Night's Dream*, I, ii, 43.

9. All quotations come from the Penguin Classics edition, Jaroslav Hašek, *The Good Soldier Schweik*, trans. Paul Selver, 1951.

10. The quotation is from Parrott, op. cit., p. 31. I am greatly indebted to Sir Cecil for much of the biographical information about Hašek in this section.

11. For the wave of anarchist actions in the 1890s and early 1900s, see Barbara W. Tuchman, *The Proud Tower*, London, 1980.

12. K.u.K. = *Kaiserlich und königlich*, i.e. 'imperial and royal'. After the Compromise of 1867, the imperial territories of Austria and the kingdom of Hungary were merged into the Habsburg Dual Monarchy. In his novel *The Man without Qualities*, Robert Musil calls the empire 'Kakania': the pun in German is that k is pronounced 'ka' and *kaka* is the baby word for 'shit'.

13. *The Diaries of Franz Kafka*, ed. Max Brod, London, 1992, p. 64.

14. Irving Howe, Introduction to *The Castle* (Everyman Edition), London, 1992, p. vi. On circumcision, cf. *Diaries*, pp. 147, 151–2.

15. *Diaries*, p. 88.

16. *Diaries*, p. 174. It seems that Kafka had found this engaging ditty in the book he had been reading, Pines, *Histoire de la littérature judéo-allemande*.

17. Karl, op. cit., p. 385, See also p. 73, quoting an undated diary entry: 'I shove the long slabs of rib meat unbitten into my mouth, and then pull them out again from behind, tearing through stomach and intestines.'

18. Bauer, op. cit., p. 63.

19. *Diaries*, p. 228.

20. Sir Isaiah Berlin, *Personal Impressions*, Oxford, 1982, p. 161: 'Famous poets were, at this time, heroic figures in the Soviet Union.'

7. Memories of the Future

1. See Detlef Briesen, 'Berlin – Die überschätzte Metropole' ('Berlin, the Overvalued Metropolis') in Gerhard Brunn and Jürgen Reulecke, *Metropolis Berlin*, Bonn and Berlin, 1992, p. 41. Briesen quotes Walther Kiaulehn, *Berlin: Schicksal einer Weltstadt*, Munich, 1976, pp. 22–3, as saying that Briesen reckons that the busy-ness of the Potsdamer Platz may well have been exaggerated. In 1926, according to Kiaulehn, there were only 49,000 cars in Berlin, or one for almost every 100 inhabitants. In Paris at the time the figure was one car for every forty inhabitants, and in New York one for every six.

2. Interview with Dr Eckart Stratenschulte, press secretary to the Mayor of Berlin, November 1993.

3. Gerhard Masur, *Imperial Berlin*, London, 1971, p. 3.

4. Dr Heinz Vestner, ed., *Berlin*, Hong Kong, 1989, p. 168.

5. ibid., p. 166. Among those exchanged there were Anatoly Sharansky in 1986 and in 1962 the U-2 pilot, Francis Gary Powers.

6. ibid., p. 171. The house is at 56–8 am Grossen Wannsee. It is a three-storey villa of considerable size, and it was used as a children's home for many years. In 1992 it became Germany's first museum to the Holocaust. It is illustrated in Tony Le Tissier, *Berlin Then and Now*, 1992, p. 439.

7. There is an extremely useful guide to the architecture of Berlin, *Kunstführer Berlin*, ed. Eva and Helmut Börsch-Supan, Günther Kühne and Hella Reelfs, Stuttgart, 1977, 1991.

8. Otto Friedrich, *Before the Deluge*, London, 1974, p. 25.

9. See, in Le Tissier, op. cit, the telling contrast between a picture of Kaiser Wilhelm I unveiling a monument to his father in front of the Schloss, surrounded by troops in parade order, flagstaffs and bands, and the modern glass Palace of the Republic erected by the GDR after the Schloss was demolished in 1950.

10. Kiaulehn, op. cit., p. 476.

11. Annemarie Lange, *Das Wilhelminische Reich*, Berlin, 1967, p. 38.

12. For example, in *Frau Jenny Treibel* and in his finest book, *Effi Briest*.

13. Masur, op. cit., pp. 86, 105.

14. Eike Geisel, ed., *Im Scheunenviertel*, Berlin, 1981. In the introductory essay Geisel describes how a French writer, Jacques Huret, found a small Jewish ghetto existing around the Grenadierstrasse in the Scheunenviertel in 1906. But the major immigration came, ironically, after the German army liberated Polish Jews by defeating the Russian armies in the war.

15. Masur, op. cit., p. 93; p. 88.

16. The poet was Robert Hamerling, quoted in Lange, op. cit., p. 6.

17. Masur, op. cit., p. 125.

18. For the following account of the abortive German Revolution of

1918-19 I have relied especially on three books: Otto Friedrich, *Before the Deluge*, London, 1974, pp. 14–78; Sebastian Haffner, *Failure of a Revolution*, London, 1973; Richard M. Watt, *The Kings Depart*, London, 1969. Haffner's book is called, in German, *Die Verratene Revolution* ('The Betrayed Revolution'), and must be read in the context of his thesis that a genuine (and by implication not necessarily undesirable) revolution took place in 1918–19, and was betrayed by the Majority Social Democrats with the help of the Freikorps, and that this made the failure of the Weimar Republic and the rise of Nazism inevitable. In my view this thesis is far too hard on the Majority Socialists, and does not do justice to the impossible situation they found themselves in; it is also, in historical retrospect, too kind to the Spartakists and the Revolution they wanted to carry out.

19. Friedrich, op. cit, p. 25.

20. Watt, op. cit., pp. 199–200.

21. ibid., p. 211.

22. ibid., p. 229.

23. The same officer who ordered the murder of Karl Liebknecht and Rosa Luxemburg.

24. Watt, op. cit., p. 235.

25. Robert G.L. Waite, *Vanguard of Nazism*, Cambridge, Mass., 1952, pp. 25–6.

26. Haffner, op. cit., pp. 131–2.

27. Friedrich, op. cit., pp. 45–6; Haffner, op. cit., 139–51; Watt, op. cit., pp. 269–73.

28. Watt, op. cit., pp. 45–6.

29. See Geisel, op. cit., especially pp. 64, 65, 69, 70 and 71.

30. The title of the first novel in Richard Hughes's trilogy about an Anglo-German family.

31. Friedrich, op. cit., pp. 200–201.

32. For example, Anita Loos, *A Girl like I*, London, 1967; Klaus Mann, *The Turning Point*, New York, 1962; Josef von Sternberg, *Fun in the Chinese Laundry*, London, 1966.

33. Vicki Baum, *Menschen im Hotel*, published in English as *Grand Hotel*. See

also Kiaulehn, op. cit., p. 542. *Grand Hotel* was later a Hollywood movie with Greta Garbo.

34. Irmgard Keun, *Das Kunstseidene Mädchen*, Berlin, 1932.

35. Golo Mann, *The History of Germany since 1789*, London, 1968, pp. 357–8.

36. Alan Bullock, *Hitler: A Study in Tyranny*, rev. edn, Harmondsworth, 1962, pp. 90–91.

37. Friedrich, op. cit., p. 127.

38. Jürgen Kuczynsky, 'Effets de crise au quotidien', Lionel Richard, ed., *Berlin 1919–1933*, Paris, 1991.

39. ibid., p. 217.

40. For the Zeitungsviertel and its lore, see Kiaulehn, op. cit., pp. 476–542.

41. Masur, op. cit., p. 201.

42. Dominique Bourel, 'Les mandarins contre la démocratie' in Richard, ed., op. cit., p. 145.

43. Siegfried Kracauer, *From Caligari to Hitler: a Psychological History of the German Film*, Princeton, NJ, 1947, is a splendid account. See also Pia Le Moal, *L'UFA, le cinéma et l'argent*, in Richard, ed., op. cit., p. 165.

44. Pia Le Moal, in Richard, op. cit., p. 167.

45. ibid., pp. 170–71.

46. I have relied heavily on two biographies of Bertolt Brecht: Martin Esslin, *Brecht: the Man and his Work*, New York, 1960; and Frederic Ewen, *Bertolt Brecht: His Life, His Art, and His Times*, New York, 1967.

47. See the excellent biography by Giles McDonogh, *A Good German*, and Christabel Bielenberg's *The Past is Myself*.

48. Le Tissier, op. cit., pp. 372–3. This is a detailed account with maps and pictures by a former British intelligence officer.

49. Tacitus, *Histories*, I, xlix.

50. The phrase *mémoires du futur* appears without context or explanation of its context in the jacket copy of the excellent collection of essays, *Berlin 1919–1933*, edited by Lionel Richard and published by Les Editions Autrement, Paris, 1991.

8. Dead Hearts and New Beginnings

1. I owe this anecdote to my friend David Butler, of Nuffield College, Oxford, who had it in 1947 from Lord Stansgate, father of Tony Benn, MP.

2. The story of the *Freihaus auf der Wieden* is told in Ilse Barea, *Vienna: Legend and Reality*, London, 1966, p. 89. Ms Barea cites an article by Else Spiesberger, 'Das Starhemberg'sche Freihaus auf der Wieden', in *Jahrbuch der Geschichte der Stadt Wien*, vol. 19/20, 1963/4.

3. The word is not strictly appropriate to car travel: it was originally the American for a season ticket.

INDEX